Praise for Lyndsay Faye:

'Lyndsay Faye is a superstar-caliber writer. She confidently and exquisitely re-creates the past while her characters live on with you in the present, the elusive gold standard for a historical novel. *The Gods of Gotham* is a gift to the genre that readers will surely relish while we wait for Faye's next one'
Matthew Pearl, author of *The Dante Club*

'A thrilling and beguiling Gothic tale of innocence, the antagonism between brothers, faith and a nation standing on the precipice of a new age . . . This is a new and exciting historical novel which has everything that will entrap a reader . . . an inferno of a book'
Crimesquad

'The sights, sounds and smells of the old city are there, they leap off the page at you and there is a lushness and febrile intensity to the writing which put me in mind of *The Crimson Petal and the White* by Michael Faber, it has the same slight edge of decadence and something vaguely rotten in the air'
Random Jottings

'I don't read an awful lot of historical crime fiction, but *The Gods of Gotham* has persuaded me that I very probably should. A fascinating backdrop, neatly observed historical detail, an intriguing protagonist, and beautifully written, with the added bonus that many of the characters speak 'flash', aka the argot of New York's criminal underworld: it's a potent blend'
Declan Burke, Crime Always Pays

'*The Gods of Gotham* was an amazing read. I loved this look at New York and its history'
a-fantastical-librarian.blogspot.co.uk

'A historical romp of a read that's as sexy as it is adventurous'
***Elle* magazine**

Also by Lyndsay Faye

The Gods of Gotham
Dust and Shadow

SEVEN
FOR A
SECRET

LYNDSAY FAYE

headline
review

First published in Great Britain in 2013
by HEADLINE REVIEW
An imprint of HEADLINE PUBLISHING GROUP

1

Cataloguing in Publication Data is available from the British Library

Hardback ISBN 978 0 7553 8678 9
Trade paperback ISBN 978 0 7553 8679 6

Typeset in Goudy by Avon DataSet Ltd, Bidford-on-Avon,
Warwickshire

Printed and bound in Great Britain by
Clays Ltd, St Ives plc

Headline's policy is to use papers that are natural, renewable and
recyclable products and made from wood grown in sustainable forests.
The logging and manufacturing processes are expected to conform to the
environmental regulations of the country of origin.

HEADLINE PUBLISHING GROUP
A division of Hachette Livre UK Ltd
338 Euston Road
London NW1 3BH
www.headline.co.uk
www.hachette.co.uk

This one's for Gabriel, who always thinks I can.

Selected Flash Terminology*

ANODYNE. Death; to anodyne; to kill.

BAM. A lie; to bamboozle.
BAT. A prostitute who walks the streets only at night.
BLOW THE GAB. Confess.

CHAFFEY. Boisterous; happy; jolly.
CHINK. Money.
COLE. Silver or gold money.
COVE. A man.
CROAKED. Dead.
CULL. A man.
CUTTY-EYED. To look out of the corner of the eyes; to look suspicious; to leer.

DANCE AT HIS DEATH. To be hung.
DEAD RABBIT. A very athletic, rowdy fellow.
DIMBER. Handsome; pretty.

FADGE. It won't do; 'It won't fadge.'

GRAFT. To work.

HUMMER. A great lie.

INNOCENT. A corpse.

---

* Excerpted from George Washington Matsell, *The Secret Language of Crime: Vocabulum, or, The Rogue's Lexicon* (G. W. Matsell & Co., 1859).

KEN. A house.
KETCH. To hang.
KINCHIN. A young child.
KITCHEN PHYSIC. Food.

LACE. To beat; to whip.
LAY. A particular kind of rascality.
LEAKY. Not trustworthy.
LEERY. On guard; look out; wide awake.
LIBBEGE LINEN. Bedclothes.
LION. Be saucy; frighten; bluff; 'Lion the fellow.'
LOWRE. Coin.
LUNAN. A girl.

MAB. A harlot.
MAZZARD. The face.
MITTEN-MILL. A glove fight.
MOLL. A woman.
MOLLEY. A miss; an effeminate fellow; a sodomite.
MOUSE. Be quiet; be still.

NACKY. Ingenious.
NIMENOG. A very silly fellow.
NOSE. A spy; one who informs.

ON THE MUSCLE. On the fight; a fighter; a pugilist.

PALAVER. Talk; flattery; conference.
PEPPERY. Warm; passionate.

RIGGING. Clothing.
RUG. Sleep.

SCRAN. Food.
SCRAPP. A plan to rob a house or commit any kind of roguery.
SHAKESTER. A lady.
SIMON. A simpleton.
SLUBBER. A heavy, stupid fellow.
SNAPPER. A gun.
SPOONEY. Foolish.
STARGAZERS. Prostitutes; streetwalkers.
SWELL. A gentleman.

TANGLE-FOOT. Bad liquor.
TOLD OUT. Beaten; defeated.
TUMBLED. Suspected; found out.

WARE HAWK. Look out; beware.
WHIDDLE. To tell or discover.

YAM. To eat.

THE COLORED MOTHER OF NEW ENGLAND TO HER INFANT

Thy sparkling eye is full of light,
Thy heart beats high with joy,
And woe, or care, from morn till night,
Disturbs not thee, my boy.
Smile now – for, o'er thy coming years,
A cloud of misery bends;
Disgrace and shame, regret and tears,
Till earthly being ends.
Whose skin reflects a darker hue,
Than that the white man wears,
And for this cause thy earthly dew
Of joy must change for tears!
For thee, from childhood's gleesome hour,
Through all thy onward track,
Are hard and bitter things in store,
Because thy skin is black!

Popular abolitionist song

PROLOGUE

O n the day the worst happened to her – and by worst I mean the tragedy you'd die to prevent, kill to prevent, the cruelty beyond endurance – Lucy Adams was working in a flower shop, arranging scarlet and orange hothouse roses whose colors could have put a midsummer sunset to shame.

How little I learned about her, that day when we met. How tragically little. The details would come later. Long after I'd told her that I, Timothy Wilde, copper star badge number 107 and defender of whomever I damn well pleased, would set it all right again. That I would stop at nothing to help her and to that end, I wanted her to spin me a tale.

Just tell it to me like a story, and I'll fix this.

God, what hubris men can achieve after six months working at a job.

An impossible job, at that. Or maybe just one too taxing for the likes of me. I'd like to say that my brother Valentine manages better, this being a fledgling star police of New York City business, but he's the captain of Ward Eight and complicated the whole wretched affair the way a kitten complicates a ball of yarn.

So, no. Wildes, in this case – the younger and the elder – made precious few sound decisions.

I could pretend that recording Lucy Adams's story is important for posterity. Justice, even. But that would be humbug. Smoke obscuring a charnel-house landscape. What truly matters just now

1

to me is that a black saga resides at the back of my eyes.

And the last time that happened, I wrote it all down.

At six o'clock in the evening on February 14, 1846, Mrs Adams stood at a worktable behind the front counter of the flower shop, peeling thorns from rose stems. St Valentine's Day had dawned frigid and clear, but now winds churned above Manhattan, and snowflakes swooned their way to Chambers Street outside the frosted display window. The shop ought to have closed an hour previous, but still swarmed with men in swallow-tailed coats demanding artificial armfuls of summertime. Scarves flapped, watch chains whirled, acres of forced conservatory flowers disappeared out the door into the snow.

Mrs Adams hummed a tune as she worked. A melody too old for a name that drifted along the exhalations of her breath. She thought with a pleasant longing of supper, for her cook had promised to stew a pair of ducks for the family, and imaginary scents of orange rind and dried mint teased at her nose.

Minutes ticked past, and still more minutes, and she began to wrap the stem of her bouquet with blood-red silk. Winding it as if casting a spell. Fingers sure and length of crimson ribbon supple as skin. It was the last time she would ever do so. The bow she tied was perfection. A soft, elegant ending.

The shop owner – Mr Timpson, a former Manchester dweller with kindly eyes and a grey, sagging complexion save for his crimson nose – tutted when he glanced at the clock next to the yellow sprays of lilies. He'd just warmly thanked a trio of departing swells with maroon greatcoats and ivory trousers, and Timpson's Superior Blooms at last had emptied. All the day long, it had resembled the Stock Exchange.

'I'll sweep up, dear,' he told his single shop assistant, Mrs Adams. 'It'll be ghastly out there in a quarter hour, and I've only to climb the stairs to reach my supper. Get along home with you.'

Mrs Adams protested that her final order for the next day wasn't quite finished. That it was only a little snow, that anyhow her house was round the corner from Chambers, just down West Broadway. But Mr Timpson insisted, with a jovial clap of his hands followed by a shooing motion. And it was late, so much later than usual, the busiest day of the year, and Mrs Adams yearned to be home.

And so she went.

The shop windows ticked past Lucy Adams's vision like the unnoticed beat of a bedroom clock as she hastened homeward. A safe rhythm, familiar as your own pulse. *M. Freeman's Old and New Feathers Emporium. Needle and Fishhook Manufactory. The Museum Hotel.* The snow whirled above the cobbles, as if gripped by an undertow, and she pulled her fur cloak close. She passed a man driving a cart piled with burlap sacks and calling, 'Sand-O! White sand-O!' A shopkeeper dove out of his dry goods store at the cry, nearly running into her. But she stepped neatly aside, and the whiskery gentleman apologized as he fed coins into the sandman's palm for the Rockaway silt that would keep his storefront pavements safe a while longer.

And Mrs Adams went on her way.

When Mrs Adams opened the door of her narrow brownstone in West Broadway, shivering as she removed her fur, silence greeted her. She dropped the cape on a damask chair in the hallway and went into the parlor. The room was empty. Mrs Adams fanned her fingers before the waning fire, pulling off her gloves. She unpinned her hat. Her eyes drifted over the pressed flowers framed on the brick mantelpiece, over the pair of tiny china horses and the single holly sprig in a vase of amethyst glass. She called out to the household that she'd arrived.

No one answered.

Unhurried, she went into the dining room. Not the echo of a whisper met her ears. She turned to climb the stairs, still cheerily announcing her return.

All was silence. A quiet deeper than death.

Five minutes later, Mrs Adams hurtled out of her house into West Broadway, her skirts in her fists and her mouth torn wide in a scream, flying through the gathering storm in the direction of police headquarters at the Tombs.

That's where I come into it. I work there.

As for me, I sat in the windowless closet space I'd the previous month eked out for use as an office, a glass of Dutch gin in my hand and a crooked smile on my ruined face, toasting the health of my friend Roundsman Jakob Piest. We having just solved a pretty thorny problem and feeling none too humble about it. He lifted his ugly wrinkled fist and tin cup, laughing like the maniac he is, and then Mrs Lucy Adams stumbled against my half-open door with a *bang*.

Can I describe her properly, as she was before I came to know her secrets? I suspect not. If secrets are gems to their owners, to be cradled in dark cases, I plundered Lucy Adams's jewel chest as thorough as a highwayman despoiling a carriage. It hurts to be a thief, when what you stole was a person's history. I am not that man. I *loathe* being that man. People, all manner and persuasion of people, want to tell me things of their own accord. Always have done, since I was a barman. Even before. But I can't stomach knowing secrets without an invitation, a wave of the hand to walk inside.

So what did she look like, this mystery of mine, before I laid bare the stories carved into her before we met?

Lucy Adams was dressed for winter so simply that every garment announced its high quality. The toe of one boot keeking out from swirls of a cobalt-velvet day dress was soaked through with snow. So she'd quit the house hurriedly, without donning rubber overboots. An ivory ermine cape around her shoulders had been tied with a violently asymmetrical red bow, and a score of other things about her that evening pleaded for help. White leather gloves gaping, their pearl fastenings loose. No hat, not even a lace cap for decency's sake and not warmth's. Just wave after wave after wave of pinned-up chocolate brown hair in the tightest corkscrew curls I've ever seen, with white snowflakes melting tenderly into them.

Something horrible had happened to her. I didn't need a

barman's sleight of hand to realize that. Lucy Adams's eyes were the color of lichen on a stone wall, mossy flecks of green shot through the grey, and they stared wide as if she'd just been pitched into the Hudson off a steamer deck. Mr Piest and I stared at her, shocked. Her lips were very full, very round, and she peeled them open to speak as if the motion agonized her.

She was beautiful. That part of the story is impossible to discount. It matters, unfortunately. She was one of the most beautiful women I'd ever seen.

'Are you hurt, ma'am?' I found my tongue at last, leaping to my feet.

'I need a policeman,' she said.

'It's all right. Here, sit down,' I said as Mr Piest scurried to pour her a tumbler of water. She seemed not to see the chair until I offered my hand, and then she went like a marionette with a novice puppeteer. 'We can help.'

'I pray so.'

Her wracked voice was deeper than her willowy frame suggested. It sent a shiver down my neck as if she could open her throat and cast ships into rocks. Christ knows enough ships were lost that night, in the storm, packed with New Yorkers who never came home. That wasn't any of her doing, of course. Most would say it was luck's, or Fate's. Or even God's. But I can't help but think of her voice that way now. The way it tugged a man, could wrench a steamer off course into cruel shoals.

'You can certainly trust us to try,' I said gently. 'Just tell it to me like a story, and I'll fix this.'

Her eyes met mine. They'd gone pale as slate.

'There's been a robbery.'

'What's been stolen?' I asked.

'My family,' she answered me.

CHAPTER ONE

The evil we complain of is increasing. Europe is flooding the country with emigrants – Great Britain has appropriated twenty-five million to deport to this country one million of Irish paupers, to compete with and destroy American labor.

Mr Levin of the Native American Party,
as reported in the *New York Herald*, 1846

I have come to know my city too well.

Not the pleasantest of afflictions. Presumably this wouldn't be a problem if I lived in a gorgeously crumbling stone wreck on the coast of Spain, casting my nets for sardines of a morning and catching strains of guitar music long into the night. Or if I kept a tavern in a melancholy little English town, pouring pints for widowers and reading poetry of an evening. I've never been away from here, so who can say? My knowledge of other places is bounded in books. It could be possible to know a city intimately and yet like it. I hope so.

No, the main trouble seems to be that I'm a policeman of Ward Six in Manhattan, the only copper star I know of assigned not to walk rounds but to solve crimes after the fact, and that so far I've not much cottoned to the content of the crimes. Not by half.

For instance, on the morning of St Valentine's Day, I awoke with
the faintly sick sensation that a law had been broken by someone or
other in this city of near half a million, and I hadn't yet brainworked
out *who*. The day before, Chief of Police George Washington Matsell
– our unquestioned leader, the charging rhino of a man who set me
up unraveling riddles – had appeared in my airless Tombs cave.

G. W. Matsell would already be impressive because he is
enormous, over six feet tall and three hundred pounds if he's an
ounce. But it so happens he's impressive because both his mind
and willpower resemble a train running under full shrieking steam.
He was a prominent justice before being appointed our chief, and
thus already famous. Since we copper stars are a controversial band
of ragtags to say the least, now he's infamous. But infamy doesn't
seem to chafe him overmuch.

I heard a scuff and looked up from my desktop. The previous
instant, my doorway had seemed a reasonable size. Man-sized,
anyhow. Now Chief Matsell stood within, and it had shrunk to a
mouse hole. He stared at me placidly. Jowls furrowed into deep
fleshy ditches and pale eyes gleaming. I'd used to walk my ward in
circles as my colleagues did, on the lookout for trouble and finding
it all too often. Since the end of the ghastly kinchin murderer
business last August, when the chief decided my brains ought to be
at his perennial disposal, I sit at the Tombs and trouble finds me
either via notes from Matsell or in person. I'm damned if I know
which is more disconcerting.

'A priceless miniature painting has been stolen from a private
residence at One-oh-two Fifth Avenue, under unusual circumstances,' he announced.

A bead-sized but tightly worked knot formed in my stomach.

'You're going to find it. Mr and Mrs Millington expect you to
call round at nine.'

'Right,' I said, exhaling hard.

'Find the thief while you're about it, Mr Wilde,' he added over
his shoulder, charging quietly away as if he'd battalions that wanted
commanding.

Easier said than done, I surmised.

I'd been among the very first copper stars, as the Common Council had only succeeded in forming the police the previous summer. And I'd a hankering to be the best of the lot. But the work was still a coat that didn't fit me, all floppy sleeves and straining buttons, every fresh problem prompting my brain to prate, *And just how will you set about solving that?*

It's a nasty sensation.

Bizarrely, I still dreamed at night of tending bar as I'd used to – of running dry of rum with Wall Street speculators piled twenty deep in a hissing, writhing snake pit before my cedar plank. Not of stolen goods I couldn't find or of street brawls I couldn't tame. Nor murders I couldn't solve. In my usual visions, my face wasn't yet so scarred by the fire that erased half of downtown that no decent watering hole would ever hire me, my home and fortune hadn't evaporated, and my keenest concern was serving champagne to stockbrokers who were already half-stupefied. Mostly I dreamed of flimsy troubles.

I say *mostly*.

I dream about police work too, every month or so, and about last summer. Of course I do. But those dreams crack my skull a bit.

Anyhow, from the instant Matsell assigned me to retrieve that painting, I commenced skirting the edges of my wits. Since my removal from the company of patrolling roundsmen and promotion to *solver-of-the-chief's-nastier-puzzles*, I'd never investigated a crime committed against our white-sugar-dusted upper crust. And 102 Fifth Avenue turned out to be within sneezing distance of the annoyingly chipper Union Place Park.

Not my sort of neighborhood, speaking economically – I've five items of furniture and a rented room above a bakery. But what Matsell says goes, and thus so did I.

Alighting the hack the morning of February 13, I shook my head at the miracle of Union Place Park. Our parks tend to become pig troughs or chicken yards within ten years' time. But Union Place clings with religious frenzy to its prim shrubbery and raked

9

walkways. The aisles whispered, *Welcome and enjoy, supposing you belong here.* Under the branches of the bare young trees, a matched set of girls wearing flounces of white lace beneath their furs laughed together in the knifelike daylight, sparks shooting from the diamonds woven into their hair.

Had I been in fit romantic condition to study them, maybe they'd not have hurt my eyes. But I continued west along Sixteenth Street, pretending as I went that there wasn't a girl across the ocean who'd long been corralling off ninety percent of the thoughts in my head.

Prime-grade, triple-purified mule headedness, my brother Val called the obsession. Unfortunately, I couldn't help myself. I wanted to plant flags for her, conquer city-states. If her mind had been a map, I'd have taken an ivory ribbon and pinned it softly and painlessly along the route of her thoughts. Barring the likelihood of that happening, I'd have settled for being the fellow to bolt her front door of an evening, as she's far more audacious than she is sensible. Check window casements, generally stand guard against the frailty of locks. That sort of thing.

Mercy Underhill was in London, though, and I was in Gotham, and so instead I rapped at the door of 102 Fifth Avenue.

The three-story house of brown stone couldn't possibly have reached its fifth year, its steps spreading in a great curved smirk between two despondent-looking stone gryphons hunched atop either pedestal. Carved teak door, window boxes stuffed with pine that somehow had sprouted gilt cones, a decorative stone face everywhere they could find on the façade to slap one. Even the roofing tiles reeked of new money. The gryphons wanted nothing to do with the place, and neither did I.

I tried the bell. It chimed like a gong summoning an emperor to dinner and the door swung open. The butler, when he saw me, looked as if he'd just glanced inside a slaughterhouse.

Granted, my winter coat is of pedestrian grey wool and was once someone else's. And granted, the upper right quarter of my face does resemble a hardened wax puddle. But he didn't know a thing about the coat's previous history. Or the face's. So he ought to keep dark about it, is what I thought.

I waited for him to say something.

He stood there. Being altogether tall and silent and side-whiskered.

So I swept my fingers toward the dented copper star pinned to my lapel.

'Ah,' he said, as if discovering the source of a pesky smell. 'You've been summoned to discover the whereabouts of the painting, I gather. A . . . *policeman*.'

Despite myself, I grinned. I was used to the disgusted tone people took with the infant police force by then, if not used to the word *summoned*, but none of that mattered. I've listened to thousands of people from hundreds of cities in my years tending bar. It was a game of mine, before. Placing them. One of many games. And apparently the Millingtons hadn't the ear to identify a Bristol man doing his level best London accent and had hired a jack-tar for a snob butler. That kittled me. The barely visible hole where the ring had once pierced his ear kittled me too.

'How's the shipping industry back home?' I asked.

If you've never seen a liveried sea dog turn purple and then an oysterish white, you're missing something splendid. His muttonchops practically stood at attention.

'This way, sir, and . . . do please let me know if my services can be of use to you.'

We entered a foyer lined with portraits of unhealthy-looking women with their dogs and their children and their needlework. An active gentleman of about fifty-five burst through the opposite door, checking a gold pocket watch. Mr Millington, it seemed clear.

'The policeman is here to see you, sir,' the Bristol butler reported.

'Oh, wonderful! What's his name, then, Turley?'

Turley's mouth worked like a pike's. The man was suffering so deeply, I solidified our new friendship with a rescue effort.

'I'm Timothy Wilde. I'll be happy to see what I can do about returning your property.'

'My word,' Millington mused as he shook my hand. 'Not what I'd expected from a note to Chief Matsell himself for help, but I suppose he knows his business.'

Unsure of which side to take in this argument, I kept mum.

'I'm due at the 'Change,' he fretted. 'So I'll just post you up on our way to the music room, the – well, how do you people put it? The stage of the crime, as it were?'

'I really couldn't tell you.'

'I see,' he said, baffled.

Mr Millington informed me en route that, upon entering the music room the previous day at six a.m., their maid Amy had suffered a fright. The Millingtons were art lovers (the chambers we passed through were drowning in China vases and Japanned fire screens and oil paintings of cherubs at their never very strenuous occupations), and each morning the precious artifacts were cleaned. *Inventoried*, I supplied in my head. Unfortunately, Amy had discovered a gap in the miniatures hanging on the music-room wall. After a thorough search, Matsell was notified, and thus I was ordered to try my hand as an art bloodhound.

Not my strong suit. I knew it sure as gravity.

'My wife is *extremely* upset over this dreadful affair.' Mr Millington's pocket watch reappeared briefly. 'Shall I tell you about Jean-Baptiste Jacques Augustin?'

I grew up pickling my brains in an erudite Protestant minister's extensive library, so I answered, 'The court miniaturist? Later official painter to the king of France?'

'Oh. Well, then.'

'What's it look like?'

As I was being told that it looked like a shepherdess wearing a straw bonnet with pink ribbons, we arrived at what could only have been the music room, as it was possessed of two pianos facing each other down like duelists, a cello, several decorative lutes, and a winged harp the size of a broom closet.

'I'm terribly sorry, but I really must be off,' Millington concluded. 'See that this policeman's questions are answered, yes, Turley? You know best what to do from here, Mr Wilde.'

I didn't. But he departed so swiftly, I hadn't the pleasure of telling him.

When his master's footsteps had faded, Turley wriggled his side-whiskers apologetically. 'About earlier, sir. I regret—'

'You could be the queen of the Gypsies for all I care. Besides, they expect it of you. That ghoul of a dead high-court judge act. Just because you can't flam me doesn't mean you're not doing handsome work flamming them. Help me sort this, and we'll forget about it.'

He smiled, showing crooked teeth that likely hadn't glimpsed public daylight since he was hired. 'I call that fair play, Mr Wilde. I suppose first you'll want to examine the room.'

Thinking it a spruce idea, I peered about. At the instruments, the bow windows, the pink draperies, the leering dragons guarding the fireplace. I wrestled back an audible sigh.

It looked like a room.

Obviously, an artwork had been removed. Eleven miniature portraits hung as a collection, most of vacuous rosy-cheeked dignitaries but some of vacuous rosy-cheeked peasantry. There ought to have been twelve, though. The third from the right in the second column was missing, and the papered wall was dirty from lack of cleaning beneath the missing painting, dark streaks mottled over the sprays of blushing tea roses. Three little parallel smears of ashy grime. I leaned closer, examining the gap.

It looked like a gap.

I lightly worried at the eyebrow bordering my scar as I went to look over the locks on the chamber's two doorways. 'Turley, the chief said *unusual circumstances*.'

'I called it peculiar myself, sir. This room was locked at midnight when I made my nightly tour. I've a key; Mr Millington has a key; Mrs Thornton, the housekeeper, has a key. They're all accounted for. And like Mr Millington said, weren't we all bleeding searched to our eye teeth and past yesterday? As if any of us would ever dream of touching this swag.'

I tossed him a wry look as I quit the second – and likewise untampered with – door lock. His stately London vowels had dissolved entirely by this time into Bristol's River Avon. I was almost fond of him for it.

'They're worth a fortune, some of them. That miniature certainly is. Nothing has disappeared before now, I take it?'

'Never, sir. There's none of us as needs the money, not in that way. We've fine victuals below stairs, three sick days a year, bonuses every Christmas. And all of us with family away home to support and ten thousand more Irish crawling into the city every day. It'd take a bedlamite to risk being sacked without a character, things as they are.'

Irish were indeed flooding New York as if a Donelly or a McKale were contained in every raindrop of every thunderstorm. No one liked them – no one save for Democrats of my brother Valentine's stripe, who liked their votes considerably – but certainly not house servants of British extraction who could be on the streets in the breadth of a hat pin should their masters take a turn for the frugal. I sympathized with Turley. His brand of animosity was practical, at least, and not the vicious anti-Catholic paranoia that makes my hackles rise.

But the Irish had commenced starving the year previous when their potatoes disintegrated. And now it was wintertime, and that particular fellow feeling went beyond sympathy. I've Irish friends, Irish fellow copper stars, and I know what missing mealtimes feels like. Val and I once made a supper out of the mushy mass of vegetables a restaurant had strained from a stock pot, kernels scraped from a half-eaten husk of buttered corn, and three street-foraged chestnuts. My older brother had salted it, peppered it, plated it, garnished mine with two chestnuts and his with one, and deemed it salad.

It was unconvincing.

'When you locked up, did you notice anything amiss?'

'It's a pity, but can't say as I looked. Last member of the household to use the room was Mrs Millington, after breakfast.'

'And the only way in is through those two doors and these two windows, unless a duplicate key exists.' I unlatched one of the bow windows.

'Aye, sir. But you police types can tell, maybe, if a key's been duplicated?'

Biting my lip in annoyance directed almost entirely inward, I leaned out, the sudden chill making my eyes burn. The alley side of the building was brick, with a single ivy strand hauling its way upward, and we were on the second floor. The other window faced frenetic Fifth Avenue. Both difficult to reach without being seen, and both locked anyhow.

Refastening the hasp, I returned my attention to what I'm good at: stories, and the people who tell them to me.

'Do the Millingtons have children?' I asked, ruminating.

'Not them. Just two sets of coronation china, a dozen Wilton rugs, five—'

'Does the master of the house have any unsavory habits? Gambling, women?'

Turley snorted. 'His notion of sport is hauling in money as if it's schools of sardines. Good at it too, as you can see. Better than most.'

'Mrs Millington. Suppose she had debts?'

'I suppose she'd draw on her allowance. Comes to a hundred a month, excepting December. Then it's two hundred, if you please, in the spirit of the season.'

How convenient for her if she ever needs a tenth silver bud vase in the shape of a swan. I glared at the nine arranged on the mantelpiece, fuchsia hothouse buds sprouting tortuously from the creatures' throats.

Then I caught sight of something more disturbing: a mirror had been hung over the fireplace.

It isn't that I was worthy of a block of marble being devoted to my face previous to the explosion. But faces are personal, and I'd

15

preferred mine intact. The reflection gave me back my dark blond hairline with its sweeping double arcs, the downward-edged crescent stamped on my chin, the narrow but curving lips above, the straight nose, the deep-set green eyes. But it also gave me a healed-over torrent sweeping across my temple, as if a penny had been thrown in a pool.

'The house servants,' I said, wrenching my eyes away. 'Who are they?'

'Myself, and at your service, Mr Wilde,' he listed, counting on his fingers. 'Mrs Thornton, the housekeeper. Agatha, the cook. Amy, Grace, Ellen, Mary, and Rose, the maids. Stephen and Jack, the footmen. Lily, the scullery maid. That's without the coach driver and grooms who bunk at the hostelry.'

'Anything you'd like to tell me about any of them? Anything . . . interesting?'

Turley dissected this. Hope shone like a distant lighthouse in my breast.

'Agatha's knee can tell her when a storm's coming,' he answered me shrewdly. 'That's always terrible interesting. It acted up something fierce this morning, so we're in for a parcel of trouble, Mr Wilde.'

He hadn't the faintest idea.

By the time I'd interviewed all of the servants and trudged in defeat out of 102 Fifth Avenue that afternoon, I had, in fact, learned several interesting things.

First off, the household had sunk into a clawing panic of self-preservationist accusations. According to Ellen (a downstairs maid), who was a breathless Cockney lass fresh from the Thames, it must have been Grace who took the miniature. Because well, *Just look at her*. According to Grace (an upstairs maid), who was a short black girl who stood always with her hands neatly behind her back, it must have been Ellen. For Ellen talked funny, and the Irish talked funny, and *Everyone knows how the Irish are*. Then Ellen had called Grace an uppity wench who went with all the fastest gadabout coloreds in the city, and Grace had called Ellen a dry little prune who'd be lucky to give it away for free disguised as a hat, let alone sell it or marry it off.

I left them both teary-eyed and regretful, staring horrified at each other from either side of the kitchen table. Each of them minus a friend.

Next I called round to the hostelry on Fifteenth Street where the Millingtons' coach staff resided. Grace did indeed have a male caller: one of the two black groomsmen, whose name was Jeb, paid his respects every afternoon and would marry her when he'd enough coin for a farm plot in Canada. The white coachman suggested as we parted ways that Jeb might have a motive there.

Predictably enough.

Blacks are accused of thievery every ten or so seconds in these parts. Almost as often as the Irish are accused of witchcraft. And I've sweated alongside too many free blacks, in ferry yards and restaurants and the like, for that not to lodge in my craw sideways. It's infuriating. They own the same wrenching ambition that drives Yidishers to sew sixteen hours a day. Anyway, I grew up haunting the Underhill rectory, and you'd be hard pressed to dig up a more bullish clan of abolitionists.

So I chalked up my interviews to less than useless and went on about my day.

Still . . . nothing any of the servants had said surprised me. This city plays with its residents a mortal game of musical chairs, and when the clanging pianoforte stops, the consequence for the loser is either a slow death or a short one. There is simply *not enough* here. Not enough work, enough food, enough walls with roofs topping them. Maybe there would be if we filled in half the Atlantic. But today, there aren't enough chairs for the tens of thousands tearing their way into the parlor for a try. And if only one seat out of a dozen is marked FOR COLOREDS, and that identical seat is the only one marked FOR IRISH . . .

Then it's a question of who pitches whom on the hardwood

first.

After some herring and potatoes at the nearest dining hall, I returned to the main house to conduct my own search, including a heart-hammering interlude digging through Mrs Millington's bureau while she was out delivering calling cards.

No painting.

I went home and drank three glasses of New England rum. That seeming the useful thing to do.

And thus, when February 14 dawned, atmosphere wildly clear with a silken grey sheet of sky spread high above, I'd the sensation that today held a trip to the barber's to have a rotten tooth pulled.

I kicked off my bed sheet. My chambers are above Mrs Boehm's Fine Baked Goods, which means that my landlady's bread ovens bake my floor in the wintertime. Bless the woman, my rooms are like June. They're also briefly inventoried: a secondhand four-poster under the window, a claw-footed table my brother scavenged from a fire, a chair I found in a ditch, a rug from Mrs Boehm's attic. And finally, a chest of drawers I'd gritted my teeth and purchased on the fourth occasion I found local insect life thriving in my neatly folded togs. The room doesn't look empty, though, maybe because its walls are plastered with charcoal drawings. I sketch scenes when I'm troubled.

I sketch a great many scenes.

The tiny 'sleeping chamber' hasn't any windows. So I've lined it with shelves, with Mrs Boehm's permission. Five books reside there at present. But I'm working on that. I'm accustomed to a much bigger supply.

A strange object that isn't precisely a book also lives there: a long manuscript I wrote about what happened last summer, as a handy alternative to screaming my lungs raw about it in a public square.

Last August, a little girl by the name of Bird Daly collided with my knees. She was brave and terrified and inexplicably covered in blood, and I'd about as much notion of what to do with her as I'd have over a malfunctioning threshing machine or a wounded sparrow. But I was broken myself, after the fire. My world had vanished. And so I would speak with Bird as if she weren't a kinchin whore, and she would look at me as if I weren't a freak, and we made sense to each other. She was running for her life from a brothel madam called Silkie Marsh, who has a fair face and golden hair and no trace of a heart that I've been able to discern.

I wrote it all down – the unspeakable mass grave in the woods to which Bird led me, everything. Unlike writing police reports, which I detest, the words emerging from my pen siphoned off the pressure in my skull by small degrees. I've no notion what to make of that stack of parchment or why I didn't burn it upon stabbing the final period into the page. But humans are largely inexplicable and I'm no exception. So there it lies.

Bird yet flits in and out of my mind like a firefly in the dim, and I'm glad of it. Often enough, I see her in person, and I'm gladder still of that. She's much more sensible than I am. But at times, thoughts come unbidden of a madam smiling at me. Not with malice either. With comprehensive indifference. As if I were a sum to be calculated or a fish to be gutted for supper. And when I think of Silkie Marsh, I shut the door to the sleeping closet, as if the manuscript about her were possessed of mystical eyes.

I was feeling just enough out of sorts on the morning of February 14 to pull it closed with a dull *thud*.

After dressing, I marched downstairs to find Mrs Boehm slamming a rolling pin with obvious satisfaction into a ballooning ball of dough. It pillowed in the center, emitting a honeyed yeast smell.

'Good morning,' she said without looking up.

Something about my landlady's failing to spare me a glance feels comforting – as if I'm *expected* to be somewhere, anywhere, and her lack of surprise means I'm in the right place. Mrs Boehm's eyes are rather too big, rather too wide, and the soft blue color of a dress wrung out to dry in the sun for too many Junes, and they'd used to track me everywhere. Keenly too. Now I could parade a brass band through the door and she'd go on sifting flour. Her hair looks grey in low gaslight, but it's a strawlike blonde, wispy as the tips of pussy willow wands, and I found myself addressing the part in the center of her head.

'Good morning. What's that, then?'

'*Hefekranz*,' she said happily. 'Special order, by Germans next door, for a birthday celebration. Sugar it has, yeast, eggs. Very rich. Into a braid it goes, then in the oven. I like very much making this. Find anyone wicked?'

Endearingly, my landlady has a taste for sensationalist literature. And thereby for my career.

I picked up a day-old seeded roll on my way out. 'I can't even find an oil painting.'

'But you will,' she called, smashing the pale ball again with a childlike smirk on her face.

Seconds afterward, I realized I'd have paid good money for that confident little smile. Without even having been aware I'd needed it. Meanwhile, I stopped, blinking up at the dawn.

I'd not the slightest idea where I was going.

Admittedly, I paced for a few blocks in grim circles, skirting the malarial murk produced by the nearby Five Points, stewing over the futility of ever returning to the Millington residence. But then it came to me: I know someone whose wholehearted passion is *finding things*. Lost objects are his relics and pawnshop records his hymnals.

Finding things is what Jakob Piest *does*.

And so I strode with a purpose up Elizabeth Street toward Mr Piest's beat. Practically whistling in relief as I went, and entirely unaware that Mr Piest and I were about to meet the most fascinating human being either one of us had ever encountered.

CHAPTER TWO

I am that rarest of deviants in New York City: one who feels about
politics the way most men feel about scraping pig dung off their
boots. My antipathy stems from the fact that I spent most of my
life thinking my brother, who is an enormous cog in the Democratic
engine, one hundred percent despicable. I'd been mistaken – Val is
only three-quarters despicable. But when he landed me a job with
the copper stars, he could only place his highly unpolitical sibling
in Ward Six.

The appointment required me, as was the case with all star
police, to live in Ward Six. Which was a shame, because previously
I'd always treated the neighborhood just as everyone else does:
avoided it. Now that I've a comfortable set of rooms and a landlady
who pours me a small beer of an evening without my asking, I can't
be bothered to find new lodgings. Anyhow, I'm mere blocks from
the Tombs. But that doesn't make the scenery any more agreeable.

As I walked toward Mr Piest's beat that morning, I turned onto

Bayard to discover a pair of flame-haired Irish girl kinchin trading their one pair of shoes. The littler stood in the gritty frozen road porridge with toes gone pearl-white, offering a supportive shoulder as her sister peeled disintegrating moccasins off her own feet and passed them along.

Red toes are the first sign of frostbite. White means worse news. Those lasses were the sort Mercy had fought tooth and claw for, risking her health for tiny skeletons with pupils like gun barrels, and I found myself wondering how Manhattan's kinchin could ever survive without her. With a hat pin stuck in my throat, but nary a spare coin, I passed them by. More Irish, scores of them, trudged in their blue brass-buttoned jackets out of Ward Six in numb search of day labor. Sans gloves, sans overcoats in most cases. Hopeful as pallbearers and shivering in the weightless morning light.

Carts sagging with bolts of gingham lumbered by when I reached Chatham Street – or Jerusalem, as many call it – and its Dutch Yidisher pawnshops, each with three golden balls painted above the door. A mayor's office employee carrying a BEWARE OF MOCK AUCTIONS sign nearly slipped on a wheel-crushed rat, its guts still steaming. Before we star police existed, my friend Jakob Piest was a night watchman and private finder of lost property, so Chief Matsell routed him along Manhattan's epicenter for fenced goods. Most shops on Chatham are respectable as churches. They sell candles, spices, secondhand rifles, jewelry from tasteful to tawdry. But a few specialize in vanished objects, goods there and gone in an eyeblink.

And Mr Piest knows them as intimately as the back of his lobster-claw hand.

I found him quick enough. Just at the corner where Chatham angles off into Pearl Street, I glimpsed an awkward sideways gait emphasized by enormous Dutch boots. Shrimplike legs came next as my eyes moved upward, then a gaunt torso in a threadbare black coat. Above all floated a chinless face crowned by lively tufts of grey hair and a top hat gone shiny at the edges. The copper star pinned to his lapel had a drip of gravy clinging to it, which wasn't exactly unusual.

'Mr Piest!' I called out. 'I need a favor if you've time to spare.'

The roundsman's face split into a grin. Scuttling around a vendor selling thread, almanacs, and games of jacks from an open box, Mr Piest wrung me by the hand.

'At any hour of any day, Mr Wilde. With relish.'

'There's been a job done on Fifth Avenue. An original Jean-Baptiste Jacques Augustin has gone missing, a tiny study of a shepherdess. Might you show me around a shelf or two?'

His fluffy silver brow quirked. 'Of course, yes, by all means. It shall be done to the utmost of my ability, this very instant. What exactly is a *shelf*, Mr Wilde?'

'Sorry, that's flash,' I lamented, passing my hand over my mouth.

I use flash patter, the argot of thieves and all other breeds criminal, when solving any crimes in Ward Six. And when speaking with my sole surviving family member, which is how I came to know it at all. It's as much style as cipher, but daily the slang creeps further into plainspoken English – one of these days, the whole country will be calling pimps *jack-gaggers* and liars *confidence men*. Enough rowdies and swells leap on board, and even low cant can turn fashionable. Using flash unconsciously felt pretty disturbing, though. Valentine hasn't an inkling when he's speaking it. Next I'd sprout flowers all over my waistcoat and a Bowery-style cigar end from between my teeth.

'I was dealing with the cutthroat breed of Orange Street counterfeiters all of last week. My proper American evaporated,' I confessed. 'Pawnshops. Can you take me round to any pawnshops that might fence paintings?'

'Why, Mr Wilde,' the wonderful old madman exclaimed, 'I thought you wanted a *favor*. What do you think my rounds consist of?'

He set off, and I followed. Aside from the usual manic commerce, most businesses were peddling valentines, of course. Turner &

Fisher sported a hideous sign offering original verses by the anemic New York University type in the display window who was churning out PROSE OR VERSE, WITTY, SATIRICAL, LOVING, COMICAL, IRONICAL, OR ENIGMATICAL. I was just thinking I'd quite enough *Valentine* in my life already, thank you, and also *May God strike me dead if I ever pay a badly shaved bean sprout to write Mercy poetry and sign my name to it*, when Mr Piest began pulling me into a series of secondhand establishments smelling of musty cloth and used metal.

I was instantly fascinated. The pawnshops each boasted floor-to-ceiling shelves presided over by a merchant whose skin resembled parchment that would disintegrate if exposed to sunlight. Tortoiseshell combs jostled against pearl-handled razors and weirdly curved knives from the East. Books were wedged into every crevice. Dusty and molding volumes sat propped against kettles, pots, lamps, clocks – and, in one notable case, stacked at the base of a stuffed grizzly wearing a rather fetching pearl necklace.

'I heard the most *disturbing* gossip regarding your rival down the road, Mr De Groot,' Mr Piest whispered loudly in one such cave. 'It seems that Mr Duitscher – who we both know owns no scruples and is a blight upon the length of Chatham Street – recently came into possession of a painting. A very *small* painting, of a shepherdess, by Jean-Baptiste Jacques Augustin. Can you credit that he would attempt to sell an item so recognizable it endangers the *entire neighborhood?*'

'Sounds like Duitscher down to the letter,' De Groot agreed. 'But I've heard nothing of it.'

'Might I then – purely as a customer, for my dear mother's birthday fast approaches,' crooned the ancient copper star, 'have a glance at the contents of your safe?'

'*Natuurlijk.*' De Groot smiled toothily.

'*Ik dank u vriendelijk,*' my friend returned.

And so it went in every establishment. De Groots, Duitschers, Smiths, Emeriks, Kieks, and Johnsons – none had heard rumor of the miniature. In one shop, we did spy a suspicious monogrammed silver tea service. But it turned out to have once belonged to the other sort of stockbroker: the kind who prefers a quick introduction to the river to a slow introduction to being hungry.

Regarding the painting, we earned not the smallest sliver of a clue.

At last, Chatham Street behind us, we stood at the edge of that cankerous blot on the face of Manhattan, City Hall Park. I discouraged, Piest frenziedly thoughtful. To our right, City Hall and the Hall of Records presided over a wintry wasteland barren of cheer, leaves, and dignity. By then the sun was high. Urchins and emigrants and addicts trickled out from the naked trees, where last night they'd made beds from stone steps and hearths from dead grass. Just south of us, the fountain that in the blazing summer had presented a dry bowl littered with tadpole corpses now sprayed malicious plumes of ice water in the faces of passersby as far off as Broadway. The molleys who congregate there – men inclined to share tenderer intimacies with other men than simply dinner and a glass or two of rum – ought to find a new gathering place, I thought. The ways of New York fountains are mysterious. Possibly sadistic.

'Thank you for your help.' I pulled up my greatcoat collar and adjusted my muffler beneath. 'Though that tack didn't go quite as I wished.'

'No, indeed! Fortunately, there is a saloon just over in William Street that serves corned beef with dandelions. Best to eat and think this through.'

'I can't take you away from your beat any longer,' I protested.

'I've a night route, starting at six in the evening,' he called back over his shoulder, hair streaming from his head like the explosion of a silver firecracker. 'My shift just ended, at ten. We've all the time in the world.'

Dark booths a single step off the ground lined the walls of Calverey's American Dining Saloon. Alcoves, really, with coarse brown plush draperies. Mildewed and cheap, though the corned beef and wilted winter greens were far better than edible. Two candles shone between us. Mr Piest had just pushed our cleaned plates aside and twitched the cobwebby curtain halfway round.

'Why can't it have been one of the servants?' he asked cannily, shoving a wooden pick into his chaotic mountain range of teeth. Just what artifact he hoped to find in there I knew not. But I wished him well with the project.

'It can. It's just . . . unlikely anyone I spoke with would risk their place. Not impossible, mind. I can be queered same as the next fellow.'

'No, not quite the same as the next fellow, in my experience.'

'Anyhow, the painting is *gone*.' I glanced downward, having appropriated the back of the daily menu and begun to sketch the music room with a lead stub from my pocket. Out of undiluted frustration, probably. Drawing settles my brains. 'It isn't in the servants' quarters, which means if it was one of them, we're already hocussed. How reliable are those pawnbrokers?'

'I'll own that it's a perpetual twelve-sided game of chess.' Piest stuck four fingers of each hand within the opposite coat sleeves. 'But I've a fifteen-year relationship with most of them. And a shared language, no less, with both the Dutch and the Yidisher vendors. My father was a Jew, you know. I fear the painting hasn't been pawned by the usual channels.'

Puzzled, I made a few calculations, contrasting what I knew of my friend's police history with the figure *fifteen years*.

'Just how old are you?' I asked without thinking.

'Thirty-seven. Why do you ask?'

I felt my jaw dropping and then shut it so fast I must have looked as if a leg cramp had seized me under the table. Not my best performance. But apparently, police work ages a man as do seafaring and the tanning industry. It seemed at twenty-eight, I'd myriad delights in store. I dug deep for an explanation, but thankfully Piest was riveted by my room sketch.

'Mr Wilde, your talents range far and wide,' he exclaimed. 'That is very fine. Now, what of the Millingtons?'

'Mr Millington went straight to the chief, after all. Seemed

26

disappointed when he saw me. And Mrs Millington . . . no. Just no. She's decorative as her house.'

'So it was stolen by an invisible being,' Piest chuckled. 'A ghost who favors collectibles.'

I smiled at that bit of foolery. Then stopped, midway through darkening the edges of the fireplace.

There was a thought. Or the beginnings of one, anyway.

'Mr Wilde?'

Closing my eyes, I passed my fingers over them. It was more of an instinct than an idea, really. But there are plenty of invisible beings in New York. We walk past them every day. They're silent as our paving stones, no more solid than the stench in the air or the shadows thrown by our lofty stone monuments. Unnoticed and unseen. And one sort of unnoticeable would surely have visited that chamber often. The room's layout required it by law.

'The wall wasn't *dirty*!' I cried, slamming my hands flat on the tabletop. 'Idiot. Of course the servants clean under the artwork, they'd pay with their hides if they didn't. I am such an *idiot*.'

Mr Piest stared, wide-eyed as a fresh shrimp. Probably wondering if I might be combustible.

'So the wall in question was . . . clean?' he attempted.

'It's the middle of the month.'

'Mr Wilde, are you all right?'

'Grace. Grace is one of two upstairs maids. Of course. That makes all the difference in the world. If I'm right, that is, and—'

'I thought you said it was none of the servants.'

'It wasn't.' I dropped a shilling on the table as Piest did the same. 'Mr Piest, I've a harebrained theory. I'm likely wrong, and you'll lose your sleep this afternoon by it. But you're welcome to come.'

I set off, faintly hoping he'd choose to find a little peace before another sixteen-hour shift.

Wasted sentiment. The man is mad as a moon-addled barn owl. I've been grateful for the fact more than once.

'I've a particular fondness for harebrained theories. Lead the way, Mr Wilde,' called Mr Piest, his boots sending terrified shivers through the helpless plank boards. 'Leave sleep to the dead, for they've no better pastime, and leave the solving of crime to Ward Six's very own copper stars!'

The hack dropped us at 102 Fifth Avenue a bit after two o'clock in the afternoon. Already the sky had turned an ominously soft grey like the inside of a clamshell, and I didn't need a cook's enchanted knee to guess that snow was in our immediate future. We bypassed the front entrance and its dispirited gryphons, for I wanted none of the Millingtons. I wanted Turley the Bristol butler, my new bosom companion, and thus I headed behind the house. Piest trotted eagerly behind me, coat collar turned up against the still but piercing air.

Buzzing with hope, I rang the service bell. Ellen the downstairs maid appeared. Eyes like dull pennies, looking not best pleased with anyone. Herself included, I'd wager.

'I need Turley, Ellen. Quietly, all right? I'm hoping this will be over soon.'

'Truly, Mr Wilde?' she asked.

'Truly.'

She quit us with the forward momentum of a jackrabbit. Barely two minutes passed before Turley appeared, sideburns bristling.

'Mr Wilde. How unexpected.' The imperious London lilt had returned, but I supposed he'd not risk talking like a deckhand in the back area.

'Turley,' I said under my breath, 'please take no interest in the questions I'm asking. Do you savvy? I ask them, you answer, and then you forget them.'

'I have not the smallest doubt of my capacity to retain a discreet silence, sir.'

'Much obliged. Now. Grace's suitor, Jeb, visits her daily?'

Turley's eyes narrowed in annoyance. 'Yes, he does. He brings poesies, notes. A valentine just an hour ago. It's all in broad daylight, visible to myself or to the housekeeper, and quite respectable.'

'Of course it is. And Grace and Amy are the maids responsible for the rooms on the second floor, the music room included?'

'Now, just one moment,' Turley objected sharply, 'you clearly have formed a mistaken—'

'When was the music room's chimney and flue last cleaned?'

He stopped.

New Yorkers abhor the threat of fire. Particularly since half of downtown vanished last July. Fires are about as popular as smallpox, and households are required by law to have their chimneys swept monthly, enforced by the superintendent of sweeps. The actual sweeping is performed by a class of emaciated kinchin who appear to remain forever childlike. That's because they find better work by the ripe age of twelve, when they've grown too big for such narrow spaces – or they're already dead. Sweeps are invisible. About as conspicuous as gnats. And the sweeps, God help them, are all colored boys. If a white sweep exists on this island, I haven't glimpsed him.

'Households either clean their chimneys midmonth or near the first, so as not to forget,' I explained, watching comprehension dawn upon the faces of Piest and Turley. 'If the flue in the music room was being serviced, and Grace stepped away – maybe to have a word with Jeb – she'd not have thought anything of it. Why should she? And then, if she discovered that the painting was gone . . . I needn't tell you what that might have looked like to some. A black maid, a black sweep, an artwork stolen when she'd left the room.'

'The accusation of conspiracy would have loomed over her the instant she gave the alarm,' Mr Piest hissed.

'I found soot on the wall where the painting had been. I'd thought it merely dirty, but that was absurd. The sweep touched the paper with his knuckles when he took the art down, and the painting was small enough to hide in his shirt or his kit,' I concluded.

Turley rubbed at his cheeks with one hand. He hadn't any gloves on, and his fingers and face were flushed with cold.

'Call for Grace. If I'm right, there's still a chance we can end this nonsense.'

Turley considered my request. Likely not trusting me, and likely afraid for his staff. I admired him for it. Then he disappeared within the house. We waited, I staring at the paving stones in breathless anticipation and Mr Piest grinning toward the side of my head.

'Have you considered delivering lectures on the application of common sense in police work, intermixed with divine inspiration?' he teased me.

'Spare me, please,' I muttered, stamping my feet against the cold as a slow smile twisted my features.

Minutes passed. When Turley and Grace did appear, my heart curled in on itself at the sight of her. Turley led her gently enough by the arm into the yard, but her entire body trembled like a bell freshly chimed.

It was the first occasion, as a copper star, I'd terrified someone. Simply due to the metal pinned to my lapel. It was a repellent feeling. As if I'd awakened another species, something with serrated teeth and long, gleeful claws. I wanted to scrape its hide off of me with a tanning knife, return to a short-statured fellow with a fresh-poured drink in his extended hand.

Doubtless Grace's discomfort was far worse. But just then, I could scarce stomach my own.

'I wanted to shield the child,' Grace gasped. 'I never meant any harm, on a Bible I didn't.'

'We aren't arresting you,' I protested in dismay.

'I'll never find work again without a character, you can't—'

'Quieter, Grace, and no one need know about it,' I pleaded.

'Just tell him what happened, Grace,' Turley requested. 'He's not the sort to rake an honest girl over the coals.'

It took a bit more cajoling. But if there's one thing I can do effectively, it's look like a dimber place to deposit a story. Where stories are concerned, I am a man-shaped safety deposit box.

The household's usual chimney sweep had been coughing wretchedly for months; and Grace, not having the heart to let him starve just yet, had convinced Turley to keep him employed. But the lad had at last disappeared – into a colored hospital ward, or a charity society, or the ground. So Grace, whose job it was to interact with other blacks, had found a new sweep.

'He was crying on the street corner with a bell,' Grace told us, wringing a handkerchief into a coiled knot. Crying out one's business is a useful if deafening practice. Everyone from milk vendors to scissors grinders screams their professions from the sides of the road. 'A quick little mite, very neat and nimble.'

'Where was he stationed?' I asked.

She shook her head. 'I won't say.'

'But you must, Grace,' Turley exclaimed.

'No. You can't send him to the House of Refuge, Mr Wilde. He'd not live through it, and I don't think he understands. I'll not use him again, I promise.'

Children guilty of vagrancy or criminal acts are meant to be sent by copper stars to the House of Refuge. I've flouted this order upward of a hundred times in my short six-month tenure, as I'm not of the opinion that cat-o'-nine-tails improve kinchins' characters. A session with one certainly didn't enhance my brother's moral stamina. Whenever I think of how close my little friend Bird Daly came to being buried behind those stone walls at the behest of Madam Silkie Marsh, the old jolt of fear still echoes through my chest. If I could raze that institution to the ground, I'd consider my life to have been a parade-worthy success.

'I would never send any kinchin to the House of Refuge,' I said grimly. 'Where did you find the lad?'

'Don't make me say it. He's not quite right, but he's—'

'I'd sooner cut my arm off than send a child to the House of Refuge,' I vowed, my hand over my copper star. 'Please, Grace. Where does he cry his work?'

Grace stared back with wide, fierce eyes. I think if she could have taken a damp cloth and wiped the answer clean from her mind, she'd have done it. She'd no earthly reason to trust me. But she'd no guarantee I wouldn't throw her in the bowels of the Tombs for disobeying me either. Finally, she answered, 'God help him. He stands at the corner of Eighteenth and Third Avenue, the poor boy. God keep him from harm.'

Grace's throat sounded as if it were grinding glass, and *harm* meant *that horrible copper star in front of me*. So I said, as Piest and I turned away, 'I've no proof, you know. I only want to talk to him.'

A humorless laugh flew from Grace's mouth. 'That you'll never do.'

'Why not?' Mr Piest inquired.

'You'll see,' she said.

Then she buried her face in Turley's coat, her body wracked with deep sobs that made me understand something I hadn't before.

I wasn't the first copper star Grace had encountered. Or perhaps heard tell of. Something about us frightened her, yes, but it was the distinct, explicit breed of something. I wondered with a ticklish sensation in my chest what it was, but she was clearly now past speech. Grace's tears, and Turley's hushed words of comfort, followed us as we quit the corridor, and above us the skies sharpened to a wicked shade of steel.

Chapter Three

He asked, 'Are ye a slave for life?' I told him that I was.
The good Irishman seemed to be deeply affected by the
statement. He said to the other that it was a pity so fine a
little fellow as myself should be a slave for life . . . They
both advised me to run away to the north; that I should
find friends there, and that I should be free.

Frederick Douglass, *Narrative of the Life of Frederick*
Douglass, an American Slave, 1845

We soon reached Third Avenue. A tensely snapped gust like the crack of a driving whip blew up the street. Third is a vast swath of McAdamized roadway, much more pastoral and less shielded by tall buildings than is Fifth. It teemed with people, for Third is one of our headiest driving courses. Omnibuses rumbled toward the Twenty-seventh Street depot, hardened American dead rabbits whizzed by in pleasure traps, and swells took their ease in carriages with gaily painted bodies that looked like so many tropical birds. Every so often, a driver would glance up at the sky. Curious as to how far he could make it before the air was pale with snow.

'I only hope the boy isn't engaged at his profession,' Mr Piest observed, clutching at his top hat as it made a bid for freedom.

I hoped the same. But I needn't have worried, or at least not over that. When we crossed Seventeenth Street, a faint chiming sound met our ears over the strengthening gale.

A tiny colored lad stood at the corner of Eighteenth Street and Third Avenue, ringing a hand bell. I put him at six years – not over, and anyhow that's a common age for a new sweep. Charcoal coated him from head to toe. Novice sweeps often exhibit one or more limbs askew from falling down chimneys, but this kinchin appeared unscathed. So far. When we drew closer, I saw that his eyes were inflamed, red and weeping and blinking compulsively. Typical affliction, considering the incessant dust. They nevertheless searched with cutting focus for potential employment. He wore his coarse hair short but unbraided, and he'd a filthy broom at his feet.

'Hello,' I said affably.

Ringing the bell a bit faster, he smiled. It didn't fool me – he was exhausted. Not to mention starving, judging by his wrists. The smile was pure sales technique, and a fine one.

'Do you sweep the chimneys in these parts?'

A nod, long lashes wicking the moisture from his brown and scarlet eyes.

'Do you know what this means?' I asked, touching my copper star.

He shrugged. But that didn't nettle me. I was constantly informing adults that the police force existed, let alone six-year-old kinchin who live in fireplaces. Then Grace's parting words echoed through my skull.

'Can you speak?' I questioned.

He shook his head and then stuck his chin up, ringing the bell beside his ear.

'That's all right, I know you can hear me. But you're mute?'

The child adopted a bored expression that demanded to know *Why the devil does it matter to you.* I exchanged a look with my fellow star police.

'That is going to make questioning him a bit of a wrench,' Mr Piest owned.

Frowning, I considered various tactics. Surely the child had never lived in an asylum where sign was taught. And if anyone had bothered to show him his letters, I was prepared to watch Manhattan's numerous stray pigs take flight over the Hudson. *Tell us where the painting is. Have you stolen any paintings of late? We'll not harm you, but we're reasonably sure you filched a Jean-Baptiste Jacques Augustin.* All sounded either brutish or ridiculous. Finally, I lowered myself to my haunches.

'Do you like art?' I asked him. 'Pictures?'

The bell stopped. Then, with a youthful happiness that would be trampled in a month's time – if not much, much sooner – he nodded.

'What sort?'

Quick as thinking, he'd set the bell down. First he drew a square before me with his fingers, and then flashed a palm. Next the shape of a vase materialized out of thin air, followed by the same brief palm-forward motion. Finally he circled his arms in an expansive flail, encompassing anything and everything, showing his palm quickly one more time to signal he'd finished and then staring at me with his head cocked.

I glanced back at Mr Piest.

'Did you understand that?' I asked, feeling a bit dizzy.

'Mr Wilde, I believe it is safe to say that I did,' he answered, equal parts admiration and frank awe.

'I like art too,' I told the sweep. 'Paintings and vases and the like. All of it.'

An honest thread of fellow feeling had burrowed into my tone. I've met plenty of queer people in my time, but never a kinchin who'd invented his own version of sign language. And a comprehensible one, no less.

'Have you ever seen a picture being made?'

This answer was in the negative. Wistful and longing.

'Would you like me to show you?'

Bell and broom scraped against the pavement as he leaped forward.

35

'Mr Piest, have you a memorandum book?'

Within seconds, I'd paper on my knee and my pencil stub in hand. The boy came round to see what I was doing, and I confess it freely: I cast out bait no fish would have been able to resist. Maybe I needed the Jean-Baptiste Jacques Augustin back, and maybe I wanted to give the kinchin ten minutes of fun. Probably both motives were true and neither pure. In any event, within a short space of time, I'd completed a small portrait of a chimney sweep.

A sweep who now stared at me with the soft light of wonder in his swollen eyes.

'What do you think?' I prompted.

The boy explored his face with his fingertips, brushing them carefully over his even brow, his sharply edged lips, the bridge of his up-tilting nose. Lacking a mirror but clever enough not to need one. A smile bloomed across his features as he searched.

I don't think I've ever been prouder of my facility myself. It's generally a useless knack altogether.

'That is the most magnificent artwork that I have ever seen,' Mr Piest announced.

Grimy fingers hovered over the memorandum book. When I moved it away, the sweep's face snapped to mine. Quivering with desire and asking the most direct question I've ever seen rather than heard.

'All right. It's yours, but I need payment.'

He seized the broom and bell.

'No, I don't have a chimney to clean. As I told you, I'm very fond of art. I've shown you a painting. Now I want you to show me one, as a trade. Have you anything worth looking at yourself?'

He lit up as only a six-year-old boy can. Before permanent lines are drawn between victims and tormentors, before suffering quite registers as cruelty. Before the falsehoods adults tell acquire a tinny ring.

Meanwhile, a generous splash of vinegar seeped into my belly. Lying to him shamed me, but I hadn't much of an alternative. And I thought to make it up to the lad.

The sweep flew across Third, barely pausing for traffic as we hastened after. A dogcart swerved, an open landau filled with champagne-swilling ladies in dark furs nearly flattened Piest, and we stopped once in the middle of the road to allow for a speeding omnibus. But all three emerged unscathed from the perilous avenue. When the boy sped north along the road's margin, we kept pace with him, the spreading oak trees casting blurred shadows into the milky light.

After ten or twelve blocks, we'd quit the developed city for the farmlands surrounding Bellevue Almshouse. We like our benevolent institutions much farther afield than our blinding rainbow array of vices. Only the fanatical reformers brave the streets as Mercy did, a basket over her shoulder and a ferocious calm in her eyes. By the time the boy veered off of Third into the woods, the streets intersecting the avenue were no longer paved. They were hints at the grid design – square forest canvases, blank pages in a diary. Now roots caught at our feet, and the slender elms and maples grew scattershot. Birds called out from the branches rendered in sable ink against the ice-hued skyline, and every so often a wild creature crashed away through the bracken. I glimpsed the red tail of a fox, trotting over the undulating ground in search of supper and shelter and rest.

Before us, the tiny black figure flew onward like a gap in space. A cutout, the silhouette of a boy running through the undergrowth.

I hadn't the smallest notion what to expect, of course. But when he'd reached our destination, I took a moment to blink in astonishment.

'By all the saints,' Mr Piest exclaimed softly.

Many years earlier, from the looks of the waxy ivy and the trailing brown vines, a carriage traveling up Third Avenue suffered an accident. Likely the horses had panicked. It happens all too frequently. The beasts had crashed into a barely visible ditch in the middle of a theoretical block within a glade no one occupied, almost in sight of the East River. I didn't bother wondering why the owners had abandoned it, for the back axle thrust at a wrecked angle up through the dead leaves. And even if no humans had died there, it was obvious from the carriage's state that horses had. Nothing sounds like a dying horse. That sort of scream sends a sick shock through your guts every time you hear it. No, the carriage had been rendered unusable.

Temporarily unusable, it seemed. The sweep trotted up to it and threw open the double doors with a flourish.

'Mother of God,' I whispered.

The carriage had been converted into a display case. Cracked pieces of bright blue pottery lined the floor, shards of green glass were strung from the upholstery buttons, singular finds including a chipped ceramic rose and a chunk of sparkling river granite rested on the rotting seat cushions. Loose chandelier crystals and broken paperweights and a slender French liquor bottle – a cherished museum of unmourned, unremembered objects. I wondered if, before he'd joined the regiment of chimney dwellers, he'd lived nearby. It was probable. But I supposed I'd never know the answer. Stray children hereabouts are as closely tracked as the ants underfoot.

The showcase's pièce de résistance sat propped against the opposite door panel, festooned with a string of cheap amber coloured beads: a tiny painting by Jean-Baptiste Jacques Augustin. The shepherdess peered coyly at us, her head tilted back against a scandalously rosy summer's evening. The curves of her fingertips and of her bosom echoed one another, and she seemed to be in the act of repressing a beautiful confession, tasting words of adoration on her tongue.

The sweep pointed at it in triumph.

Reaching, I plucked it from the glittering yellow glass. When the boy's face tensed with worry, I took a seat on the carriage's footrest and hung my wide-brimmed hat from my knee.

'This came from a house on Fifth Avenue. You cleaned their chimney, didn't you?'

He rubbed at his eyes with ash-covered hands. Stared up again – not at me, but at the painting.

'You must have known it was stealing, lad. Why should you have taken their property?'

Furiously, his little fists rent the air. He made about a dozen stabbing finger points in all directions, then circled one hand with the other in a gesture of endlessness and concluded with a fraught, exasperated wringing of his fingers.

'I know they've more art than they know what to do with. I'm sorry. But this painting already has a home.'

The vitriol in his raw eyes was fully deserved on my part. So it burned me all the worse. I'd tricked him, and now he'd cottoned to the fact. Worse still, I understood him perfectly: the tender young shepherdess was far more passionately beloved in a ruined carriage than she was in that snob art warehouse on Fifth Avenue. I wished to holy Christ I'd never heard the name *Millington*.

Tearing my sketch from the memorandum book, I passed it to the scowling youth who stood digging his boot toe into a patch of frozen earth.

'This is yours. I'm not going to punish you for stealing, but you must promise me never to do it again. Scavenging is one thing, but thieving could get you croaked. This is your first and final art theft.'

He reached for his portrait. Like enough thinking my art better than no art at all, and already deft at quick choices.

'Promise me,' I insisted.

The boy did, with an enraged little shrug. He wiped his eyes with his sleeve. Though he wasn't weeping, or not any more than he did perpetually.

'What's your name?' Mr Piest inquired. 'I am Jakob Piest, and this is Timothy Wilde.'

The child's face fell. He gave a pained blink, staring at a moldy wheel spoke, before shoving both hands hard into his pockets.

I'd thought him an orphan. There's an independence about us, and a gravity, that's unmistakable. But at least Val and I had been old enough to own our names, no matter that we'd nothing else. Old enough to remember the family who'd named us, as well. A name can make a man. I couldn't imagine being robbed of anything more personal.

'Surely they must call you something, where you live now,' I reasoned. 'What does your sweepmaster call you?'

A shudder passed through him. It left the boy wearing a grimace as if he'd like nothing better than to peel himself out of his own skin.

'Never mind,' I said, before his expression could bring any more of an ache to my ribs. 'What sort of name would you like?'

His eyelashes fluttered, soot-dusted and feathery. The line of his mouth grew a shade less taut.

'Capital idea, the very thing!' Mr Piest agreed.

'Sweepmaster be damned. It'll belong to you. What's the bulliest name you can think of?'

The boy took his time about it. Solemn as gravestones, lips pressed into a line. Finally, face all curiosity, he pointed at the shepherdess I held.

'The man who painted this? His name was Jean-Baptiste Jacques Augustin,' I answered.

The kinchin's eyes closed as he rolled the sound of it to and fro in his mind. Meanwhile, a wild woodland happiness swept through me. A pleasure like sharp country wind and blown-open winter skies. I'll never forget the look I shared with Mr Piest a moment later. Warm as a wordlessly shared flask. And all thanks to a chimney sweep.

'Do you like the name Jean?' I questioned.

From the smile that transformed his face, like a pure crescent moon when the clouds have been swept away, I believe that he most assuredly did.

'To the Millingtons,' Mr Piest proposed in my office, raising his cup of gin, 'and the ways of old Gotham. In particular, to fat rewards and those who offer them!'

We'd all quit the woods as plump snowflakes began to whirl around us in the late afternoon. Crossing Third Avenue in the accepted semi-suicidal fashion, dodging hacks and gleefully reckless vans. I'd watched the crystals settling, and thought about names and their absolute importance to their owners, and felt pretty near to delighted. We celebrated Jean-Baptiste's self-christening by buying him the thickest bowl of oxtail stew I have ever seen summarily destroyed and then lingered over the occasion, sluggish with warmth and with firelight.

I'd have done better by him than a hot meal if I could. Children are remarkable creatures, hurtling through savage landscapes of sudden laughter and sharp heartbreaks. It gnaws me bloody to see the city stretch them into leaner, taller, grimmer animals altogether. And there was an innocence to Jean-Baptiste, that wide joy at tiny blessings, I'd have liked to see preserved longer than the next fortnight or so. But taking it upon myself to relocate each and every destitute kinchin I come across would be akin to kneeling at the shoreline and forcing the Hudson back with my fingertips and my will, and at least this one was employed. Housed with his fellow sweeps, presumably, if neither fed nor loved. And thus I shook his hand outside the low saloon, and my fellow copper star flipped him a shilling, and we parted ways.

Piest and I returned to the servants' door and handed the painting over to Turley. He vanished, returning with a drawstring purse.

'Didn't you know there was a reward?' he'd asked in response to my complete incomprehension.

So Piest and I split fifty dollars, bestowed for our facility at *finding things*, and he immediately bought the oddest-tasting Dutch gin conceivable. It warmed the throat in a friendly fashion, tasting of dark bread rather than pine.

My Tombs cave had never looked brighter, as the wind howled beyond the great walls like a wolf baying madly at the heavens. I was rich enough to buy thirty or so used books, pay Mrs Boehm for the carpet I'd borrowed, and set some aside. I was intoxicated with competence at my profession. Mercy Underhill was in London, which meant Mercy was presumably contented. And it was snowing, so I wasn't unduly worried that my brother's engine company might be fighting the raging house fire that would finally leave me the only Wilde in New York.

That is to say, I was about as happy as I ever am. Happiness not being any great knack of mine.

'To the Millingtons.' I touched Piest's cup with mine. 'To not having suffered the honor of seeing them again.'

'Oh, come,' he chuckled. 'We must view the Millingtons in light of their generosity with rewards and the unlikelihood that they will ever pose us any . . . unfortunate questions.'

'I'm being an ass,' I agreed. 'To Jean-Baptiste and the artistic soul.'

'Hear, hear!' My friend sloshed more gin into our cups.

'To that shepherdess,' I added. 'Whoever she was. My God.'

Cackling in a nicely filthy fashion, Mr Piest drained his spirits.

'Shouldn't you be sleeping?'

'Yes!' he cried. 'Yes, Mr Wilde! But I so seldom work with watchmen – police, I beg your pardon, old habits – who can differentiate between their arses and their eyelashes. It's exhilarating. The last time I—'

My door burst open.

The woman standing before us was uncannily striking. She'd richly golden skin that, when paired with grey-green eyes and hair the color of imported chocolate, would arrest the attention of male passersby and female alike. Universally.

'I need a policeman,' she said.

She didn't. She needed a miracle.

We soon had her seated, with a cup in her unsteady hand. Her distress was a horror you could taste, thick and sluggish as a slow death.

When I asked her what had been stolen, her answer was *My family.* That statement hung gruesomely in the air for several seconds.

'I don't understand,' I said.

'My sister and my son,' she gasped. 'Delia and Jonas. They're gone. Delia stays with me when my husband is away, he travels for his business, and she – she was watching my—'

The tin cup fell to the floor with a light clatter as she covered her face with her hands. Her shoulders trembled in concert with her breathing, ripples over the crests of shallow waves.

'Have you searched—' Mr Piest began.

'I need *you*, Mr Wilde,' she said, looking up at me fiercely.

My showing at comprehension was already landing at about nil, but I'll admit that staggered me.

'Why do you say so?'

'I know who you are and I know what you've done. You must help me.'

My lips parted to say *Of course I will*. But they were a fair distance from my cartwheeling brain. I hadn't the slightest idea what she was talking about.

'They steal people.' Tears filled her eyes, a tincture of misery and rage. 'We're wasting time.'

'But how—'

'I ought to have been at home by then. They'd have stolen me too, and you'd never have heard a word of this. When I did arrive, my cook, Meg, was bound and gagged on the floor of the pantry and my family was gone. They don't want Meg, she's lame in one foot, not worth their trouble. I asked a policeman in the front hall where Timothy Wilde was, and he sent me here.'

'And I'm glad you did, but—'

'You saved Julius Carpenter.' She launched herself from the chair, grasping both my lapels.

Then I managed to grasp two things I hadn't previously.

My friend Julius Carpenter, the quietly brilliant colored oysterman I'd worked with when I was a relatively untroubled bartender, landed in trouble last summer. A pack of starved Irish caught the notion that burning him at the stake would be rare sport. I'd disagreed and been near roasted over it. Not that I'd minded, seeing as Julius had saved me from the fire downtown by sending my brother to dig me out of the smoldering rubble. If we were

43

counting notches, Julius and I stood dead even. So there was half the mystery solved.

The other half of the mystery ought to have been obvious. If I'd been looking as closely as I like to think I do, anyhow.

Lucy Adams, with her honey skin and green-flecked eyes and gorgeous tangle of brown hair, might have claimed Italian parentage. She might instead have been of Spanish descent, though her voice proved a northern American birthplace. And then again, she might have been the exotic blending of a Welsh mother and a Greek father, or a Sicilian and a Swede. But she was none of those combinations. The reason I'd been so damnably slow to comprehend her spine-melting panic was that I didn't much care one way or another *what* she was.

But Lucy Adams did. She cared a great deal. Because Lucy Adams was black.

Not above a quarter, likely less. I'd have guessed at an eighth. A fraction black is still black, though. Legally speaking.

Then I grasped why she wanted my help and none other. My fellow copper stars are half wholesale decent folk and half plain villains, granted. But the slave-catching industry – which was the subject we'd been discussing all that while – isn't just *legal*.

It's law enforcement.

I pulled her hands off my coat, but only so I could have a grip on them. 'You're all free New York citizens, I take it.'

'We hailed from Albany originally. My grandparents bought their freedom some sixty years ago. Slave agents care nothing for that, when the chance for profit is high enough. Delia and Jonas would be worth—'

'How long have they been missing?'

'Two hours by now.'

'And how old is your son?'

'Seven,' she said, nearly choking on the word.

'Wherever he is, he's with your sister, and we'll soon find them. Mr Piest, I can't ask you to join us, but—'

'If I report to the chief regarding our success today, I ought to be free if it's to assist you,' Mr Piest returned, shoving our cups in my tiny desk drawer.

'I'd be grateful. Where are we going, Mrs Adams?'

'To see the Committee. My house, Eighty-four West Broadway between Chambers and Warren. You must knock exactly six times, sir, in sets of two.'

With a small salute, Mr Piest scudded away. Leaving me to dazed wonderment over who the devil *the Committee* was and what temperature of hot water I'd just landed in. Mrs Adams took my arm, and we plunged through the door after him. We hurried through stone corridors out of the massive combined prison, courthouse, and ward headquarters, I making every effort to ensure my new acquaintance didn't plunge headlong down the stairs wearing sopping dress boots.

Then something peculiar happened.

At the mouth of the exit hall, a burly redheaded copper star by the name of Sean Mulqueen peered after us, unmoving. Eyes narrowed in nail-sharp Irish scrutiny. He was flanked, as I'd often before seen him, by a hulking black Irish and by a native New Englander with an eerily rosy, youthful face, both of them Ward Six roundsmen. I nodded to Mulqueen, as I knew him slightly. Whenever we'd spoken, he'd struck me as forceful-minded beneath the layers of gristly muscle.

'Friend of yours, Mr Wilde?' he surmised.

'Crime victim.'

'Oh, then ye had fain be getting on. Best o' luck,' he added, voice quite inscrutable.

'Good night,' I called back as we quit the granite fortress and found ourselves smothered in darkness.

Mrs Adams's grip tightened as we negotiated the eight slick steps down to the cobbled road. Two gaslights shone nearby, but the rest had blown out due to cracks in the lamps. We hurried south along West Broadway. The snow tumbling beneath what light remained looked faerie-touched, sinister. Shards of airborne glass keen to slice a person in ribbons.

'Were you anxious over harassment from slave catchers?' I questioned over the din of the gale. 'Had they threatened you?'

'No. They needn't have. I've been terrified for years that this moment would come one day.'

'Why so?'

'That's easy enough to answer, Mr Wilde.' She pulled her fur tighter around her regal neck. 'I've been kidnapped before, after all.'

CHAPTER FOUR

*I felt of my pockets, so far as the fetters would allow – far
enough, indeed, to ascertain that I had not only been
robbed of liberty, but that my money and free papers were
also gone! Then did the idea begin to break upon my mind,
at first dim and confused, that I had been kidnapped. But
that I thought was incredible. There must have been some
misapprehension – some unfortunate mistake. It could not
be that a free citizen of New-York, who had wronged no
man, nor violated any law, be dealt with thus inhumanly.*

Solomon Northup, *Twelve Years a Slave*, 1853

To the south of our city exists a land as unlike ours as it is
possible to imagine. A country of lush fields, soft-voiced
belles, easy graciousness, and mist-shrouded nights that whisper
like the heat of a lover's breath against your neck. There are moss-
draped trees there, I hear tell, and slow winds, and blue skies. And
in that land flourishes a trade that festers like an open cancer in our
national skin.

We don't think about that land very often. Or most of us don't,
anyhow. It might as well be a separate nation.

I've met a great many Southerners here. Poured neat bourbons
for them, added mint to their water in the summertime, talked with

47

them of books and of horses and of trade. Some of them are kindly and genteel folk who would serve up a feast to any flea-ridden midnight stranger who knocked at their door and then ask the chap to stay over for the week. Some are fiery scoundrels who'd as soon duel you as shake your hand. Exactly the same as New Yorkers, therefore – pretty evenly divided between knights and knaves.

With one cardinal difference.

In the North, blacks are a free but steadily trod-upon race. And in the South, they are livestock. Cattle, but a universe of suffering worse than cattle: cattle that can think. Our small but vocal set of abolitionists are at pains daily to point this out, and they get putrid tomatoes and jagged rocks lobbed at them for their trouble.

The rest of us simply don't want to dwell on it. We're cowards of the human imagination. Soft as fresh cheese. We don't want to think about breeding people as if they were racehorses. We don't want to think about kinchin pried from their mothers and traded for farm equipment. We've no desire to think about branding fellow humans, nor of laboring in the Louisiana sun in an endless daily cycle, nor of being flogged to death if the party objects too loud or too often to this scheme, nor of escapees being torn apart by dogs. So the general population doesn't think much about it. And grows hotly annoyed when forced to pry open an eye and stare slavery in the face.

That would be one reason we loathe slave catchers.

New Yorkers enjoy being told what to do about as much as we enjoy a plummeting stock market. And thanks to the Fugitive Slave Act of 1793, we're required to hand runaways over to Southern slave agents as if we're returning a spooked thorough-bred. In 1840, a shockingly moral Albany law granted alleged fugitives in New York State the right to a jury trial. And in 1842, *Prigg v. Pennsylvania* nationally revoked the right of any colored fugitive to a jury trial. Thus, in 1846, up is down and straight is crooked and black is blacker than black has ever been. Right and wrong are left suffocating, beached fish in a barren legislative no-man's-land.

It's all so illogical that every man does pretty much as he pleases. And that was my plan, as Lucy Adams rapped carefully in three sets of two upon her lightly snowbanked front door before turning her key in the lock.

To do as I pleased.

Damask curtains masked the windows in her parlor. The gas burned low. Barely a yellow flicker to mark the furnishings or the floral carpet beneath my feet. The fire in the grate had been stoked up, though, sending restless shadows dancing across the comfortable chamber. A profound sense of emptiness, of something *missing*, permeated the room. I'd have thought I'd intruded upon a wake, but wakes are considerably noisier.

Three men rose to greet us. All of them black and one of them known to me.

'You've found him, then,' my friend Julius Carpenter said to Mrs Adams, shaking my hand. 'How are you, Timothy?'

I smiled despite the gravity of the setting. When we'd worked together at Nick's Oyster Cellar in Stone Street, which seemed millennia ago, Julius shelled upward of a thousand gleaming oysters a night. He's quick and contemplative, with a calm, round face and deep-set eyes under inquisitive brows. My friend wore the clean but loose-fitting clothing of a carpenter after work hours, and he'd fragrant tea leaves braided into the rows of his hair. If it was a shock to see him, at least it was a pleasurable one. We'd worked together for so long, I think the pair of us could still serve a hundred stock jobbers blindfolded and never break a sweat. We're sympathetic that way. In tune.

'Julius, what in hell are you doing here?' I gripped him by the arm. 'And what have you been doing with my reputation?'

'Nothing it didn't deserve, I calculate. Everyone, this is Timothy Wilde, Ward Six copper star. Meet the Reverend Richard Brown and George Higgins, of the New York Committee of Vigilance. And the third member would be me.'

City dwellers are inordinately fond of committees. Committees for temperance and against it, organizations supporting everything from the expulsion of the Irish to all-vegetable diets to secret fraternities. But I'd never heard of this one. 'You're part of a club?' I asked.

'No, a cause. We do what we can to keep free blacks alive and well and in the North, where they belong,' Julius explained. 'People of color run the risk of capture every time they step outside. We do what we can to reduce the danger. It's all run on a volunteer system, and any donations go toward keeping the streets safe. Mainly organizing patrols and night watches in colored neighborhoods, providing legal advice to blacks who find themselves in hot water with slave agents, that sort of thing. We try to take care of our own.'

'You're an unofficial watchman?'

I shouldn't have marveled, for Julius is square as they come, but the thought took a moment to settle. Smiling gravely, he tapped his forefinger against his chin, a wonderfully familiar little gesture he employs whenever I am surprised for no good reason.

'But for how long?'

'Nigh about three years by this time, I'd figure.'

'Why didn't you tell me?'

Julius shrugged one shoulder. 'I didn't want it getting around. You remember Nick – fair enough as bosses go and always paid us on time, but he liked me better the less he saw of me.' My old friend brushed his palms down his shirtfront. 'Sit down, everyone. There isn't much in the way of time.'

We seated ourselves – Julius and I in a set of matched armchairs with our backs to the fire, and Mrs Adams, Reverend Brown, and Mr Higgins spanning the settee. Richard Brown was thin and scholarly, with the bulge of a miniature book straining his waistcoat pocket, though I didn't need the tiny Bible or Julius's introduction to set him down as a minister from eighty yards. His face was worried but strangely peaceful – as if he'd accepted that the outcomes of his trials were in other hands than his.

50

George Higgins was much more intriguing a fellow. Taller and thicker built, with a kingly jaw and a very dark, almost blue-black complexion. He wore a carefully trimmed beard, a silver watch chain, and a green silk cravat, though his hand was calloused where it dangled from one crossed knee. The calluses could have meant anything – local blacks tend to average three jobs at minimum. But this Mr Higgins was wealthy. Had the watch chain possibly been an inheritance, I wouldn't have leapt to such a conclusion, but it was fashionably long and slender. Anyhow, silk cravats are capable of surviving a single New York month at best, and his gleamed sumptuously at me. He'd widely spaced, clear brown eyes with something flintlike gleaming at the back of them. They scraped over me as if uncertain what lay beneath my skin.

He was anxious, and not from abstraction or gallantry. He was anxious personally. I wondered for whom.

'Post me,' I requested. 'Mrs Adams told us that her sister and son have been kidnapped for more than two hours. As reported by her cook, Meg, who was forcibly tied and left within the house.'

'Meg went home just now, shaken up and with a stiff leg but otherwise fine,' Julius answered. 'Seems that two men, one with a Colt pistol, barged into the house after she answered a knock at the door. Tied her down and tossed her in the pantry. She heard one or two screams, then nothing.'

'Can she identify the assailants?'

'Oh, we know who they were well enough.'

'I mean, could she peg them in court as kidnappers of New York citizens?'

If I'd stood up and blown a shrill whistle blast, the others couldn't have looked more dumbfounded. The expression melted into anguish on Mrs Adams's face, rancid disgust – quickly mastered – on Mr Higgins's, and simple disbelief on Julius Carpenter's.

'Your friend the copper star is a real prize, Julius,' George Higgins drawled.

'How would he know, after all?' Julius leaned forward with his fingertips touching. 'Timothy, how well Meg saw them doesn't matter. Black testimony isn't admissible at fugitive slave trials. Only a white can officially identify a black in court. As for a black identifying a white kidnapper – I've never even heard it tried.'

My jaw dropped for long enough to say, 'But that's ludicrous.'

'Yes, that's rather the point, isn't it?' Mr Higgins asked acidly. 'Mr Wilde, we're grown men and not afraid of facing down these vermin, nor fearful of a fight if it comes to that. But we want this rescue to come to some good, you see. We don't need your help doing what's right. We've done that before, a score of times. We need your help doing what's legal, now there are copper stars.'

A score of times.

'You've rescued upward of twenty people?' I asked, startled.

'We've begun to, though not all were saved in the end,' Reverend Brown confessed. 'Sometimes we succeeded, but as for the rest . . . their court cases fell through. The poor souls are in Georgia or Alabama by now, may God grant them strength.'

I passed my fingers through the arch of my hairline, skimming normal skin and skin resembling badly cured alligator hide. This assembly was clearly better than capable of minding their own affairs. If the fact they'd no legal way of doing so made me ill, it must have sent a brushfire burn through their guts when they looked at a pint-sized white star police.

Six raps spaced into pairs reverberated from the foyer, and Mr Higgins pushed to his feet with a worried glare.

'It's my colleague, but let me be sure,' I said.

When I threw the door open, it was indeed Piest, half-frostbitten and his squashed face red as a boiled lobster. He stamped his boots and followed me into the parlor without a word wasted.

'This is Jakob Piest, as good a copper star as you'll find,' I said, making the necessary introductions. 'Now. Obviously, I'm at sea here. Who's responsible, and what have you done in the past to counter them?'

Reverend Brown put his elbow on the arm of the settee, a finger tensed before his lips. 'Their names are Seixas Varker and Long

Luke. Slave catchers, they would tell you. We would say otherwise.'

'They're snakes,' Mr Higgins snapped. 'And we're wasting valuable time.'

Mrs Adams shuddered.

'Well, whatever their species, their names are Seixas Varker and Long Luke Coles, and I believe they hail from Mississippi,' Julius put in smoothly.

'Where would they have taken their captives?' Mr Piest leaned with one shoulder against the doorway. 'And what can we do about it?'

'We've one great cause for hope tonight.'

'What's that?' I asked.

'The storm,' Mrs Adams whispered, touching the curtain.

Beyond the pane, snow poured like grains through an hourglass, wind whipping drifts into sinuous eddies that broke in white-crested waves. It was terrible out there. And getting worse. Already, ships had dashed themselves to pieces along our coastline and sailors with talismans clenched in their fists searched the horizon in vain for a lighthouse, a harbormaster, a haven, a crest of rock. To no avail. February 14 of 1846 was a cruel night. One that would be long mourned. But even if I didn't yet know of the massacre the Hudson had wrought, I took their meaning plain.

'I'd suppose kidnap victims are normally spirited away without bothering over a trial, if possible,' I ventured. 'But no sane person would dream of setting sail in this weather.'

Julius nodded. 'Varker and Coles have a side business in wine distribution. They've a dockside shop in Corlears Hook, equipped with plenty of bottles in the front and a cell in the back. They hold people there when a ship isn't ready to hand.'

'And that's *legal*?' I demanded.

A host of simmering looks met my eyes.

'Next time I say something stupid, cuff me in the ear,' I requested of Julius. 'What's first on our agenda?'

'Lucy needs a hiding place. This house isn't safe,' Julius answered.

'But I'm going with you,' she said with a deadly look in her eyes.

'That would be an insane risk,' I objected.

'He's right.' George Higgins dug his nails into his palm. 'There could be violence. And so we really ought to be *leaving*. Where's best for Lucy to wait?'

'The station house, for my money,' I said, rising.

'No!' she cried, aghast. 'No, not the Tombs. After sending Meg for the Committee, I came there for *you*. They'll—'

'Not that station house.' I exchanged a look with Julius. 'I've a suggestion. No offense meant, but you said *legal* help. Think of the copper stars as your hired bruisers. If a fight breaks out and we get the worst of it, you men throw down gloves – but if not, it's cleaner to leave any milling to the star police. Tell me I'm wrong.'

A seething sort of trouble percolated in Mr Higgins's eyes, but Reverend Brown set a hand on his shoulder. 'If we're wanted, we'll fall in,' the clergyman agreed.

'Aces. Mr Piest, how are you at pugilism?'

'Ah,' he said doubtfully. 'Well. Very *willing* to employ fisticuffs in a good cause, Mr Wilde, in fact none more willing, but—'

'There's a kinchin at risk here, and the kidnappers are armed, and visiting the Hook is its own set of risks. Mr Piest, we're fetching one more copper star.' I offered my hand to Mrs Adams, who took it without looking at me. She'd gone quiet as a stone.

'Then we three will go at once to the wine shop and keep guard.' George Higgins leapt up, pulling on his gloves. 'If something should happen before you arrive, Mr Wilde, I warn you – we'll do whatever we must.'

'I certainly hope so. We'll meet you there in force and storm the gates. Mrs Adams, we're taking a hack to the Ward Eight station house.'

'And why Ward Eight?' Higgins queried pointedly.

'Because Mrs Adams doesn't trust copper stars, and you don't trust copper stars, and I need another copper star who's flash on the muscle and runs a loyal station house. That means the captain of Ward Eight. Think of him as my brother instead of as police if you like,' I suggested as we all converged on the door and the tempest beyond. 'Or as a Republic of Texas-sized version of me, whatever you please. Just so long as we get your family back, Mrs Adams, I don't mind if you think of Valentine as a trained grizzly.'

'And anyway, that wouldn't be too far off the bull's-eye,' Julius muttered amiably as we shut the door behind us.

Hacks were scarce in the violence of the storm. But so were pedestrians, and within ten minutes I was seated in a drafty cab with Mr Piest and Mrs Adams. Our hacksman must have driven close to blind despite his lamps, for the snowfall formed an arctic curtain of bitter lace. More than one bone-snapping bump sent Mrs Adams's hand clutching for the strap handle.

But she said nothing. And comfort unasked for is often comfort unwanted. So we listened to the whistling gusts until the driver reined his horse, cab wheels skidding dangerously and the half-frozen creature whimpering with nerves. Prince Street was drowning in white. After paying the driver his two bits with a few pennies extra to wait for us, I could scarce find the neat brick station house's door.

Inside, the fireplace crackled hotly behind the hinged pine countertop with the quill and inkstand where my brother was meant to be presiding. Granted, according to my pocket watch, his shift had just ended. We'd passed nine o'clock at night by then. But the station felt oddly abandoned, for the roundsmen were freezing their eyebrows off trudging in circles and their captain was nowhere to be seen.

I gestured at the bench. 'Make yourselves comfortable. I'll just check the office.'

Mr Piest commenced a slipshod but kindly meant tale of the formation of the copper stars to the hollowed-out Mrs Adams as I set off. Halfway down the hall, I paused. A muffled scraping noise met my ears. Then a chirping birdlike giggle. I threw open the office door.

My brother Valentine was seated in a wide oak desk chair. So was a ravishing girl of about twenty. Plump everywhere that mattered, red-gold hair falling about her bare shoulders, with her back to Val's chest and her left arm crooked up around his neck. Laughing as if the fact of his palm cupped inside the swell of her canary-yellow corset was more amusing than anything else she could think of.

Maybe she was right, and she couldn't. But I didn't have time to talk it over.

'Jesus Christ, Val,' I growled. 'In the *station house?*'

'Timothy!' Val waved a friendly cigar at me with his free hand. Not bothering to desist any activities being performed by the other. 'Tim, meet Miss Kelly Quirk. Kelly, this is my brother – as plumb a pin basket as they come.'

After those few seconds, I understood the following pieces of truly disturbing news.

First, from the languor of his towering frame and the constricted pupils within the vivid green circles of his eyes, my brother had just indulged in the usual evening recreation: sipping enough morphine tonic to float a barge down the Hudson. Second, from *plumb pin basket* – which loosely translates from flash into *good little brother* – the upswing of an absolutely soaring state of loose-limbed euphoria was gaining momentum. I can force sobriety on the man during the downward spiral, but not before. That would require divine intervention, and God doesn't indulge me on that particular front. Last, he'd been scraping his fingertips through his dark blond hair, sending the tip of his widow's peak up in a boyish scruff, which meant that a hefty dose of ether had also been involved.

Ether makes Val tactile. Before he starts seeing things, that is.

Of the six substances Valentine combines with morphine that I've documented, ether is trickiest to navigate. I loathe the stuff. Literally anything could happen to him – from loss of consciousness to winning an impromptu boxing match to deciding that wearing clothing is a hypocritical act. If I'd been anxious before over our mission, now a spoiled lemon had magically appeared in my gut.

'Miss Quirk here was nabbed on suspicion of stargazing.' The near-scarlike bags beneath Val's eyes quivered with amusement. 'She's explaining why she's no bat, and I think she's got a nacky argument. Where's the whoring if it's for free sport and not a little hard cole clinking in the pocket?'

Kelly Quirk nodded sagely, then emitted a happy squeal that presumably had something to do with my brother's whalebone-obscured right hand. I wasn't eager to dwell on the subject.

'You. *Out.*' I jerked my thumb at the door. 'Charges are dropped. Congratulations.'

Her mouth curved into a tiny pout. 'I want to *stay.* I *like* him. What's wrong with your brother, Valentine? He's not a molley, is he?'

I'd a pretty tart reply on my lips as to which one of us could be accused of amatory tendencies toward men with any validity. But I swallowed it in the nick of time.

'Can't I stay?' She fluttered her eyelashes at me. 'I like you too, you know.'

'Christ almighty,' I groaned. '*Get out*, or the vagrancy charges are reinstated. I'm sorry. Have a pleasant night.'

Frowning prettily, she retrieved her long-sleeved jacket bodice and flounced her way through the door. Sticking her tongue out at me for good measure.

'What in hell, Tim?' Val crossed his boots on his desk and tugged his ivy-patterned waistcoat down. 'That's sound police work I was—'

'What did I do to deserve you?' I demanded of no one in particular. 'I need you. I need you *now*. And here you are, useless as a dead clam. So I ask again, what in holy hell did I do to deserve you?'

'Probably nothing,' he owned generously as the cigar end landed in the side of his mouth. 'That's a wet streak of luck, my Tim, and no mistake.'

Mr Piest's clanging crowbar footsteps sounded behind me in the corridor. 'Mr Wilde? A young female just passed us by who seemed—'

'She's on her way out,' I hissed. 'And we are in serious trouble.'

'What sort of trouble? Good evening, Captain Wilde.'

When Valentine clapped eyes on Mr Piest, his expression shifted from annoyance to confusion. To my dismay, it was the cast his face takes when he's so marinated in chemicals that he's seeing dragons and sphinxes roaming the streets, and is reluctant either to mention or to scrutinize them. Why the look should be directed at a shriveled roundsman was beyond my study, however. Particularly when they were already acquainted.

'What species is it?' Val queried, glancing in my direction.

My jaw came up, newly furious.

'My guess would be barnacle,' he added thoughtfully.

Searching for the choicest words, I was about to tell my brother just what species of morphine-soused prick he was when Piest started laughing.

'Captain Wilde, it is an enormous honor to see you again. *The* Valentine Wilde – undisputed hero of the Broad Street fire, defender of the Irish, tireless advocate for the copper stars, and the pride of Ward Eight. Don't chastise yourself over not recalling me. Since the star police formed, I work from time to time with your very talented brother here. Shake my hand, sir, shake my hand.'

Valentine's bemusement slid into a half smile as he pulled his feet off the table and complied. 'You're the old Dutch toast who found the final piece of the kinchin murderer puzzle last August. I remember now. By Jesus, but your face gave me a turn.'

'Good God. You might be a bit more delicate with a mate of mine,' I exclaimed.

'This doesn't need delicacy. It needs an oyster knife, or possibly a nutcracker. But if he's O.K. by you, then he's O.K. by me.'

'Remarkable!' Mr Piest exulted. 'Simply first-class, Captain Wilde. 'O.K.,' you say, which I presume to be letters of the alphabet? What can they mean?'

'It's just flash,' I snapped. 'It's short for *oll korrect*.'

'*All correct?*' Mr Piest repeated, looking happy as if he'd stumbled upon a warehouse packed to brimming with fenced goods. 'Wouldn't that be A.C.?'

'It can *spell*,' my brother rejoiced in a whisper, equally delighted.

Mr Piest made a far lower bow than ever ought to be directed at my disgraceful sibling. Then they stared at each other, grinning in childlike joy.

'Are you through now?' I wondered in desperation.

'So, you need me,' Val recalled. 'Are you going to tell me about it, Timmy, or are you going to stand there like a lamppost?'

I passed a moment gnawing on my own tongue. My brother calls me *Timmy* to infuriate me. He does so because it works. Every single time. Crossing my arms in a physical effort to subdue the smolder in my breast, I reviewed my options. The main point seemed to be whether or not a morphine-drunk Valentine was more valuable than an absent Valentine.

Unfortunately, the answer was yes. Even a half-crazed Val is better than no Val at all. It's one of the most intolerable things about my barely tolerable elder brother.

'Can you walk?' I demanded.

He scowled. 'Of course I can.'

'Can you think more or less clearly?'

'Presently, I think you're a milky little sow's tit.'

'Can you fight?'

'Christ have mercy. Will you listen to the puppy? I can always fight.'

'Will you come with me?'

'I'll mull it over.'

I seized his arm and dragged him into the hallway. When he could see the otherworldly Mrs Adams, who sat frozen in grief on the bench against the wall, her almond-shaped grey eyes pinned to the floor and her chaos of curls glittering with half-melted snow, I pointed.

'Will you come with me to do a favor for *her*?'

Valentine scratched lazily at the nape of his neck. Ruminating, no doubt. Or debating whether or not she was a wood nymph.

Who in his right mind could say? Then he slapped me on the back so hard that my teeth clacked together.

'You should have tried that argument first, young Tim,' he advised over his shoulder, winking. 'Would have saved yourself ten minutes. Let me get my coat.'

CHAPTER FIVE

They are called slave-traders, and their occupation is to kidnap every colored stranger they can lay their hands on.

E. S. Abdy, *Journal of a Residence and Tour in the United States of North America, From April 1833 to October 1834*

Valentine employed the shrillest whistle I've ever heard to summon a roundsman. That copper star received strict orders to guard the woman in the office, and to bring her coffee and hot chestnuts to boot. Our poor hacksman, meanwhile, shivered pathetically as we three star police climbed back into his vehicle. Lurching forward with a grinding, sliding motion that smacked Mr Piest's head against the door, we rode in haste toward Corlears Hook. There had been ample room for three to sit abreast in Mrs Adams's company. But with Valentine's sprawling bulk to accommodate – not to mention his weighted walking stick – Mr Piest wedged his feet together while I in the center performed my gamest impersonation of a tinned sprat.

'This falls shy of ideal rattle weather,' my brother observed, meaning *hackney cab* by *rattle*. 'The sleighs will be out by morning. Now tell me what we're about.'

'We're lioning a pair of slave catchers,' I answered.

'Slave catchers,' Val repeated slowly. My brother is extremely fastidious about food, and he used the same timbre of voice he would have spent on *turned fish*. 'Right. When a human parasite crawls into my fair state and tells me the laws of his backwater swamp are trump and that I'd best flash my ivories and bend a knee about it, I'm itchy to lion him too. But why are we lioning these *particular* blackbirders, in a snowstorm?'

'Mrs Adams – did you notice anything about her?'

'That she's colored? I do own eyes, thank you.'

'These slave catchers figured her family for some ripe valuables. But they operate out of Corlears Hook. And one has a pistol. And so I need you.'

'We're actually interfering with a catch?'

'A shamelessly illegal catch, yes.'

Valentine blew out a sharp gust of frustration through his teeth. The collar of his blue velvet greatcoat is tastefully lined with short fur, and the ether was compelling him to run his knuckles across it repeatedly, as if he were petting a cat. The gesture took on a worried sharpness.

'What?' I prompted.

'Nix.'

'No, what is it?'

'I'm just grateful you waited until I was off duty to spring this scrapp on me. That's several shades more discreet than you generally are, and it was keen of you to take care about it.'

'I didn't,' I said, baffled. 'I took this hack straight to your door.'

Valentine winced, and then he laughed heartily, expressions which on him go perennially hand in glove.

'That sounds more like you,' he admitted, wiping the pained look off his face with one hand as he tried to angle himself meaningfully in my direction. His largest success was at knocking my knees with the pearl-topped cane. 'Listen to me, bright young copper star: we aren't abolitionists.'

I stared at him, the severe jostling of the cab the only reason I didn't let my mouth hang open. Mr Piest glanced at my brother in near-equal shock.

'You're pro-slavery?' I demanded.

'Slavery is a putrid blot on the mazzard of this country that's going to bring all hell and fiery brimstone down to raze the land. Sooner rather than later.'

'So you're anti-slavery?'

'Any freeborn American possessing eyes and ears and a half ounce of brains is anti-slavery. Yes, you despicably rude insect.'

'Then what—'

'I said we aren't abolitionists. We're Democrats.'

I sensed Mr Piest relax against the seat, apparently satisfied. For my part, I was ready to wrestle my brother into the snow.

'First of all, never speak for me. Ever again,' I suggested. 'Second, bugger your buggering Party and all the buggering thugs you call pals. Third, why are we talking about the Party?'

'Because the copper stars are largely Democrat run and Democrat populated,' Mr Piest put in. 'God knows most Whigs loathe us, and the American Republican Party is all but washed up. Though it hadn't occurred to me, I do take your meaning, Captain.'

I didn't. But I was determined to work it out. And quickly too, for my brother was shooting me optimistic looks. As if I might possibly have been born with the intellect of a catfish, but he held tenuous hopes.

Then the obvious dawned – bright and painfully clear.

'The Irish,' I conceded. 'Your voting majority. Every Irishman is a Democrat, and the Irish compete with the blacks. Fine. Why not gain some black voters to make up the difference?'

This time it was my turn to be stared at as if I were some monstrosity from Barnum's American Museum.

'Timothy Wilde, I will slap the stupid out of you if it is the last thing I ever do,' Valentine vowed. 'Blacks can't *vote*.'

'Of course they can,' I said, frowning.

'They're held to a property requirement. Whites can vote, if citizens. Blacks can vote if citizens who also own a minimum of two hundred and fifty dollars in property.'

My head listed back against the cab interior in considerable disgust. I live on fourteen dollars a week – four dollars more than the roundsmen – because Matsell seems to think the denser of the two Wildes something special. So if I counted up all my earthly goods, the sum of them would maybe total forty-five dollars. Maybe. That's including my half of the fifty dollars in silver that Piest and I had left hidden in my office.

And I am richer by far than almost every colored person I have ever met.

'Can any of them vote?' I wondered bleakly.

'Maybe two hundred or so of around ten thousand. And they sure as hell is warm don't vote Democrat. The Liberty Party, now *there* are some abolitionists.'

'The whole process is a repulsive circus. I'm far more of an abolitionist than a Democrat.'

'Well, that's bully, Tim. But I'm a Democrat,' Valentine snapped, glassy green eyes flashing. 'That means the repulsive circus is why you've a roof over your head and bread on the table and it has been ever since you were a younger and very slightly smaller half-witted idealist, so forgive me my loyalties to the freak show. It kept you alive. That was the *point*. God forbid you be grateful, I owed you worlds over. But if you're an abolitionist, you are mouse on the subject. Can you manage just *that* much for my sake? We are the fucking quietest abolitionists in the world. Do you savvy?'

Trying not to flinch – and failing – I nodded. Meanwhile cursing myself for not treading carefully with Val where mingled ether and morphine are concerned. Ether sometimes makes Valentine sentimental.

And this, it seemed, was my lucky night.

My brother fancies himself responsible for burning our house down with our parents inside it, when I was ten and he all of sixteen, by means of an accidental fire in our stable that took place near our supply of kerosene. I discovered this fairly salient point last August. But God forbid either of us mentions it. And in front of a third party, no less, who was studying his fingernails and doubtless comprehending next to nothing. I deeply wanted to say *It was an accident*, and I wanted to say *I'm still an abolitionist but I'm also an idiot*, and I was even suddenly tempted to say for the first time *I realize now how ferociously you fought for me despite the fact you're a comprehensive bastard*. I didn't, though.

The things my brother and I don't say could pave over the Atlantic Ocean.

'This is the Hook,' Val announced abruptly with a final unconscious brush of his fingers over his collar. 'Every man look to his coattails. They come up on you like river rats in this stretch of town.'

I don't often visit the Corlears Hook portion of the East River docks anyhow, but the storm had rendered it unrecognizable. We stood where Walnut and Cherry intersect, facing the slips of the waterfront two blocks distant. The sluggish East River swells, the cloud-piercing masts. But the snow had erased us, actors and stage alike. It was everywhere, even coating my eyelashes. It banked against the sailors' bawdyhouses, gifting them with chaste white doorways and dazzlingly pure caps for their sagging rooftops. Ordinarily, Corlears Hook is barely walkable for the Irish streaming off the docks into the waiting menagerie of rouge-smeared ladybirds. But that night, save for one unfortunate bat stumbling along with a tattered shawl atop her head, all was quiet save for the wind. Peaceful and weirdly lovely. Even the passing mab looked like a Madonna, the rank rag covering her head shining with a virginal halo of ice.

Within twelve hours, it would all be sooty as Jean-Baptiste's jacket elbows. But for now, the city had been wiped ruthlessly clean.

When we'd crossed Cherry, our companions came into view. The three men stood stamping their boots, eyeing a shop that fronted Walnut Street. Sallow gaslight trickled through its curtains, sullying the clean midair snow.

'Anything peery, Julius?' I asked.

'No one in and no one out,' Julius returned. 'How d'you do, Captain Wilde.'

'Julius Carpenter,' Val marveled. Adding for my hearing, 'Is he actually here, or is he somewhere else and only looks like he's here?'

'He's here,' I sighed.

'But whyso?'

'Vigilance Committee. They know what lay to make, so we're their men this evening. Does that sound agreeable?'

Despite the conversation in the hack, I wasn't much worried over the question. Val has always liked Julius Carpenter, and after the fire, that liking took on the solidity of a debt. But Julius is also the only man alive who's ever beaten my brother at three consecutive poker games, and ether makes Val capricious.

I'm not overfond of ether where Val is concerned.

'Thank Christ,' Valentine said dryly. 'And here I thought Tim was in charge. That's a ponderous weight off my mind.'

A smile crept onto Julius's face.

'I take it the direct route is the safest, George?' Reverend Brown questioned.

'Personally, I don't see any point in subterfuge or elaborate scheming.' It was an arsenic-laced tone. George Higgins was a man, I thought, with blood on his mind. 'Julius? I'd sooner trust your judgment than mine any day of the week.'

'We knock on the door, the copper stars introduce themselves, we leave with Jonas and Delia, devil take the hindmost,' Julius proclaimed.

'Well, if a thing's to be done, best to be started at it.'

So saying, Valentine sailed across the intersection, kicking through the snow as if he were on Jamaica Beach in mid-May. I scrambled after him, the others following. When he reached the door, Val pounded thrice with the stick that was ten times more a weapon than an aid to afternoon walks. Looking of a sudden to be pretty fond of our project, passing his tongue over his lips like a wolf smelling rent flesh.

That worried me. Almost everything about Val worries me.

'Why don't I do the talking? Just at the start,' I hastened to add.

With a flourish that would have been much more effectively sarcastic if he hadn't been neck deep in narcotics, Val stepped to the side. The door opened, a tall but lanky creature in its frame.

'Who's this?' he snarled. 'What's it all about?'

I pushed inside with Piest. When the scoundrel cursed and moved to bar our way, Val's fist landed *bang* in the door's center like a battering ram and the shop entrance became much more definitively *open*. Julius, Higgins, and Brown filed within, leaving the gatekeeper spluttering like a rasher of bacon hitting the pan.

'Just who in hellfire do you think you—'

'Star police,' I answered.

Valentine stepped inside last of all and shut the door. He then latched it, spreading his stance in his finest dead rabbit style and beginning to toss the head of his cane from palm to palm like a metronome. Most of Val's intimidation techniques irritate the living spit out of me. But that one is plenty chilling, so I approved.

'We won't take up much of your time,' I said, glancing about the room. Stacks of pine crates, presumably full of wine bottles. Planked and sawdusted floor. Soot-spewing lamps mounted to the walls, a desk with two clay cups and a half-full wine bottle on it, a pair of chairs, and not a comfort else. 'Long Luke, I take it?'

'That's him, all right,' George Higgins answered me. Making it sound as if I'd just called the man an absolutely vile name.

And maybe I had. Long Luke Coles was taller than everyone save Val, but his neck about matched the circumference of my brother's wrist. His lanky blond hair was tethered with a plain black ribbon, and he'd an equine face and indifferently arranged teeth. But most unnerving of all were his eyes. They tracked constantly, switching from one to the other of us and even between my left eye and my right. Snakes flick their attention helter-skelter so, and the Committee had been right: a more snakelike individual than Luke Coles I'd not yet met. Something about him wanted squashing in the head with a garden shovel.

'Luke, now what's all this fuss over?' The voice was elegant, unhurried, and deeply Southern. 'My word, we've callers. And in this weather too. What can I do for you?'

Val's eyes flashed up from his pearly cane top to the newcomer who'd just emerged from the interior doorway. That tiny glance told me he supposed the greater of the two threats had just arrived. Carefully, I took the fellow's measure.

My brother, as so often happens, was dead on.

'That makes you Seixas Varker,' I surmised.

If Long Luke was a snake, Varker could easily have been the gopher it lay in wait for. He was certainly of a dull brown hair color and a healthy pinkish complexion. He was nearly as short as I am, but boasted considerably more well-oiled flesh than I'd care to lug about and seemed closer to forty than to thirty. Meanwhile, his features puzzled me. They were handsome if overfed: fine nose, even jaw, clear dark eyes. But I felt a peculiar repulsion at the sight of him, though he smiled with thin, well-shaped lips as he spoke.

Then I realized that the smile itself was wrong. Insincere, but far worse in another way: purposeless. If it had been a deliberate mask, I'd have taken it in easier. No, smiling was just what Varker's face did when he was inwardly shaking like a rat in a burrow. That smile had the stench of fear all over it – he hadn't calculated the expression at all. I realized my brother wasn't wary of Varker because the slave catcher was fearless. The way my brother is wary of his former mistress Silkie Marsh, for instance, because she isn't tethered to earth by anxiety or affection as normal mortals are. On the contrary. Val had snuck a glimpse of him because Varker was *gutless*.

That makes two men in the room who could try anything at any moment, I thought.

A snowlike bead of cold sweat formed on my upper neck.

'I take it you're in the business of capturing escaped slaves,' I began.

'Do you now?' Varker exclaimed softly. 'But I run a wine store, Mr . . . ?'

'Timothy Wilde. And you also collar runaways. That's a fact.'

'I see, I see, someone's told you about me,' he reflected. 'Well, I'd be foolish to deny it, then – but I don't like to brag of doing my civic duty, sir. I'm sure you understand, a fellow agent of the law like yourself.'

I let that one go by unanswered.

'But you're right, Mr Wilde – I do what I can to restore people's lost property, give the coloreds the means to go back home where they belong. They're downright grateful for the opportunity, you know, and I can't say as I blame them a bit. It's mighty cold in New York, isn't it, and mighty hard living. Have you brought me some prodigal sons, then?'

I could practically hear Higgins's teeth grinding behind me, while the Reverend Brown and Julius remained impassive.

'You know us well enough by now,' Julius said quietly.

The smile floated on Varker's lips, bobbing like an apple in a barrel. 'Know you? I may have seen you hereabouts before, but can't say as I recollect specifics. Oh, just a moment – aren't you associated with some sort of free Negro club? That was it, wasn't it now? Well, you're . . . certainly something, a credit to your race. I don't see what you're doing here, however, nor why you've a trio of copper stars.'

'How the devil does a shell *make* mother-of-pearl?' Valentine suddenly wanted to know, eyes following the decorative tip of his cane. 'Call me a simon, but I can't savvy it – seems to be spun out of light and seawater. Is that possible?'

No one had an immediate answer to this question. Least of all me.

Long Luke barked a laugh, eyes flying madly from one to the other of us. 'What's wrong with *him*?'

'He's a man of science,' I bit out.

'Did the pair of you visit a house in West Broadway today and take custody of two alleged runaway slaves?' Mr Piest inquired, setting us back on track. I could have kissed the ugly lunatic. 'A woman and a child of seven?'

'Did those darkies tell you that?' Varker mused. He'd been standing near the door, but now he approached us. 'If I were you, I'd think mighty hard before listening to anything they have to say. I haven't seen a liar yet can beat a free Negro at telling tales. And even if we did, well then – why the fuss? You can't blame a man for wanting his property back, can you? Or us for doing lawbreakers a kindness and helping them find their way home?'

Julius took a single step and was at my side. I'm grateful to say so, because whatever was about to emerge from my mouth would have been breath wasted.

'Enough. Through that door and on into the back,' he said, angling his chin. 'That's where we'll find them.'

'If anyone did happen to be back there, it would be a misguided ingrate with no legal right to set foot on this here soil,' Varker said, smiling and smiling and still smiling. 'And you'd do well to mind your tongue, boy, before someone comes along to mind it for you.'

I'd like to say that all hell broke loose at that instant. But it didn't, not really. It just appeared so.

As the talk had seemed tranquil enough for a set of men who loathed one another, I hadn't noted Varker edging silkily toward his desk. I ought to have done, though. Simultaneously, my brother behind me had ceased his study of the miraculous capabilities of mollusks and had begun slinking forward. If I'd grasped either one of those clues, nothing would have been startling about what happened next.

It was barely possible to register Varker's hand tearing open his desk drawer and retrieving a Colt revolver. He didn't capture my eye for long, though. That's because Valentine's weighted stick was already tracing a blurred arc above his head.

The cane struck the back of Varker's wrist with the firecracker snap of a delicate bone breaking.

Varker howled an instant later, and the gun fell heavily. He began gasping in a wounded, panicked fashion, and for the best of reasons: Valentine had his broken wrist pinned to the desktop, pressing with both palms on either end of the leaded cane.

I think everyone save me took an awed breath, and Long Luke shied away in fright. I couldn't find it in me to blame him overmuch. Whimpering, Varker looked up at Val and made a timid effort to pull his hand free.

We heard a grind of loose bone, followed by a tiny shriek. My throat constricted.

My brother is a dangerous man.

'I haven't been paying attention,' Val remarked in a conversational manner. 'Damned if there wasn't something else on my mind. So tell me – what play were you aiming to make with that snapper, drawing it like a heathen without a fair warning?'

Sickly sweat had broken out all over Varker's pudgy face. The smile was gone, replaced by what had always been beneath it: purblind terror.

'No play,' he panted. 'I was afeared for my life, and – I meant nothing, sir. Please let me—'

'It's only that I've heard tell of coves in this ward who'd quiet a rabbit first and let the river solve what followed. You weren't thinking along those lines, were you? Making us easy and then trusting to the devil?'

'No, no, as a gentleman—'

'A gentleman? A *gentleman*, he says. Do you know what I think of blackbirders?'

Valentine was smiling himself by now. A terrifying smile, an ocean's distance from Varker's blankly scared smirk. Varker said nothing. Probably couldn't, by then.

'I think they're men who couldn't scrape together enough coin by whoring out their mothers and elected to try a less noble profession.'

'Do you now,' the slave catcher moaned. It wasn't a question. 'Well, that'll give me something to sure enough ruminate on.'

When I reached for the pistol and slipped it inside my coat, Val let him go. I think that's what he'd been waiting for. Varker fell into the chair, cradling his hand with his mouth hanging open. The Committee of Vigilance kept their peace. Possibly horrified, possibly preferring to have broken his wrist themselves. I could sympathize in either direction. Val is a simon-pure, dyed-in-the-wool thug.

'Quick,' Julius said, starting forward.

'Can you and Piest manage here?' I asked Valentine.

My brother crossed his arms, draping the stick over one shoulder. 'If me and the sea urchin couldn't lace this pair of maggots, I'd throw myself in the river and save them the trouble.'

I rushed with the Committee into the adjoining chamber. It proved a wine storage space, lined with crates wrapped in grey wool blankets. But in the opposite wall loomed a door. It was locked, with a small iron bar drawn through a bolt.

Not a lock meant to keep filchers away from your property. A way to keep your alleged property *in*.

The Committee men outpaced me by yards. George Higgins threw the bolt, diving within as his friends did the same. I followed more slowly. Pretty sure of what I'd see and equally sure I'd not stomach it well.

That was a selfish reluctance. But then, I'm not any too adapted to police work.

Very little light spilled through the doorway. But what light there was illuminated a godless scene. Bare walls – though here and there old blood spatters gleamed, their mute throbs yet permeating the air. There was nothing else in the room save for chains. And by nothing, I mean a vile and merciless *nothing*. No pallet, no sink, no chair, no window. No lamp. No chamber pot.

Nothing.

Just a room with four walls, one air vent, and many shackles fixed to the plaster with hooks.

I'd been on the verge of telling my brother that he'd overplayed his hand, but that room snuffed the feeling. Only a devil could have imagined the place. And only a human could have actually made use of it.

In the corner, a boy had curled himself into the smallest shape possible, as if he were nestled in a shell. He was gagged with a cotton rag and tethered to the wall with a leg iron. Reverend Brown had already reached him. Touching his arm, speaking in soothing tones.

The woman – likewise gagged, and chained to the opposite wall – was fighting against a pair of wrist shackles as if she could saw through them using her own flesh. George Higgins reached out, but she thrashed away from him unseeing. Fighting anyone and anything that touched her.

Then I saw why. The top six buttons of her dark green bodice had been ripped open. Methodically too. The fabric was intact.

'That miserable worm,' I said through my teeth.

'Delia? You're all right now.' Higgins changed his posture. Curved it into a calm, quiet shape and backed away a few inches. 'It's me. You're all right. It's George.'

'Get those things off her. She's hurting herself,' Julius called out as he cast his eyes about for a pick or a tool or a crowbar.

He was right. George or no George, Delia was determined to snap the shackles off her wrists and lose no time about it. No matter how many bones she shattered.

I left the room. Half tempted to rip Varker's hand the rest of the way off. But that wasn't as important as snatching up the set of keys I'd observed hanging from a hook in the shadowy corner of the storage room. As I returned, it occurred to me that barreling forward like I was about to thrash someone senseless wouldn't calm anyone, and so forced myself to slow down.

'Here.' Kneeling next to the boy, I unlocked the rankly sour metal cuffs and then tossed the key ring to Higgins. Jonas and his aunt had been taken without their coats, and the child shivered uncontrollably. Whatever heat permeated the other two rooms was lost through the prison's air vent. I shrugged my greatcoat off and the minister wrapped it about Jonas's shoulders.

'There now,' I heard Higgins say as more chains fell to the ground. 'You'll be all right. It's nearly over.'

I levered myself to my feet. Julius had succeeded in untying the fabric forced between Delia's lips, and Higgins held a flask to her mouth. She was no less lovely than her sister – though smaller framed, and with a generous splash of freckles surrounding her dark brown eyes. Once free of the shackles, she calmed considerably. Or it seemed she did. I'd have taken in her mental state much better if my eyes hadn't kept dragging themselves down to the blood streaming from both wrists.

'I'm going out there for a last word with Varker and Coles,' I said with deliberate, nigh jaw-snapping calm.

'Steady on, Timothy,' Julius warned. 'When everyone is well enough to walk out of here, we'll leave as fast as we can manage.'

My feet carried me back into the front room of the wine shop without measurable help from my brain. It being too occupied with wondering whether burning the place down would be at all satisfying. I found Mr Piest keeping a cool, silent watch in the center of the room. Valentine leaned against the desk, one of the cups in his hand and the half-full wine bottle by now quite drained.

'Everyone healthy?' Val asked, setting the cup down.

'Healthy enough.'

'They're escaped slaves!' Long Luke whined. He sat huddled against the wall. 'Aren't they, Seixas? Seixas says they are. You lot can't take them. You *can't*. *Prigg versus Pennsylvania*—'

'It's entirely illegal,' Varker managed to hiss from his chair. 'Monstrous, on my word it is. You can't just steal a pair of reclaimed runaways from their legitimate captors.'

'How legal is it to attempt to rape a New York citizen, would you say?' I shot back.

Varker's lip curled, half pretended outrage and half hot shame. 'I never – of all the *revolting*—'

'*Attempt*, you said?' Valentine asked me darkly. I nodded. 'That's flash, then. Because frankly, this talking shit sack rubs me a bit wrongways, and if it wasn't *attempt*—'

'You subject me to the basest of slanders!' Varker squealed. 'I – a man has to check, doesn't he, see that he's collared the right—'

'I have an idea.' My brother set the toe of his boot on Varker's

74

chair seat between the Southerner's ample thighs. 'Give the useless bit of meat between your teeth a holiday before I feed it to the nearest stray pig along with the useless bit of meat between your legs. How does that suit you? Because it suits me right down to the ground.'

Silence gathered around us. Thick and hostile as the snow without. Long Luke subsided into a furious quiet like a kettle just turned off, while Varker directed his eyes to the floor.

About ten seconds later, the Committee men appeared with the stony-eyed captives. Jonas in my coat, and Delia in George Higgins's far superior one. She'd lifted her nephew into her arms. The five traveled around the desk, giving the slave catchers a wide berth but paying them not a single dram of attention otherwise. It was admirably done.

Only Delia looked back at Varker. But that glance seared the air like a lightning bolt. I found myself shocked the expression hadn't blasted a hole square through his skull.

'Right, then,' I said to the slave agents. 'The pair of you are under ar—'

'Finish that sentence and I will rearrange your teeth,' Val growled. 'They'll say they misidentified their captives by accident and be out of the Tombs in jig time, and the Party will have our bollocks.'

'Or worse,' the Reverend said quietly, 'they'll put up a fight for them and these folk will starve in a Tombs cell until they're subjected to an identity trial.'

'She's the victim of assault,' I spluttered, 'and—'

'Attempted assault,' Val corrected me. 'Get that to stick in court, why don't you.'

Buzzing with outrage, I slowly realized, was accomplishing nothing. And when I looked to Higgins standing next to Delia, expecting to find him an ally, he remained silent. Only glared back with the sort of long-suppressed fury that could wear a fellow's bones down to silt. Forcibly calming myself once more, I turned away.

'It's your decision. Are we through here?' I asked Julius.

'We're through,' he agreed.

'Bully. Tim, return the maggot's pistol,' Val ordered. That made not an ounce of sense to me. When I didn't oblige quick enough, he added, 'It's *stealing*. Hell if I care, but I know you do. Toss it in the road if you like.'

My brother was right, so I walked to the entryway and opened the door, throwing the Colt into the snow. A chill like the hand of sudden death swept into the room. Julius led Delia and Jonas out, followed by Higgins and Brown. We copper stars filed more slowly toward the exit, eyes locked on Long Luke and Varker.

'I'd get that hand looked at if I were you,' Valentine suggested as he motioned me and Piest outside, standing in the threshold with his fingers on the knob. 'I'd also forget we paid you a visit. Evening, all.'

The breath of relief I sucked in when we dove into snowdrifts once more burned my throat. But it felt free, fierce, downright glorious. No matter that the cold sliced so deep into my bones as to be painful. Our hacksman had long since saved himself and his horse, so we hastened up Walnut Street toward Grand, where if we were blessed by sublime luck, another desperate cabman might be trying to snatch the last of the fares before the sleighs had been turned out. We hadn't gone a block before I heard a very familiar sound from behind me.

'Why are you laughing *now?*' I demanded of my brother.

'You were going to steal that sick son of a bitch's revolver.' When I glanced back at him, he was shaking with mirth and wincing as if he'd been shot.

'I was not,' I retorted. My heart wasn't in it, though. He'd just thrown me his scarf and then yanked his fur collar up around his ears.

'You were,' he gasped. 'What we just did is bollocks-out illegal, and *then*, young Tim, you wanted to leg it with a bit of fast swag. I knew you had it in you.'

'Had what, Captain?' Mr Piest asked, beginning to chuckle.

'A taste for mayhem, buried deep down. Eh, Timothy?'

Mr Piest gave a muffled snort.

'Were you keener to pawn it or keep it? You, my Tim, are one shady palmer of illicit goods,' Val concluded with wicked delight.

'It isn't funny.' I wrapped the extra scarf round my neck, grinning reluctantly.

'No,' Valentine agreed. And then he laughed all the harder.

Chapter Six

*Had New-York, been but free from colored people, how
peaceful would she be! What a saving to her people in
expense of a police! Had Philadelphia – ditto! But New-
York, not being so overstocked as Charleston and New
Orleans, leaves some difference to her credit. Still she is
quite lamentably stocked, and hence her violent reputation
throughout our union.*

John Jacobus Flournoy, *An Essay on the Origins,
Habits, &c. of the African Race: Incidental to the
Propriety of Having Nothing to Do With Negroes,* 1835

At the Ward Eight station house, I knocked, pushed open the
door to Val's office, and sent Delia and Jonas inside. Trembling
and wet but undisputedly free. Lucy Adams released a cry without
any sound to it. As her family flew toward her, a smile broke over
her face that could have lit the Astor House for a year.

The knot just at the base of my own throat went slack far too
quickly, unspooling at a reckless speed. After handing over the
station house's medical kit for Delia's wrists, I shut the door behind
me and slumped against it.

Mercy, I thought, *would have been proud of that night's work.* I
pictured her as she'd looked when gliding into rank rookeries and

78

cellar hells. Madly fearless and half-smiling, passing out bread and salt and soap with no regard for the skin shade of the recipient in question. Poor and well-off alike thought her as deranged as she was generous, and she'd terrified me on behalf of her own health. And I'd adored her for it.

Sucking in a breath, I headed back down the hall.

'I owe you one,' I said to Valentine, who'd pulled up his tall chair behind the front counter. Setting my hat on the wood, I rubbed at my ruined temple. Of course the instant I'd stopped tensing my right eye in mute worry, half my head throbbed in dull, half-hearted revenge.

My brother and I were alone by that time. En route to Grand Street, Mr Piest had peeled off in the direction of his own night circuit – stalwart as ever, though bleary about the eye. The three Committee men had recognized quicker than I'd done that no cab would take all of us and few enough would take the three of them in any case. To my stifled but cinderlike embarrassment. So they'd made the gentlemanly offer of parting ways, after I'd vowed to see the family to a temporary haven in the absence of Charles Adams. And thus the two living New York Wildes – one jelly-spined in relief and the other jelly-spined for self-inflicted reasons – had whisked Delia and Jonas away in an indecently bribed hansom. Paid for by my far flusher older brother. That was irritating. As is everything else Val does.

'As if I did that for *you*.' Val smirked, resting his elbows on the counter. 'If a riper moll exists than that Mrs Adams, I will eat an unsalted shoe.'

'She's married,' I said with a scowl.

'Hasn't troubled me before now. Oh, for God's sake, dry up, I'm not going fishing in that lake.'

'Thank you. Wait,' I added. 'Do you usually – not that I'd mind.'

'Mind?'

I never had minded, had been raised – so far as I'd been raised at all, which was a piss-poor joke – not to care in the smallest. About amalgamation, that is. Blacks and whites exchanging intimacies. Val and I hadn't money enough to be snobbish toward any living beings save lice when I was a boy, and the Underhill patriarch who took us under his wing was a radical Protestant zealot. Anti-amalgamation sentiments are for people with embroidered cushions and lace antimacassars, or else the sort of low clods who insist Africans are a type of monkey.

'If she wasn't married,' I explained, 'I'd not care. If you—'

'Leave off your face before you make it even more of a smashed pudding.' Val slapped my hand away deftly.

'Don't talk about my face.'

'Don't tug it like a pervert with a gratis spy hole, then.'

'Sod off. But – I mean to say, do you?' I inquired none too clearly.

'Sleep with black women?' Val by now looked entirely baffled. 'Last time was two or three months back, so far as I can recall. Why?'

And there we were. The only surprising thing about the conversation was that I'd bothered asking. Valentine can't be arsed over the gender of his bed partners, as I'd learned to my shock the previous August. So the race could hardly give him pause. I considered adding amalgamation to Val's list of scandalous acts and found I couldn't be bothered. Narcotics, alcohol, bribery, violence, whoring, gambling, theft, cheating, extortion, and sodomy had all alarmed me at one point or another – amalgamation was a trip to the American Art-Union to survey the placider landscapes.

I'm supposed to mind, though. I'm supposed to mind, according to some, a very great deal.

In 1834, we hosted one of the most enthusiastic riots Manhattan has ever witnessed. As we've quite a collection, that's saying something. One of our leading white abolitionists invited a black clergyman to church one gorgeous spring morning when the great blue bowl of the sky was cupped tenderly over our holy Sunday goings-on. And not only to hear the sermon, but to sit in the abolitionist's very own pew. When the white congregants made to shuffle their guest into a colored pew, their minister made the mistake of protesting that Christ Himself must have been of a Syrian complexion.

The implication that Jesus our Lord might have been anything other than pale as a dogwood flower set off such a chaos of violence, arson, and general savagery that we got to the point where handbills with planned routes for havoc were distributed in public marketplaces. No police, of course, so the New York First Division cavalry finally quashed the uproar. And on every sneering rioter's lips was the word *amalgamation*. I was sixteen years old, Valentine twenty-two, and I can still hear their voices – swollen thick with tar fumes and whiskey and spite.

Let the amalgamators have their way and no place will be safe for our women, not even our churches—

Blondes are particular susceptible, they say, it's the very blackness as does it, how opposite they are, a blonde girl will turn fascinated and then—

Did you know that their lady parts can rip it right off a man, though if you ask me any amalgamator who suffered that would get what's coming to—

It's mainly Irish who'd sink so low, and just think of the brutes they'll be breeding, between colored brains and Irish character I can't bear to—

'Anyhow, it isn't my appetites that need palavering over,' Valentine declared with a bruising finger jab at my chest. 'You, young Tim, need a ladybird.'

I wrenched my brain dizzily onto this new topic.

'Oh, God. We aren't discussing this,' I protested in genuine alarm.

'What sort do you hanker after? I know plenty of pretty lunans would leap at the—'

'No. Please, no.'

'If you get any more stiff-necked, your spine will snap like a wishbone. We're finding you a moll. What about that landlady of yours, Mrs Boehm? Widows, eh?'

'Leave my landlady out of whatever this is.'

'But you'll admit she's a charmer, if you like the bony sort of bloss. God, don't you ever wonder what that mouth would look like—'

'Stop talking.'

'Mercy Underhill isn't in London *waiting for you*.' Val was quiet but certain, as if reading tides from an almanac. 'She's just living. As she's always done.'

'Fuck ether,' I said with deadly sincerity. 'The morphine I can manage, but—'

'Or here's a suggestion – why don't you wait until your nuts shrivel off and then mail them to Mercy by transatlantic post as a remembrance? Because that's more or less what you're doing now.'

'That isn't the way it is.'

'And I say you're wrong, and you'd better change the way it is, my Tim, or it's a sorry pass you'll come to.'

As far as I can tell, I didn't want to throttle him just then because he was obnoxious, or sailing on a sea of pleasurable poisons, or even because he was my brother. I wanted to throttle him because I suspected he was right.

Part of the problem was that I couldn't picture a girl wanting someone so scarred up that his only waking thought other than *Mercy Underhill* was *police work*. And my stomach flopped like a fish every time I imagined trying my luck with an actual girl and finding out I was right. But as for the other part of it . . .

The space Mercy's absence created in me was a voracious hole. Not a neutral erasure, but a gleaming black bonfire. Had I taken a keek in my chest, I'd have seen bluish flames skittering along ribbons of ebony pitch. The sensation was pretty specific. It wasn't just about my libido, on my life it wasn't – she'd been my closest friend. I missed Mercy as if she were a phantom limb. So rather than dousing the dark inferno, I kept shoveling fuel like an engineman. Terrified by the nullity that would be left inside me if ever I lost it. Trivia fed the fire – that Mercy had once crossed this street with me, that she was obsessed with first snowfalls, that she stared down torch-wielding brutes as if they were bowling pins, that she'd always passed me any pieces of parsnip from her plate with a wry smile of distaste.

So possibly, I'd have been better off scouting out a cure. It's a ridiculous affliction, being unable to glimpse a waterfront without calculating the number of waves between myself and her. Ridiculous, and impractical. New York is an *island*. But I was so far advanced a case that the usual sciences seemed not to apply.

'Gentlemen, it would be a miracle if I could express my thanks to you,' a velvety voice announced.

Mrs Adams stood before us with her kin. Viewing Lucy and Delia next to each other, I suddenly knew just what their mother looked like – tall and graceful, with generous lips and cheekbones like the gentle sweep of a bough in an apple orchard. Lucy's pale eyes and Delia's blithe freckles were the only striking differences between them. Mrs Adams stood about two inches taller than her sister, clutching at Delia's elbow as if her sibling might be whisked away again.

The kinchin was barely visible in his mother's skirts. But the fraction in view looked a fine boy. Clever hands, thin frame. Quick, curious brows under a mop of dark curls. Jonas was very like his mother, though with a wider-set mouth and perfectly round blue eyes.

'No thanks necessary,' I assured her. 'I wish I could take you home, but you heard Julius and the other Committee men. It's not safe before your husband returns. We need to find you temporary lodgings. And I need your statements, even if they're to be unofficial – if Varker and Coles are kidnapping free blacks on a regular basis, I have to spread word at the Tombs. Apologies for making a wretched night even longer.'

Jonas – or the pair of eyes afloat in a sea of cobalt velvet – commenced studying me over. As any practical person will do when confronted with the natives of a hostile foreign land.

'Are we really meant to find a hotel in this weather?' Delia asked worriedly.

'I can escort you,' I offered.

83

'That's a ripe peach of an idea,' Valentine sniffed. 'Why don't you prance up and down the streets in a blizzard with three people who've no luggage – and two of them no winter coats? You'll find a proper hotel in seconds.'

'They can't go home until Mr Adams returns, not with that pair of mongrels loose.'

My brother shrugged in agreement. I didn't add a principle that I was only just beginning to grasp based on my conversation with the Committee men: *and anyway, the word of two colored women isn't worth a straw against the word of two white men.* If only a white could identify a black in a court of law, I wanted the family as far away from the courthouse as possible. Varker and Coles, I theorized, could be dealt with in due course. Personally.

'We'll go to church, Lucy,' Delia suggested, fingers tracing her sister's hand. 'I'm sure they'll let us heat one of the choir rooms.'

'Our church will be locked this time of night,' Mrs Adams answered doubtfully.

'But it's only ten blocks, and it's true, we've no coats, and—'

'Right,' Valentine declared in what I think of as his *political* voice. It's the tenor he uses to convince Irishmen they'd best turn out on Election Day or the Party will suffer crushing defeat. He lifted the hinged countertop. 'I am *famished*. A dose of kitchen physic is what's called for.'

My head spun a bit. Even if nearby restaurants remained open, I doubted many of Ward Eight's were unsegregated. We could bluff our way in, but there's always a risk when blacks pass for white and no one looked to be hungering for excitement.

'There's an eating house near the Hudson slips on Charlton Street that might do for everyone,' I said skeptically. 'But—'

'No, not Radolinski's rat hole,' Valentine scoffed. 'Their dumplings are always lumpy, how I'll never know, and their veal sauce tastes of bear grease and shame. I've got plenty of scran at my ken.'

'Good night, then.' I nodded. 'I'll let you know—'

'Are you lot coming? Or are you going to drag these perfectly decent folk through the snowdrifts like a cat with a dead bird?'

Absorbing the fact Val had just invited us to his residence a block and a half away on Spring Street didn't take long. The fact I was so glad of it bustled me thoroughly, though. After *not abolitionists*, for one thing, and *Mercy isn't waiting for you*, for another.

'That would be much appreciated.'

'Then leave off your fireplug imitation and walk,' he ordered.

I did. As for the exhausted crime victims, they trusted me on a basic level by then, and so they followed.

That was a pity. Not only for me, but for them as well.

And I do think of them as well. Very often. If I'd known the sort of trouble that would follow Val's simple act of decency, I'd have wished my brother a heartless cad in fact and not in theory. Instead, I took Mrs Adams's arm and walked straight out the door toward the ice-sharp edge of the known world.

'You owe me two, now,' Val pointed out, winking.

'I'll remember that,' I replied.

And I did.

'Talk me through it from the beginning, slowly,' I said to Delia – who was unmarried, apparently, and whose name was Delia Wright.

'You look troubled.' She took a deep sip of hot Souchong tea.

'I detest writing police reports,' I admitted, fiddling with the quill. So tired that I could barely hear myself explaining my innermost thoughts to a stranger. 'Particularly when I'm recording conscienceless things. It's as if – I can't explain it. As if when I officially document them, they have to stay with me. Or I give them permanence, or . . . I know it doesn't make sense.'

Sitting at Val's oak desk in his parlor, sipping tea whilst sizzling sounds drifted with the smell of browned onions from the kitchen, I'd begun to feel less like a Timothy Wilde-shaped ice sculpture. And strangely communicative. Mrs Adams, who kept running her fingers through Jonas's hair, was with him in the kitchen helping

Valentine do whatever he was doing. I'm dead certain Val liked that arrangement. Delia Wright sat before me in an overstuffed chair, still wrapped in Higgins's coat. Neither of us wanted to encounter her torn dress buttons just yet, I believe, though the room was warm. Nor the white strips of bandaging dividing her arms from her hands.

'As if you're deliberately memorializing something that oughtn't be remembered at all,' Delia said softly.

'I've never phrased it that well.'

We fell silent again as Delia gazed about the room. Valentine owns the second floor of a brick rowhouse in Spring Street – a large kitchen, a parlor with a dining area, and two bedrooms, all of them scrupulously clean. The second bedroom doubles as an office and is stuffed with Democratic Party paraphernalia that has a disturbing tendency to encroach on the rest of the house. For instance, above the sparkling freestone hearth, a framed sign announces THE DEMOCRATIC PARTY IS THE TRUE VOICE OF THE PEOPLE, and the one above the striped armchair Delia occupied reads THIS HOUSE VOTES LOYAL DEMOCRAT. As if that was in question. I'd mock him for it, but there's no reasoning with a man who has a four-foot painting of Thomas Jefferson in his bedroom. Opposite an oil study of an American eagle armed with arrows in its talons.

'Please tell me about it, howsoever you like.' I dipped the quill in the inkpot. 'Take your time.'

Delia took an abrupt interest in the edge of her saucer. 'I'd walked Jonas home from school – I teach at the Abyssinian Church along with Reverend Brown – and we were in the sitting room roasting some chestnuts. I like to stay over when Charles is away. The men knocked and when Meg opened the door, they forced their way inside.'

'Had they other accomplices?'

'No. It was just Varker and Coles. I told Jonas to run, but Coles caught him and tied his hands behind his back.' Her expression went brittle, eggshell thin. 'I tried to tear him away, but I couldn't

86

manage it, and by that time Varker was back from shutting Meg in the pantry. Varker pointed the gun at me. Then he said if I kept struggling, he'd take it out of Jonas's hide.'

I'd no wish to snap Val's quill, but that was getting to be a difficult job. 'You might have seen that Varker's wrist is shattered. I don't know if you remember. Anyway, I'm pleased to tell you about it.'

Her brown eyes sparked. They were very dark, but lit from within, a late-October sort of color. 'Whose doing was that?'

'My brother's.'

'I'd have killed him,' she said. Flat and even. 'If he'd touched my nephew, I'd have murdered him. I don't care how. I'd have found a way.'

I touched the feather to my lip. Delia Wright, I concluded, was a decidedly different woman from Lucy Adams. Mrs Adams's terror for her loved ones had seemed a bottomless pit. Freefalling, almost unmanageable – I was amazed she'd acted as courageously as she'd done. Deeply admiring, in fact. I'd seen such fear in those grey eyes, fear churning and depthless as hell itself. It had rendered her exhausted afterward. Near mute. Delia, though – now the shock had worn off – was furious.

'I shouldn't have said that,' she owned with a half smile. 'You're an easy man to talk to.'

'I'm a rosewood secretary,' I found myself confessing ruefully. 'All neat little drawers and dark cubbies people lock their bloodied knives in. I don't mean to imply – God, I'm sorry. You're easy to talk to yourself. And you won't find I've any sympathy for that worm. What happened next?'

'They took us away in a carriage. It was all very fast. After they locked us in that room, they left us in the dark for hours, chained to opposite walls. I kept talking to Jonas, telling him to move, that he'd grow too cold otherwise. Reciting poems to him, stories. When Varker came back, he'd evidently been drinking. He told me he needed to test the quality of the merchandise.'

I got it all down. And in my horridly clear handwriting too. But

I might as well have been trying to draw blood from the paper, I gripped the quill so hard.

'Then you men arrived. That part . . . you're right, I don't remember as clearly. I'm sorry.'

'Don't be. Miss Wright . . .' I hesitated. 'Your sister said something to me earlier, something she hadn't the time to explain. Have slave catchers kidnapped her previously?'

The look that crossed her face was sky wide, enormous – it didn't fit within her round lips, within the sun-dappled skin at the edges of her eyes.

'All three of us were stolen. When we lived in Albany. They meant to auction us at the Capitol. Not Varker and Coles, of course. Others like them. Charles Adams encountered us there and arranged for our release when he learned we were free. Oh, didn't you know?' she continued when I frowned in confusion. 'Charles Adams is white. Apparently someone or other forgot to mention that to you.' When Delia Wright encountered no worse than a raised eyebrow on my part, she exhaled, her mouth melting into an amiable curve. 'Afterward – they grew to like each other. He whisked her to Massachusetts after proposing so that all would be quite official. Not like these common-law marriages the State of New York ignores so resolutely. Thank God he'll return in two days' time.'

She was right, of course. Miscegenation is illegal in our state, but prosecuted almost never. Copper stars have only existed for six months, after all, and laymen who object to interracial union would generally rather die than acknowledge it exists. So plenty of poor whites and blacks set up housekeeping, either legally by way of Massachusetts or practically by means of sharing a bed. But for people of Charles and Lucy Adams's obvious means – it was unusual. Extremely. No matter how pale she was, or how radical his abolitionism.

I was about to observe this fact when footsteps sounded. One set neat and delicate and the other smaller, like its echo. Mrs Adams approached Val's dining table carrying a pot with a golden crust crowning it, her burden flooding the air with the scent of butter, Jonas trailing three feet behind her. It was an improvement, those three feet. A recovery. Jonas had a full, somber mouth, the upper lip quite as wide as the lower, and he seemed to have abandoned my overcoat in the kitchen. He gave his aunt and me a brief smile.

'*I* put the crust on the pie, and did it perfectly, and I marked it with an X,' he announced.

'Well executed, Admiral Adams,' Delia replied. Adding to me, 'Jonas currently boasts a fleet of nine boats.'

'Toy boats,' the lad explained soberly.

'I worked on a ferry myself as a boy and loved it,' I told him.

'Mr Wilde, I've never seen anyone make a shortcrust in under ten minutes, nor season a pigeon pie with white wine, but I can tell you the results seem to be spectacular,' Lucy Adams said with a weary smile.

Val appeared, setting plates and a formidable knife on the table. 'Pigeon is subjected every day in this city to undeserved atrocities.' He then wandered over to the desk with a hand cocked on his hip, reading my report over my shoulder. A flicker of revulsion tugged at the sack beneath his right eye.

'Pigeons deserve our respect,' Delia affirmed, taking Jonas's hand and going to the table. 'I've had terrible pigeon more times than I care to recall. I try not to dwell on those memories.'

'I once had pigeon at the firehouse I thought was strips of boiled belt leather. Boiled, but *dry*, you savvy? Ought to have been impossible, speaking scientifically.'

'A miracle of culinary arts. I can't think of anything fouler tasting than bad pigeon.'

'All bad food is close akin to a bad tumble. Not only personally offensive, but a horrifying waste of time.'

Following this exchange, it grew impossible not to smile. I couldn't even manage to temper my expression with a sourly angled eyebrow. Valentine reached for the inner pocket of his swallow-tailed jacket and produced a silver flask, unscrewing the top as it emerged. He took a pull, then dangled it before my nose. I accepted, ready to celebrate the bizarre sensation of actually liking my elder brother by pouring what turned out to be flash quality rum down my throat.

'I haven't had your pigeon pie in years,' I recalled.

'Then you'd best look lively,' he advised, 'before I yam it all.'

I wish that I'd felt as if dinner that night was something to be savored. But I fancied it repeatable – my brother laughing regretfully, two beautiful and clever women speaking in low but determined swells, and a kinchin who shyly amazed us with his facility at dangling a spoon from his nose and then described the outlandish histories of the boats in his fleet. If I'd known how fast it would pass, swift as a New York springtime, I'd have paid better attention.

I ought to have paid better attention to all manner of things.

After we'd tidied the kitchen, just as I was beginning to fret over finding a decent hotel in a blizzard, Valentine appeared in his parlor with coat, muffler, and top hat donned.

'Where are you going in the middle of the night?' I asked. Not a bit certain I wanted the answer.

'I do have *duties*, you know. When you barge in like a freight train and squander hours of my time, they still exist afterward. I'm on shift with the firedogs.'

I enjoy Val fighting fires about as much as I enjoy him taking ether, but held my tongue, knowing it a lost cause. 'We'll be off, then, to find—'

'My brother,' Valentine said clearly to the exhausted family behind me, 'has the manners of a brained squirrel. I'll rug at the engine house tonight and tomorrow. Extra libbege linen for you lot is in the trunk in my bedroom. I don't need to add that it's a flasher play if no one knows you're here. Here's my spare key.' Metal arced through the air and landed on the table. No one touched it. 'If you must leave, leave only by the back exit, and look sharpish first, and best not to touch the laudanum on the bookshelf, that's . . . special.'

With this earth-shattering announcement, he was out the door. If Valentine had announced his permanent defection to the Whig

Party, I don't think my face would have behaved any differently.

'My God,' Lucy Adams breathed.

I dove after my brother. After scrambling down the short hall, I found myself addressing his broad back as he descended the stairs.

'That's awfully generous of you.'

'I sleep at the engine house plenty often, anyhow.' He glanced back, an evil smile curling upward. 'I'm ruminating on a way you could keep warm yourself tonight, Tim. It's a long, cold walk back to Ward Six. And the sister seems like she could use some comfort.'

I bit the tip of my tongue, understanding dawning.

'You are a horrible man,' I decided.

'I'm a philanthropist. Give her a taste of the Wilde tonic and see how she perks up again. Try to draw it out a bit if you can manage to after so long, there's a devilish little trick with a pinky finger where if you—'

'Everything about you is wrong.'

'No, I gunned her over pretty thorough, and she looks a sweet, soft handful of all that's right in the world to me.'

'I'm not—'

'Just because I savvy you're right-handed doesn't mean you need to work the wrist until *everyone* knows it.'

The right hand in question, which I had admittedly grown to know better of late, clenched into a fist.

'We're never speaking of this again,' I snapped, turning on my heel.

'Sleep well,' came the infuriatingly cheery reply.

I barged back into Val's ken looking like a thundercloud had just gone eight rounds with a hurricane, but no matter.

'The place is yours for two nights. I'll be back to escort you home.'

The sisters stared at each other, as dumbfounded as they were relieved. Jonas made a happy dive for the fireplace and commenced poking at the logs to send brilliant starbursts up the flue. Mrs Adams shook her head in glad wonderment before hastening after him, murmuring something about the dangers of rogue sparks.

Delia removed Higgins's overcoat, not so much as glancing at her ruined buttons. She hung it on the nearest chair. That was another recovery, and one I loved seeing.

'When Charles is home, you'll both come to West Broadway and be thoroughly feted,' she said, smiling. 'Between Meg and Lucy and myself, you won't know what to eat first, nor will your brother. I'll try not to tease you over it and confine myself to heaping roast pig on your plate.'

'I'd like that,' I said. 'I'd like it tremendously.'

Then I went home through weird and wild streets that shone like a full-scale model of New York City carved from ice. All windswept, all abandoned. All mine for once. In seconds, I was snowfrosted and heavy limbed. I didn't care, not about the bone ache or the wind searing my eyes or the fact that my brother is despicable and incredible in equal measure. I didn't even care that the snow was piled against my door in Elizabeth Street and that residents are required to clear their own sidewalks as I walked round the back and gamely found Mrs Boehm's snow shovel. The world was spinning the way I wanted it to that night, and I'd helped to give it the hard push. For the second time in as many days, I was about as happy as I ever am.

Which ought to have been my first warning: that never lasts very long.

CHAPTER SEVEN

*Alas! that we are called to witness American Christians,
who are prepared thus to sacrifice long-cherished
friendship, ardent and sincere affection, patriotism,
country, conscience, religion, all! all! to this visionary and
necessarily fruitless war against slavery!*

David Meredith Reese, *Humbugs of New-York: Being a
Remonstrance Against Popular Delusion Whether in
Science, Philosophy, or Religion*, 1838

When the worst happened to me – and by worst I don't quite
mean unendurable, just grimmer than anything I could
have imagined – I was trying to solve another mystery entirely. A
mystery that was also a miniature miracle.

The morning after the snowstorm, my eyes slitted slowly awake
when dawn's pale glare cannoned off the drifts and through my
window. Rolling out of bed, my feet hitting deliciously warm
floorboards, there wasn't a thing I wanted from life but a word with
Mrs Boehm, a day-old roll, a hot cup of coffee, and a new puzzle
from George Washington Matsell.

Downstairs smelled of the sweet onions Mrs Boehm had cooked
down and then stuffed into some sort of bread, the name of which
always seemed composed entirely of consonants whenever I asked

her about it. Mrs Boehm is half Bohemian and when talking to herself, divides her vocabulary between that language and German. She owns three dresses, to my knowledge, and that morning she wore the plain navy twill with white buttons running from the genial scoop collar down to her toes. The one that makes her hair marginally less ashen but her eyes marginally less blue. She seemed to be awaiting me, for she glanced up just as I finished adjusting the knot in my cravat. The set of her generous mouth seemed troubled.

'Are we at war with Mexico over Texas yet?' I quipped. 'Or is it with England, over Oregon?' We'd been flirting dangerously with both for months.

'There are many dead along the Hudson. In the storm. Ships, everywhere crashing. And a new harbormaster who did not know his business.'

'My God. Was it in the *Herald*?'

'Germans next door.'

This was Mrs Boehm's most reliable source of information. I had the *Herald*, she had *Germans next door*. I sat down at the worktable, for I wasn't due at the Tombs for an hour yet.

'Herr Getzler, he works repairing the steamers,' she said. 'Engines and such. Losses were very bad, he said to me. Thank you for last night clearing snow.'

'You're welcome.'

'You've a letter.'

She nodded at a piece of folded correspondence resting on the table.

My heart almost stopped.

No, not quite right. It expanded like a balloon and then commenced pulsing painfully. But that's not quite sufficient to the purpose either, now I think on it.

I could have had a hundred hearts, and they wouldn't have been sufficient to the purpose.

Handwriting is a curious thing. Mine is neat and scholarly, as if I'd been whipped about the palms for forgetting to add proper flourishes to my capitals, and that was never the case. I stopped schooling at age ten and commenced devouring the Underhill library wholesale at fourteen. Whether my young self cultivated a steady hand or it was born in me, I'll never know. The evidence has been erased – I remember that my mother's receipts for muffins and fried rabbit and the like were neatly penned, but my father was a farmer, and I've no notion whether he had his letters at all. My brother's is shockingly unlike him but very like mine. Regular as typesetting, largely untroubled.

Mercy's looks like a spider's web if you had collected its inky threads in the tenderest fashion, rolled them into a ball, and then tried to spread them out again over a piece of paper. Slightly mad, entirely unreadable.

To anyone save me, that is.

'Best it would be if you read it, I think.'

Mrs Boehm sounded amused. I pulled the letter toward me. 'Where's the envelope?'

She shook her head. 'There was none.'

'How could this have been delivered from London without any envelope?'

'It's from London?'

'Yes.'

She jutted her angular chin as if to say *Read your letter, you ninny.* So I did.

Dear Timothy,

For a man long used to being addressed as *Mr Wilde*, there was a toweringly spectacular start.

I've taken up residence with a cousin of my mother's in Poland Street, near to the heady curve of Regent Street where the world spins a bit faster than it does everywhere else and the boulevard can't help but bend to centripetal force. Letters addressed to 12C Poland Street will find me should there be anything you might wish to write about. And supposing that you'd prefer to forget about me, which I don't like to think of, I'll simply presume that you are still writing me notes but have consigned them to bottles. I walk a great deal by the Thames and shall keep an eye to the water for them if I fail to hear from you by more conventional means.

I pressed a hand over my lips, guessing my expression to be a bit rich for the breakfast table. Whatever it was. *Letters in bottles and walks by the grey winter river*, I thought. That was Mercy right down to the ground.

Cousin Elizabeth is married to the owner of a quaint little museum of saleable curiosities. Arthur, by inclination if not by trade, is an ardent painter, so to make up a little of my board I've taken to opening the shop in the mornings, dusting and nattering and exploring and reading and writing and generally pretending it's actual work until midday, when Arthur arrives. The leaded glass of the shop door is curved, with tiny bubbles marring the clarity, and if I look through it, I feel as if I am back on the steamer from New York to London, all mist about me and ocean and space and unknowns, and I remember how easy I thought it would be to fall into the waves with arms spread wide and drift down into the cool darkness where I would stop seeing the things we saw and stop remembering who was responsible for them. I don't look through the glass of the shop door very often.

Arthur, I thought.

What precisely was cousin Arthur like, and did he believe in marital fidelity? As for the sudden fall into cool, dark water . . . by the time I realized I was gnawing on my knuckle, it was due to my tasting copper, so I stopped. I glanced up at Mrs Boehm, who stood peering into the hot depths of her bread oven. I kept going.

I volunteer feeding soup to the destitute at several churches in the East End and the men and women wear the same look they did back home, half hungry and half ashamed of being hungry, and I wish I could tell them all that God dearly loves to bless the poor, but perhaps as few people believe that here as they do in New York. The rest of the time I walk, and think, and muse over words. The stories I write here do queer things, beginning as a tale about a seamstress who sews 'I love you' in matching thread into the linings of every waistcoat she makes for the merchant she adores, for example, and ending as a conversation between the clever mice who watch her at work and know that the merchant runs his fingers over every stitched letter, but says nothing because he realizes he will die within the year.

I'm not any better when it comes to my poetry either. The phrases that look nicely crafted at first dissolve into nothing upon a second reading, and so I thought I should try my hand at writing letters. Forgive me for it, if you find this unwelcome. We had always used to tell each other of all the mundane breadcrumb-teakettle-washboard little details of our lives, and I feel here as if everything is slightly transparent, and I myself entirely so. There isn't any weight to me since Papa died, and perhaps if I tell you that this morning I found in the shop a little tortoiseshell box and inside was a clockwork bird painted like a rainbow, and I polished it until it shone, then that will have been real. Or I will be real, or something better approximating myself. Sometimes I think someone else lives here now.

If I read this over, the meaning will melt and I may possibly become a pillar of salt, and so I'll send it without looking backward. I hope you are well – I hope so not often, but once and continually. If you wish me not to write, please don't tell me so. Just burn them unread.

Nearly invisibly,
Mercy Underhill

'Mr Wilde, are you all right?'

Mrs Boehm was speaking to me, apparently. Or so I gathered from the pale shadow brushing my jacket sleeve.

'I – yes,' I said. 'I'm fine.'

I wasn't. Something was pooling in my breast, hot and treacle-thick and bitter like burned sugar.

'From who is this letter? May I ask?'

'From a childhood friend of mine. She lives in England now.'

'And she is well, this friend of yours?'

When I didn't answer, a steaming cup of tea appeared in my peripheral vision. I think I thanked her for it. I hope so.

After all Mercy went through last summer, Reverend Underhill's death and previous to that his descent into madness, I couldn't be surprised that she felt less than her usual self. She'd survived her own beloved father nearly killing her, after all. And I'd probably have been unhinged at abandoning everything and everyone I knew. She's always been one of the bravest individuals of my acquaintance, however, and so she'd fulfilled a lifelong dream and simply left us. Abandoned America for the land of her mother's birth. I don't think she could stomach the sight of Manhattan anymore. I didn't blame her for that, didn't blame her for the sort of courage it took to leave us all behind. Leave me behind. But I felt a frenzied surge of ownership after reading that she was in any way unhappy.

It's my job to see that doesn't happen.

'So she is not happy.' Mrs Boehm leaned with her bony hips pressing against the chair opposite me. 'I am sorry. Can you do anything?'

I rose to slide Mercy's letter into my allotted drawer of the sideboard. Thinking of our breadcrumb-teakettle-washboard trivialities, all the nonsense we'd used to share on a near-to-daily basis. If one person on earth has catalogued the things that lift her spirits, I am that man.

And I can write a letter as well as the next fellow.

'I certainly intend to try,' I answered, passing my fingers over Mrs Boehm's hand as I set out for the Tombs.

'How is it can a letter travel across the ocean without an address or stamp?' she called after me.

'Magic,' I answered, donning my coat. 'Dark alchemy. Fey spirits. True love. I haven't the faintest idea.'

* * *

The Tombs loomed above me like castle ramparts rising from the drifts. Feudal, vaguely warlike. Generally a crowd of babbling misfits occupies its front steps – attorneys and bail runners and reporters and street rats, all about their inexplicable business. But the snow had muffled us, gagged the hubbub with a wet white cloth. No one was there. Which made it all the more surprising when I'd reached the entrance and a voice plucked me from the reverie, *Are envelopes ever stolen when letters are delivered, and if so, why in hell—*

'Mr Wilde.'

I skidded to a halt. 'Mr Mulqueen. Good morning.'

Sean Mulqueen had last addressed me when I was escorting Mrs Adams from the Tombs; previous to that, we'd spoken twice. About the pernicious nature of too-tight boots when walking in circles for sixteen hours, when we were first appointed roundsmen. And then about the remarkable nature of the telegraph and when it would be finished and whether it might destroy civilization, et cetera. He's a County Clare man – of medium height but broad shouldered, ruddy hair cut above his ears, ears tilted backward like a hissing cat's. He looked plenty pleased about something. I've seen butchers mull over slaughtered steers in like fashion.

'I think ye'll be finding that Chief Matsell wants a private word,' he reported.

'Thank you. Regarding?'

'A source o' great pride it has been, to watch you rise so quick and easy to the rank of . . . well, what, in fact, are you?' His lips cracked into a smile. 'But that's all like enough to be over now, more's the pity. Sometimes fast flames make for spent fuel. I'm sure ye'll find work elsewhere quick enough, a handsome lad like yourself.'

I took a small moment to stare at him in astonishment. Apparently, the man loathed me. And here it had never occurred to me that other copper stars might envy my tiny office and my lack of rounds.

No response seemed possible. Nodding, I made for Matsell's

office. Strains of Mercy's letter still floated through my head like the imprint of a midnight waltz the next morning, but now the wracked poetry was mingled with more present concerns. Hall after hall glided past, all unfeeling stone built far too wide and too tall for a man to feel comfortable within. At length, I knocked at a door wearing a huge brass plaque that boomed GEORGE WASHINGTON MATSELL: CHIEF OF NEW YORK CITY POLICE in my face.

'Come in.'

I entered. Cautiously. The chief's fire blazed recklessly, and I held my hands out toward it. I'm strangely fond of Matsell's office – the surprising lack of stray paperwork on his desk, his namesake's portrait, the scandalous reading material that lines his bookshelves. Pamphlets about female reproduction, about capital punishment, about the underworld, about every unfashionable thing. Our chief is an intellectual omnivore. He has a room at City Hall as well, but the Tombs nook is much more like him, the neat rows of scientific journals brightly illuminated by the enormous window. Chief Matsell himself sat at his desk, scribbling entries in his dictionary.

That's a pet project, but a useful one. It's a criminal lexicon explaining the vagaries of flash language. The fact that *shady glim* means *dark lantern*, and *brother of the bung* means a *brewer of beer*, and so forth. He means it for use by green copper stars. The sort likely to meet with a knife in the neck when they first encounter a dead rabbit. Part of me inwardly cringes from the thing. If you could spare yourself the sort of topics Valentine and the rest of the flash speakers palaver over . . . well, wouldn't you?

'Mr Wilde, you are about to explain several things to me. And with complete candor, or you will deeply regret it. Sit down.'

I sat, keeping well mouse. Trying to get ahead of Matsell in a conversation is tantamount to shoving the spike down your own throat to ready yourself for the roasting spit. When his eyes rose, I could see clear as the air between us he was deliberately reading me.

Clothing, hands, shoes, face, the whole inventory. The fact that he didn't bother to hide his scrutiny from someone who'd instantly notice it set my teeth on edge a bit.

'You found the missing painting,' he began. 'The copper stars have received a glowing letter of thanks, and doubtless you – and Mr Jakob Piest, I take it – were rewarded handsomely.'

'It was a very successful enterprise,' I said, already baffled.

'Hm. Possibly you don't recall that I also asked you to apprehend the criminal responsible.'

That one took me a moment. I hadn't any lay planned out, and faced the prospect of bluffing my way through a pair of threes. Where the chief is concerned, I'd sooner have stared down a wild boar.

'I do recall,' I owned apologetically, my mind scrambling for a story – any story that made sense, save for the one that had actually happened. 'I'd just ask you to ruminate over the sort of folk who might find themselves inside the Millington mansion. People who live fast lives, accumulate secret debts. It might not be a good idea for us to arrest such a fellow. If he was a valuable sort to the Party, and the situation has been handled.'

His eyes raked over me. Ever so marginally fond below the scraping tines. But maybe I was imagining that.

'I'm not going to swallow a word of the shit you just fed me,' he said.

I wouldn't have either, in fairness. But I'd never lied to Chief Matsell previously. So it had been worth a try.

'Do you see any reason why I should trust you far enough to let you shield a thief, Mr Wilde?'

'Not any reasons for trusting me that you don't already know about. Sir,' I added quietly.

The chief knew of which I spoke. He'd seen those nineteen tiny bodies in the woods, and he dragged that anchor about just as I did. He knew what Silkie Marsh was capable of. He knew the evil shape under her creamy skin as precious few of us did. He shared my buried secrets. Another man might have thrown me out on my ear, but Matsell looked as if that option was untenable, and he felt considerably irked by the fact. He glanced up at George Washington as if requesting strength from a deity and then leaned back in his enormous chair.

Well, it has to be enormous, after all. He is the living incarnation of a scholarly bull elephant.

'Fine. Bugger the Millingtons. The second question will be considerably worse going,' the chief advised, eyes blazing. 'Did you enter a private business last night and physically assault its proprietors, stripping them of their weapons before absconding with their property?'

I've been struck by multiple facers in my scant days as a copper star, but that one landed on the jaw. 'Not as such—'

'I ask because two entrepreneurs – one whose wrist is *very* badly broken, by the way – have been to see me early this morning. They imagine that you removed from their possession two runaway slaves, grossly injuring their persons, and they want you sacked.'

'I see,' I replied. It had sounded more eloquent in my head.

'So you're following me thus far? The scenario sounds familiar?'

'Yes, and I'll explain, sir, but did they name anyone else they wanted sacked?'

'They did,' he shot back coldly. 'Two other copper stars. But I assumed those claims to be preposterous, because I am convinced you acted alone. Shall I look into them further?'

'No! No, I was alone. There was an altercation. I . . .'

Glad as I was that the deluge was landing on my shoulders, and not Piest's or Val's, feeling like a cornered possum isn't my strong suit. So I decided to grasp the nettle.

'Damn it, are you an abolitionist or not?' I questioned.

His eyes narrowed yet further. 'Slavery is a repugnant institution, one that will eat away at this country until it is left a cracked shell.'

My lungs thawed a bit. 'Yes, that's what Valentine says. And I agree.'

'Enough to steal a pair of runaways from their lawful captors?'

'That's unadulterated hocus. They're New York citizens, as sure as I am. I was consulted by a family member and by the Committee of Vigilance, who vouched for the captives' identities.'

Digging a vexed thumb into my opposite palm, I awaited his answer. Chief Matsell merely smiled indulgently. Then his attention wandered. I'd placed my greatcoat and hat on the back of my chair when I entered, and he commenced eyeing my black frock coat appraisingly, as if judging its resale value. I returned his stare, entirely befuddled.

'Might I pour you a drink?'

'If you want one yourself, I can't say as I'd mind,' I admitted.

Matsell hoisted his leathery bulk and poured two large tumblers of what smelled like New England rum. Then he held a hand out.

'Mr Wilde, might I examine your jacket?'

'Why would – all right.' I peeled it off my arms. Determined with every ounce of dignity I possessed not to ask Matsell directly why he wanted to study a secondhand swallow-tailed coat.

As it happened, he didn't want to study it.

Without ceremony – as a matter of fact, without hesitation, without the smallest pause – my chief threw my coat in his fireplace.

For a moment, I gaped at him. Thunderstruck.

'What in Christ's name do you think you're doing?' I cried when I found my tongue.

It was ablaze in seconds. Ruined an instant later. More than half ash by the time I'd rounded the desk corner with a vile expression on my face and was halted by an enormous hand against my chest.

'Don't stop me, *fight* me,' I snarled, pure instinct having taken over.

'You don't want me to.' Matsell gripped me by the shirtfront and threw me back three or four staggering feet. As I recovered, ready to fly at him in earnest, he asked placidly, 'What was that coat made of? The fabric?'

'What in sodding hell is wrong with you? Cotton,' I growled, again clenching my fists, 'and you—'

'I am giving you a taste of what your life will look like after the war against our Southern brothers breaks out.' He seated himself as if nothing had happened. 'After we lose. And we may well lose, if a war is fought.'

'You want to make a political point and you're vandalizing my clothing to do it? Not that I'm surprised,' I sneered. 'That's just the sort of thuggery your precious Party relies on to make arguments.'

'How do you find the rum, Mr Wilde?'

Matsell reached unflappably for my tumbler.

He flung the glass within the fire in a flaming spurt of orange. That was when the real trouble started. The alcohol's fumes mingled with the smoking cotton to create a noxious cloud that made me altogether sick in the gut.

Loathing unrestrained fire isn't something I can help. But God, I wish it were. If I could treat fire as I treat large men like Chief Matsell who know how to kill small men like me, for instance, I'd be well served. If I could walk into infernos in a sort of unholy rapture as Val does in his twisted notion of a lifelong penance, I'd be insane, all too true, but at least I'd be a man about it. The fact I can't will be a misery that commenced at age ten and will end when I am still and cold and fed to the wildflowers.

In seconds, I found myself gripping the edge of the nearest bookshelf. White-knuckled, bile frothing at the back of my throat, vicious as a rabid dog.

'Touch me and I'll break one of your fingers,' I coughed as a giant figure cautiously entered my vision.

It didn't touch me. Matsell strode to the door and flung it open. Smoke rushed out and air flooded in and I turned to where the bookshelf met the wall and gagged once, quiet as I could.

Air, I thought while sucking it in, and *More air*, and then, *I will mash my chief's face into a loyal Democratic pudding*. A minute passed while I pondered along those lines. But blessedly, as the smoke cleared, rational thought returned. I shifted to see that Matsell had resumed his seat behind the desk. Time appeared to have gotten itself muddled, though, for two rum glasses rested on its surface once more. With a rum bottle between them.

'Sit *down*,' the chief said.

Not at all gently. Thank heaven for that. If it had been gently, I might yet have laced him down to sinew – or tried, rather. Wearing shirtsleeves and a waistcoat and feeling ridiculous over it, I complied. It wasn't a sure bet I could stand up much longer.

'You are one of my most valuable copper stars.' The chief pushed the drink toward me with two fingers. It was gone in an eyeblink, and he poured me another. 'You are not *invaluable*, however. Neither am I, come to think of it. But here is my point: ask yourself where cotton comes from. Where rum comes from. Tobacco? What about sugar?'

'From people treated worse than their masters' dogs,' I rasped out, eliminating my second glass of rum.

'Precisely so, And what about the industries employed to refine and distribute all of these examples? Or the Northern companies that sell mills and engines and ships and weapons and hansoms and liquor back to the South? Who sews with the cotton thread? And who wears the clothing? Have you given any thought to Wall Street a mile or two away from us, and how they make their living?'

'I was more concerned with saving New Yorkers from a fate worse than death.'

A silence settled over us. At last, I raised my head and breathed a steady, clockwork breath. Strangely, Matsell no longer looked angry with me. And by a second singular blessing, he didn't seem to be pitying my weakness either. His eyes shone and his broad hands were clasped together. Whatever he was about to tell me, he believed it.

'One day, there will be a war over slavery. I see no route around such an eventuality, though many do, and often propose asinine stratagems to keep peace in place. This heinous struggle over Texas is an excellent example. But when war comes, do you covet my position? Would you like to preside over Manhattan's lawkeeping when its shipping industry is gutted and its steamers rotting in the harbor, its poor unburied in the streets as they are back in Ireland?'

My kerchief had been in my frock coat, unfortunately. So I

pressed my shirt cuff to the edges of my ruined face instead. Pondering.

'If you do,' Matsell concluded, 'then you are not the man I thought you were.'

'Are you asking me not to interfere with slave catchers who kidnap New York citizens?'

'I am asking you to cease assaulting Southerners who are doing their jobs. If the press got wind of such, the Party could lose everything, including the police force. Don't think Mayor Havemeyer is at all fond of us. He isn't. You need to follow the law.'

'*Prigg versus Pennsylvania*.' The words were bitter as the smoke I still tasted in the air.

'You insult me, Mr Wilde. I much prefer our local Albany laws to the horse manure they so constantly churn up in the Capitol.' Matsell's eyes twinkled. 'Of course every alleged runaway has the right to a jury trial in my city. Now. Are we clear?'

'We're clear,' I said. Looking pretty haggard over it, I'd wager. 'But I'm not returning people to the likes of Varker and Coles.'

'I'd imagine those *particular* people are quite untraceable by this time, already in Canada where they cannot be retrieved.' Matsell shot me a meaningful glare.

'They're long gone,' I assured him.

'Grand. Go to Eighty-five Bayard Street, if you would, it's an establishment I know for a fact has been selling liquor without a license for six months, and none of my roundsmen can ever manage to locate their cache.'

Donning my overcoat, I noted in a side-eyed fashion that Matsell was regarding me with a highly satisfied air. That of a man who'd worked through a thorny conundrum.

'Yes?' I said snappishly.

'Nothing. Only I'd wondered just what it took to slow you down, Mr Wilde. Now I know.' I must have scowled, for an answering smile creased the deep folds of his face. 'Please, it's a perfectly reasonable thing for your chief to be apprised about. On your way to Bayard Street, feel free to stop by Chatham with a bit of that reward money and find yourself a new jacket. I haven't the smallest doubt,' he added with wry but final emphasis, 'that it will be made of *cotton*.'

It took me an hour to find a black secondhand coat with tails of a length that didn't make me look like a kinchin of twelve or an undertaker, sold to me by a bleary-eyed old Yidisher tailor who likewise lacked stature. The coat, as predicted, was made of cotton. It took me all of half an hour to discover the secret store of liquor in Bayard Street and to write out a ticket. I honestly can't recall how I went about doing that. The deciding factor had something to do with a neat assembly line of spotless new canning jars, and the sorts of vegetables that actually grow in February.

The next day, February 16 – my sole weekly day of freedom – Charles Adams was due back. So I set out for Val's house at dawn, struggling shin-deep through gaps in sidewalk-clearing etiquette. The snow was a dull grey by that time. Littered with frozen newspapers, chicken bones, liquor bottles, worse. The light in the streets I passed through seemed the color of regretful ghosts.

Knocking at my brother's door, I received no answer. But I was due back at home shortly to receive an illustrious visitor. So I announced my presence by stamping my overboots on the straw rug in the hall and then went in anyhow. The door was unlocked.

'Mrs Adams,' I called out.

No response.

'Miss Wright, we must see what we can do about getting you home.'

Nothing.

'Valentine!' I attempted, annoyed.

I didn't find my brother. I didn't find Delia Wright or Jonas Adams either. What I did find sent a shock through my chest as if someone had bashed my exposed heart with a pine plank.

I never wrote out a police report regarding that February

morning. Thank God. But if I had done, it would have gone something along these lines:

Report made by Officer T. Wilde, Ward 6, District 1, Star 107. On the morning of February 16, I arrived at the residence of Captain Valentine Wilde to escort Lucy Adams, Jonas Adams, and Delia Wright to their home in West Broadway. Upon finding the rooms empty, initiated a search and noted signs of a violent struggle in the master bedroom of the house.

I discovered the corpse of Lucy Adams in Captain Wilde's bed, in a state of considerable disarray, with a cord wrapped tight around her neck.

As for Delia Wright and Jonas Adams, they had vanished without trace.

Chapter Eight

*They know too well which side their bread is buttered on
ever to give up these advantages. Depend upon it – the
Northern people will never sacrifice their present lucrative
trade with the South, so long as the hangings of a few
thousands will prevent it.*

The Richmond Whig, 1835

For at least ten seconds, I couldn't comprehend what I was
looking at.

There was Val's little walnut bedside table, upended and its
crystal decanter of some spirit or other – whiskey, from the woody
scent – smashed into a hundred dreamlike shards upon the floor, as
if a society woman's diamond necklace had exploded. That much I
understood. There was Thomas Jefferson rendered in dramatic
brushstrokes, gaping up from the floor. I could manage that too.

Then I forced myself with every ounce of willpower I own to
understand the central figure in the landscape and felt my legs turn
willowy.

Lucy Adams's golden skin had gone blue at her lips and her
fingernails. Her motionlessness was final, permanent – she looked
as if she'd never moved at all. There was a cord wrapped twice
about her neck, ends dangling, and it took me less than an instant

to understand it was the brown silk tie from Valentine's robe.

It was suddenly necessary to place one hand at the edge of the bed while the other grasped my own knee. In the back of my mind somewhere, in a place that wasn't plunging like Niagara Falls, I wasn't keen to lose sureness of step anywhere near a carpet of malicious glass shards.

If I only shut my eyes for a moment, I thought madly, *this will go away.*

I was mistaken. When I opened them, I spied one of the vilest things I've ever before witnessed.

Her eyes were likewise wide open. But that was quite usual, I'd recently found, for the violently dead. She was dressed in her underthings – corset undone and sagging low, chemise unlaced, most of her chest exposed though the flimsy silk shift was still draped over her sprawling shoulders. Neck bruised purple and still darkening. I'd seen that before too, as a copper star. Twice. In an evil brothel in Orange Street it took me three weeks to dismantle permanently.

But I also thought I saw scratches running along her chest. Not new scratches – these were bloodless old ridges like the footprints of dry creekbeds, done long ago. Years, if not longer. Silvery ridges of healed-over skin, probably long forgotten by their owner. Why I should still be able to see them puzzled me. Then I realized the scratches were knife scars. And not ordinary knife scars either.

Knife scars I could read, running in two lines across her breast.

as many as I love I rebuke and chasten
be zealous therefore and repent

Whatever expletive I meant to employ is lost to time, for it burst against a closing throat.

There are moments when I simply stop seeing things clearly. After reading that phrase carved years before into Mrs Adams's flesh, there was nothing but the horrible floating sensation of a fever dream, all sparkling black periphery and melting shapes. I was in a badly directed stage panorama where Mrs Adams spoke fragmented scraps of Shakespeare while swallowing knife after knife after knife, points protruding from her full belly. When I pleaded with her to cease, I found that my mouth was missing. From nose to teeth proved merely sealed-over skin.

That all made equally as much sense as a strangled Mrs Adams in Val's bed with writing carved into her, though.

'Pull yourself together,' I hissed, swallowing an enormous portion of brandy.

The sick feeling receded in time with my thudding heartbeat.

I sat in Val's parlor, staring down at his oaken desk. Outside, the sky was brightening mercilessly. Burning the safe, private holes away. A minute had passed, perhaps. Maybe two.

I needed to do something, and quickly, for there was no sign of my brother and nothing about this made sense. Nothing. Not money, not love, not politics, not God, not any of the reasons I've decided people kill each other. Mrs Adams dead was not only tragic. It was incomprehensible.

You need to move, I thought. *Fast.*

Here's the wretchedest thing about what followed after: I didn't even think twice about it. Once I realized what that body meant, the shadow its shape would cast, I set to. With vigor and willpower. It would be pretty admirable to say that I ruminated over the moral implications of taking an obviously murdered corpse away from where I'd found it.

I can't, though. Because I knew in my bones Val hadn't done this. No matter how morphine crazed or black minded.

And even if he had done, I was not about to watch my brother hang.

The blood flowed back into my shock-numbed hands. I knew *exactly* what to do. Supposing there was time.

Racing into the bedroom, I found Mrs Adams's blue dress crumpled in the corner. I carried it to the bed and drew my fingers gently down her eyelids, closing them. Next I returned Val's brown silk tie to its dressing gown. Swift as I could, I dressed her not-quite-cold form, inwardly cursing the intricacies of female costume.

It needn't be perfect, I repeated over and over again. *It need only be finished in time.*

As I closed the buttons over her neck, the admonishment stared back at me obscenely. *Love. Rebuke. Chasten. Repent.* I thought about how frightened Lucy Adams had been when her sister and her son had been taken. How her world had split visibly – ruptured and commenced wildly hemorrhaging.

I've been kidnapped before, after all.

'You can't hear me,' I murmured when I'd got my breath back and was winding her up in a blanket. 'But if I ever meet the dog who did that to you, I'll leave some marks of my own in his hide.'

For convenience's sake, I opened the front door of my brother's lodgings before lifting Mrs Adams. Her face was visible within the grey wool, but little else. I walked down the stairs, carrying her narrowly enough in my arms that her head rested on my shoulder and her feet wouldn't snag on the banister rail. When I reached the ground floor, I made an about-face toward the rear exit, hoping to God someone or other had shoveled it clear.

I reached for the doorknob with my freer arm, the one supporting Mrs Adams's knees. The frosty air seared the sweat into my flesh as if the skin were burning. Little rivulets of molten lead creeping down my neck. Kicking the door shut behind me, I crossed the yard. After my brief waking nightmare, and my words to her in Val's room, nothing hurt as it ought to. Not while I was about a very specific and important task.

It would hurt, though, I suspected. Later. I suspected my absolute failure to protect her and her family would hurt a great deal.

Leaving the tiny back courtyard behind me at a gate tinged with gore-colored rust, I entered the alleyway that would take me through rear yards and away. Here the snow was half-melted, not shoveled, salted, or sprinkled with ash or Rockaway sand. Twice I staggered, and once I caught Mrs Adams's gorgeous fanfare of curls on a nail thrusting savagely from a discarded door frame, only noticing when a tendril tore away.

I'd have hated myself for that. But I hadn't the time.

Broome Street borders Val's dwelling to the south. It was populated with newsboys piping out headlines, chestnut vendors, sleighs gliding by in the snow. Our incessant street advertisements, all the howling posters plastered to boards suspended above the sidewalks, seemed maudlin and hysterical in the delicate light. As I walked, I peered out from beneath the brim of my hat, studying passersby. Expressionless, meanwhile. Functioning exclusively as a conveyance and a spyglass.

An adroit-seeming oysterman looked me over as he approached. His cart was glass fronted, boasting trays of oysters on ice, racks of ginger beer, and a steaming pile of hot peppered biscuits that would be sold within half an hour. He squinted at me. Resting my cheek against Mrs Adams's hair, I began talking, just loud enough to be heard.

'Don't fret yourself, dear, you're merely overtired. A fainting spell is nothing to be ashamed of. We'll soon have you home.'

The oysterman huffed sympathetically. And then we'd passed each other, each man vanished from the other's vision in a fraction of a moment. Tens of thousands of other strangers – the strangers on the harmless days who watch me sip coffee and visit the barber and buy the *Herald* when I haven't a corpse with me – have glimpsed me once and never again. I hoped to Christ he was of their sort. A unique encounter, fast and unrepeatable.

I struggled onward for several more blocks.

I am a conveyance. And a spyglass. Nothing more.

When I knew my legs were near to faltering and reminded myself that falling with a body in my arms would effectively derail my plans, I turned into the next alley. Hoping. Maybe praying, a little, if prayers can be released into the air like Mercy's letter, without any designated address. There are too many avidly worshipped gods around here to risk offending one of them.

But either one of them heard me or I was in luck.

From the instant I'd understood my role in the tragedy, I'd dreaded the appearance of a large rubbish bin. Either I would *make myself do it*, actually throw Mrs Adams away as if she were a gnawed chicken leg as I'd seen done to helpless others, or I would have to pass it by and admit to myself that my fastidiousness meant more to me than my surviving kin. Neither seemed an agreeable option. I know that bones aren't people – bones bearing soon-to-be-dissolved flesh still stitched over them aren't legacies, aren't keepsakes, aren't even a decent approximation of the torch that once burned within the sum of their parts.

Still. A rubbish bin. There is such a thing as honor, after all.

But here before me, in an alley in Ward Eight near to the Hudson, was my answer.

The shanty in the passage clearly housed newsboys. They'd built the tiny structure of river drift, mismatched planks joined to honest branches and logs. It was covered in paper, layer upon layer of newsprint. Eight or ten of them, if they arranged it right, could probably sleep in a huddle within, all shivering against one another until they vibrated themselves to sleep.

Well, at least I'd be giving them a headline.

I left her there, gently curled into herself. She wouldn't be suffering from the cold. It was the tiniest mercy I could think of, but by then my muscles shook like the laundry rags fluttering in the wind above me, and so I thought of it again and again. *She isn't cold.*

She isn't ever going to be cold anymore.

The rest of my journey back to Val's house must have been uneventful. I don't recall it, though. None of it imprinted upon my memory. The Hudson could have been on fire, and I'd never have registered the fact.

I closed Valentine's door. Just breathing. For a moment only, I came apart as if I'd been constructed of loosely looped cotton string. After the shuddering gasp had passed through me, I stepped firmly into the small foyer.

Tasks, I thought. *More tasks.*

Not a single object in Valentine's rooms escaped my scrutiny. A few things struck me as odd. For instance, whoever had knocked over the table hadn't agitated the rug beneath. Nothing had been taken, so far as I could tell. No rooms disturbed other than the bedroom. And even the bedroom wasn't disturbed in any great fashion. His morphine tinctures and their complementary morphine-tablet brethren were safe in their brown glass apothecary bottles, waiting to serve whether a sip of sugary venom or a swift-swallowed poison pill seemed better planning, neatly aligned in his carved curio case with the butchered thirteen-segment DON'T TREAD ON ME viper carved into the lid. Deeply familiar, those bottles, harmless as bullets. The knives in the kitchen were neatly slotted in their pine stand, save for one resting on the table. It was perfectly clean, though, so I imagined it must have been set there to dry. The ladies had remembered to water the rosemary bush in the window.

All was in its rightful place, more or less. Apart from the world being splintered to pieces.

None of it meant anything. But it, all of it, might mean everything. I never knew such things until the very last moment. And one day, when my luck runs out, I won't know what things mean until it's too late.

After cleaning up every trace of chaos as frantically as an underhousemaid who'd offended the mistress, I quit Val's ken with the intention of locating him in the swiftest manner possible. But on my way to the stairs through the carpeted hallway, I heard the front door of the building opening. As I reached the upper steps, a stocky man approached the lower, placing his hand on the rail. I kept right on going. We met in the middle, looking each other over. Neither with a particularly fond eye.

'Mr Mulqueen,' I said.

'Mr Wilde.'

He glanced at my copper star. I glanced at his. It was pinned to a thick brown sack coat, and he wore a blue jacket of Irish manufacture, all pointed tails and brass buttons. His star wanted polishing, but so did mine. Mulqueen has green eyes, much paler than the bottle color my brother and I share. They glistened with something wary.

'Any idea where my brother is hiding himself at the moment?' I asked.

Mr Mulqueen had been a step below me. Apparently that didn't suit him, because he abandoned the rail to drift toward the wall and join me. I wasn't much fussed by his being taller again. In fact, I walked two or three casual steps farther down, just to show that we were mates and I was short and also leaving. His oddly tilted ears burned red from the wind, and he peered down at me with a sour expression.

'Looking for him, are ye?'

'I thought I'd drop by. It's my day off, you understand. Care to lift a pint down the street?'

''Tis nine forty-seven in the morning,' he answered, pocket watch in hand to dryly illustrate this fact. 'And I don't drink.'

'Ah. Well, if you're after my brother, he isn't in, I'm sorry to say.'

'I'm here due to there bein' a report of a disturbance. In your brother's very rooms, can you believe it. Seems there was a fight o' some kind, maybe a violent one, and they're after me sortin' it out.'

'There's no one in, I tell you.'

'Well,' he said with a smile tender as sandpaper, 'lucky thing you're here, and like enough to know where his spare key is, and we can sort it proper between the pair of us.'

I assumed a worried air. That wasn't a long walk, for I'd never been so worried in my life. Trotting back up the stairs, I studied Val's door, wondering how feasible its being left unlocked would look when I opened it. His spare key had been bestowed on Mrs Adams, of course, and despite a search I hadn't an inkling where it was.

There was nothing for it, however. I tried the knob and swung the door open. Affected a bit of puzzlement. Mulqueen likewise raised an eyebrow, but then he strode over the threshold.

He examined each room by turn. I stayed by the doorway. Skeptical and irritated. When he returned from the bedroom, I snapped my watch shut in mild reproof.

'There must ha' been some mistake, to be sure,' Mulqueen murmured. 'As ye said, there's nary a soul here. If that were a prank, 'twas a poor one, eh?'

'Very. A very, very poor prank. Who alerted you?'

'Oh, we all have our little sources, Mr Wilde. Someone thought there was a row, you understand. Just a citizen doing their part. A relief, though, to find naught amiss after all. Best be off, then?'

Despite the fact that he made every nerve in my body stand up and clang like the City Hall cupola fire bell, I couldn't have agreed with him more. We returned to the street in silence. Val's door was left unlocked again, but I couldn't be bothered about it. If a poppy freak broke in and stole his morphine supply, well, then I would simply have to shake that man's hand.

'Afternoon,' I said, touching my hat in the briefest possible gesture.

'And to you, Mr Wilde. Oh,' he added, turning back.

I likewise paused. The morning sun etched every detail of him into my brain, from a barely loose coat button to the almost imperceptible stain at one side of his mouth from chewing tobacco, and I wanted the blankness back. If I was seeing everything again, clear as I normally do, my day was about to get painful. He wore three heavy golden rings on various fingers, and his watch chain was likewise creamy yellow ore.

Odd, on a policeman's salary. To say the least.

'Whatever happened to that negress?' he asked. 'The crime victim from t'other night?'

'I haven't the faintest idea. I removed her from a slavers' den, as you've probably heard. But after that, I don't know. She's gone.'

'Pity,' he said, smirking coolly. 'She was an eyeful.'

Another curt good-bye followed, and I fled.

Something resembling panic was creeping along the backs of my eyelids. As if I needed a reminder that I was vexed, my scar twitched in petty mockery and I shoved my fingers against it, warding off the tension that would set my head pulsing. I needed my brother. I needed a plan. I needed to blast this day to pieces and sink it beneath the waves like a pirate-ravaged schooner. I needed a cave to crawl into and think things through before the soft edges of the panic hardened and closed round my neck like a noose.

She's not cold, I thought as the panic's slack grip tightened its reins. *She'll never be cold anymore. And for all you know, you'll never be warm again.*

A conference between my brain and my feet to which I was not invited determined that I should go home before I gave the entire affair away by exploding into slivers of ash on some street corner or other. I'm not sorry to have missed the discussion. When I opened my front door, I entered a hearty cloud of orange rind and cinnamon.

After hanging my hat, I found myself peering down at a small girl of around ten or eleven. It's impossible to be sure. We don't know her birth date. It occurred to me that she ought, as Jean-Baptiste had done, select one herself. Bird Daly is an equally discerning, independent-minded sort of creature.

'Hello, Mr Wilde.'

The grin she was wearing belonged on a promontory along the Hudson, to stop more ships being lost in inclement weather. She has a dazzling smile when she likes, and she likes more often now. It changes her entire face, the pale, sober square of it softening into gentle curves. Bird's dark red hair was done in a prettily worked single plait, and she wore a warm woolen dress of a scarlet hue that didn't match her tresses in the slightest, having likely come from a Catholic charity box. She resides at the Catholic Orphan Asylum for schooling and takes what comes. The object being that once she's schooled, she can take what she likes.

When her grey eyes met mine, the joyful expression crashed to earth in a meteoric descent.

'Mr Wilde?'

'It's all right. I'm happy to see you. I'm just . . . happy about nothing else at the moment.'

'What's happened?'

'Is there tea?' I asked of Mrs Boehm. My voice sounded strangely distant. 'Or barring tea, will you pass me the whiskey bottle in my cupboard?'

Mrs Boehm made a familiar clucking noise that meant she was very concerned about something, but would defer discussion for the moment. Water from a pitcher promptly splashed into a teakettle. Walking to the table, I sat down and palmed a hand through my dirty blond hair.

Bird's fingers lightly brushed my shoulder. Seconds later, whiskey appeared before me.

A culinary project of continental proportions had been undertaken on the bakery table. The end result looked as if it was going to be tea cakes. Little trays had been set out, dotted with pools of spices and zest and thick batter. Then I recalled that it was Monday, and Bird was missing school in order to visit us thanks to the generous nature of Father Connor Sheehy, and understood.

'The cakes are for your classmates?' I asked. I didn't bother hazarding a smile. Bird can read me clear as she can a Democratic political poster.

Bird's snub nose twitched as she worked out how best to handle me. Interrogation versus patience seemed to be at war in her head. Having once been a kinchin-mab, she's very good at it – the handling of people. Children who earn their living in brothels surviving the attentions of adult men have to be good at such things. But my friend Bird has a knack all her own.

'I thought it would be a flash lark, and Mrs Boehm didn't mind.' She squinted, dimpling.

I released the breath I'd not been aware I was holding. Apparently she was going to allow me to pretend that life was normal, at least for a few minutes. A pinched look of worry had settled between her eyes, but she gamely dipped a wooden spoon in the bowl of batter and passed it to me. I wish to Christ that Bird Daly had never been imprisoned and used like an animated doll for men's amusement. The thought of it will never cease to make me ill. But her strangely adult gravity can be an unexpected reprieve at times, and I found myself grateful, though I'd have traded it for a display of childish temper in an instant.

Dutifully, I tasted the spoon.

'Either you or possibly Mrs Boehm is the best baker I've yet encountered,' I decided. My small friend smiled, a real one. My taller friend shot me an anxious glance.

Later, I mouthed.

Nodding, she set the teakettle on the stove.

I thought about being a child, and not one like Bird: one with parents. As I once was. Helpless and happily unaware of the fact because someone else was doing the protecting. Then I thought about Jonas Adams. His fleet of wooden ships and his shy smile and his round blue eyes. His exceedingly foreboding absence.

Taking a breath deep enough to reach my toes, I wrenched myself back into some approximation of attentiveness.

'You've been studying sewing,' I mused.

Bird's lips pursed. 'How do you reckon?'

'Because you've two pinpricks on the fingers of your left hand, and no one told you that you ought to finish off a button with the little knot on the underside instead of the top of your sleeve.'

'And so? You've been spying like a simon-pure nose,' she scoffed.

'Why the devil do you say that?'

'Mr *Wilde*. It's from the charity togs. *Anyone* could have been learning to sew on this frock. You passed by the schoolroom, and you looked through the window last Friday. I spotted your hat. It *was* me mending it, of course,' she added ruefully. 'I'm rubbish at sewing.'

Smiling didn't seem quite so difficult suddenly, though I knew the sensation would be very short-lived. 'Tell me about school,' I requested.

She pegged me for desperate, so she obliged. Bird is generous like that.

Some time later, when the cakes were cooling and awaiting decoration, when I'd listened to her tales of earthworms and grammar and the horrible boy who called her a beetle-eyed vixen, I was near enough to myself again. Mrs Boehm likewise listened attentively, nodding when I advised that the horrible boy ought to be teased mercilessly for paying any attention to Bird whatsoever and questioned in the closest detail in front of his mates as to why he was looking at her in the first place. Apparently, whiskey at my elbow and a pair of watchful allies are all it takes to pull me back from the edge of mental ruin. That was a nice thing to know about. Comforting.

'Are you growing to be happy there?' I asked.

A second or two passed before Bird's chin jutted up and down in a forceful nod. 'I'm very happy. You'd not believe how happy. I'm chaffey as you please.'

Biting my lip, I hesitated. Bird isn't allowed to lie if it's for my sake, since I'm keen to shoulder whatever burdens she passes me. But Bird hammers lies into shields to hide behind, weaves falsehoods into little ships to keep herself afloat, and I couldn't spot out whether that last fabrication had been for her or for me. Nor how to ask without bullying her. Beneath the queasy anxiety over my discovery that morning, it mightily troubled me.

'Mr Wilde,' Bird whispered when Mrs Boehm had stepped out to feed the yard chickens. She hovered, thrumming with unspoken questions, a few inches from my right elbow.

'Yes?'

Her voice fell yet further. 'Something happened to you. Was it something like . . . did you find more kinchin, say? Buried in the woods?'

Bird and I tend to stay about a foot away from each other – she carries herself as if an invisible battalion surrounds her, and I understand why. That is, we keep our distance barring exceptional circumstances. But this was one, for I'd neglected entirely to imagine what she must have been thinking. So I smoothed a tiny strand of her hair behind her ear in apology.

'That's not going to happen anymore.'

'Do you promise?'

She said it guiltily. As if her enduring fear might offend me. That broke my heart a little.

'I said it already,' I replied as Mrs Boehm returned. 'I don't need to promise.'

I hit some mark or other, whether or not it was the bull's-eye. She nodded. Satisfied, at least for the next five or six seconds. And then, because in several ways Bird and I are very alike, I realized that I needed confession too, of a kind.

'Bird, might you go up to my room and gather the charcoal and paper? We'll draw something.'

'Do you really want those things?' she couldn't help but ask me.

'No,' I admitted.

I'd made it the most obvious ruse possible, knowing she would see through it. Bird – as a deft and experienced liar – can spot a hummer a mile away. But she went anyhow, because Bird is plumber than most anyone else I can think of.

'*Bitte*,' Mrs Boehm hissed on the instant Bird had vanished up the stairs to my room. She sounded almost angry. I wondered why. 'What in God's name has happened?'

Softly as was possible, I spilled the story wholesale.

If I could say why I did that, I'd be deeply comforted. At knowing my interior so well and all. I can't, though. Maybe the events were too big for me and would have seeped out through little splits and fissures if I hadn't employed the more usual outlet of my mouth. Maybe Mrs Boehm was a woman to whom the worst had happened already, the unendurably worst, and I didn't fear hurting her. Her husband and child were dead, after all. Whatever it was, I posted her entirely. Telling the tale was insane, I know. But it felt like necessity nevertheless.

'And so I'll be damned no matter what happens, probably,'

I realized.

She twitched an eyebrow, half-seated with one lean flank on the kitchen table.

'Worse things there are to burn for,' she concluded, 'than family.'

Footsteps approached. Bird deposited the bits of charcoal before me with a long-suffering glare that understood her absence had been what was needed and not means for creative expression. I was about to apologize to her, and tell my friends that I must go find my sibling with all possible speed, when a heavy *thud thud thud* fell on the front door. My feet were under me in an instant.

'Stay back,' I said.

Mrs Boehm crowded Bird away with shooing sounds while I considered my likeliest weapons. The cleaver looked tempting. I was well spooked by then, after all.

'Mr Wilde! If Mr Wilde is at home, answer for God's sake!'

The voice was familiar. My spine still felt taut as a kite string in a whirlwind, but the immediate sense of danger lessened. I pulled the door wide.

Mr George Higgins, vigilance soldier by night and by day occupied at a highly lucrative profession I'd not yet divined, stood before me. He looked terrible. In fact, the poor man seemed as much in shock as I was. With a sick sensation, I imagined our distress stemmed from the same cause and wondered how he came to know of the tragedy.

'I scoured the Tombs in search of you.' Spent, he leaned with one palm against the door frame. 'It's so huge, and I couldn't find you anywhere. At last I discovered your address.'

'Bird, I'm sorry,' I called to the anxious girl behind Mrs Boehm's rail-thin arm. 'Something has happened, and I need to fix it.'

Her lips tensed into a line. *Of course*, that look said, *something has happened. You utter nimenog. I've been managing the wreckage of you all this while.*

'Whatever you need, the answer is yes,' I told Higgins. But I knew what it was. Or I thought I did. By then I supposed that Delia and Jonas must have informed him of the murder.

'Come with me back to the Tombs, then, at once. We've wasted far too much time. Though God knows – I only hope there's something you can do. I fear there isn't.'

Your brother has been arrested, I thought, *and will now rot in a Tombs cell until they hang him. If he's wonderfully lucky, his neck will snap and spare him the—*

'Varker and Coles are old hands at their particular brand of villainy, after all,' Higgins spat out.

'Varker?' I repeated. My arms were arrowing into coat sleeves.

'Varker has him. It may well be too late already.'

'For Jonas Adams?'

'What? No,' Higgins said, looking agonized. 'For Julius Carpenter.'

CHAPTER NINE

*There are few men so hardened against the claims of our
common humanity, so utterly lost to the sympathy of
nature, as to aid the slave agent in his work of blood. It
requires those extraordinary samples of human depravity,
which have lately disgraced our city, as police officers and
judges, to accomplish such deeds, at which the mind
naturally revolts.*

*The First Annual Report of the New York Committee of
Vigilance, for the Year 1837, Together with Important
Facts Relative to Their Proceedings*

My circuit at the towering Egyptian-style sepulcher of the
Tombs is pretty well established. There's my closet at the
end of a narrow passage. There's the open quadrangle at the center
of the massive hive, where the sky seems very far from the earth
and the gallows is assembled on hanging days. Hangings are popular
sport among the more vicious of our residents, and the more
curious, and among the young philosopher types who imagine
they're *more fully experiencing the world.* I avoid watching the life
snuffed out of rogues whenever possible. But the open square is the
quickest route to the prison, and – since I've made a fair number of
arrests in my six months here, for all manner of crimes – I use it

frequently. Then there are the cells themselves, where I bury people alive.

As for the courtrooms, I'd scarce set foot in them. We'd been addressed by Matsell on day one in a courtroom, but apart from that, I'd only twice been called to give material evidence. The fact I was entering unfamiliar territory didn't do much to ease my heart, which clenched and unclenched like a piston propelling a steam engine.

I live five minutes' hard dash from the Tombs, and Higgins and I took the distance at a jackal's pace. We talked as best we could, though winded. But there wasn't much to say.

'We'd a meeting last night to discuss things,' Higgins gasped. 'The rescue, the Committee, the – well, in fact—'

'Me and the copper stars. And?'

'Julius never arrived. We thought him late or ill, but on my way home afterward, I checked at his lodgings. He hadn't returned from work at all. He's been employed at a chairmaker's shop since winter set in and construction slowed. I went there at once.'

'Did Varker and Coles take him quietly?'

'They dragged him into the middle of the street, put a leg iron on him, and told passersby he was a runaway from Florida. His employers were surprised. But he hasn't worked there above two months. So they let him go.'

Stone loomed grimly above us when we reached Franklin Street, blotting out far too much sky. The weird, upward-tapering windows of the Tombs are the height of its full two stories, barred in iron and casting judgment on all who pass antlike through the prison's monstrous entrance columns. At the threshold, Mr Higgins stopped me.

'I went to his house already.' Reaching in his navy greatcoat, he pulled out a folded piece of parchment. 'You take his free papers.'

'Gladly. But why—'

'Because I'm *not white*, Mr Wilde.' His words were bullets, all velocity and sharp points. 'I can't legally testify as to his identity.

Do you think I'm too stupid or too cowardly to act as witness myself, if I could? Are you really that dense?'

'All right. You could be a gentleman about it,' I shot back.

A bright gleam of well-aimed meanness shot through that remark. One I regretted the instant it left my mouth. I like to think of myself as an agile-brained fellow. And so embarrassment – like hurt and helplessness – translates to anger somewhere between my gut and my tongue about nine times out of ten.

As for Higgins, his eyes turned cindery. 'Could I *really*, Mr Wilde? Be a gentleman? Heavens, just thinking on it . . . you truly suppose so, sir?'

'Oh, for God's sake, I didn't mean—'

'Yes, you did. You could be a man about it.'

Holding your tongue by nearly biting it off isn't pleasant, but I prevented making a further ass of myself. It was a near thing, though.

'In any case, do you think the way I conduct myself has any effect whatsoever on whether or not I am considered a *gentleman?*' he growled.

I looked George Higgins over. He was finely clad, tall and agile and self-made. His beard was so meticulously trimmed it looked *cultivated*, a hedging mask over his rather inscrutable features. As dark a man as I'd ever seen and as poised a one. There had been something about the way he'd said *Delia, it's me* at that wretched slavers' den that had positively glowed with urgency. Passion, perhaps. I wasn't yet certain. He wasn't a docile chap by nature, and neither was he a scrapper, like my brother and me. He was a reasonable man who'd been told countless times, in our rules and our practices and our speech, that he wasn't a man at all. And it ate away another piece of him every single morning. Tiny holes dotted his heart and his mind as if they'd suffered an infestation of moths.

'I'm sorry. Fair warning, calling me dense again would be a bad idea even though you're entirely right.'

'You'd better try harder, then.'

He was off again, at a clean, smooth stride through the stone halls. I am a mustard-tempered-enough idiot that some further stupidity might well have emerged from my lips, but Higgins stopped before a wide door.

My companion entered, beckoning me into the courtroom. Many heads swiveled from the audience benches in our direction. Most native, some Irish, some tourists. A number of uppish sorts educating themselves so that they could better endorse whatever social opinions they already held. Tight-collared ministers, foreign businessmen with wax in their hair and perfume on their wrists, bespectacled spinsters devoted to serious and salacious causes. Others were poor, and cold, and simply wanted benches. Up on the dais, next to the American flag hanging bright with optimism before the whitewashed walls, sat the judge.

Judge Sivell, I thought, though in truth I knew him only by sight. His reputation is for impatience and querulousness, tempered by an almost secretive streak of good sense. His robes seemed to hail from the eighteenth century, and his powdered wig was squashed and yellow with use. A very prominent hooked nose was just then directing his gaze to me as if he were looking down a rifle sight. Hurrying to the front with George Higgins, I sat down, and then spied Julius in an elevated prisoner's chair to my far right. A copper star hovered behind him, bored and half asleep.

God help Seixas Varker if he ever meets me alone in the dark, I thought.

They'd done a flash job of it. Julius's togs had been taken, replaced with loose cotton rags that looked exactly like what a New Yorker would costume a runaway slave in if producing a melodrama at Niblo's Garden. His shoes were likewise missing. I wondered how they'd muscled him into the disguise and then took a deep breath because I didn't need to wonder for very long. He held himself like a wax statue, as if any movement might set something bleeding. My friend sat straight in the chair, not touching its back, leaning one elbow on the arm with a finger over his lips. Doubtless several things wanted saying that he was busily forcing down.

'As you were telling us, Mr Varker,' the judge coughed, having glared at me sufficiently.

Varker had spied me as well, of course, and his simpering look shifted into an uneasy smile. If he thought I was daydreaming over my fist meeting the pink folds of his neck, he was spot on target. His wrist had been bandaged and splinted from palm nearly to elbow. It was the only cheerful sight in the room. Long Luke Coles lounged on a bench, skinning me with his eyes.

'Yes, sir,' Varker continued. 'So as you've seen, this letter from Mr Calhoun St Claire commissioning me describes the accused to perfection. And as much as I disrelish discussing it, this is not the only occasion on which Coffee St Claire, the runaway you see before you, has escaped the St Claire estate. He began as a house slave, but soon proved to be most intractable, Your Honor. By the age of twelve, he was set to fieldwork. When he behaved well, he would be rewarded with housework for a time, but rebellion and indolence always sent him back to the cotton fields, I'm sorry to say. The St Claires almost despair of reforming him, but have prevailed on me to return him to his home, to his wife and his three children, and see whether Christian forgiveness and generosity may prevail at last. They think it not impossible, sir, though their fondness may sound foolish to some.'

Julius had begun to look like a man in a bear trap attempting to ignore the metal sunk in his leg. A thin sheen glazed his temples, an unholy amalgam of pain and disquiet. I felt a palely echoing twist in my own gut.

How clever they're being, I thought. How very many questions they'd just forestalled in a single statement.

How do you know it's Coffee St Claire? *Oh, he answers this description perfectly.* What was he running from? *Fieldwork is a hard path for a useless gadabout like him, though the diligent thrive at it.* But if he's a cotton picker, why does he carry himself so proud? *Trained to be a house slave.* Why does he speak like a New Yorker? *Well, I've said he's run away before now, and he lights straight for Manhattan every time. He's learned to ape high talk.* Why should they

129

want him back, then? *These folk are Bible-fearing caretakers, and they trust this wretch will do right by them one day, repay them all their kindnesses. Do right by his wife and sons as well.*

I stood.

'I beg your pardon, Your Honor, but this man's name has never been Coffee St Claire. His name is Julius Carpenter and he's a free citizen of New York.'

Judge Sivell's attention returned to me. 'And just who—'

'Timothy Wilde, copper star One-oh-seven, sir. I have his free papers.'

'That's preposterous.' Varker's lips tugged up as if something had curdled at the back of his throat. 'I regret to state that Mr Wilde holds an unfortunate personal grudge against me, sir.' He glanced meaningfully at the splint. 'He is a mightily violent and hot-tempered *abolitionist*, you know.'

A murmur passed through the crowd. I turned back, curious. The talk proved too low to hear, but a good many lips were visible, and barmen worth their salt don't need to actually hear a drink order to understand it.

These dreadful warmongers.

They'll not stop before blood courses through our streets.

Pity they don't channel their energies into worthy causes, like the Colonization Society. When we've sent them all to Liberia, our troubles will be over.

'This isn't about abolition,' I announced, admitting to nothing. 'It's about identity.'

'Well, of course it is, Mr Wilde,' Judge Sivell sniffed. 'It is also about due procedure, which may be superfluous to point out now that you are trampling roughshod over it.'

'I'm sorry for interrupting, but I'm prepared to swear that's Julius Carpenter. I worked with him for years in an oyster cellar before the fire. My word against Varker's ought to be enough.'

'And what about *my* word? Ain't that good for nothing?' Long Luke whined. 'I back Mr Seixas Varker one hundred percent:

we've caught Coffee St Claire, and the day he arrived in New York too. Just look at the creature.'

'You're his partner, of course you agree with him,' I shot back.

'All of you keep your peace this instant,' the judge hissed shrilly. Tossing his head, he sent his wig an inch or so askew of true north. 'Can any of you provide an *unbiased* witness as to this man's identity? Not one who stands to profit, Mr Coles, nor who wishes to further a deranged cause, Mr Wilde.'

'Why, certainly I can.' Varker bowed, exiting the witness box. 'Thank you very kindly for coming, Miss Marsh.'

Pivoting in disbelief, I saw her. I think my brains came unraveled a little. Distantly, I realized I'd an ivory-knuckled grip on the wooden barrier before me.

Not that, I thought. *God in heaven. Anyone but her.*

I'd not seen Silkie Marsh in two months, not since last I'd checked to ensure her brothel met my personal age standards. She looked neither wealthy nor fashionable enough to be a brothel madam that day. Low, cheap-cut shoes revealed themselves as she approached the witness box, and her beige walking costume was quite plain. She passed me by without a glance. That didn't queer me for an instant though.

If Silkie Marsh was here, it was about me. The woman wants me dead. And barring dead, eviscerated and longing for the grave. The scent of violets lingered behind her as if it were an artfully crafted curse, conjuring her voice in my head.

I wonder if you know, Mr Wilde, just how very far a man can be ruined without being killed. You'll understand what I mean one day.

'Has that woman ever testified for Varker before?' I whispered to Higgins.

'She's one of his regular performers. What, you know her?'

Madam Marsh sat down. Her movements were hesitant, as if the courtroom unsettled her. She'd gathered her blonde hair at the nape of her neck beneath a hat with a single feather, her sweet face was free of rouge and kohl, and her lips formed a regretful pink bow. I wondered if Valentine had ever found her thus, unadorned

131

and fresh as May, when she'd been his mistress. It was like watching a viper slither into a lambskin and then gaze prettily at you. She ought to be beautiful, I admit, as milk skinned and delicate featured as she is, but all it takes is her looking right at you for the illusion to fracture.

Silkie Marsh's eyes, pale hazel with a startling ring of blue at the centers, met mine for a moment. It was like staring into a bottomless pit.

'Name?' the clerk inquired.

'Selina Ann Marsh.' Her lashes fell shyly. 'Most know me as Silkie.'

'Residence?'

'I live on Greene Street.'

'In just what sort of house?' I demanded.

'Quiet!' Judge Sivell snapped.

'He's right. Mr Wilde and I are acquainted. I keep a club of sorts there . . . for gentlemen.' Her face colored as if she were a girl of seventeen. 'I didn't like to mention that in court, Your Honor, for I'm a lawful woman otherwise, and a great friend of the Democrats. Mr Wilde's brand of abolitionism – he is most passionate, sir, regarding vice as well as slavery. I'm sorry for it, but my presence offends him.'

A skittish hummingbird thrill shot down my spine. Because that was *masterful*. In seconds, she'd turned me from a disreputable abolitionist into a religious fanatic. Where lies are concerned, Silkie Marsh is twenty-four-karat talent. Uncharitable whispers drifted through the court.

'And what have you to do with any of this?' Judge Sivell asked Madam Marsh, shuffling papers.

'Mr Varker here sought me out, saying he may need my help to see justice done. I find myself acquainted with many Southerners, you understand. Upstanding citizens to a man, Your Honor, and very dedicated to keeping the peace between our lands. So I came to know these gentlemen, and also . . . Mr St Claire himself is known to me, sir.' She hesitated, wetting her lips. 'He once called upon me when in New York for an extended stay – there was no vice in it, I assure you, as I was hosting a small affair for Party contributors and he'd business with some of the gentlemen. That troubled colored boy was with him, to be auctioned on their way back through the Capital. I later heard that Mr St Claire had a change of heart when it came to the point of actually selling Coffee, however, the dear old gentleman. I admired him greatly for his temperance and patience.'

I felt like clapping. Or clapping her in a Tombs lockup. One of the two, at any rate.

'This is ridiculous,' I said sharply.

Judge Sivell's beaky nose swiveled, ready to impale me on its point. 'My courtroom is *ridiculous*, Mr Wilde?'

'No, but listening to a parcel of pure flam from a brothel madam—'

George Higgins, behind me and just to my left, kicked my shin so hard I nearly stumbled.

'Closing statements,' the judge droned. 'I have cases of considerably more import to try today. This ought to have taken five minutes. Miss Marsh, have you anything further to add?'

Silkie Marsh shook her head, eyes downcast as if in shame at being the center of attention at a public proceeding.

'Mr Varker and Mr Coles?'

The fixed smile pinned to Varker's rosy cheeks brightened to actual joy. 'I'd never dream of wasting your time further, Your Honor. The facts of the case sure enough speak for themselves.'

'Thank you for your consideration,' Long Luke added with a revolting flourish of his hat.

'You, then.' Judge Sivell swung his attention to – of all people – Julius Carpenter. 'Have you anything to say for yourself?'

Julius looked at the judge. His eyes were bloodshot, carriage agonized, attire smeared with God knows what and hanging in tatters. But his voice, when he spoke, was the same eloquent instrument I'd been half listening to since I was all of seventeen years old.

'I was born and bred here. Never seen Florida in my life,' he said. 'And I could act like a big man, tell Your Honor that I don't care about what they've promised they'll do to me if I testify in court that I'm free. But that would be a lie. I could even tell you I don't care what they've done already, when I refused to admit I was Coffee St Claire. But saying I don't mind being handled worse than a thieving cur for knowing my own name would be perjury.' He leveled a stare at the two slave catchers. 'My name belongs to me, and it's Julius Carpenter. If what they want is the skin off my back, they can have more of it. But they can't have my name.'

The air shifted, a tangible change in mood. Judge Sivell looked almost sympathetic. 'I'm sorry for your state, but by the looks of things it can't be helped. Let this be a lesson for you as an honest Christian. You'll grow used to plantation life again soon enough, I'd wager.'

'*Do* something, you idiot,' Higgins hissed at me in desperation.

'I have this man's free papers *in my hand*,' I insisted, waving them as if they were a battle standard. 'All signed and in perfect order. If you would only *look* at them—'

'Free papers can be forged, and you have proven yourself to be a biased party, Mr Wilde,' the judge answered. 'I have told you more than once to cease disrupting proceedings.'

George Higgins jumped forward. 'I've known Julius Carpenter since we were children at our lessons. He's my closest friend. We were born on the same street, I'll swear it on a Bible.'

'Inadmissible. Come now, whoever you are, you know better than to put your oar in where it isn't allowed.'

Julius closed his eyes. Not a flinch or an admission. Just as if he couldn't be expected to watch any longer while his life was surgically extracted from his person.

'Thank you for your wisdom in this matter, Your Honor,' Varker called out, gathering his belongings with his uninjured hand. Coles, by his side, grunted hearty agreement.

Silkie Marsh had disappeared by this time. Silent as the devil and twice as wicked.

'Pistols on the way to the ship it is, then,' Higgins grated out. He meant it too.

Think. I shut my eyes as Julius had, holding the rail before me with both hands as if on a ship's deck in a tempest.

Think, you cocky little runt, if you're so bloody clever. Think.

'Very well.' The judge belatedly adjusted his wig. 'As to custody, this man is released under supervision of Mr Varker and Mr Coles, to be escorted to—'

'*Look at his feet!*' I cried.

All eyes turned to me. Meanwhile, I was past caring about procedure. I thrust the free papers at Higgins's chest for safekeeping and vaulted over the barrier to stand in the open between Julius and Judge Sivell.

'This man is meant to have been captured on his first day in the city.' The words came tumbling helter-skelter, even as I thought them. 'Look, his togs are falling off. He's penniless. He made it from Florida all the way to New York, running through fields and swamps and forests. I admit he may have ridden partway, but never the entire distance, and *he hasn't any shoes.* Look! Take one single look, I'm begging you. Are these the feet of a shoeless field hand? Are they the feet of a barefoot runaway?'

Judge Sivell raised himself from his chair to peer over my head. Grasping in a pocket for spectacles, he slid them up the formidable cliff of his nose.

The feet in question were not merely clean. They were uncalloused, neither scraped nor blistered, and owned the narrow appearance of having been thrust into boots for upward of three decades.

When Julius left off studying his toes, he looked up at me and winked.

Judge Sivell removed his spectacles and resumed his seat.

'Mr Varker,' he said ominously, 'are you attempting to make a fool of me?'

Pandemonium of a chattering, speculating kind erupted in the courtroom. I could hear Varker expostulating, Coles emitting a string of profanity and threats in my direction. George Higgins followed me over the railing and set the papers before the magistrate.

The chaos settled seconds later, with a rap of the gavel. Judge Sivell studied the paperwork as Higgins, Julius and I studied him. The silence was thicker than blood.

'Mr Varker, doubtless your enthusiasm is commendable,' Judge Sivell announced, passing Higgins back Julius's certificate. 'But if I discover you have made such an egregious mistake again, I will grow very uncivil. This prisoner is free on his own recognizance. I will adjourn for ten minutes, and then hear the next case.'

'Oh, Christ,' I muttered senselessly, and resumed breathing. The room buzzed around me, a wasps' nest freshly kicked.

'We need to get him away from all this,' Higgins said in my ear.

In truth, Julius looked close to collapse. Higgins took his arm and began walking while I opened the little gate in the railing that neither of us had previously bothered over. The hostile skepticism of the crowd had disintegrated. Spinsters wept, foreigners took notes, gentlemen glowed with civic pride, poor laborers hooted about freedom and republicanism and booed the slaveholding tyrants of the South. It was all very fine.

'Are they on our side now?' Higgins marveled.

'I wouldn't exactly set my watch by them,' I answered. 'Julius, when you were held captive – were you alone?'

'As alone as is possible.'

So they aren't imprisoned in Corlears Hook, I thought. *Where can they be? Already aboard ship? In hiding? Dead?* The slave catchers were attempting to regain the attention of the judge, and thus didn't hinder us making for the door. For an instant, I thought to confront them.

Tell me what you've done. Tell me where you've taken Delia Wright and Jonas Adams or I will make your life a hell.

Tempting. Had I not just that morning removed a corpse from Val's bed. Caution muzzled me. With an uncomfortable churn of the stomach, I realized I couldn't even tell the Vigilance Committee men what I'd discovered. Not yet. I'd have confided in Julius alone in a heartbeat, but he needed medical attention. I elbowed two weedy British tourists – abolitionists keen after an interview for their circular – to the side, and we hurried toward the exit.

'Did you have to wait until the *very* last moment, Timothy?' Julius inquired mildly.

Higgins laughed at this, a short and dry exclamation. 'He took his time all right. But when you're not being dense, you're extraordinarily keen, Mr Wilde.'

'So my brother tells me. Often.' I couldn't even object to being ragged, relieved as I was. 'How far can you make it sans shoes?' I asked Julius.

His answer would have been *As far as needs going*. The man is stubborn as a canker sore. It's one of the reasons I like him so thoroughly. But Julius Carpenter lost consciousness less than a second later, so he was saved the trouble of replying to my inane queries.

I kept Julius under guard in my office while Higgins ran for a stretcher. A wheelbarrow, a handcart, a sleigh. A dog and a sled. Anything. Thankfully, when he proved unsuccessful, the pair of spindly British abolitionists still lurking about like playgoers at a stage door offered their private carriage to convey the freed man to the residence of Mr George Higgins. That gentleman – of course he was a gentleman, the things that emerge from my mouth at times genuinely frighten me – having insisted that Reverend Brown's medical care would be much preferable to suffering the smallpox aroma wafting through the colored wing of New York Hospital.

Higgins was right. So I didn't argue with him. Learning quickly is one of the few redeeming aspects of my character. Anyhow, from my own brief but careful emergency investigation in my office, Julius's injuries required more nursing than doctoring. They seemed to be upward of forty lashes, a head injury that explained the fainting spell, and a cigar burn on the right forearm.

I've no wish to diminish the extent to which those injuries pained Julius. They must have been excruciating. But they hurt me too, in another sense, and George Higgins was likewise inwardly smoldering when between us we deposited our friend on the seat of the abolitionists' carriage. The starch-collared Britishers looked as if they'd won a lottery prize of some sort as they drove off. That was bully. At least someone was having a pleasant afternoon.

The plummeting violet darkness of February greeted me when I found myself alone on the Tombs steps in the late afternoon, staring at the tracks left by the enthusiastic abolitionists' carriage. Finding Val could wait no longer. Diving back into Franklin Street, I headed north toward the Ward Eight station house. A narrow alley divides the block between White and Franklin, a common shortcut for the copper stars, and I took it, pulling my muffler up to my ears and attempting to ignore the faintly nauseous feeling of not having eaten since dawn.

Then a shadow crossed the path ahead, and I paused.

A hulking figure loomed at the end of the alleyway. Its posture in stillness was weighted to one side – a threatening, almost feral stance. Nevertheless, there was elegance in the curve of the heavy hand, in the unhurried gravity of such a large, potentially clumsy form.

I'd envied that unstudied air of cool savagery for decades. Even when it infuriated me.

'Val,' I said. A monumental weight left my shoulders just at the sight of him. Only to crash back into place.

He didn't know. Couldn't know.

'Evening, Tim.' My brother's voice was calm. But he doesn't normally stand like a pugilist for my benefit, and there was no one else in the corridor. 'I gather you've spent your holiday at policing.'

'Valentine, I found—'

'Nish,' he interrupted, ordering me quiet. 'I was looking for you, and I went to your ken. That Mrs Boehm is a square shakester, blew the whole gab.'

So he did know. Mrs Boehm had told him. I didn't have to say *strangled to death* again, or *left the corpse in an alleyway under some old newsprint* either. My brother made a neat about-face and exited the passage the way he'd come while I struggled as usual to keep up.

'Where are we going?'

'Someplace safe where you can whiddle me the whole scrap.'

'Good,' I murmured. 'That's good. Then we need to find Jonas and Delia. If Coles and Varker have them, I don't know where. They aren't at the wine shop by the docks. We need to start searching.'

'So we will, once you've told me the tale.'

'Val, Silkie Marsh is involved in this somehow. She just testified at the Tombs for Varker and Coles.'

Valentine stopped dead in his tracks.

'Silkie Marsh.'

'Yes.'

'Silkie – who loathes us from cap to boot soles – has joined ranks with the blackbirders. The blackbirders we bunged up proper and then robbed of two captives.'

'Apparently, she often provides testimony for them. And it's three, now. I've just helped recover Julius Carpenter.'

This information required a moment for Val to absorb.

'Are you *trying* to get us croaked?' he wanted to know.

'Of course I'm not—'

'Close your head. Of all the – Jesus, Timothy. The theme is *ware hawk* from here, do you understand me?' Val demanded, plunging into the void of another corridor. 'Silkie Marsh. Doesn't *that* beat the Dutch. Christ almighty, Tim, if the pair of us are still healthy by the end of this week, I will be very pleasurably surprised.'

Chapter Ten

He chained the large boys two and two, but not the small ones. They travelled generally on bye roads. Were not permitted to talk to anyone they met, always encamped out. Were severely whipped by Johnson, for saying we were free.

1826 interview with kidnap victim
Peter Hook of Philadelphia

My brother kept to back alleys at first, where snow lay piled in chest-high drifts against weeping brick walls. In the middle of the corridors, the ice runoff had mingled with the perennial dank mud and melting rubbish and chicken blood and animal manure to create a truly awe-inspiring mash of the sort referred to by political cynics as 'corporation pudding'.

Once we reached the open road again, my eyes flitted uselessly from stranger to stranger. Needing to glimpse Delia's serene beauty beneath every winter bonnet, Jonas's small round face above every child's scarf. Wondering how to search for two missing persons when my parameters were New York City.

If they were still in New York at all. Shivering, I trotted forward in a quick burst to catch up with Val.

If they are on Manhattan Island, I will find them, I vowed to the air. *I will find them if I have to search every house from the Battery to Chelsea and back again.*

We were deep in Ward Eight on Mercer Street and half a block away from Valentine's engine house by the time I realized that was our destination. I avoid it, habitually. In fact, I've only been inside twice, having previously imagined that Val was a fireman due to hateful bloody-mindedness, and not due to ingrained lunacy and a blighted conscience.

It's not actually clear which is worse. I've been trying to work it out and have come up nix.

The firehouse for Knickerbocker Engine Company Number 21 is brick, two stories, with a carriage-style portal for the engine. They keep that fantastical machine glistening like a dragon lurking in the dark of its cave. Manhattanites adore firemen. The dead rabbits of the engine companies are exempt from conscripted military service, from juries, and from eighty or ninety percent of our laws. And – like my brother – the balance of the firemen earn their rum and oysters by politicking. Engine companies are a veritable scoundrel's brotherhood. I didn't wonder that Val found his the safest port in a storm. Every mother's son of them has broken a man's pate or smashed a fellow's nose at one time or another, since the glory of dousing a fire rests in who claims the fireplug with a barrel and a set of brass knuckles first. Rascals to a man, I mean to say. But they also walk into sheets of flame when citizens are wailing inside fiery death boxes, their axes swinging while sparks rain down on their long leather helmets.

And so they are adored. And every week, another dies, smothered in the bowels of a blazing warehouse or toppled from the remains of a charred ladder.

It's tempting to ponder arranging somehow for Val's leg to be amputated – just the one – so he couldn't run head down into hellscapes any longer. Until he physically can't anymore, he will be the most recklessly brilliant firedog this heartless city has ever birthed. And I will loathe that fact while absently owning that it is admirable.

We entered by the side door next to the shuttered archway for the engine and kicked off our overboots. They didn't bear close scrutiny. Val hung his hat and fur-collared greatcoat on a peg in the short hallway. He wore his fireman's togs beneath, I saw, an indifferently buttoned shirt of blood-red flannel neatly tucked into perfectly brushed black trousers.

'Have you even been home yet?' I asked.

'No. I'd the Sunday labor appointments yesterday. And after Mrs Boehm spilled this afternoon, home seemed a nasty prospect. She is a dimber slice of creation all round, Tim. How she manages to have a perfect arse when the rest of her is thin as a stick is beyond me entirely. I may well take the plunge myself, seeing as you've turned monk. What's the story, lads?'

We'd entered the engine room, which was populated and the reason I failed to defend the honor of my landlady immediately. Or to ask Val what *Sunday labor appointments* meant. Leather fire buckets lined one wall, hung from brass pegs, and a healthy supply of pine ladders reposed beneath them. There the engine sat, painted scarlet and black and ivory with the gaudiest brass fittings imaginable, resembling a garish version of a child's seesaw mounted on enormous carriage wheels. After attaching the apparatus to a street-side fireplug, two men operate the brakes, pumping the wooden arms from either side to send Croton water gushing through the hoses. Two volunteer firemen lounged in armchairs before the crackling hearth playing at piquet, cigars tucked in their mouths and braces hanging round their knees. One of the card players, a sandy-haired fellow who flashed the glint of two gold front teeth at us, jumped up in greeting.

'Val, there's a family of Paddies out back, claim they can't wait till next Sunday. It's probably gospel, they're short as pie crust. I've warned them off twice, but – oh, hello, Tim,' the oddly familiar fireman greeted me.

'Tim, you remember Jack,' Val said dryly. 'Last you were here. Eighteen thirty-six, thereabouts.'

'It's not decent, Val, them skulking about the alley fixing to die any second,' Jack continued. 'When I said the copper stars would have them for vagrancy, they said so long as it was you, they'd risk it.'

'A family? How many men?'

'Two.'

'Well, that's something. Don't let Riley bilk you at cards when you still owe me three dollars. Step smart, Tim, we're for upstairs once I settle this.'

I followed him to the back of the building, dodging sandbags and lengths of neatly coiled leather hose, passing shelf after shelf packed with cured leather helmets and mysterious cogs and nozzles. When Val opened the back door, an arctic gust invaded the engine house.

'Aye?' he prompted, not unkindly.

Outside waited four individuals. The sun had abandoned us, so they were lit meagerly by the faint orange echo of the fireplace beyond. Thus I'd no notion whether they actually had skin the complexion of lard or no, but they seemed pale as is possible. Directly before us stood the father. Irish by feature, with wiry russet hair, sans gloves and clutching a swaddled baby. Next came a frail grandfather of approximately sixty years who'd sensibly wrapped himself in burlap. A little redheaded girl stood before the men. Dull of eye, sunken of cheek, clutching a pail. She shook from head to toe in a thin cotton summer dress printed all over with lilac plumes. When Valentine revealed himself, the breadwinner of the family stared up at him as if my brother were the risen Christ.

'Captain Wilde! Thank you for seein' us, sir, and on such a night.'

'Fit to freeze you right down to your pocket ends,' Val agreed. 'Friends of the Party, I take it?'

'Oh, aye, none stauncher.' The man nodded frantically. His hand was cupped over the baby's exposed ear, with its head pressed to his shoulder.

'Glad to hear it. Applications for day labor along with

complimentary supper, rum, and hot Newark cider are distributed at the Knickerbocker Twenty-one on Sundays directly after mass at St Patrick's, as I think Jack informed you. Rain or shine, sure as the post. You're better than welcome. I think we're due for leg of mutton this week.'

'Please,' the man whispered. 'It's nay for me.'

'Is this Sunday?' Val insisted. Again, not unkindly.

'Have ye any work at all? I'll fetch, carry, clean, shovel. Muck out your gutters. Your stalls, your privies. Anything for a shilling. Even for sixpence. Name it.'

'Unfortunately, we're fairly spruce just now.'

'Do y'fancy a tune, then? A finer voice for a ballad ye've not heard.'

Val laughed, wincing sympathetically. 'I set up no less than forty-eight of you with casual labor yesterday. It was a *Sunday*, to begin work this morning. I've no fresh positions the next evening, not in winter when the construction's stopped. I wish I had, believe me.'

'Two such loyal voters as ye've ne'er seen, sir, that's me and my da here. Democrats to the very bone. We've nary had milk in three days, and my Alice is passed on.' He shifted his hand so it covered a sliver more of his infant's face. The babe was still as death. 'Mary here has some coal she found in the road. Don't ye, Mary? Will ye buy coal from my daughter, sir, as a Christian?'

Valentine glanced down into the emaciated girl's bucket and heaved a dark sigh. '*Jack!*' he shouted over his shoulder. Then his green eyes shifted back to the emigrant. 'Can you actually sing?'

The unfortunate man launched into a rivetingly melancholy Gaelic lullaby. At least, I think that's what it was. Its life was cut short soon after birth. As often happens in these parts.

'Enough, *enough*. Jesus, but that was high ropes. You've a pipe organ in there and no mistake. Right. Can you sing that way on a Sunday?'

The man's face fell into a waxen mask. 'Yes, sir.'

Jack appeared, smiling inquisitively.

144

'Hand over my chink,' Val ordered. Grumbling, Jack obliged, passing him three dollar bills and then wandering off again. 'Here's an advance.' My brother tucked the money into the Irishman's sagging coat pocket.

My disbelieving eyes attempted to blink away what they were seeing. It was a huge sum – a week in a room with a roof if they weren't particular about bedding, company, or privacy. And a hot meat pie a day if not full meals. The Irish family seemed to find my brother equally in a state of delirium, the child lurching forward to deliver him her small treasure trove. Val neatly snatched the coal bucket from her hands and passed it back to the father with a meaningful shake.

'I said *advance*, not payment, we're not half through this cold spell.' When the emigrant opened his lips to protest, my brother's quicksilver temper finally frayed. 'Don't be thick – do I *look* like I need coal? Learn to pay attention or you'll find this an unlucky neighborhood. Listen, I don't want you now. I want you on Sunday, warbling ditties of the mother country all through the hot supper, giving us a bit of cheer. Do you understand the word *Sunday* at all?'

'God bless ye, sir,' whispered the old man. 'I'll light a candle for ye at St Patrick's when I've means.'

'Thank you,' his son cried. 'I'll sing such tunes as will make your voters fall at your feet, Captain Wilde.'

'Good Christ. Sing such tunes as will make my voters *cast votes*. Thank you for your support and good health to you, patriots,' Val said, and then emphatically shut the door.

He turned. Only to discover I was staring at him as if he'd produced a dove from his top hat. I may as well have just watched Valentine Wilde fly.

'That's a natty imitation of a dead trout, Tim,' my brother said testily, setting off for the staircase we'd passed on our way inside.

I couldn't help myself. Because *charity*, in New York, is synonymous with *setting bones out to attract the rats*. Particularly where the Irish are concerned. And my brother, for all his scorn and his swagger, had just exchanged hard cash for . . . nothing at all.

Not a gesture I'd expected of him, and not one we'd often encountered when reduced to living by our wits.

This is the way I understand folk who accept a leg up from time to time: it isn't that we aren't industrious, or that we expect charity we don't deserve. It's mainly that human creatures want to live, and – when we can't come by flour, or heat in the silvery frosts – we fight. Some fight by stealing (that was primarily Val's territory). Some fight by seeking out charity workers (as we'd both done on occasion). The unbalanced, disreputable charity workers who didn't insist you were scrubbed gleaming and already healthy. Most Bible-fearing benevolent types figure that poverty is a sign of moral weakness and disease evidence of God's thorough dislike for your person. And best not to cross God, after all, not when He handpicks the wicked meant to writhe for their sins. Only the fanatics fail to equate suffering with vice, and my childhood friend Mercy Underhill had grown up to become just such a rare and liberal-minded font of generosity.

As had Val, apparently. The shape didn't quite fit between my ears. I hastened after, catching him at the stair.

'Are you some kind of . . . of almshouse administrator?'

He scowled over his shoulder. 'Of course not.'

'You just gave your own money to a penniless emigrant. On condition he *sing for you*.'

'A penniless *voter*. Part of roping them in, isn't it? I'm the police captain of Ward Eight and its Party boss, not to mention the senior Knickerbocker Twenty-one engine man.'

'That means you're a dead rabbit, not a charity director.'

'Yes, I am a dead rabbit. And the things you don't know about politics would run Harper Brothers dry of ink.'

'Then aren't you going to tell me about them?'

'No. You treat this place like a quarantine hospital. And since you know nothing about politics, then nothing about politics should surprise you.'

I confess myself stung. And over accusations of political apathy, no less. Scrambling up the stairs, I searched for a hole, any hole, in his weary-sounding statement. None seemed apparent.

The upstairs room proved cosier than the engine shrine. Night tapers flickered in brass sockets along the walls. An iron pot on the hearth emitted a heady smell of rich brown stew that set my stomach roiling. Bunks had been attached to the plaster, the way berths are rigged in a ship, which explained where Val had been sleeping. Without preamble, he ladled some stew into two wooden bowls, produced pewter spoons from a drawer, and took a seat at the table in the center of the room, shoving an abandoned card game, several dice, an empty corn whiskey bottle, a box of cigars, and a copy of the *Herald* aside.

Too topsy-turvy to continue fighting, I sat down and ate. The stew proved one of Val's standards, veal with beer gravy. It was perfect. Of course it was. I began reading the *Herald* upside down, as I'd missed it that morning, my eyes at once drawn to THE TERRIBLE STORM. Sixty men from the doomed packet ships had been killed in the gale, and ten vessels foundered, amounting to upward of half a million in damages. Possibly, we were at war with Mexico. Possibly, with Great Britain. Sighing, I turned the paper over to reveal an advertisement for imported Turkish leeches. That was better. At least leeches aren't lethal.

'Why were you looking for me?' I inquired when we'd both pushed our bowls away and commenced staring at nothing.

'When?'

'This afternoon, when you went to my ken while I was at the Tombs. What did you want?'

Valentine rubbed at the bags beneath his eyes with a sweep of his fingertips, yawning. 'Oh. Nothing. Just passing the time.'

That was about the dustiest thing I'd heard since leaving the courtroom.

'I actually want to know.'

'I actually just told you. Christ's left nut, you can be *such* a sack of drowned kittens, Timothy. Oh, excepting when you're antagonizing murderous culls or transporting corpses, presumably all because you've developed some sort of death wish.'

'That's a vile thing to say, and you know it,' I choked out. 'I'm not the one with the . . . Moving her body was—'

Stopping seemed best at this juncture. My throat had inconveniently grown splinters. Val opened his mouth, but then wisely shut it again and instead poured a generous pair of whiskeys.

'It was horrible,' I finished when he'd sat down again.

'I know it was,' he said quietly. 'That took a mountain of nerve, and I'll not forget it. Ever. Now, tell me what happened, and don't be gripe fisted about the details.'

I did. From Val's disordered bedroom, to the encounter with Sean Mulqueen, to the long walk through the cold with a body in my arms, to the trial and the unexpected appearance of Silkie Marsh. When I was through, half the whiskey bottle was gone, and I'd finally begun to feel warm again. Val leaned back in his chair, drew another toward him with his boot toe, and put his feet up, looking as perplexed as I'd ever seen him.

'My turn, then. I've a bit of good news,' he said. 'First of all, your lay worked. A couple of hours ago, after I'd been to your ken, a news hawker ran screaming to one of my copper stars about a dead woman in an alleyway. The roundsman carted her back to the Prince Street station house and sent for me.'

Thank God, I thought. My imaginings since leaving her there had conjured nothing save ghoulish body snatchers and corpse-scavenging rats the size of chickens.

'The roundsman was Glazebrook, which is a rich streak of luck. He is as lumber brained as they come. If Glazebrook could locate his own arse in the dark without a candle, I'd be considerably surprised. Naturally, I took over the case. So as it happens, thanks to you, I've had a perfectly valid chance to study her over.' Val flicked a vesta against the tabletop and pulled a cigar from his loose shirt pocket. 'Dead since about dawn, according to the coroner.'

That figured. She'd been barely cold when I'd arrived. 'What else?'

'She wasn't raped, for one. For another, there's no bruising on her body, so whoever caught hold of her did it neat and fast.

Obviously, she was strangled, and strangled something fierce – I'd not think a moll would be capable without a struggle that would leave other marks, so we're after a man, and a ruthless one. Neck was nigh crushed.'

'With the tie from your dressing gown.'

'Dainty touch there.' A crooked smile formed. 'That means one of two things. Either hushing her was unplanned and he used whatever he could lay hands on, or someone wants me to dance at my death.'

'Don't joke about hanging. And it must be the former – that he used whatever he could. No one save us knew she was there. Not even Piest. And even apart from my moving the body, you must have an alibi,' I argued. 'Who was keeping you company this morning?'

My brother grew distracted by a smudge of soot on his sleeve. After contemplating it, he looked up.

'Actually, I was alone,' he reported. 'Taking the air along the Battery. Seemed a flash day for a stroll.'

The most enormous silence I have ever heard spread between us. In seconds, that silence had spread over the entire United States, past Texas, and on to Oregon.

When Val is lying, he looks at something irrelevant, and then he looks you bright as brass in the eye. He'd never tried it on me before. But I'd seen it done a hundred times. An invisible hand took hold of my guts and squeezed.

'My God,' I whispered. 'What have you done?'

'Nothing. Why should—'

'You're never alone.' I gripped the cup of whiskey with both hands and watched the caramel-colored liquid tremble in concert with my fingers. 'You're here, or at your police station, or at the Liberty's Blood saloon, or at a Party meeting, or at a race or a boxing match with your pals, or annoying me. You *loathe* being alone. The only time you're ever alone is when you're asleep – no, ninety-nine percent of the time you've company in bed as well.'

'Well, I was alone early this morning, so you can stuff that wheresoever you like.'

I stared at Val's face, aghast. His was deliberately blank. 'I can't credit it. I *can't*. You actually killed that woman.'

Val's lip snagged viciously, destroying the unsettling expression of neutrality. 'Dry up, you stunted little weed, I did nothing of the sort. I was putting myself through a few paces down Battery Park way.'

'Wading through the remains of a snowstorm.'

'Timothy, I'm a grown man, not a hothouse lily.'

'Valentine, *tell me*,' I begged him. 'If someone saw me, if I made a single mistake, if you're suspected, you'll have to give an account of yourself—'

Valentine actually snorted. 'Thank you kindly for explaining the intricacies of our judicial system, my Tim. And all this time, I'd supposed we still decided guilt by whether or not people with millstones round their necks sink or float.'

I sat forward with my hand to my snakeskin-textured brow. That my brother is impossible is a principle akin to daylight following nightfall. But apart from a single ghastly secret that ought never to have been one, I've always known all there is to know about the man. Unfortunately.

'You lie to plenty of other people, but never to me. Why start now?'

He pulled his thumb along a seam in his tailored black trouser leg, considering. 'Because you are being a rash on the hindquarters?'

'Val, consider how helpful it was the *last* time I failed to grasp a significant event in your personal life.'

A sharpish flinch crossed my brother's face. But then he threw up his arms to their full wingspan and linked his hands behind his head in a neat little gesture of unconcern.

'My alibi is unimportant and will never be presented in court,' he announced pleasantly around the cigar.

The steel bands encircling my stomach loosened a fraction. 'Bully. What is it?'

'*Irrelevant*. Also uninteresting, and no longer the topic of our conversation.'

'Did it have anything whatsoever to do with Mrs Adams's death?'

'Did someone replace your brain with a parrot's?'

'Was it illegal?'

Frowning, Val thought it over, the deeply scored bags beneath his eyes contracting. 'Now, that's a maybe. Could well have been. Probably so.'

Though hardly surprising, I couldn't call that piece of news helpful.

'So you're telling me that although you are never alone, you have no alibi for the morning a woman was strangled in your bed, because you were doing something *else* that was criminal.'

Val grinned, a look on him that's always carnivorous somehow. 'Young Timothy Wilde, copper star, solves another mystery. We'll put it in the *Police Gazette*.'

My fingers squeezed themselves into angry, helpless little balls.

'It would give me tremendous pleasure just now to tell you I hate you,' I hissed.

'Better let fly, then. It's all bob to me.'

I don't hate my brother, though I think he expects me to. But I'm often pretty tempted to punch the airy, uncaring expression right off his mouth. I've done it before and will doubtless do it again, though I tend to come off the worst in such matches. But on this occasion, my head descended to where I'd folded my arms on the table. It seemed a likely place to settle while I worked out whether I wanted to drink all the whiskey in Manhattan or throw Val out his firehouse window.

'None of this makes sense,' I protested to my boots in despair. 'You didn't strangle the murdered woman in your bed, but you won't tell me where you were at the time. No one save us knew she was there, but someone found and killed her. Some sort of struggle knocked over your bedside table and your painting, but there are no signs on Mrs Adams's body of having resisted attack. Varker and Coles have good reason to want revenge on us – and on Julius too, for that matter – but no reason to hush someone who's worth a mint to them alive. Were Delia and Jonas dragged off somewhere? Are they the reason the furniture was disarranged? And just where in sodding *hell* does Silkie Marsh come into it?'

A humorless laugh sounded from the other side of the table. 'I can tell you *that* much, Tim. Where she comes into it is where we start to worry.'

'Just how bad would it be if you presented this alibi to a jury?'

'About as bad as you're supposing. So we won't.'

Breathing deliberately through my nose in an effort to slow my heartbeat, I tried for several minutes to calculate what ought to be investigated first. That is, apart from investigating Val.

'You're right, you know,' I heard my brother remark at length. 'I never noticed I hate being alone, but I do. My thoughts are very . . . loud.'

Lifting my head, I set my chin on my arm.

'That was good, earlier,' I murmured. 'What you did for the Irish family. I didn't mean to rag you. You probably saved their lives.'

'Dead men can't vote,' Val pointed out blankly.

'Neither can girl kinchin.'

'You calculate they'll recall me fondly when that kid's in her grave?'

'I don't care what you say. It was still top marks.'

'You should see me on Sundays, when the crowds come,' he sneered. 'Then I do it in choir robes and a halo.'

'Mrs Adams said she'd been kidnapped before, Val.' My voice fell still lower, and I let my temple list to one side. 'That writing. God, that writing. You saw it.'

As many as I love I rebuke and chasten, be zealous therefore and repent.

'I saw it,' he answered, also hushed.

'What does any of it *mean*?'

Val stood, dousing the cigar stub in his empty whiskey glass. He arched his back in a lazy stretch and then angled his head at the bunks along the wall. 'Get a little sleep. We've a great deal of work ahead.'

I stifled a yawn. 'I don't need—'

'You're obviously past clear thinking, mulling over whatever happened to Lucy Adams long ago and far away from here. Have a rest. Keep arguing with me and I'll make your face more of a burnt soufflé than it is. I don't want that kind of challenge. I'll wake you in a couple of hours.'

What Val said carried weight. He knows me, and I *was* drifting, facts flying past my lidded eyes in chaotic swarms, and I unable to pin any down. Part of my befuddlement was shock seeping out of my bones. And part of it was probably whiskey. Still, I'd never have obeyed that order, not with – as he'd said – so much to be done.

If not for a tiny suspicion hovering at the back of my mind.

So I removed my boots and crawled into a bunk. For five minutes, I listened to the muted rustle of Val reading the *Herald*. And then the quiet puffs from his lighting another cigar. Slowly, my breath evened out. Then it deepened. My fingers relaxed, and my eyelids stopped nervously fluttering. For a quarter of an hour, perhaps, I drifted in a cotton-headed reverie, the hissing and popping of the firewood my only indication time was passing. For all appearances dead to the world.

I wasn't, though.

So when the creak of the door met my ears – the sole indication that silent feet had exited catlike down the stairs – I did the only sensible thing. I threw on my boots again, laces flying through my fingers.

And I followed.

CHAPTER ELEVEN

We wonder that the stones of old Bunker Hill do not cry out, when the Union, cemented with the dearest blood of our fathers, is thus publically assailed. But on the whole, this mad folly of the silly fanatics, will operate better than the sly, underhanded works. The people can see their designs, and shun them. It will work out its own cure; in a few years, these ravings will be forgotten, and the men who uttered them will have been consigned to an unlamented oblivion.

Regarding abolitionism; *The New York Herald*,
February 17, 1846

Widely spaced bootprints in the snow, those of a man determined to reach his destination with efficiency, proved my breadcrumbs through the forest when I'd exited the engine house. A tiny jewel box of a one-horse cutter flitted past me, the black stallion's footfalls muted as sleigh rails skimmed the packed grey powder. Ward Eight is well maintained by comparison to my dung heap of the Sixth, and so sporadic gas lamps shone down upon shuttered shop windows and ice crystals dripping from awnings like so many salivating fangs. Muffled strangers hastened past. A butcher with a tweed coat, an Irish peasant clad in the soft, tilted hat and corduroy breeches he'd worn when he stepped off the ship. I followed the path of the footmarks quiet and quick as I could. Before long, however, I reached the wide intersection of Mercer and Houston, and all possibility of tracking disappeared in the riotous snow heaps edging the roadways.

Thankfully, my brother is unnaturally tall. His high black hat bobbed steadily along Mercer, and the pearl head of his stick gleamed in reflected light from the snow. Avoiding a trio of free-roaming pigs and a man scattering white ash with a shovel, I followed Valentine across Houston.

My mind felt slick, frictionless as the ice beneath my boots. What business could my brother have, plunging into Ward Fifteen? At its center is a tranquil little park called Washington Square, saturated with greenery in the summertime and serene in its frosted winter repose, where Mercy Underhill had once flown whenever her mind was unsettled. At the thought of Mercy, a thorny twinge struck me that I wasn't writing the most heartening letter ever set to parchment. The sensation required considerable quashing. But quash it I did, for Val had no call to visit the rowhouses of Washington Place, nor the quaint Dutch Reformed Church, nor New York University with its parapets and pale students rushing about on stalklike, hose-covered legs.

No, Val's business is of a more visceral cast, generally speaking. And so I glided along behind him. Half sick over what I might discover.

He turned left on Amity Lane, just before the square. Bare elms with eerily frost-crusted branches were now our only observers. We passed several mews, the backs of the buildings inscrutable, shriveled ivy vines crawling up the brickwork. I kept my distance now, hugging the shadowed wall. A dog howled, longing for the moon's return, for the clouds lay thickly over us, a smothering weight that could come crashing to earth at any moment.

Val pushed open a whitewashed gate. When he'd shut it again, I crept forward, putting my eye to the slats. A path had been shoveled through the snowfall between the house and the alley. Pulling a key from his pocket, he unlocked the door at the top of four wooden steps and went inside.

I don't want to know, I thought.

But I had to know, of course. So I crossed the yard and tried the door. He'd left it unbolted.

Carrying a leaden weight in my belly, I went inside.

I found myself in a darkened hall littered with umbrellas and boxes and overboots. Val's were propped neatly in a corner. Further along, light spilled through a doorway, pooling on the hardwood.

I walked along the corridor and into the unknown.

The second I passed the threshold, an enormous arm hooked round my throat. I shoved myself backward, but to no avail. My assailant planted his feet and then swept a boot against my ankles, sending me sprawling to the floor.

Stars burst before my eyes. Then I shook my head, clearing it.

'Was that *really* necessary?' I gasped.

My person seemed unharmed, but a mouthful of carpet isn't high on my list of ways to spend an evening. Twisting onto my back, I glared up at Valentine with lovely visions of pummeling him to a pulp clouding my sight.

'Was it *really* necessary to trail me as if I were some kind of wounded deer?' Val snapped.

We were alone in an empty parlor. Eerie doesn't begin to describe it. More crates lined the walls, two valises and a steamer trunk resting on a dining table alongside a single pair of men's kidskin gloves, far too small to fit Valentine's hands. Why my brother and I were staring daggers at each other in a set of rooms someone appeared to have just moved into was beyond my fathoming. A pair of sky-blue armchairs flanked the fireplace, and the windows were hung with coral damask. But very few furnishings were in evidence. The hulking object draped with a cloth before the window could only be a piano, I surmised.

Not that a piano was comforting. Val doesn't play the piano.

'Where in bloody hell are we?' I rolled to my feet.

'Are you aware of just how oafish your bird-dogging skills are?' My brother stood with his arms crossed, looking tragic. 'I told you I'd wake you in an hour or two. And so you charge after me like a riled steer. Can a man run a single errand in peace?'

'Not while you're still lying over where you were this morning.'

'Because murdering helpless molls is *just* my style. You vile little tadpole.'

'No, your style is to cripple Whig Party thugs and occasionally blackbirders, and poison yourself half to death, and bed anything that moves, and *never lie to me*.'

'If you think I'm going to be interrogated by a doltish runt, you—'

'Oh, for God's sake,' came a beautifully cultured voice from an interior doorway. 'He was with me this morning. I've moved into a new flat, which is a dreadful enough business without doing it alone. If Val hadn't helped, I should have simply burned all my belongings and begun again.'

'Jim,' I said. Then, 'Hello.' The smile on my lips spread until it was an idiotic smear of a grin. It wasn't worse than what I already knew of Val at all. It was just . . . more of the same. 'Good lord, of all the secrets. It's nice to see you.'

'Likewise,' Jim said, mystified.

Gentle Jim, as he's called, was taken aback by my good spirits. Admittedly, some men might take more hostile exception to the chap with the indelicate attachment to their only brother. Myself, I can't be bothered.

Where Val is concerned, warmhearted molleys are the least of my worries.

My brother's friend is a Londoner. Slender and articulate, accent imported direct from the Halls of Parliament. Rather arch. Arch suits me fine where Jim is concerned, though, because he owns a ready smile to make it up to you. I often wonder how he lives and what he does. It's my opinion, based on particular creases at the edges of his melancholy blue eyes, that eighty per-cent of his thoughts remain in his head. He wore fitted trousers,

an indigo shirt, and a maroon dressing gown of Chinese patterned silk, hastily tied. Jim has dark, burnished hair, and those
high-boned features that only rest well on Englishmen and on
everyone else look either wicked or feline. Now that he holds a
romantic interest in Valentine rather than a recreational one
(which from my guesswork seems to have happened two or
three months back), he tends to treat me as if I were a fragile
document, to be pinched at the corners and held to the light for
examination.

Not that my brother would term it romantic – and, in fairness,
Jim is subtler than most. I simply happen to be uncomfortably
familiar with obsession and its miens. He emerged from the
doorway. One hand on his hip, posture hesitant. As if it were my
new digs being invaded and not his at all.

'Valentine doesn't bed *anything* that moves, Timothy,' Jim said
testily. 'He does draw the line at undomesticated mammals. Risk of
hydrophobia, and all that.'

'Satisfied now? You wanted my alibi, and there he is.' Val threw
himself into one of the armchairs, slouching disgustedly. 'When a
pal needs his entire ken moved, it takes time and muscle. So when
my shift at the engine house ended yesterday, I capped in with Jim
and we put our shoulders to it.'

'So it was work, then.' I eyed him, doubtful. 'Not . . . leisure.'

'Just as you say.'

'Not that there were no events of the nature you're referring to,
rather later.' Jim coughed, looking somehow both vulnerable and
ferociously determined. 'I think your brother is loath to discuss
having passed the night here.'

My eyes flicked to Valentine, who appeared not the smallest
degree discomfited.

'I helped him move a *piano*,' he explained.

Reflecting over whether to inform my insane brother that most
men tend not to accept French favors from svelte artistes as a
reward for moving furnishings, I determined to refrain. My head
ached. It didn't need a mental image of the erotic tasks Gentle Jim

158

enjoys setting his mouth to, not when my brother was involved. And not when it had recently occurred to me that my brother is a very . . . reciprocally inclined individual. Proud of his bedroom prowess. Disinclined to owe debts.

'That thing is *heavy*,' Val continued, pointing, 'and there was a stairway—'

'All right, all right,' I protested. 'Stop telling me.'

'You're the one who wanted to know every detail of the possibly illegal thing I was doing, you utter cow pie.'

'Well, now I want less details.'

'Oh, come off it, Tim, it's just a lark. He's my closest mate. So what if we like a bit of—'

'It's definitely illegal, no maybe about it. Has that occurred to you?'

'Well, I'm not very likely to *arrest* him, am I?'

'Not him! You!' I all but shouted. 'It's punishable by ten years' hard labor!'

'That's scarce ever enforced and you know it. Are *you* collaring me? Anyhow, *buggery* is punishable by ten years hard labor. It isn't as if I'm bending the boy over the kitchen table. *We* happen to prefer—'

'For heaven's sake, cease tormenting your brother simply because you can,' Jim interjected, drawing a softly shaped hand over the back of Val's neck before falling into the other chair.

Valentine blinked, baffled. Clearly that particular thought had never occurred to him.

Jim stood up again. 'Oh, bollocks. I'm sorry, Timothy. There isn't another—'

I silenced him by drawing up a sturdy-seeming crate full of papers and seating myself. He forbore speaking further in favor of gnawing thoughtfully at his lip as he reclaimed his perch at the edge of his armchair.

'Well,' I said. Calm. Friendly. 'I have one question.'

'Admittedly a lower figure than I had anticipated,' Jim muttered.

'Jim's tastes are no secret to anyone. Neither is the fact that you're pals. You're not exactly careful about any of it. For God's sake, you have his house key.'

'Those aren't questions,' Val retorted.

'Is it safe to say your Party friends know you're . . . close?'

Jim shifted. 'I take your point. And yes, I should think so, I'm afraid.'

Setting my hat on the floor, I rubbed tiredly at my eyelids. 'Then you're right, Val. That would have made for a truly regrettable alibi in the public courts.'

'I don't like to – that is to say, Timothy?' Jim began.

'Yes?'

'Why are you trailing Valentine to my new flat? And why on earth are you asking him about an *alibi?*'

I studied my brother's elbow while Val scrutinized my right knee.

'Val, you didn't just say something about *murder*, did you?' Jim added softly.

A few false starts hampered us. But we bit the bullet and told him everything. Jim fared better than I'd expected. Partly I think he appreciated that, when my brother had scented a sharp miasma of danger after hearing the name *Silkie Marsh*, he'd decided to apprise Jim for caution's sake. But mostly, I think I'd under-estimated him. Just because a fellow has smooth hands doesn't mean he's a stranger to violence. Supremely regal accents often belong to men whose heads are being nicked off by a silently descending blade.

So I stopped treating Jim as if he might be a bloom waiting to wilt. Hoping he might do me the same favor.

When all had been discussed to everyone's satisfaction – that is, when we were all mortified and Jim had opened a bottle of gin and passed it round, sipped from the endearing Oriental soup cups that were all he could find – Val and I finally formulated a plan.

'Right.' I levered to my feet with a will renewed. 'We'll try to catch a public sleigh, though walking isn't out of the question.'

'Hold there, bright young copper star.' Valentine pulled out his pocket watch with a frown. 'Ten o'clock at night. No. God, no, not now. Meet me at seven at the Tombs, Franklin Street entrance. We'll start then.'

'There is a *child* out there somewhere, possibly about to be shipped off to Georgia to be tortured for the rest of his days, and you're worried over a sound night's sleep?'

Val blinked at me sadly. 'No, you donkey. I need time to *identify the body.*'

'Christ.' My brain staggered, then fell back into step with Valentine's. 'You're right. We can't possibly begin the search before you identify her. Do you need help?'

'Better if I sort it, all told.'

'What do you mean, *identify?*' Jim asked Valentine. He'd turned greyish at our tale but remained remarkably still, like a fencer at the start of a duel. 'You knew Mrs Adams.'

'Chief Matsell is kindly overlooking our bully little crime spree Tim here orchestrated down at Corlears Hook, which is how we landed in this pile of manure in the first place. Presently it's the blackbirders' word against ours we were ever there. Piest would stand by us, he's the square species of lobster, and we all know what colored testimony counts for. But the chief will be told out for certain if we can't stick to the bam. Supposing they tumble on me—'

'If Val's suspected,' I interrupted for Jim, whose nose was wrinkling in puzzlement, 'we'd better have kept to the same line of lies all along.'

'Thank you.' He tossed me a lofty smile. 'I do tend to keep better pace with the conversation, but we aren't often speaking of crime.'

Val smirked. 'Sorry, Jimmy, old habits.'

'Apology not necessary, but entirely accepted. Just a moment. I'd not thought that, for copper stars, bending laws was quite so . . . frowned upon as for citizens? I hope I don't sound overly blunt, but why should it matter that what you did at the slavers' den was illegal? Copper stars answer to copper stars, after all.'

'Copper stars answer to the Party. It doesn't matter a straw that it was illegal,' Val agreed. 'It matters that it was against our platform. And anywise, not yet knowing who's leaky . . . before we question outsiders, I'm going to need a story about discovering the innocent's name. Safer all round.'

'Innocents,' I said as I returned my hat to my head, 'are corpses.'

'That's positively ghastly,' Jim remarked.

'Yes, it is. Evening, Jim, and apologies for invading your ken like a barbarian.'

'Oh, invade away.' He put a wistful hand on his knee and tucked himself farther back into the chair. 'You may be the most civil barbarian with whom I am acquainted.'

'You haven't known him for long enough,' Val sniffed. But there was no malice in it. Just habit. Giving them a small wave, I turned away.

How Val meant to identify Mrs Adams, I didn't ask. Now I'd a moment to myself, I knew precisely what needed doing. Trudging up and down the streets of Manhattan in search of a woman and child was practically impossible before Val had identified Mrs Adams and I could consult the Vigilance Committee as to likely hiding places, and then interrogate Varker and Coles with a plan in my head and the ground firm under my feet. Not a soul had been imprisoned with Julius and I couldn't yet ask her friends where Delia lived. Better, as my brother had suggested, to wait a few hours. But day and night, in every season, in the company of others or alone in the filthy, glittering streets, the bones in my fingers throb to be doing something toward making Mercy Underhill happy. The thought of a specific task, one that she'd all but requested when she hinted she hoped I'd write to her, was thrilling. Half crusade and half prize already won.

'Be careful,' I said at the door. 'About all of it.'

'I'm always careful.' Val's indistinct smile turned wolfish. 'You just haven't noticed that yet.'

* * *

162

I hailed one of Kipp and Brown's public sleighs at Broadway and crowded into the huge ten-horse contraption, wedged on a seat between a skinny snake-oil salesman who'd thickened his hair with shoe polish and a shopgirl with glazed eyes. Both looked as if February had been the month they'd at last been forced to buy coal instead of hot lunches. Both had visible holes in their boots. Both wore cotton.

Drifting, I imagined the world Matsell had described, the one without cotton to wear or sell or cut or sew. The sleigh's lanterns shone like polished bells and its bells rang bright as lanterns, and the shop windows in the great stone buildings flashed past in a streak of gold. And then I was home, having walked east along Walker dreaming of a Party boss with his moneybags stuffed full of cotton, cotton bursting from his seams and pockets and ears and mouth. A scarecrow. A puppet hero with glass-bead eyes.

The bakery was dark. Mrs Boehm retires early and is up before dawn. But I found a tea cake shimmering with pink sugar crystals, under which lay a note. Half prim, clear handwriting – left hand, I noted, smiling – with Germanic a's. Half loopy scrawl of a ten-possibly-eleven-year-old girl.

Mr W—

You are presented this cake with our compliments, as you were called away. Some artistic disagreements we would have been glad to consult you over arose, but in the end results are very fine you will agree.

MR WILDE this one is yours tho I'd wanted yours to be bigger I tried but it wouldn't rise you see and was sticky in the center. Next I come we are bradeing bread like hair. Won't that be interesting I think it can't be done but MRS BOEHM says wait and see.

– Mrs E. Boehm
– MISS AIBHILIN ó DáLAIGH

Unlooked-for kindnesses can cut deep as cruelties if they come at the wrong time. It was a sweet note, but it robbed me of half my spine. Anger and fear can wind a man up, propel him forward. That small piece of gentleness deflated me as if I were a tent collapsing. So I tucked it inside my new frock coat and headed upstairs after retrieving Mercy's letter. I wrapped the cake in a napkin. Something about its innocence burned my eyes.

Lighting the lamp, I pulled my rush-bottomed chair up to my table. I waited for words to come, rubbing a quill over my lower lip, staring at Mercy's tangled penmanship.

Nothing happened.

You can write police reports about kinchin whores, kidnapping, assault, and murder, but you can't write ten words for her sake. You're a prize catch, Tim Wilde.

Helpless to do any better, I read Mercy's missive again.

. . . perhaps if I tell you that this morning I found in the shop a little tortoiseshell box and inside was a clockwork bird painted like a rainbow, and I polished it until it shone, then that will have been real. Or I will be real, or something better approximating myself. Sometimes I think someone else lives here now.

Ten minutes later, I discovered I'd sketched a clockwork bird in the corner of my blank sheet, my chin in my hand. It was the identical bird she'd described. I knew for a fact. It must have been the exact duplicate, a portrait of a treasure I'd never seen – because that's just the sort of thing Mercy would put in a story, and alongside the blood in my veins, her tales occupy a separate system of channels. Her ink has long pulsed through my frame. I wondered what it meant that she couldn't feel her own stories, couldn't find them real, and I practically taste them.

There was a thought.

The salutation daunted me. But I'd nothing to lose, and anyhow she knew I loved her. So I took a deep breath and the quill struck the page, words falling in measured, careful rows.

Dear Mercy, who will never be invisible to me,

Last week, I was engaged to find a stolen painting. I despaired at first, but ultimately there was an adventure in the woods and a happier end than I'd ever expected . . .

Then I told her of the miraculous disappearing transatlantic envelope. And of Val's Irish family. And of Bird's cake.

I signed it *Yours, Timothy.*

I dreamed that night Mercy could draw. She can't – she pens the most ludicrously deformed sketches it was ever my privilege to laugh at. But in my vision, she was painting a shepherdess with ribbons in her hair, on a canvas ten yards wide, against a fantastical violet and green sunset.

The dream didn't turn ominous until the peasant girl came to life under Mercy's fingers. She smiled cruelly, while her flashing eyes promised that the rush of a first kiss would be delivered over and over and over again. I tried to warn Mercy to stop painting Silkie Marsh's likeness – that it was dangerous to reproduce her, that I'd a manuscript I worried might be cursed. But the words caught in my throat. By the time I'd managed to call out, Madam Marsh had already stepped off the canvas and was walking away from us with a pleased glint of intention in her gaze.

'I ought to tell him, I think,' I announced to my brother the next morning. 'I've been dreading it, so I must be obligated. He'll want to know . . . God, what will Charles Adams want to know?'

Valentine didn't answer. I don't think he was listening. He shrugged in a twitchy fashion, tapping his stick against the pavement just outside the Tombs. His silence didn't much bustle me, considering the time of day.

The garbage my brother ingests is always obvious to me – I can practically see tarry slick pumping through the thick bluish vessels of his neck, whatever o'clock it may be – but before noon, it's obvious to *everyone.* The light of early morning never treats Val cordially. His hat hadn't a wide enough brim to shield him from pinkish dawn sunshine, a glare that shone perversely cold but still dazzling. I could have weighed the bags under his eyes on a scale, and the eyes themselves were shot through with blood beside the clear green. He'd reverted to Bowery style, with an amethyst cravat and a turned-down shirt collar, waistcoat teeming with foxglove sprays. Which could only mean he'd taken the tiger by the tail and returned home.

'I mean to say, it isn't—'

'If you could close that gap in your head for thirty or so seconds, I'd be much obliged to you,' Val suggested, leaning on his stick in earnest.

I sighed, crossing my arms. My annoyance highly grating and all the more abrasive for being so familiar.

'World spinning?'

'Shut *up*.'

I obliged. It's generally faster. Anyhow, my brother had apparently spent the previous half hour at the Tombs requesting of Chief Matsell that I help the captain of Ward Eight investigate a shocking crime. A crime that, *if the press got wind of it*, could greatly unsettle the locals. Considering the public scrapes I'd been entangling myself in lately, I'd have been flabbergasted if Matsell ate a word of what he was fed. But he trusts Valentine. And so I was now assigned to solve the murder of a beautiful mulatto female who'd been found tragically strangled in an alleyway between King Street and Hammersley.

I studied my brother, who was still the color of glistening chicken fat.

'Ready yet?'

Val blew out a breath and started walking. Steady enough for travel, if not a tightrope. 'Fire away.'

'I mean to say, it isn't as if we can tell Charles Adams the truth.'

'If Charles Adams doesn't know *something's* afoot by now, he's spooney,' Val noted as we strode along Franklin toward West Broadway. 'His wife disappeared from both her ken and her graft, and hasn't been seen since. With his stepson and sister-in-law, no less.'

'I'd be worried half blind if my wife disappeared from her house and her work, but that doesn't mean he knows she's been murdered. Or that his stepson has vanished.'

'True. Unless Delia and Jonas fled home yesterday and informed him, that'll be a surprise.'

I nodded, it having likewise occurred to me that our missing acquaintances might simply have returned to West Broadway. 'Did you identify Mrs Adams?'

A pair of mabs passed us by with their arms linked, faces painted white and scarlet like divas in an opera. Franklin Street was already alive with traffic, the milkmen and stevedores and chandlers on their way to a day's wages passing the gamblers and bartenders and faro dealers stumbling home for a few hours of sleep.

'I didn't identify Mrs Adams. Glazebrook did, when he came on shift.' Val rolled his eyes heavenward and then winced at the light. 'I could replace that roundsman with a wheel of cheese and no one would notice until the cheese solved a crime. I asked him to go through her togs for me in search of clues, and can you believe the luck? Her calling card was in her dress pocket. *Mrs Lucy Adams, Eighty-four West Broadway, at home Tuesdays and Saturdays.*'

I smiled at my deranged, brilliant sibling. 'Aces. Was it printed or handwritten?'

'Don't cast doubts on my thoroughgoing nature, Tim. I used printer's blocks. It took me twenty minutes. They're only a hair crooked.'

We turned onto West Broadway. On the opposite side of the street stood a clock-and-watch emporium, while beside us a window hung with dozens of gilt and silver cages trembled with the fluttering of dozens of pet birds. Many well-dressed blacks traversed the sidewalks alongside the whites, dark men in fine chequered greatcoats and brown-eyed women with hand-tooled scarlet leather shoes nudging at their lace skirts. Poorer blacks too – hacksmen combating the lingering snow, servants and grocers and one sheet-music salesman out crying his wares. But the street was highly respectable. It beat my neighborhood by leagues.

'That's the house.' I nodded at it, recalling the fraught meeting in the midst of the storm. 'Wait, that's him. It must be.'

My first glimpse of Charles Adams was from just across the street. He proved a white man of medium build, with a hearty complexion and neatly cut brown hair and side-whiskers. A pair of silver half-spectacles rested on his slim nose, and his chin was adorned with a goatee that was well on its way to wholly grey. Tucking his walking stick under his arm, he turned back to lock his front door.

Then I lost my focus on him entirely.

The house's windows had been covered. Not draped in black bunting, as with mourning, but boarded with thick wooden shutters bearing heavy locks. Empty houses are secured so, to prevent sixty or seventy Irish taking up residence and using your fainting couch for kindling. Then Mr Adams faced the street, in an overcoat of beige wool, and I saw he wore no mourning band. Whatever his strange business with the house, he knew nothing of the fate of his wife.

'I wonder why—' I began, stepping out into the street.

A fist of iron closed around my upper arm. I landed behind a billboard claiming that Galvanic Rings could cure heart palpitations, rheumatic pains, and general nervous derangement at one go. I wasn't sure that was possible. But I was dead certain that if my brother manhandled me one more time, he was going to happen upon my knuckles in his eye unexpectedly.

'What the hell is the matter?'

I twisted free. Valentine peered down the road, following the easy progress of Charles Adams's camel-colored coat and navy top hat.

'Not sure I savvy where to start.' Cautiously, he emerged from behind the advertisement. 'Eighty-*four* West Broadway. I'll be damned. I knew it sounded familiar, but I couldn't place it.'

'What are you talking about? Start with whatever just turned you into a spooked colt.'

'All right,' he returned placidly. 'That is not Charles Adams. That is a man by the name of Rutherford Gates, and he is a Democratic Party state senator to Albany. Now, wipe that look off your mazzard. You are about to learn how to bird-dog *effectively*. Why I didn't school you before now will be an everlasting puzzle to me.'

Chapter Twelve

I'll tell you a good joke. The other day I saw a strapping fellow standing on the Corner of Franklin-street, with his back to me. I walked quietly up, and taking him roughly by the collar, saying 'Oh, I've got you at last, you runaway scoundrel.' If I had fired a pistol near his ear, he would not have been more frightened; breaking away from me, he left a dusty streak after him towards the river.

—William M. Bobo, *Glimpses of New York City by a South Carolinian (Who Had Nothing Else to Do)*, 1852

As I shadowed Valentine, who was shadowing the man I'd supposed to be Charles Adams, I thought, *They can't be the same fellow – Gates and Adams. It's impossible.* The men must have been friends, business associates, perhaps even kin.

Surely.

I didn't want to mull over the alternative. The alternative was a tar pit of no small proportions.

'Where then is Charles Adams?' I attempted.

We'd just reached Anthony Street, heading eastward. Val whistled through his teeth at a news hawker, the lad's throat bulging as he bellowed over the possibility that we may, if not now then all too soon, be at war with either Mexico or England. My brother tossed the lad a coin and rolled the newspaper, stuffing it in his inner pocket as he spared me a glance that looked – to my deep consternation – almost patient. Fully alert, anyhow. Having a target to tail had livened him considerably.

'Wherever Charles Adams might be, that was Senator Gates's ken. I've been there before. Such an out-and-outer you've never seen. Muscat, prime rib, ice carved into the shape of a swan.'

'I've been there before too. Lucy Adams lived there.'

'Then our stocks have just taken a turn for the bearish, supposing you hankered after a happy ending.'

'How do you know they don't share that townhouse? Adams and Gates?'

'Because I can tell which way the wind is blowing, particularly when it's sending shit in my eye.'

Why I wanted so badly for there to be a Charles Adams, and for him to have loved his wife, I don't entirely understand. After all, I'd have been forced to inform a soon-to-be-grieving widower of his loss. Yet I longed for that outcome from the marrow in my bones to the prints of my fingers.

Because if there was no Charles Adams, there was no Lucy Adams either. There was only a living, breathing, beautiful lie who wasn't aware that she was a heartless ruse personified and not a wife.

Not living and breathing any longer, I corrected myself.

Gates was still in sight when we reached Broadway. The street beyond the flagstone sidewalk was packed with sleighs, single-horse cutters skirting past the massive vehicles in deadly spurts and starts. A swarm of people surrounded us. Black people, white people, every sort of human wearing every cut of cloth and every style of hat yet invented. A Mohammedan with his head neatly wrapped jostled my arm and murmured a polite apology, just as I gripped the collar of a figner – a child pickpocket to the uninitiated – who'd taken instant advantage of my imbalance and sent grubby fingers into my coat. I tossed him back into the river like an undersized fish.

'First,' my brother said, stepping around an enormous pram draped in pink satin, 'stop *looking* for him. See with the sides of your vision. Thankfully, we're on the Dollar Side. Savvy?'

Val was peering at the shop windows as we progressed. The west side of Broadway is colloquially called the Dollar Side for its plate-glass-fronted shops brimming with English jewelry and French silk and Belgian lace and Italian statuary. On the Shilling, or eastern side, chophouses and saloons and steps leading into subterranean oyster cellars prevail. And in the polished glass, I realized I could spy Gates as well in reflection as I did in plain view.

'Stop walking like that, you ninny. You're squandering the fact you're small. It's flash that you're small. Head up, shoulders out, as if you want to be seen. Then nary will see you.'

Unaware I'd been skulking, I straightened up like a bantam rooster.

'Notice we're twice as far back as you were when trailing me. That was journeyman's work. Stay alert but stay distant.'

Dodging a group of gabbing Spanish tourists who all seemed to be pointing in different directions, I recalled a ghastly stretch of three hours when I was five, on the July afternoon when eleven-year-old Val decided I needed to know how to swim. He'd dragged me down to the shore from nearby Greenwich Village, tied a rope around my waist, looped the same rope around his wrist, and thrown me in the Hudson. Eight times. I caught the gist of it after that.

'Val, he's stopped,' I hissed.

A trinket in a window had arrested Gates's interest. As we approached, he proved to be studying ornamental cigar boxes.

'Break your stride and I will break your ankle,' my brother said affably.

We breached Gates's shadow and emerged from the other side. After about ten yards, my brother cut past a parson wearing homespun, nearly sending the poor hayseed into the gutter, and stepped to the curb. Val's stick shot up through his fingers and flashed above his head like a torchlight as he finally glanced back the way we'd come. But now – due to the sluggish traffic and the way his body was oriented – he for all appearances was seeking out a sleigh for hire.

'When you do look back, have a reason. Never keek over your shoulder.'

Just as Gates caught up to us, Val glared impatiently out at the choked roadway. He then made a small circle, slid the leaded stick back down through his fingers, and resumed our pursuit when the distance was safe. It was like watching a ballet savant. If ballet were based upon sneakthievery and rowdyism.

Half a block farther along, Val muttered, 'I knew it. That uppish peacock. I could have taken us straight here and saved the botheration.'

'I'd not have learned bird-dogging.'

'Fair play, then.'

'Where . . . oh,' I breathed as Gates entered the Astor House hotel.

Most of Broadway's edifices, both on the Dollar and Shilling sides, are built either of sandy stone or of brick and mortar. The Astor House is a pink-granite behemoth, scrubbed and eager as a debutante with a paltry dowry, finished ten years ago at the apparent cost of three or four equivalent European palaces. Facing City Hall Park, its entrance is flanked by four great pillars, the building itself occupying the entire city block between Broadway, Vesey, Church, and Barclay streets. At six looming stories, it looks as if America's first multi-millionaire had dumped a cartful of moneybags at an empty lot to see what sprouted. Which is exactly what happened, so far as I know. They probably employ more laundresses than Ward Six does copper stars.

Gates slowed before the carpeted entrance, checking his watch. But Val plunged ahead while the senator's head was down. I found myself within a disquieting land of piercing crystal chandeliers, polished gold monocles, potted palms, and ruby-draped white throats. The society women slid about with blank expressions meaning *I will do you the honor of allowing you to stare*, while the men of business somehow managed to look both impatient and bored, sipping from snifters and trimming their cigar ends. My brother ambled through the lobby toward the sunlit courtyard in the center of the opulent monstrosity. Finding an emerald settee commanding a view of the entrance, he took a seat, pulling the newspaper from his jacket and leafing through its pages. I joined him.

'And finally,' Val said, eyes not leaving the page, 'the very best way to trail a rabbit is to arrive at his destination first. Saves them getting peery.'

'What now?'

'Now you keep your mouth shut as much as is possible for you. Here he comes.'

Gates stood casting his eyes over the room. A colored waiter of military bearing marched by, effortlessly balancing a salver of what smelled like clam soup. The quirk of the Astor is that if you stay there and you want something – any something, day or night – you get it. I presume such services cost copious chink, but I'm not in any position to know. When Gates proceeded toward the bar, my brother lowered the paper with a snap.

'I'll be damned. Gates! What a streak of luck. Just the man we were looking for.'

Rutherford Gates veered our way with an open smile. From closer up, I saw that his goatee was neatly waxed, his brown eyes radiating good health and good cheer. Thrusting a palm at my brother, he tucked his left thumb under his braces. The right thumb did likewise after he'd shaken Val's hand. Why every politician on the face of the earth feels compelled to copy this mannerism I do not know, but I will ache with curiosity over it until the day I die.

'Captain Wilde. What a pleasure. Good lord, I haven't seen you since last year's elections. And this is . . . ?'

'My brother, Timothy. Another copper star, as you can see.'

'Pleased to meet you,' I said.

'The pleasure is mine, Mr Wilde. Always happy to meet an ally. I do take it, seeing who your sibling is, that you're one of my voters.'

Having never voted in my life, I merely nodded.

'You said you wanted me, Captain?' Gates took a seat on a chair next to the settee, gesturing magnanimously for us to sit as well, as if he were visiting royalty or possibly the owner of these specific furnishings. 'Gearing up for spring elections soon, and all, I'll be seeing more of you, no doubt. We can't have eighteen thirty-eight happening again.'

Val raised his fingers to the bridge of his nose in what seemed genuine distress. 'Do not speak of that year. It puts me off my appetite for days at a time.'

'What happened in eighteen thirty-eight?'

Valentine placed his boot over my toe and pressed down painfully.

'I was very ill that year,' I explained. 'Scarlet fever.'

'We nearly lost him,' Val agreed. 'Had to take a rest cure in Savannah. He drifted in and out, as helpless as a babe. He's never recovered entirely. Has these sudden fits, eh, Tim?'

'Fits.' I glared at him. 'Yes. On occasion.'

'My sympathies.' Gates smiled at me, wise and generous. 'Well, in eighteen thirty-eight, the Whigs secretly imported hundreds of men from Philadelphia, set them up in boarding houses, and paid them to vote against us. And it worked beautifully. The bastards.'

'That's revolting,' I said, sincerely.

'I know. *Why* didn't *I* think of it sooner?' Val lamented. 'We're flush with lowre, we can afford our own Philadelphians. It was disgraceful.'

'You mustn't blame yourself, Captain,' Gates soothed. 'We are at least still gratifyingly fiscally solvent. In fact, I'm meeting with a major contributor. I fear I've only five minutes to give you gentlemen.'

'Here's the gist of it.' Val leaned forward with his elbows on his knees, pressing the tips of his fingers together. 'A moll was found in an alley near the river yesterday. Strangled to death. Foul piece of work.'

'How dreadful.' Gates pulled a silver case from his waistcoat and offered us French cigarettes. Hands steady, gaze dispassionately interested, mouth in a neutral line. I declined to smoke and Val readily accepted.

'We've done a little digging. And the worst of it is, Senator Gates, I've reason to think you knew the victim. She was a high yellow colored woman, around thirty years, dimber lass – really, she made quite a picture. Sound familiar?'

Gates paled. The cigarette in his fingers dangled unlit. I stared voraciously, ravenous for details – for every twitch of his lips, for the subtle tremor at his temples. A thready pulsebeat fluttered in his throat as he swallowed. 'You can't possibly mean my housekeeper, Lucy Wright?'

Housekeeper. *God in heaven*, I thought.

'I think that might be just who I mean,' Val said evenly. 'We identified her this morning.'

'Oh, God,' he said. 'God, that's . . . oh, *Lucy*.'

He sure enough resembled a man whose spine had just been yanked from his torso. Pain had speared him, and it was quick spreading. Gates's hands shook. He looked at them helplessly, as if they belonged on another animal.

'When was the last you saw her?' Val asked.

Gates's head fell forward, his eyes closing. 'I hadn't seen her since returning from Albany. I'd assumed that she'd found new lodgings, you see. I never dreamed harm could have come to her.'

'Steady on, Senator,' Val said when our subject appeared to lose all powers of speech.

I don't like scrutinizing folk in distress, and it seemed the fragmenting man before me was in enough to splinter apart. It was evidence, though. So I took it all in as best I could. 'Any changes to the household recently?' I inquired.

Gates lifted his eyes a fraction. 'About a month ago, she found a position in a flower shop – Timpson's, near to my residence. Of course I congratulated her and of course I allowed her to remain for as long as she needed to find a respectable boarding house or a set of private rooms. Poor Lucy. Are you certain that it's her?'

'Yes. And Lucy was your housekeeper, you say.'

'She was, but she found work in the flower shop much more to her tastes. Oh, God. You must find the monster who did this, Captain. You must find him at once.'

My heart was hammering. Charles Adams had rescued Lucy Wright from a gang of kidnappers and later married her. Rutherford Gates had a housekeeper called Lucy Wright who had left his service in favor of work as a florist. Whatever breed of lies we were dealing with, they were the sort that sink their teeth in and leave you bleeding.

Valentine pulled out his little notebook. He never needs to write anything down, but I think he likes the effect. 'Lucy Wright. Spinster?'

'Widowed, with a child.'

'Previous residence?'

'She was originally from Albany.'

'How long had Mrs Wright overseen your ken?'

'Two years, all told. I was very fond of her.'

'Seemed the sort of lass it would be easy for a man to grow fond of.' Val smiled salaciously, flicking a vesta with his thumbnail and lighting his cigarette. He leaned forward and did the same for Gates. The man obviously needed one.

'Lucy was lovely, yes,' Gates said with some care. His hale complexion had grown moldy. 'If you're suggesting that my relationship with her was in any way improper—'

'Oh, I'm not *suggesting* it,' Val said in a remarkably bold display of cunning. 'Don't tell me you had that thoroughbred under your nose for two years and never took a ride.'

My hackles rose at Val's language – but the foul tone aided the greater good, for Gates's pallor shifted to a stunning shade of crimson.

'Are you accusing me of something, Captain?'

My brother splayed a hand over his chest, all innocence. 'Senator, I'd never dream of it. But were you in a position to *know* Lucy? Her friends? Enemies? Where do we start?'

Gates shuddered, looking stricken. 'I'm sorry. This is such a shock.'

'That's fair,' I allowed, aiming for kindly and landing at civil. 'Take your time about it.'

'You're right, of course.' Gates cast a look at my brother, a *We all of us have our little foibles, do we not* expression. 'We were . . . intimate on occasion. We kept it secret, and I hope I can trust you to do the same. Lucy spent the majority of her time within the walls of my home with her little boy. She was terrified of slave catchers, you see. As many Africans are. She was once the victim of a vile kidnapping attempt from which I extricated her. That's how we met, in fact. Lucy lived in mortal fear of being snatched up again. When she found the position at the florist's shop, I was terribly proud of her. It seemed that she was finally making a recovery.'

Val blew out a smooth circle of smoke, watching its lazy dissipation with considerable interest. 'Before she was killed, her sister and son were netted by blackbirders.'

I shot a glance at my brother, surprised at the admission. Likely because my head was spinning. Gates's tale was so close in character to what I'd supposed to be the truth that I felt in a dreamscape. Gates, meanwhile, dropped his own cigarette. Gutted, for all appearances. My brother calmly stepped on the glowing point.

'No. Please tell me—'

'The Wrights afterward escaped to a safe location. Two days later, Lucy Wright was put to anodyne with a cord round the neck, possibly in an alleyway, possibly somewhere else. Delia and Jonas Wright are missing. Might you know whereabouts they are?'

'I can't imagine.'

'Nary a suggestion?'

'I wish to God I had one. I don't even know where Delia Wright resides, only that she teaches school at the Abyssinian Church. This is all so shocking.'

'Shocking is about the color of it. And here's what I'm wondering, Senator.'

Gates tugged at his goatee, looking as if he might sully the flawless reputation of Astor House by being ill on its finely worked carpet.

'Yes, Captain?'

'I'm wondering what you want me to do about it.'

Val propped his elbow on the arm of the settee and continued smoking reflectively. I hadn't known where he was leading before, but now he'd arrived, I saw his ploy for the brilliantly simple scheme it was. If Rutherford Gates had returned home, somehow inexplicably discovered Lucy at Valentine's, and killed her in a jealous rage – all of which fit, people kill for love every day of the year and the world keeps turning – then his response to Val's question would be telling.

I know nothing of this affair. But please drop the case, for the sake of the Party.

'Please do all you can.' Gates slumped back, mouth slack with grief. 'I arranged to have the house closed up this morning – I'm so often traveling between here and Albany that I'm thinking of selling it, and after all, my housekeeper had given notice. Living in a hotel seemed much easier in the interim. When I found no one home, I pictured her settled elsewhere . . . the mistress of her own establishment. Happy. I can't stomach it. Find the son of a bitch who did this, Captain, and hang him.'

'Oh, there you are, Rutherford. But I fear that I interrupt you.'

Animal apprehension slithered across my shoulders. Silkie Marsh stood behind Val, dressed in her usual splendor – black satin with jet beadwork, lips artfully rouged, a pale fur cape the exact color of her pale golden hair. She was addressing Gates, but naturally she was looking at Valentine. Madam Marsh sees people the way most people see cobblestones – as a means of getting somewhere. But she once had Val, and she wants him back, the way a child would want a toy simply because they've been told they can't have it any longer. She'd worked a spray of tiny scarlet hothouse roses into the artful sweeps of her hair that made me think of sprayed blood.

'Silkie.' Val smiled, still languidly smoking. 'What a pal you've been to the Party this year. They've all but built you a shrine at the Hall, dear little duck. You've been plumping our coffers something admirable.'

'I couldn't think of doing anything less.' She placed a hand on his shoulder. He ignored it. So she shifted her attention to me, smiling as if he'd leapt up and embraced her. 'And Mr Wilde. I gather your efforts to redeem Mr Carpenter were successful. It is the last time I'll trust Mr Varker's word, of that I assure you.'

'I take it you only imagined meeting Coffee St Claire,' I couldn't help but mention.

'I was convinced it was the same man, but now I understand that I allowed myself to be led, I'm afraid.' She cocked her head, dimpled and wide-eyed and soft as a razor. 'You must think me a foolish, impressionable girl, Mr Wilde.'

'That is the *last* thing I think of you.'

Blushing as if at a compliment, Silkie Marsh turned to the senator. He mopped his face with a handkerchief, pushing his half-spectacles up his nose. 'Rutherford, darling, I won't ask what you were speaking of, but you seem most . . . troubled. Are you all right?'

'Yes, yes. I've had a bit of a shock, I fear. Nothing to speak of.'

'Nothing but murder,' Val said brightly.

Emerging from behind the settee, Silkie Marsh eyed us in either real or feigned wonderment. The woman is such a creature of clockwork, mimicking humanity by means of wax and paint and cogs, that it's almost impossible to tell when she's lying or simply parroting normal sentiment.

Rutherford Gates, meanwhile, was turning blue.

'Murder?' she echoed.

'You're familiar with the concept,' I reminded her.

The vivid circles within her dappled eyes froze over. 'I'll await you in the restaurant, Rutherford, and we can discuss fund-raising. If you are able. If other business detains you, I'll simply take advantage of their excellent chef. Valentine, might you consider my house at Greene Street for a Knickerbocker Twenty-one event soon? My girls and I would be delighted to provide a little cheer, entirely gratis, of course.'

'Gratis, you say?' my brother mused.

'Always for you, Valentine,' she murmured.

'Well, they do say you get what you pay for. No.' Val crushed the cigarette in a discreet crystal tray. 'No, I would not.'

Shock would be the mildest word for my reaction. I'd never seen him so openly reject an overture in my life. Silkie Marsh colored again, this time naturally. A sheen of tears sprang into her eyes for good measure. Nodding to Rutherford Gates, she hurried away, silken coiffure bobbing in a sea of similarly artful heads.

'Thank you for speaking with me,' Gates said, rising. If we'd insulted a pal of his, he seemed game to ignore the fact. 'I really must meet with Miss Marsh, as she's contributed healthy sums to my campaign in the coming spring. But keep me informed. Please.'

'You'll be in town for the Party ball a week from now?' Val inquired.

'Yes, though Albany will doubtless require me in the meanwhile. I'm staying here at the Astor when in Manhattan. Room three thirty-seven. Don't hesitate to contact me.'

Gates departed. He left behind him a visible aura of grey unease. When the senator had caught Silkie Marsh up at the restaurant entrance, she smiled, taking his arm. They proceeded into an exotic realm of terrapin and goose liver and capon. Neither of them honest. One of them, at the minimum, a ruthless killer.

I hadn't decided about the other quite yet.

'I don't suppose we should be surprised Gates and Silkie Marsh know each other?' I ventured.

Val shook his head. 'They've been pals for years. So have I, for that matter. We're all cut from the same cloth.'

'No, you aren't. Would you call them friends or friendly?'

'Friends.'

'That worries me tremendously.'

'That's because you, my Tim, are sharper than the average fence post.'

'Have you spotted the lie yet?'

'The only hummer I know he just delivered was that they were intimate *on occasion*. I told you I wouldn't go sniffing after Lucy Adams, and that's because she wasn't the casual sort of ladybird. She was a one-man moll. Worried at her wedding ring as if it eased her, nary a disloyal thought in her head. They went to it regular if they went at all, though I never spied her at his ken.'

My scar needed some vicious rubbing, so I started in. Val, for once, ignored me. After he waved his fingers at a waiter – Irish this time – a pair of brandies were shortly thereafter clasped in worried grips. I drank, not caring what it cost. Anyway, Val would pay for it. He's the Democrat, after all.

'Motive, Val,' I said under my breath.

'Motive,' he sighed. 'Don't I know it.'

A politico, I thought, *rescues a beautiful woman. He's entranced. He likes who he is in the story because it's the wrong story he's telling. He supposes himself the hero. He imagines the narrative is printed in great block letters, with pictures rendered in blinding splashes of color. Fantastical portraits of knights drawn in his image. Of dragons slain, the glory of the conqueror. Of swift, heartbreaking love. And then he finds himself married – perhaps – and only a politico after all. With a wife, now.*

Seixas Varker and Long Luke Coles wanted Lucy alive so as to make a swift, rancid profit. Val and I and Piest and the Committee men – at least to my knowledge, God knows my acquaintance with Higgins and Brown was brief – wanted her safe. I assumed Silkie Marsh was acting true to form and assigned her the role of *perpetrator of whatever evil is foulest* and left it at that. These circumstances, barring extraordinary new evidence, led to one conclusion.

The only person I'd yet met who could have wanted Lucy Wright dead was Rutherford Gates. When an election and a secret marriage had entered the picture, anyhow.

Val tossed several coins on the pewter salver, rising and buttoning his coat. 'The poor fish seemed shocked enough. Whether shocked that she's croaked or shocked we wanted a chat with him over it, though, I couldn't say.'

'Could the sisters have known about all of this? Found Gates out long ago, and kept mouse for the family's sake?'

'No way to be certain just yet. But if they were mum in the name of peaceableness, that tack seems to have gone south.'

'I'm for the Committee of Vigilance,' I said, following him out the great glass-paned door. 'The remaining Wrights need finding, and finding now.'

'Then I'll explore a few notions of my own.'

'Which?'

'Ones I'll keep snug over for now.'

Irritated and worried, I blinked up at the sun, stepping to the edge of the paving stones to allow the scores of beaver-hatted gentlemen and fur-caped ladies to pass me by. 'Do I have to tell you to be careful again?'

'No. I just gave the middle finger to Silkie Marsh, major Democratic contributor and present or former darling of every Party boss in Manhattan I can think of. *Careful* won't serve the purpose. We sort this quick as possible or there'll be hell to pay.'

Val touched his hat brim and set off, swinging his stick like a dandy out for a lark. He was right, of course. Time was a precious commodity. I hastened off alone, ruminating over names.

Wright or Adams, I thought as I drew closer to Julius's ken, having sent word the night before requesting an audience with the Committee. Her murder couldn't be unraveled until I knew which it was. And I would find it out, I determined, as I recalled the weight of her nearly cold body and the depth of her richly dark voice. I would know her name, and like a key it would unlock every obstacle that barred me from the answer. And heaven forbid I leave a mystery unsolved or a strongbox unopened.

Learning people's secrets, God help me, is what I do.

CHAPTER THIRTEEN

No grand inquest has for years had the courage or virtue to find a bill of indictment against a kidnapper, however plain and undeniable the proof of his guilt.

James G. Birney, 1842

'George, if you don't sit down and take a breath, you're going to do yourself an injury,' Julius announced from where he sat propped against his desk.

Julius and Higgins had absorbed my tale – that their friends had lodged at Val's for two nights; that Lucy had been found strangled in an alleyway; that the others were missing; and that Charles Adams seemed to be a fictional character – with the quick-smothered grief mastered by people who constantly absorb tragic information. Yes, tears sprang to Higgins's eyes, to be swiftly blinked away again. And yes, Julius's jaw clenched so tight I'd feared for his teeth. But neither was a stranger to barbarism. I could practically see the groove that trickling cruelty had eroded in Higgins's skull. He paced the room as if enough circles could erase Lucy's death and erase me from Julius's ladder-back chair. My delivery of the news hadn't exactly endeared me to him. And the Reverend Brown was attending a deathbed and thus unable to sprinkle water over the hot coals of Higgins's temper.

To stop myself staring, I studied Julius's home. He lives in Ward One on Washington Street, in a boarding house catering to unmarried black men. Boarding-house living is practical and collegiate, and pleasant smells of stewed mutton and hair oil and ninepin cigars filled the halls. We were on the third floor, the window overlooking dozens of masts in the quays, though not so many as at the eastern docks and not so many as in fairer weather. They still looked like so many spearheads, somber and warlike.

I think if George Higgins could have torn one off and charged into battle with it, he'd have done so in a heartbeat.

'This is a *message*, Julius,' he bit out. 'To us, from Varker and Coles. That supposing we interfere further, we'll find our friends lynched and not just sold down the Mississippi.'

'You could be right,' I reflected. 'That never occurred to me.'

'*Nothing* occurs to you.' Higgins made an abortive gesture that clearly wished to be a fist flying at my eye. 'It never occurred to you that we'd have started searching for Delia and Jonas an entire *day* sooner if you'd done us the courtesy of telling us our friend Lucy is dead, for instance. It never occurred to you that we might in fact *care* she's no longer for this world.'

'That occurred to him,' Julius put in evenly.

'Did it occur to him that Delia and Jonas might be in a slave market in the Capitol by this time?'

His voice broke, the faintest hint of a hairline fracture. So now I knew. There are particular ways a man has of saying names. His *Delia* sure enough resembled my *Mercy Underhill*.

Higgins wasn't near through with me, though. 'We are speaking of a child of six, and a woman who was already nearly violated by the likes of Varker. So this *copper star* is your friend, you tell me, Julius. And he probably saved your life yesterday. Fine. What possible excuse can he give for—'

'Lucy Adams wasn't strangled to death in an alley.' I shivered as I said it. But there was only one thing to be done. 'She was killed in my brother Valentine's bedroom. Val never did it. Even apart from the fact he was with a friend, my brother would never harm a woman. Someone is trying to ruin us all. I can't make you trust me, but I can give you the square truth.'

I remember the explosion that disfigured me last July as being silent – a tremor so deeply felt that hearing the blast was superfluous. My statement sent a similar shock through the room.

Julius uncrossed his arms and gripped the edge of his desk. He wore only trousers, braces, and white shirtsleeves. Though he seemed much recovered, I can't imagine jackets are comfortable when your back resembles a shallow-ploughed field. 'And you moved her,' he said to me.

'I hid her in a shelter the newsboys had made. Covered in a blanket. I'm so sorry.'

George Higgins took two quick steps in my direction and then stopped. Plainly wondering whether killing a New York City policeman would be his style or not.

'I never did it lightly. I don't know how many people you have, but I have one,' I told him.

Confession of a sort had almost been a foregone conclusion when I'd arrived at Julius's digs to talk murder. But that second admission had been wholly personal and rawer than the fact of the terrible thing I'd done. My tone shifted the disgusted look in Higgins's eyes to blank surprise.

'And we're simply . . . we're meant to *take your word for it?*' Higgins spluttered in disbelief. 'That your brother is innocent? That dandified morphine freak who smashed Varker's wrist and *liked it?*'

'Remember when you called me dense? And it was true?'

'Yes, perfectly.'

'Calling my brother names that accurately describe him are every bit as flash of an idea. I want this crime solved, but Val wasn't responsible.'

Higgins turned to look at Julius while unmistakably addressing me, still visibly battling *smash-the-copper-star's-eye-against-his-brain* urges. 'So I'm meant to simply take as given the lofty grandeur of your white abolitionist morals—'

'My morals stem from poverty, not from affluence.'

'How very biblical of you. In that case, you'll inherit the earth one day, no doubt. Oh, just a moment, your kind already—'

'Stop,' Julius ordered sharply. 'This isn't about either of you.'

That landed with a resounding clang. Higgins and I looked at each other, then looked away, then felt angry at ourselves for looking away and glared at Julius. It was a pretty little morris dance, all told.

'Valentine Wilde doesn't enjoy fighting people who don't fight back,' Julius added, rubbing at a linen compress tied over the cigar burn on his forearm. He wasn't calling attention to it – Julius can shell oysters like the devil himself for a reason. His hands take pleasure in movement, are fond of being busy. 'Man to man? Certainly. As for women and children – it's beneath him, George, even if the fellow does own a taste for blood and narcotics.'

I sighed. 'Yes, that's – thank you.'

The room fell silent. A gently ticking mantel clock counted out tensely drawn breaths.

'Timothy, are you suggesting that someone, rather than sending us a message, sent your brother one?' Julius pondered.

'I don't know. No one knew Mrs Adams was there. Though Varker and Coles knew just who was involved in rescuing her kin,' I realized. 'So it's not impossible that they guessed at her hiding place. It was the *reason* for her being dead baffled me. Until Rutherford Gates came into it. Please, tell me anything you can.'

'So you can make new discoveries and fail to apprise us?' Higgins demanded. 'So you can treat us like partial men? Do you know what I do for a living?'

I shook my head. Not having been able to work that question out for the life of me. And desperately curious over it, to boot.

'I'm one of the first graduates from the Institute for Colored Youth in Philadelphia, but I trained as a shoemaker because work for educated Negroes does not exist. When I'd saved enough money to leave for Canada, I went to Julius here to say my farewells. He mentioned that most of the drunks you two used to serve were stockbrokers, and I've always had a head for finance. Julius found one who'd speculate my money exactly as I like provided he kept a third of my profits. Fellow called Inman. Even minus thirty-three percent, I've ample money to live like a king. I can't testify in court, I can't eat a meal at the Astor, I make two-thirds of what I ought to earn on Wall Street. And you, Mr Wilde, *will not* keep delivering me half the information and then a day late. Not where Delia is concerned.'

Dazzled, my eyes flew to Julius. Last I saw Inman, I was passing him a plate of oysters with sugared vinegar and his fourth champagne bottle, and he was shrieking at me that Sam Morse's telegram could make me rich in the amount of time required to take a morning piss.

'It's true,' Julius chuckled. 'I'd thought best not to mention it at the time.'

'In fact, I don't know quite why I just told you all that,' Higgins admitted.

'My fault, not yours.' I waved my hand dismissively.

'Never mind, everyone tells him things,' Julius agreed.

Memories flooded back to me unbidden, of Nick's Oyster Cellar and what our lives had looked like. *Julius, laughing fit to burst because I'd opened a champagne bottle with a saber and drenched three stockbrokers. Julius, beating Val at poker when my brother had stumbled into our establishment so drenched with opiates he could barely see me. Julius, bored and tapping a rhythm on the bar with his palms I couldn't parse to save my life.*

'You don't know Timothy, George,' Julius said. 'He's not an angel. But I know him, and I'll spill if you won't.'

'And I'll tell you everything,' I vowed. 'As soon as I learn it, from this point on.'

We were quiet for a while.

'If you ask me, Lucy was married for a fact,' Higgins announced, seating himself.

He did it for Delia. Not because he trusted me and never because he liked me. He did it because suffering my company might – just might – make a difference for her. I often don't care for people at large, but the sublimely individual things they do will never cease to quicken my heart rate.

'Are Rutherford Gates and Charles Adams the same person?' I asked. Grateful for a place at the table, however despised my chair.

'Must be.' Julius ran his fingers across his mouth in thought. 'We've known Lucy two years, and only ever met her husband at their ken.'

'Two inches taller than me, brown hair, greying goatee, half-spectacles?'

'That bastard,' Higgins growled. 'That filthy bastard.'

'Could his wife and her sister have been aware of his second identity?'

'That's a sizable lie for an entire family to keep.'

'Maybe easier for three than for one?'

Higgins shook his head, wincing a little. 'They never spoke of politics, never blinked an eye at his tales of the open road. It doesn't match. And when Jonas went to school of a morning, his aunt walked with him. Delia sometimes sent the lad home in the company of the reverend or another friend, but I could count the times I've seen the boy with his stepfather on one hand.'

'I need facts, dates, but better yet, a story,' I pleaded. 'I'm much handier with those.'

Julius glanced at his ceiling, considering. 'Round two years ago, I was contacted by a woman who'd just married in Massachusetts and now lived on West Broadway. Asked me to tea. Her family, not to mention George here, was part of the Reverend Brown's Abyssinian Church.'

'But Lucy attended services without Gates?'

'Why, Mr Wilde,' Higgins drawled, 'you'd never suggest a white man and a colored one share the same *church pew*, would you?'

'Heaven forbid,' I agreed. 'Tell me about the meeting.'

'Friendly enough,' Julius replied. 'Lucy was . . . skittish. Very recently, she'd lived through an abduction. So she wanted to contribute to our Vigilance cause.'

'For safety's sake?' I questioned.

'Could be. I think . . . like-mindedness would be closer. She wanted to talk with people who understood. Knew the way her outlook had changed.'

My thoughts flashed to letters carved in a woman's chest and a wide-eyed panic that made all the sense in the world in retrospect.

'She introduced herself as Lucy Adams, and that mongrel introduced himself as Charles Adams.' Higgins abandoned the chair to resume prowling. 'He seemed as passionate about our cause as she was.'

Several items of note emerged from the ensuing conversation. Lucy, after having been kidnapped outside of Albany with Delia and Jonas for sale at the Capitol, had been altogether crippled so far as venturing outdoors was concerned once the family was transplanted to New York. Barely keeked her head past a drapery for fear of being spied by wholesale villains. But the marriage itself never suffered a wrinkle over her reclusiveness, so far as the Committee men could tell. Adams – Gates, as we began to call him – had seemed besotted with his supposed wife. At least, insofar as Julius and Higgins could report from their own interactions with the couple inside the walls of 84 West Broadway.

'Who else was generally present, when you were entertained there?' I asked.

'Delia, Jonas. Between three and five other friends from church,' Higgins answered.

'All black?'

He nodded once.

'And when Gates hosted the rare political soiree, you were never invited.'

'Thought him a salesman for a new French-designed mechanical sewing apparatus, the lot of us,' Julius reported in an arid tone. 'He traveled a great deal in that line of work.'

'How could he have hid Lucy on the few occasions Party members were present?' I marveled, half to myself.

'I can answer that,' Higgins replied readily. 'Lucy detested being around strange white men. They frightened her. Gates would simply have sent her upstairs with the boy, dismissed the cook, and done just as he liked – she'd not have marveled over a feast being delivered for his clients.'

I sat with my eyes closed, a despicable picture forming. 'Tell me how often she left the house.'

'For church, weekly, with Delia and Jonas. That was at first. She grew more relaxed as time went on. Less fragile,' Julius recalled.

'Whose notion was that? The solitude?'

'She'd every reason to be cautious,' Higgins answered. 'And that lying snake supported her, or seemed to.'

'Supported her caution or *his* secrecy?'

Higgins descended, weary eyed, into another of Julius's hand-worked chairs.

'Was she ever in public with Gates – on his arm, as a couple?'

'Can't say as to that,' Julius replied slowly. 'I'd guess at a *no*.'

'God, this is hideous,' Higgins lamented. 'How could I have been so blind?'

'She'd been hurt beyond our imagining when kidnapped,' I posited. 'Gates genuinely feared for her, perhaps. The rest was a wet tissue of lies, and she never knew who he truly was. But suppose he did care about her and Jonas's well-being: who could say which motive for hiding in a townhouse played the bigger role? What I can't ignore is that Gates would be far more likely to panic over a real wife than a misled housekeeper. Because God knows it looks to me as if Gates either killed her or paid someone else to do it, considering what happened last month.'

'Last month?' Julius repeated.

'She got a job.' Higgins's eyes grew wide. 'Outside the house, where she could speak to anyone. Lucy was hired on at Timpson's. I'm going to wring that mongrel's neck with my bare hands.'

'Gates claims his housekeeper, Lucy Wright, was glad of a better position,' I reminded them. 'Finding her own digs, her own life. Was their relationship over?'

'Not so far as Lucy knew,' Julius said.

191

'Did Gates object to her finding work?'

'Not as she ever mentioned.'

'Did anyone set eyes on Lucy, Delia, or Jonas after the night of the abduction? Did they go to church on Sunday?'

Higgins shook his head. 'They must have kept indoors – for all the good it did them.'

Unable to keep still any longer myself, I wandered over to the fireplace, hearth neatly swept with a poster bearing the emancipationist emblem AM I NOT A MAN AND A BROTHER? tacked over the mantel. Several other objects rested there. With a start, I recognized the turnip used to gag Julius the previous summer, along with a brick with a smear of blood on it, a leather tawse, a rock the size of a child's fist, and the set of tattered clothing he'd been forced to wear in the courtroom, folded in a compact pile. I recalled asking my friend in August why in the devil's name he carried the turnip in his pocket, walking away from the construction site where he'd nearly been burned to death.

Because I'm still here, he'd answered. 'I got a brick, a leather strap, and a rock from a slingshot too, all on a shelf. But look at me. I'm right here.

'Wringing Gates's neck isn't our first order of business,' Julius reminded us, smiling at me when I turned away from his macabre collection.

'We have channels,' Higgins agreed. 'Systems in place to try to bring people back when we act fast enough. It was the courts entering into it we were worried over when we consulted you, Mr Wilde. Copper stars are . . .' He hesitated, seeking out the right word. 'A new variable. We didn't know quite what to make of you all.'

My thumb traced the star pin, as if I needed reminding it was there. 'We know Varker and Coles are connected to Silkie Marsh, and that Marsh is also connected to Gates; we don't yet know whether Gates and the slave catchers have ever exchanged words. But the kidnapping and the murder, so close on each other's heels . . . it can't be coincidental. We need more evidence. I don't care if you send me to hell itself – all I ask is that you permit me to help fix this.'

'And if they're in South Carolina?' Higgins asked in the tone of a man who could very possibly have lost everything. 'The storm has long passed, ships in and out of the harbor just as usual. What if they're gone?'

'Then we'll not rest until we've tracked them,' I answered. 'And in the meanwhile, redirect our focus to your earlier suggestion. The one involving Rutherford Gates's neck.'

I left the Committee men by way of the burnt district. Wound tight as a fishing line and needing to think things through. A list in my pocket naming Lucy's few close contacts promised me immediate work, but another line of inquiry nagged at me.

Mulqueen, my mind kept insisting. *Mulqueen at the scene of the crime.* I'd been in such a whirlwind when he'd appeared on Val's steps that I'd failed to press him. That was unconscionable. If he was involved – sent to find the corpse or even returned to check his handiwork – I would run him to ground. And if not, I needed to press him over who'd given the alarm. From the looks of Val's room, there had indeed been a struggle. That boded ill for Delia and Jonas, who could well have been dragged out by their hair. There would have been noise. Val, who is sly if not a bit discreet, would need to question his neighbors – possibly one had, in fact, alerted a copper star.

But Mulqueen was my responsibility. I hastened my steps, for snow had begun falling again, fat flakes caressing the edges of my hat.

The fire last year destroyed thirty buildings in a charred swath of destruction that will doubtless awe us for decades. My walk through the blankness was disquieting, for many walls yet crumbled while half-conceived replacements rose in skeletons beside them. Scattered construction continued, mostly of the demolition variety, for the ice made brickwork difficult and third-story aerial acts downright suicidal. I avoided Stone Street, where I'd lived before.

I think I'd a right to. Instead, I watched men with strong Irish jawlines and coal-black hair pushing handcarts filled with smoky waste along the cobbles. Their hands were flaking and bloody from the cold. But they'd buy bread for their kinchin that night.

I wondered how many of them Val had employed. I wondered why I'd never questioned why everyone treats him as if he were a deity. Mere pugilism could never have accounted for it, nor firefighting fame. Then I wondered why I work with such apparent enthusiasm at being a first-class idiot.

In Cedar Street, I stopped before the whimsical façade of the new post office. It's fronted with thousands of gilt-edged panes, numbered windows into tiny worlds, where the merchants can peer to see whether they've any correspondence. Mercy decreed it magical when it opened and promptly mailed an anonymous love letter to a businessman she didn't know, just to see it lodged in its little glass cage. I went inside and passed ten cents to the clerk to mail my letter to London. Thinking it more efficient than her suggestion of a bottle hurtled into the sea.

I felt better after that – like a man with one mission accomplished.

Thoroughly snow-caked by the time I reached the Tombs, I headed for the records room. Mulqueen's route took him down Orange Street, through the sinkhole of the Five Points itself. Rendering it nigh impossible for him to have arrived at Val's by happenstance.

Frowning, I shut the ledger and hurried to my private nook to check whether I'd any communiqués. There were two, in fact, on my little pine desk. The one in Matsell's braying hand demanded reading first.

Wilde,

Judge Sivell has asked that I pass along his compliments to you over justice served. He also desires to fine you for contempt of court. Your brother has promised me a full report within the week regarding what in hell is going on, and thus – because he often knows our business better than we do – I have agreed not to question you for the time being. In the meanwhile, be aware that your position is as precarious as the existence of the copper star force itself, and that turning runaway slave trials into three-ring circuses is not appreciated by the powers that be. You tread a thin line. A very thin line indeed.

As for me, I likewise congratulate you over freeing an innocent man. Sivell believes I have docked you a week's pay. I will dock you a month's pay and take the remaining balance out of your bollocks if you make me look in the smallest degree foolish. I haven't looked foolish since 1822.

Expectantly,
Chief of Police G. W. Matsell

I blew out a breath and tucked the note in my pocket. It would never do for him to barge into my office and see it in the dustbin. The next was from Piest, in angular writing slanting weirdly to the left.

Dear Mr Wilde,

I hear stirrings afoot, patriot, which disturb me greatly in mind. Since our escapade, I have myself largely eluded censure, but rumors grow apace regarding your own heroic role. I would be the lowest of dogs not to inform you of such. More cannot be said here, wariness is the handmaiden of courage, as you know, and I will impart to you greater detail at your earliest convenience. You know where best to find me, and as the reverse is untrue, I urge you to seek me out with all timely haste.

Best regards,
Jakob Piest

Ten seconds passed wondering whether Piest's warning should produce laughter or heart palpitations. Calling it a draw, I slid it next to Matsell's. Piest went on shift at ten, and I could find him somewhere along Chambers Street.

I cut south through the Tombs. The wind picked up when I

195

stepped beyond the shelter of thick granite walls, tunneling through the streets, keening like a wraith. I followed Leonard Street to Centre, pausing for the train to pass. It was brimful with passengers, its horses shaking the snow from their shaggy manes as they hauled the tram cars north.

In the cancerous epicenter of Ward Six, not far from my lodgings, I began my search. Twice over, I walked Mulqueen's route, once in each direction. Twice over, I endured the stench of Paradise Square – the heart of the Five Points, paved in shit of many origins and populated by the shades of what were once emigrants and blacks. A body lay sprawled beneath the bone-colored edifice of the Old Brewery that I at first took for dead, but merely suffered starvation and alcohol stupor. It was a mulatto boy of about eighteen. If he was lucky, he would survive and come morning pawn his shoes for another jug of spirits. If he wasn't, he would be in the ground the next day and not alone in that destination. His thin shirt and blue trousers were crafted of cotton, and he cradled a bottle of rum under his elbow.

You're making yourself insane, I admonished, walking along.

Frustration mounting, I commenced keeking into saloons. Mulqueen claimed not to drink, but that meant nothing. Bartenders are community emblems, and I sharply wished of a sudden to be one myself again. There's scarce any responsibility in pouring whiskey and bending an ear. Plenty of saloonkeepers I spoke with knew of Mulqueen, but it wasn't until I entered a long, low hall where an Irish lad scrambled after dinted ninepins for the bowlers that I learned anything useful.

'You want Uncle Ned's, Orange just south of Bayard.' The barkeep spat on his floor. 'Mulqueen's there, sure enough. If not *policing*, you understand me.'

I didn't entirely. But I had my suspicions. Some of the new star police spend their hours wearing grooves in the pavement. Waiting patiently for trouble. Some of the new star police go looking for trouble, demanding payments from unlicensed liquor salesmen, brothel madams, and faro sharks – anyone involved in illegalities who'd prefer to ante up than suffer arrest. One sits in a closet until he's wanted and then attempts to unravel mysteries with a woeful lack of skills.

I presumed Mulqueen's technique involved a system. One that furthered the Mulqueen cause, and the Mulqueen cause alone.

Uncle Ned's proved unprepossessing. Typical of the Five Points, though. Four bowed stairs before a peeling green door. The building was constructed of salvaged boards, of every thickness and color, cobbled together into walls. Gnawed husks from the hot-corn vendors were scattered helter-skelter to keep the stray pigs hale. Peanut shells and piss and ash and delicate new-fallen snow all trampled together, as is everything left in these streets.

Inside, though, was another story. The fire popped madly. Upon a small raised platform, a colored fiddler – shirt sopping, copper brow dappled with sweat – played a jig as if schooled by Hades direct for the purpose. It was enthralling. The walls and ceiling gleamed with whitewash, and above the sanded dance floor hung a broad wrought-iron chandelier packed with blazing tallow candles. As for the dancers careening about, I haven't words for the atmosphere of mingled desperation and joy they produced.

A uniformed British naval tar not yet dispossessed of his sea legs was attempting an Irish wedding dance. Laughing in fits whenever he fell. A dozen or so actual Irish, both red and black, spun about like dervishes. Clad in the colors of a kinchin's toy top, ending a grueling day's work with grueling play. I soon identified the hall's true source of income as the liquor shelves at the opposite end of the room. Dead Bowery rabbits and scarlet-shirted firemen sagged against the bar, cheeks blazing with liquor and song. A black chap with a pine-scented spruce beer strolled by, bobbing his braided head. Races of every hue surrounded me, including an Indian with a frock coat buttoned over buckskin trousers. Most patrons whirled about with feet tattooing rapturous rhythms. Others watched, entranced.

One reclined, presiding.

Mulqueen wasn't the only copper star present. He'd claimed the room's sole oaken bench and was flanked by his two roundsmen associates, men I'd once given collegiate nods when we'd spied the stars pinned to each other's jackets. And there Mulqueen sat – cigar in his mouth, glass of Croton water at his elbow – sampling what he supposed were the wares.

A colored girl of seventeen or eighteen years stood before him, eyes trained on her own forearm. Mulqueen's fingers crept steadily up it while he held her limp wrist in his other hand. The touch screamed possession and threat beneath a very thin veneer of lust. All the many people not looking at the bench did so in a studied, frightened fashion, as if avoiding the sight of a syphilis sore. The picture told me a story, clear as if it had been printed in the *Herald*.

Mulqueen uses his copper star to bully Five Points girls into bed with him.

My next thought was – admittedly – neither cautious, nor very considered. It took the form of a resolution and went about as well as most of my plans tend to go.

And I am going to do something about it.

CHAPTER FOURTEEN

*Of course the negroes form a large and rather controlling
portion of the population of the Points, as they bear
brutalization better than the whites, (probably from having
been so long used to it!) and retain more consistency and
force of character, amid all their filth and degradation.*

George G. Foster, *New York by Gas-light: With Here
and There a Streak of Sunshine*, 1850

'But I didn't bring my papers, sir,' the brown-skinned girl said to
the police officer who held her tethered by the forearm as if
she were a calf.

She wore an orange dancing dress of cheap nankeen and had
tied her thick black hair down in front with a purple cloth. Her
voice chimed out high and distinctly Southern – Georgia, or
thereabouts. She wasn't a New Yorker.

But neither was she an escaped slave, for that matter.

I don't understand the instinct that resides in men like Mulqueen.
The urge to rend something lovely until it is in tatters, and you
have accomplished a raw physical victory wholly of your own
making. Torn what was whole once. Sometimes I think it's mindless
behavior. Beastlike brutality of the sort of that left a Bible verse in
Lucy's skin. Other times I think it's a foul perversion of the drive

that led me to carve HENRY WILDE, SARAH WILDE, VALENTINE WILDE, TIMOTHY WILDE in the elm tree by the gate of our burned shell of a house in Greenwich Village. Something to stake my claim in time and place. Bleed out the grief. I'd been vicious with that penknife, stabbed at the tree as if it had wronged me. So either the trait of wanton destruction is animalistic or entirely human.

Just then, I didn't care.

'I never do carry free papers.' The girl's feet wavered back and forth. Debating whether allowing Mulqueen temporary use of her arm or ripping it away would be the faster route to escape. ''Cept when I leave town, for the roads aren't safe. You've got to believe me.'

'I'd like to be thinkin' you've all the proper free papers.' A smug gleam lit Mulqueen's brow, and his backward-tilting ears glowed pink, painted by the fire. He called to mind a ginger cat preening itself before the hearth. 'But your voice, my dear. 'Tisn't a *local* sound.'

Her lower lip trembled. 'When Dad bought his liberty from the Greens nigh two years gone, they sold me to him for half price. Only two hundred. They always thought kindly of him. Please let me go. My papers are at the house.'

'Maybe 'twould be quicker if you and I were to have a private interview, settle this matter between ourselves?'

'Stop touching her,' I said.

Mulqueen's smile soured. A few of the nearer dancers stopped dancing. The many-colored people not looking at the bench suddenly failed to look at the bench with much more absorbed concentration. The fiddler played on, jerking his elbow like a figure atop a music box.

'Mr Wilde,' Mulqueen greeted me. He didn't relinquish the girl's arm. 'And why should I do such a thing?'

'I told you to.'

The two other copper stars exchanged predatory glances. I'd no notion of their names. But one was small and piggish, almost infantile – native by his looks. The other was black Irish, pale as the whites of his cold, sober eyes, with a fist about the size of my head.

'Oh, to be sure, ye did,' Mulqueen reflected.

He forcefully flung her arm away, and she staggered back with a startled cry. The fiddler stopped. Then the dancers stopped, straining for breath.

Mulqueen's pale green eyes dragged over me. 'Do you mind tellin' me, Wilde, just who the fuck you think you are?'

'I need to ask you a few questions.'

'What if I don't find myself in much of a mood to be answerin'?'

I thought that over.

'Get out of here,' I said, turning to the girl. 'Run.'

She kept running right up until she was gone. That was the last pleasant experience I was to have for a spell.

'Now you'll be less distracted,' I noted.

What in hell are you doing, my head supplied. Unhelpfully.

Mulqueen stood. His fellow copper stars likewise rose. The one who looked liked an ancient scarlet baby was practically spitting at me, and the black Irish cohort stared greedily at the veins in my neck.

'Did those stray pigs outside look hungry to you?' the Irish fellow asked his countryman.

'They always do,' Mulqueen replied.

The bartender, at whom I hazarded a questioning glance, was colored. A little more than forty years old, with grizzled grey hair like a snug cap. His eyes burned brightly, a stark line etched between them. I looked him square in the face, and he nodded. And then, after a brief but blinding vision of Grace of the Millington household, the maid who'd been so very ardent about me *not* finding a nameless black chimney sweep, it all made a bit more sense. As did the golden rings adorning Mulqueen's fingers, and the watch chain, and – now I'd noticed it, or perhaps it was new – a small diamond tiepin.

'This is your regular game, isn't it?'

Mulqueen pursed his lips.

201

'You're in league with Varker and Coles,' I decided. 'Of course you are. Christ, it's so simple.'

'I'm not in *league* wi' anyone,' Mulqueen spat, 'though aye, our paths often enough cross. Varker and Coles see that runaways are returned. But bringing fugitives to justice is never a *game*, is it now?'

'Fugitives, my eye. What's your share of the take, when you turn in an alleged slave?'

'They're only *alleged* slaves to wee little nigger-loving aboli-tionists who sit on their arses at the Tombs until Matsell's prick wants servicing. To me, they're stolen property. And I a lawman, and all.'

Doing figures in my head, I'd soon enough calculated the economics. Extorting petty chink from stargazers and gambling hells wouldn't bring in nearly the money earned each and every time Mulqueen and his ilk collared a supposed refugee. I wondered how many other copper stars were in the same business, and I felt faintly ill.

'Advertisements for runaways in the papers usually offer twenty to sixty dollars reward,' I mused. 'Quite a sum. But if you captured a man and simply shipped him south and sold him – a healthy male slave is worth what? Six hundred dollars on the open market at the Capitol? Four hundred for a woman? More if she's pretty? Even if Varker gives you only ten percent of *those* figures, it makes for some thick honey.'

'What does this puppy want to ask you, Mulqueen?' the baby-faced copper star wanted to know.

'Hell if I can say as I care.'

I'd riled a bull. Mulqueen's nostrils pumped like bellows. Prudent dancers edged out the doors while the Bowery rabbits in the corner chuckled morbidly. Clearly making bets with the firedogs as to how quickly I was going to die.

'I wanted to ask about your anonymous warning of a disturbance the other day. In Ward Eight. My brother's rooms, a mile or so from your own rounds. Who was it posted you?'

My fellow copper star just smiled. That annoyed me.

'You,' I announced, 'are wearing the wrong badge.'

'And how so?' he questioned, smile widening.

'I thought men who raped penniless local women were generally of *British* extraction. Maybe you'd look better in a Royal Guards uniform.'

That was a mistake. An already enraged man doesn't require the single insult equating him with his worst enemy to be hurled gleefully in his face.

'We're headin' outside,' Mulqueen decreed. 'Ye'll be wearing a wooden coat by morning, Wilde.'

His cohorts beamed. My heartbeat all at once seemed to be emanating from my throat, a disconcerting sensation. So I ignored it. Meanwhile making an about-face and heading for the door to be pummeled into a mash.

The bartender, wringing out a slop rag, followed me with his eyes. 'Good luck,' he murmured. 'Get him against the wall if you can, and may the best man win.'

I managed a faint nod, knowing him a friend. And I don't mean to suggest that no measures against Mulqueen had already been taken inside Uncle Ned's. They had, and long before my arrival. There had been a hundred whispers I'd catalogued, dozens of glances. Several girls who'd entered and then silently backed out the door again due to unknowable signals.

No, the problem was that Mulqueen was a copper star. And we needed copper stars. And no one had yet gauged what to do with the crooked ones.

The late evening air gnawed the tips of my ears, and I tasted the leathery scent of coal smoke outside. Behind me, the Bowery boys and the engine runners trickled after us with the more aggressive of the Germans, ready to watch a sport that wouldn't have looked out of place in a Roman amphitheatre. Smallpox posters were plastered over the decrepit structure opposite Uncle Ned's, warning that symptoms begin with weariness, dizziness, chilliness, vomiting, and many other unpleasant complaints. Not a far cry from how I myself was feeling just then.

Supposing you do have smallpox, at least you'll be dead before you pass it along.

The bystanders formed a wide ring. Mulqueen, ten or so feet distant, had never looked healthier. He pulled a tin from his coat and lodged a plug of tobacco in his cheek. Then he replaced the tin and drew a biggish jackknife instead.

I soberly considered taking to my heels. But Mulqueen was going to fight me. One way or another. And I'm keener to catch a shiv in the heart after having landed a jawbreaker or two than find a shiv in my kidney when I report to work of a morning. Anyway, my blood was up, and I'd one advantage Mulqueen wasn't aware of. Yes, I was smaller than he was. I'm smaller than everyone. Yes, there were three of them and one of me. But Mulqueen wanted my guts unstrung like so much scarlet holiday ribbon for his personal trophy, so I'd likely be grappling with him alone. And I knew something he didn't.

After Valentine Wilde teaches me something, I am very, very good at it.

Six months after our parents died, Val commenced lessons in pugilism – not by request, mind – by periodically punching me in the ribs. I loathed him for it. I was heartsick and puny and livid, and I'd used to fight him like a rabid rodent, with head and feet and teeth. Much later I realized that I was never more than a bit scraped up after these interludes of higher learning. But the outcome of warding off an attacker who is larger and stronger than you hundreds of times is that you learn every filthy trick left out of the rule book.

Which might have been the point, come to think of it.

So I fight like a fork-tailed devil when riled. And just then I was in pretty warm rage.

I sidled warily round and got the stairs behind me. That earned me a sneer from Mulqueen. Then I reached back toward the ruined banister and yanked a spindle from the rotting wood. The end came free with a nail or two attached.

'Two dollars on the dwarf,' I heard from behind me.

'I'm five feet four,' I said irritably. 'That's hardly—'

I didn't have time to say anything after that.

Mulqueen charged with his head down, wielding the knife low and sidearmed. When I dodged him, I nearly slipped on greasy chicken bones, but managed to come up swinging with both fists on the makeshift club. His arms were longer but so was my weapon, and he eyed me as I danced away.

Keep moving. Mulqueen was clearly slower than I was, judging by the first volley. *If you can exhaust him, he'll make a mistake.*

Growling, he dove at me. This time I let him in closer before spinning away with torso hunched backward, just shy of his blade. My balance was off, but I swung the club anyhow and caught his calf with the nail.

Scattered applause followed first blood. Mulqueen came forward with teeth bared. Twice he swung, each thrust blocked by the end of my club. Then he lunged forward, catching the end of my makeshift weapon one-handed and wrenching my arm nearly out of its socket.

I gave him a fight over it, though. When I'd torn the banister free, I took the hardest swing I could and caught him where his neck met his shoulder.

Unfortunately, the beam splintered into so much kindling.

As for my opponent, a blow to the neck didn't vex him too sorely. He coughed, tossing the knife from hand to hand. Hoots followed my disarming, a high cackle from the piglike copper star.

'Now you're dead, little mouse,' Mulqueen snarled.

I hadn't any choice. With a crazed yell, I hurled myself at him.

His knife was up in an instant, flying toward my ribs. I was counting on that. A last-moment burst of speed into the circle of his arms allowed me to clamp his elbow with my left underarm, pinning it to my side as my hand gripped his tricep. He knew just what to do about that and immediately turned the blade in his grip down toward my kidneys. Planning to slide free and stab.

That was before I used his trapped arm as ballast. I put every ounce of strength I owned into swinging my other hand, landing a blow to his ear with my palm that reverberated like the crack of a rifle.

Mulqueen screamed and dropped the knife. Naturally he did. I'd probably burst his eardrum.

I didn't have the chance to celebrate, though. My own mazzard was mashed into Mulqueen's throat, watching the blood trickle down his skewed earlobe, the pair of us locked in an ugly dance too close for fists.

I drew my neck back. He spat the tobacco plug at my eyes, missed when I slammed my forehead into his collarbone hard enough to hear a subtle *crack*. For perhaps thirty seconds we grappled, bloodthirsty shouts deafening us. Then his knee slammed into my hip with swift, brutal speed. That freed him enough to land an elbow in my eye.

The world spun as if the Earth had bucked me free, and my back hit the frigid slush.

Gasping, I fought my way to my knees. My left eye refused to open, the traitor. The question of why I was breathing without any hands crushing my neck puzzled me. Mulqueen must have wanted a rush of hot innards and gone back for the knife. Surrounding screams ranged from *Stand up, you puny rabbit!* to *Get him against the wall!* to *Fetch the shiv and open him up!*

I pushed myself to my feet.

The black Irish copper star was handing the knife to his crony. Clenching his fingers around the handle, Mulqueen walked toward me. Blood from where I'd bitten my own tongue pulsed weakly into my mouth, a testament to the fragile way mortals are constructed.

You're going to die in Five Points of all places, I thought. Vaguely insulted.

Then I realized that someone was still shouting, 'Get him against the wall!'

And I finally savvied what he might mean by it.

If I was going to die anyhow, weaponless and half-blinded, it was worth a try. Cowering, I backed away from my fellow copper star.

I let my limbs tremble and I let my scraped hands shake. My whole posture turned to a limply drawn plea for clemency. I went about as boneless as a filleted trout as I retreated. That kittled Mulqueen, as I'd thought it would.

Twenty feet distant.

'Not so very cocksure now, are ye?' he sang out, advancing.

Slowly, I drew nearer to the filth-smeared wall of Uncle Ned's. I couldn't get Mulqueen against it, not positioned as we were, him bearing down with a knife.

But I could get him close.

'You've won, all right? For God's sake let me be.' Wrenching my greatcoat off, I held the wool before me like a shield.

Ten feet distant.

Mulqueen howled with laughter. He liked me begging. He liked me in a fight the way he liked his women in bed. Powerless and pleading for clemency. It was revolting.

'I'll let you be when your guts are steaming, wi' my boot ground into them.'

Two feet distant.

My back hit the wall. I crouched, flinging my greatcoat over my head like a kinchin afraid of the dark. I was far from a hundred percent certain that the voice demanding I get Mulqueen backed against Uncle Ned's intended the strategy I now suspected. But supposing I was wrong, I wouldn't have long to fret over my mistake.

If this tack fails to work, please don't allow Mercy or Val to hear I was slit open cowering like a rat.

A footfall crunched into the snow just in front of me.

Then a small point of pain seared into my upraised hand, the one holding my coat. A splash sounded. A window slammed shut above my head. Someone started shrieking, a garbled, agonized noise that pierced my head like a lance.

Flinging myself sideways, I landed hard on the snow. My coat hissed when it hit the wet. The reek of old kitchen grease, oil that had fried fish and pig knuckles and sheep guts and God knows what else besides countless times, had bloomed in the air. I thrust my right hand into soot-colored snow. The tiny oil burn dulled with shocking swiftness.

Mulqueen didn't fare so well.

He was flat on his back when I turned. The screaming had stopped. Bystanders flitted about, darting like so many hornets. A woman was sobbing, her shoulders cradled by a gentleman friend who gazed over her head in rapt disgust. When he pulled her aside, I saw my fellow copper star in broad view. Just as the smell of fried flesh reached my nostrils.

Then I wasn't crouched in the dung heap of Five Points anymore. I was downtown, seven months ago. The world was a water-ruined painting, blurred and somehow all the more nightmarish for lack of specifics.

You were happy. Or something similar. You were accustomed to what your life looked like. And then part of your face was missing, and since then you've never once felt anything other than a carnival freak.

And it hurt when it happened too. It hurt like all hell.

I lifted my head. The two copper stars Mulqueen ran with were rushing to pack snow about their friend's head and neck.

It wouldn't make a difference. I'd seen the cracked surface, red as a steamed apple and peeling backward from the gums. From the eye sockets. The jut of the Adam's apple.

I spat at the ground before my stomach began making its decisions without me. It was planning a bald play for independent living. Staggering to my feet, I craned my neck up at the window where the pot of hot oil had appeared. It was dark. The room was likely empty by now, the pot warming a quantity of soup. Belatedly, with a howl of rage, the pink-faced copper star rushed for the entrance to Uncle Ned's, meaning to vent his rage against dark-skinned skulls.

No one minded him. And I was dead certain he'd not find any blacks remaining. Only the closed window marked the silent wrath of that community. Its resourcefulness and its will.

'You shouldn't still be here,' the bartender said.

He spoke from inches away as I gazed numbly upward. I turned, startled.

'I think you just saved my life. So neither should you.'

'Right you are. Let's see about fixing that situation.' The line between his brown eyes had smoothed out.

My own eyes – or eye, rather, as the left was swollen shut – swept back to where Mulqueen lay in the mire, boots askew, the black Irish copper star shouting at the firemen for an ambulance. Two of them sprinted away. Mulqueen's breath had grown shallow, though his fingers yet twitched. The inelegant motions of a ruined body. Boiling oil had coated his head, his neck, his upper chest.

'It's only hours, if that, before this place is torched or far worse,' I realized. 'A white copper star attacked at a black establishment? There will be mobs if we're lucky. A riot if not. Either way, the Points will be hell on earth before morning.'

'That all depends.'

'Does it?'

'Yes,' he said, snugging up his collar. 'On whether the culprit is arrested. If the killer is locked up, a considerable number of people in these parts will rest easier.'

No words came to me. *A considerable number of people.* He was talking about his family, his friends. Hundreds of threads of deep love and light acquaintance spreading like a delicate net through his home, which unfortunately happened to be the Five Points. A net he'd knotted, rewoven. Battled for.

'And you've found the culprit. Haven't you?' he questioned.

I just breathed, staring at the man. His grey hair, his lined face now lax and peaceful, his neat wool collar and his dark rum-hued skin. My heartbeat had tightened to a stabbing ache.

'Please don't do this. I don't want to—'

'I don't give a tinker's damn what you want.'

'But why?' I needed to know. 'I mean, who?'

'That's fair. My niece Rosie,' he answered, nodding. 'She's yet in the city, thank the Lord. Though in a family way now, and the babe half Irish copper star. I was planning on poison, or maybe a pistol, but when opportunity knocks . . . and you're a fine fighter, thankfully. Now, go on with you. I don't calculate to stand around in the snow telling you your job. Make it loud and make it clear, Mr Wilde. Make it *count*.'

His hand, when I gripped it, was warm, the wrist strong from handling countless liquor bottles, the fingers rough with thousands of healed-over nicks and scrapes.

Very like mine.

I seized him by the arm, considerably less cruelly than we made it look, and shoved him against the wall. That had to look heartfelt on my part and humiliating on his. So I took him by the collar and shook. Not hard. Just visibly.

'You're under arrest. Suspicion of attempted murder,' I shouted.

All eyes turned to the pair of us.

'Is that the best you can do?' he scoffed quietly. Then he spat at my shoes.

So I forced him to his knees into the snow.

'Apologize,' I growled.

'I'd sooner apologize to a pig.'

I wondered what brand of weak-livered coward it made me, the fact I wanted nothing more than to beg him to stop. Wanted to curl up for good and all in a meadow where roots would grow over me.

'I'll have you over a sawhorse longing to die.'

His laugh echoed down the street. 'Burn in hell.'

Setting the toe of my boot between his shoulders, I kicked him face-first in the mud.

I pulled off my muffler. Satisfied by then, the bartender said nothing as I knotted the scarf about his wrists. I led him away through the crowd. Or he led me, probably. It wasn't a long journey – barely a block or two divided us from the prison. But I could scarce see, and he was in the lead, after all.

Later, when I wrote out the paperwork for his arrest at the Tombs, my hand began to burn again. A drop of oil about the size of a bean had landed on it. Watching my writing spread like a plague across the parchment, penning *The suspect has made a full confession, but acted entirely in the defense of Timothy Wilde, copper star badge 107,* I welcomed the ache in my skin as a distraction from the ache in my chest.

It didn't hurt nearly enough.

When I went home that night, Mrs Boehm was sitting at the table with a plate of sweet biscuits, sipping a small glass of gin as she paged through a magazine full of ladies' fashions and lurid scandals. The plain center part in her hair was imperfectly combed, and her skin seemed thinner than usual. I hoped nothing ailed her. She glanced up with a remark upon her lips that shriveled to nothing at the sight of me. I seem to have that effect on people far too often of late.

Equally wordless, I located the household laudanum bottle and soaked a clean rag with it. Pressing it to my hand, I sat down.

'I don't know if I can do this anymore,' I told my landlady.

Mrs Boehm subjected me to a close but gentle study. That of a botanist with a bloom, or a girl feeding leaves to a butterfly in a jar. Then she cupped her chin in her palm, her mouth curving down at its edges. The fingers of her other hand reached for my wrist and pressed briefly.

'Can anyone else, then?' she asked, voice rough.

'I don't think so,' I acknowledged.

'And the *this* you mean – must *this* be done?'

'Yes.'

'Then you will keep going.' Her wan blue eyes were fixed to my scar. The one on my face, that is. The one that matters. For once I didn't mind someone staring at it – her gaze is too soft to have any weight.

'Keeping going is terrible.'

'It is,' she agreed. 'That is why I admire you, Mr Wilde. It is much easier to stop.'

My single operative eye slid shut.

I thought about the fact that Tom Griffen (the bartender's name, apparently, was Tom Griffen) was unlikely to sleep that night, the first of God knew how many passed in the Tombs before I could free him. If I could manage to release him at all. I thought about being homeless – about the way it feels to fear sleep because your hands have gone numb, the sensation of drowning in darkness – and longed only to find Jonas Adams. Wherever he was. To find him and Delia, and make something warm again, when the world entire seemed to have turned so irrevocably cold.

After that, I even thought about Mrs Boehm's fingers on my wrist. The way they'd felt sanded smooth of prints, as if dough had refined them to a floury blank.

How long I sat thinking, likely half-concussed by Sean Mulqueen – the late Sean Mulqueen, I'd learned just before quitting the Tombs – is a mystery. But by the time I looked up again, she was gone, and the taper on the table had been allowed to gutter, drowning in its own pool of wax.

CHAPTER FIFTEEN

*The North, in many respects, does the bidding of the
South; they are Slave-hunters for their masters, the
Slaveholders.*

William M. Mitchell, *The Under-ground Railroad*,
1860

The following day, February 18, Lucy – whose name was of
paramount import and yet eluded me – was buried in the
African cemetery. The Reverend Brown performed her last rites in
a morning brittle with spider's-silk frost. Apart from George
Higgins and Julius Carpenter, few attended save for friends from
the Abyssinian Church. Julius sang a hymn of the exquisitely sad
sort, too ancient to trace, its origins forever obscured by the
numberless others who've used its chords to cradle them when
they are suffering.

Or so I heard secondhand.

I was in George Matsell's office, suffering another sort of torture
entirely, seated in a chair. George Matsell stared down at me, arms
crossed. Coolly dispassionate and carved from the same grey rock
on the same scale as the Tombs he presides over.

He took Mulqueen's death and my explanation of why Tom
Griffen ought to be set loose very quickly, if not summarily and

without further ado, in good stride. My chief's acceptance of what was doubtless a horrid scandal likely had to do with my face, which now boasted a cobblestone texture on the one side, and a swollen, purpling effect on the other. I made a pretty nice picture. So my attempted murder wasn't in question.

Thankfully, he'd plenty of other reasons to be peppery at me.

'So after I told you to keep your head down, you supposed it was a good idea to investigate Lucy Adams's death by visiting a saloon famous the world over for lewd dancing and assignations between open amalgamators?' he questioned.

When he put it that way, brows beetling and consonants harshly clipped, the argument that I am dense took on new weight.

'You care about amalgamation?' I couldn't help but wonder exhaustedly.

'My voters do. Explain yourself.'

'I was searching for Mulqueen and I found him. The rest just . . . happened.'

'And why did you require Mr Mulqueen?'

I worried at my bitten tongue, wondering if Val had made any mention to Matsell of a corpse in his sheets. Unlikely, after the trouble I'd gone to over transporting her. And the trouble Valentine had gone to over 'identifying' her.

'We've exposed a conspiracy, I think,' I replied with care. 'I believe that Mulqueen collared alleged runaways, not taking any trouble over who they were in fact, and turned them over to Varker and Coles. He practically admitted as much to me. Delia Wright and Jonas Adams had been kidnapped by the same individuals, and I thought there might be a connection.'

Matsell ruminated a bit, and then – At last, thank God, you're not sacked today, I thought – sat down in his wide desk chair.

'Are you suggesting that one of my copper stars spent the majority of his brief career at selling coloreds down South?'

'And made a tidy profit at it. You ought to look through his togs. He'd expensive taste in jewelry for a policeman, that much I can tell you.'

'And just what *aren't* you and your brother telling me?'

For an instant I thought his eyes twinkled. Then I informed myself sternly that I was going mad. Realizing that our chief had proven himself on multiple occasions to be a friend to both Wildes, however, and knowing my entire investigation to be built on a fraying tightrope, I decided to come clean. In an extremely limited sense.

'On the day Lucy Adams was murdered, Mulqueen visited my brother's rooms looking for a disturbance, claiming he'd been given a tip,' I answered slowly. 'You should know that Lucy Adams had just spent two nights at Val's for the sake of caution. I was looking for my brother when Mulqueen arrived. Neither of us found anything there. But it made no sense, sir. He ought to have been in Ward Six, and when I questioned him, he refused to answer me. And now he can't.'

'Yes, I can see how terribly inconvenient his death was for you.'

'I hope you know from looking at me that I'd not choose that specific fate for anyone deliberately. But he was a rapist and a slavemonger for a fact. I'm not weeping over him.'

Raising his brows in surprise, Matsell decided I'd a valid point and gestured for me to continue.

'The murder of Lucy Adams and the kidnapping of free blacks are related somehow,' I announced. 'But the pieces won't fit.'

Matsell rocked back in his chair, frowning. 'I need you to settle this before word of it reaches the press. You are right about one thing – any roundsman using his star as carte blanche to turn slave trader isn't worth the breath I'd waste in firing the wretch. I'll not tolerate New Yorkers of any color being snatched from the streets. Now, just where are you regarding the Adams murder?'

Drawing a long breath, I launched into deeper waters. The ones with undercurrents and riptides of a nastily political, dare I say *Democratic*, hue.

'Lucy Adams was Senator Rutherford Gates's lover. Possibly his wife, under an alias. Sir.'

George Washington Matsell looked as if he'd swallowed a

rancid oyster. I felt about the same and so sympathized with the man. In ten minutes I'd related the details, while my chief stoically absorbed them. Like a bloated spider suspended in his labyrinthine web.

'In my opinion, it comes down to whether they, in fact, married.'

'A point of salient interest, yes,' Matsell said faintly.

'I'm not so thick that I don't realize this is a nightmare from your perspective.'

'I . . .' Matsell grimaced in frustration, turning momentarily aside. 'Thank you. Even apart from the way things are fixed in Albany at present, and Senator Gates's quite key role as regards upcoming legislation, that . . . that is very bad news.'

My chief's voice was thunder-dark and thick with worry. I didn't blame him. Vices in and of themselves are almost badges of honor amongst the scoundrels of the political machines – you whored down the Bowery like a kitchen maid doing the marketing, you gambled away hundreds in rooms with locked doors and then earned it back in bribes the next morning, you drank enough champagne for your brains to feel they were melting come daybreak and then drove off the tremors with a hot mug of rum. If you were my brother, you hosted firemen's balls with a chime-voiced beauty on your arm and then spent the night tangled with a slender young man whose shirts smelled of your cigars. The existence of a Mrs Charles Adams wasn't a question of vice, though. It was a question of outrage.

Marriages matter to politicians. They reflect purpose and intent – are badges of respectability. Those wives have sweet smiles and domestic accomplishments, have memorized poetry and pianoforte airs, can quote the Bible while mixing a deadly whiskey punch for the lads. For Democratic Senator Rutherford Gates to have married an African and then lied about it would have been spitting in the eye of every principle of civic decorum we hold dear. And when principles are spit upon in New York, nothing is resolved with harsh words or formal reprimands. The populace makes certain that traitors to *the way things are done* will be punished with brass knuckles and brickbats, by proxy if not in person.

Opening a drawer, Matsell flipped through a daybook. I glimpsed several political fund-raisers, dozens of Party meetings. 'Rutherford is up for re-election in the spring. And when Silkie Marsh's involvement is considered . . . you're certain she was paid to testify for Varker and Coles?'

'On multiple occasions.'

Chief Matsell sighed bleakly, eyes on his memorandums. I'd no hardship divining his thoughts. Yes, Matsell and Val and I are aware Silkie Marsh is a conscienceless aberrance of nature. But she's plush enough lining for Party pockets that trumpeting the fact without any evidence would have made the star police look either mad or ineffectual. No one else knows her as an animated cancer. Or if they do, they're mum about it. So crossing her is, in a word, problematic.

When Matsell looked up, his eyes were steely. 'Mr Wilde, I need you to grasp that you do not make it easy for me to keep you employed. Don't suppose Party headquarters is unaware of the abolitionist policeman who invades courtrooms and slavers' dens. In fact, as a personal apology to me for my trouble, you are attending the Democratic Party's gala ball on Saturday the twenty-eighth of February. And you'll look as if you're enjoying it. That's a direct order.'

My expression must have turned an unlikely combination of mulish and appalled, because Matsell began to laugh.

'Welcome to my world, in which one must retain the favor of one's employers. Solve this crime, report to me and me alone, and in the meanwhile, do not harass Coles and Varker, do not bully Rutherford Gates, do *nothing* of which your brother would not expressly approve. Captain Wilde comprehends that milk comes from cows, eggs from chickens, and police funding from politics.'

I turned to go, seething.

'And Mr Wilde?' I paused midstride. 'Tom Griffen stays where he is. After you solve this case, perhaps I'll change my mind. Who can say?'

'You – are you holding a man hostage to keep me in line?' I stammered.

'No. I am holding a confessed murderer behind bars to keep you in line.' Smiling coldly, Matsell adjusted his wide grey lapel. 'It's going to work too. That's the wonder and the beauty of it. Good day.'

I found myself on the other side of Matsell's door, a thousand prickling barbs lodged under my skin as if I were a straw man hoisted on a stake to frighten away the crows. But Party or no Party, there was work to be done. I'd reached the echoing staircase at the end of Matsell's corridor when I encountered a welcome surprise – the cannonade of mighty boots preceding him, grey hair streaming in lanky will-o'-the-wisps.

Mr Piest came to an ungainly halt upon the landing. 'Thank heaven,' he exclaimed. 'They told me you'd be with Matsell. Are you all right?'

'Just a bit dented.'

'I heard about Mrs Adams. I was very sorry over it. Mr Wilde, I have recently burgled your office.'

Descending the stairs, I joined Piest, who looked more than usually depraved. His thin hair obviously hadn't been combed in days, streaming about his shoulders in a ragged mane, and his eyes were bulging out of his chinless mazzard. Having clapped him on the arm, I awaited more conversation. Not having had much luck with the previous statement.

'I've been searching for you everywhere,' he said querulously. 'It's too late now, of course, but I swear I did my best. I tried to write you as well, but you were deeply embroiled in—'

'I'd have come to find you last night if Sean Mulqueen hadn't decided to kill me, but what in God's name are you talking of?'

He deposited a quantity of bills in my hand. The exact balance of my reward from the Millington business, which had been locked in my desk drawer. Then he trotted back down the stairs the way he'd come.

'Perhaps, Mr Wilde, it would be better simply to show

you. Though it pains me, as a fellow copper star. It pains me very much.'

'What does?' I asked, alarmed.

But he only shook his thistledown head.

We'd soon reached my mouse hole. About a dozen copper stars murmured in its doorway, peering within by turns, and the sight sent a fresh swell of worry through me. Mr Connell, an Irish roundsman with a square head, scarlet hair tied back in a neat knot, and a strong taste for dog races, loudly cleared his throat when he spied me and the rest fell silent. I like Connell tremendously. We both read the *Herald* back to front every morning and often share a copy for economy, and he'd once told me a series of limericks that were so bawdy I still found myself smirking at odd moments.

'It's nary any mystery who's done it, Mr Wilde,' Connell said. 'Whether we can make them pay for it – 'tis another affair entirely, I'm afraid.'

I elbowed my way into my office. And promptly stifled a gasp.

It was thorough work, whoever had done it. The chair and the little desk were strewn about like so much hurricane wreckage in a childish display of wanton destruction guaranteed to chafe my hide. I'd dragged the desk with Piest's help out of a back room at City Hall. Its shards glared up at me accusingly.

That was nothing compared to the rest of the room, though.

Val's company taught me most of the filthy slang that exists in the American tongue. But the heights of profanity someone had attained when decorating my walls with scarlet paint set a new standard. The whitewash was covered with invective so hateful it burned my eyes. The word NIGGER-LOVER, and the consequences of being a nigger-lover, seemed thematically paramount. Various sexual acts of a nature distasteful to me personally were suggested for my final hours on this earth, before I was to be strung up by the neck or possibly burned to death. The author – *no, authors, two styles of writing, one generally written lower on the wall* – wasn't entirely consistent regarding how I was to be slaughtered.

That didn't matter. The effect was still alarming.

Resting on the ruined desk was a kinchin's stuffed doll. A hideous disfigurement had been painted over its face, but that pointed detail was secondary to the fact it had been pinned to a board through its torso.

'All right, move along with you all,' came Mr Connell's voice. 'Ye've seen Wilde's office and it's better than a trip to Barnum's. Enough. Kildare, if you could stay a moment? We'll have to plan out what to do.'

Feet shuffled. A low whistle or two pierced the air. Moments later, only Piest, Connell, and Kildare remained.

'You knew this was going to happen? How?' I questioned when I registered Piest's hand on my shoulder. 'Why—'

'Mr Wilde, may God strike me dead if I had known what they planned and failed to tell a brother in arms of the danger. No, on my honor, I did not. But I was in the common room, and heard snatches of a conversation, and . . . and you were not here. I could not be sure of myself. I wrote you the note and I burgled your desk. Better to take precau—'

'Thank you. Who was it?' My voice had thickened to a nasty tarlike consistency.

Piest's grip on my shoulder flexed harder. 'I've already found a supply of whitewash, Mr Wilde, and we all of us would be happy to—'

'Bugger whitewashing, I want to know who did this.'

'That the men in question were planning *something* I am certain, but that they actually enacted—'

'Oh, sure enough, they were simply palaverin' over teaching Wilde a lesson, and then by complete coincidence, someone else broke in,' Mr Connell sniffed.

Mr Kildare, the highly competent roundsman whose beat bordered mine when I'd trudged in circles for sixteen hours a day, tapped his fingers against the door frame. ''Tisn't as certain a thing as ye'd like to think, Connell. Piest is right. More than one person has cause. Wilde isn't exactly popular.'

'He's not *unpopular* either. Friendly enough fella, and a good heart and all. Just . . . folk are a wee bit leery. He not bein' a Democrat, and us loyal Party scrappers to a man.'

'There's more to it than that, by Jesus.'

'To be certain. On account o' he's exceptional.'

'*Favored*, some would say.'

'Only the petty sort.'

'Will someone for the love of God tell me who wrote *Wilde sucks nigger cock* on my wall?' I exclaimed. 'Here, why don't I start? One of them is only a bit taller than I am and left-handed, and the other five feet eight or nine and probably born in Ireland, since *indorser* is slang for a molley only in the British Isles and in flash it means—' I snapped my fingers. '*Oh*. Mulqueen's friends,' I realized. 'The rabbits he ran with in the Five Points. They must have been doubly eager to be about this business after last night. Who are they?'

I ground to a stop with all of them staring at me, the Irishmen baffled and Jakob Piest beaming as if at a child performing a complicated aria before family guests.

'My name is Virgil Beardsley,' came a smoothly rounded voice. 'And this is Mr James McDivitt.'

Whirling, I saw the formidable black Irishman from the night previous – whose name was apparently McDivitt – standing beside Beardsley, the overgrown tot with the perfectly round face. They stood just beyond my door. Evidently having awaited my arrival. Glaring at me as if a man could peel the skin from another's face with a withering expression alone, not needing cooking oil.

'You destroyed my office,' I observed.

'You don't know that. *Someone* did,' Beardsley returned. 'And *someone* ought to be given a medal, if you ask me.'

'There's to be a ceremony for Sean Mulqueen at St Patrick's in the morning, sharp of nine, and a hero's send-off we'll give our countryman. Ye'll be present, I trust?' McDivitt asked, shifting his attention to the other men in the room.

Mr Kildare shifted his feet. 'Them as can, McDivitt, them as can.'

'Them as have Irish blood in their veins will turn out for a patriot dead at the hands of a crazed colored assassin. I wonder,' he added, 'if we might have a tiny word with Wilde here? Alone, like. Mr Wilde, you're coming with us.'

'He is doing nothing of the kind,' Piest declared.

I'd have found some choice words myself for McDivitt and Beardsley, for the scoundrels who'd defiled the only working space I'd ever been able to call my own with any truthfulness. But to my shock, Piest, Connell, and Kildare now blocked my view of them in a tightly spaced wall. Arms crossed, shoulders thrown back. Looking ready – eager, even – for a fight.

It rendered me entirely tongueless. That sharing a newspaper and flask, or a difficult job and a common desire to make our city a bit safer, cemented men together. That I'd never been in a class at university, or attended a church, or joined a gang, or run with firedogs – and yet here were people who preferred me alive. Other than my family. When I hadn't asked for help and couldn't pay them a red cent for it.

The prospect was frankly dizzying.

'We'll say good day, then,' Connell declared to Beardsley and McDivitt. 'To see the pair o' you – mourning as you are, and Mulqueen not even in the ground, may God rest him. We'd nary dream o' taxin' you further. Go see to the plans for his wake.'

'And if we've a different agenda?' Beardsley growled.

'It's Wilde's wake I'm looking forward to, to be sure,' McDivitt added.

A tiny, hard-edged *click* sounded. Paler than a rifle bolt, unmistakably a small hand pistol being cocked.

'I hereby declare that I am drawing a deadly weapon, and one I do not intend to use unless my hand is forced!'

Mr Piest, in a development that unknit my muscles from my bones and left me gaping, had pulled a small and extremely ornate gold-plated gun from his coat. The weapon seemed half of a dueling-pistol set, supposing fashionable French heiresses with tiny puppies in their laps require dueling pistols. He aimed it at the ceiling, his face tucked even farther back into his neck than was usual. A squeamish expression. It was clear as glass he didn't like touching the thing.

'You have a *gun?*' I demanded witlessly.

'Oh, praise mother Mary, that sorts us,' Mr Kildare said, well satisfied. 'McDivitt and Beardsley, stand against either side o' the corridor, if you would. We are leaving.'

They did as they were told, backing away with loathing on their faces. Connell and Kildare exited first, then myself, and finally Piest. Looking for all the world as if he were wielding an enormous scorpion and didn't much care for the sensation.

'Say your prayers, Wilde,' Beardsley called after me.

I don't generally have any. But the suggestion wasn't without merit.

The four of us made for the nearest exit, earning plenty of questioning looks from clerks and copper stars and lawyers with powdered hair. By the time it occurred to me that it must have seemed I was being kidnapped by a wrinkled Dutchman, we were outside in the thin, wintry air.

'Mr Piest.' I caught him by the elbow. His gangly limbs were stiff, hair writhing in the faint wind. 'They aren't following.'

Lowering the pistol, he heaved a deep sigh.

'Why do you have a gun that could double as a Russian samovar?' I wanted to know.

Piest chuckled, shoving it deep in his threadbare frock coat. 'I found it this morning. Arrested the fellow too. I simply haven't returned it yet.'

'Is it even loaded?'

'I don't know. Firearms agitate me, I confess it freely. How does one check?'

Connell was howling with laughter by this time, Kildare chuckling as he rubbed at his side-whiskers. Stifling a smile, for Piest was reddening, I cleared my throat.

'Listen, I wasn't expecting you fellows to . . .' To my dismay, I felt a blush creeping up the back of my neck and began again. 'That is, you needn't have taken my part in there, and it was . . . thank you,' I finished, giving up on a bad job.

Kildare shrugged. 'Mulqueen was a right bastard, McDivitt a dumb beast hitched to his cart, and Beardsley . . .'

'Beardsley is a walking arsehole,' Connell finished.

Piest appeared dumbfounded. 'Mr Wilde, you wear the badge of the star police with the utmost honor, and I personally consider it much to my own credit that I was able to assist in any way. Despite my . . . reluctance when it comes to weaponry that may or may not explode.'

'Ye may wish to give the Tombs a bit o' distance, mind,' Connell advised, frowning.

'We'll show Matsell your office,' Kildare added. 'He'll never mind you keepin' snug for the time being.'

I stared up at the Tombs from under the brim of my hat. It's a savage place, really. Sweltering in summer, frigid in winter, reeking perpetually of filled-in swamp and unfiltered despair. Delivering people into its clutches always wrenches my guts wrong, and it's a seven minute walk at a ready clip to buy a decently brewed cup of coffee. Mine, though. The Tombs was *mine*. I felt quarantined, excluded, and wanted very badly to make someone pay for it. I knew just the proper scapegoat too. I shook hands with my colleagues. Putting some warmth in it, for they'd just proven themselves a set of admirably square fellows.

'Take care, Mr Wilde,' Piest called after me gravely. 'Be on your guard and contact us at once if you require any assistance. You'll do nothing rash?'

'Of course not,' I returned, marching through the ivory-hued winter morning in the direction of Silkie Marsh's bawdy house in Greene Street.

CHAPTER SIXTEEN

Nothing delighted the mistress so much as to see her suffer, and more than once, when Epps had refused to sell her, she has tempted me with bribes to put her secretly to death, and bury her body in some lonely place in the margin of the swamp.

Solomon Northup, *Twelve Years a Slave*, 1853

A portrait of Silkie Marsh hangs in her foyer above a potted fern with leaves as fragile as a half-remembered dream, and I looked over it as I entered. She wears an emerald dress in the oil study, lying on a simple black divan, ethereal blonde hair falling about her shoulders, her eyes fixing the viewers with breathless anticipation. The painting is a flawless copy. That isn't because the artist was a genius, though he was certainly competent. But unlike most painters, who require both poetry and skill in order to invest their subjects with lifelike animation, he had an easy job of it.

There isn't any soul residing behind Silkie Marsh's eyes to paint. So the likeness is more or less exact.

In her parlor, I studied myself in the floor-length Venetian mirrors that line her walls. I didn't look too well. Chest tight and lips furious and eye still swollen shut. A girl of sixteen or seventeen was reading a novel in one of the armchairs, its purple upholstery rich as the petals of spring irises. Glancing at the copper star, she bit her lip in distress.

'I don't mean you any harm,' I assured her. 'But tell me truthfully – how old is the youngest person employed here at present?'

'I think Lily's fifteen,' she murmured.

'No kinchin?'

She shook her head.

'Good. Please tell your madam Timothy Wilde wants a word.'

I hadn't long to wait. Silkie Marsh appeared within three minutes, wrapped in a red-velvet dressing gown with hints of rose-hued satin keeking through the gaps. Hair braided in a long plait down the side of her neck, lovely face affecting blank curiosity.

'Why, Mr Wilde, what an unpleasant surprise.' She went to the carved sideboard next to the pianoforte and poured a pair of brandies. 'Are you here to stampede through my rooms in a misguided search for kinchin, as you did last time? I assure you, the exercise is unnecessary. I have learned the value of hiring girls who own greater experience in the art of pleasure. Would you care for a sample?'

'I'd care to know what the hell is going on.'

She passed me the snifter, which I took. I needed it. And I don't fear her harming me, not directly – she's vowed to ruin me, but that wouldn't prove much entertainment for her if I weren't around for the ordeal. Her eyes with their narrow circle of clear blue within the hazel lingered on my face.

'I wonder who's given you a beating,' she said pleasantly.

'No, you don't.'

'Oh, Mr Wilde.' She laughed, an effortlessly musical sound. 'You've always been far too clever for a simple girl like me. You're right. The late Mr Mulqueen appears to have made a thorough job of it. He was quite the model of a copper star, wasn't he? So dedicated to his work.'

I went to the chair the stargazer had been occupying and sat.

'And how is the eccentric Miss Underhill faring overseas?' she asked softly, reclining on the settee and swirling the liquor cradled in her bone-china hands.

My head snapped back a fraction. That disgusted me plenty. Because I ought to have been expecting the question. The one Silkie Marsh knew would mortify me, calling to mind as it did my first foray into the brutish destruction of a woman's privacy.

I'd discovered Mercy there the previous summer, the night her father burned her novel to ash. She'd hidden away in one of Madam Marsh's back bedrooms. In a gentleman's company. Well, I can hardly say *gentleman*, since no gentleman would demand such favors in return for the money she needed to escape the cascading ruin of Reverend Underhill's mind. As for me, I'd played the territorial canine baring its little yellow teeth, ruining trouser legs and acting a tragic nuisance. The realization that the woman you love is as worldly as you are ought to be shocking – according to spinsters and newspaper moralists. But I grew up in the mud. I'm no clerk with a dry little bottle-brush moustache wanting a silent mouse to cook and scrub and lie still for me. Why I'd supposed Mercy free from the most predictable desire imaginable is outside my own reckoning.

What I do understand is that I treated her shamefully when she needed me most. An atrocity tailor-made to knock me windless just thinking of it. So of course Silkie Marsh had brought it up.

She ran a finger along the lip of her glass. Waiting me out. Head tilting gently, mouth pointedly not smirking at me. As if she'd decided to be *kind*. Meanwhile, my patience was worn to a tender nub, and my options limited, and we were not discussing Mercy Underhill.

'Whatever game is in play here, you're behind it,' I said. The expression of sad patience remained. 'You've connections to Gates through Party ties, to Varker and Coles through money, and you seem to know all about Mulqueen's doings as well. My career has taken quite the plunge since this began. You're terribly pleased by that, I imagine. And when I say *game,* I mean exactly that – we're all tin soldiers for you to smash into one another.'

'You give me immense credit for being a master puppeteer.' She made *puppeteer* sound complimentary. 'Are you here to congratulate me, then?'

'I'm here to question you. And you're going to tell me the truth.'

'Why should I do such a thing?'

I leaned forward. 'Because you'll enjoy it. Just like you've savored watching me bleed.'

She sipped her spirits, lashes lowering on an exhale when the brandy slid down her throat, looking as if I'd just kissed the hollow at the base of her neck. A glimpse of the golden glow of pleasure the men who bought her were allowed to see. But I was getting the genuine and not the fabricated article. I don't know whether or not Silkie Marsh enjoys renting out passion. I can't imagine she possibly could, though she's rich enough to pick and choose her partners. But she as sure as politics is crooked relishes games. Particularly when she's the stick and I the spinning hoop crashing along the thoroughfare.

'Here's what I think,' I mused. 'I think that when I ruined your business selling corpses of stifled kinchin, you wanted a new source of income.'

She inclined her head, waving her snifter under her nose.

'Varker and Coles offered to pay you to wrongly identify kidnapped blacks. There's an enormous amount of money in it. Mulqueen provided the copper star presence and helped to capture the merchandise.'

'All true,' she said sweetly. 'You're really doing very well so far. Pity you had to drag your magnificent brother into such a sordid matter.'

She'd meant to bait me and nearly succeeded. But it was actually an opening. I took it.

'Pity he's aware you're behind it all. It hasn't seemed to endear you to him. Do you know, I have never once in my life seen him turn down a free fuck.'

Her eyes turned instantly to glass. Not with moisture, but with a hardness like polished crystal. I could see myself reflected in them, being torn oh so slowly into ribbons.

Now keep talking, I willed her silently. *And tell me something. Anything.*

Silkie Marsh chuckled gently, unwinding her slender legs. 'It's sweet really, how often you speak of your brother, Mr Wilde. But you actually want to know about Lucy. Don't you? You want to know how she died. I do assume that you know *where* she died, though not many do.'

My breath seized.

Of course she knew. *Of course.* She was behind it all, must always have been behind it, had been the author of the most putrid narratives I'd ever learned in my life, and for all that she wanted Valentine back, she wanted me crucified and then resurrected so she could do it again. I'd a horrible sensation that everything I touched from then on would crumble and decay, that I was a plague-ridden stranger in the midst of a healthy town.

'How generous of your brother to offer his rooms as a haven. Valentine is nothing if not predictably gallant where beauty is concerned.' Acid bled through the creamy tone, but an instant later she was composed again. Gleeful, even. 'You're perfectly right, Mr Wilde, what fun. I'm enjoying this *tremendously*.'

The blood quickened in my veins. Impossibly, my scheme was actually working. Silkie Marsh so enjoys tormenting me that simply paying her a call was illuminating the conspiracy in sharp flashes of lightning in the darkness. Glimpses. If I could only get the right angle on the landscape, I could learn everything.

'Just a moment. You didn't kill Lucy – is it Wright, or Adams?' I amended.

'That question is impossible to answer.'

Surely it wasn't, but I let that go. 'You never murdered her. You're not strong enough for that kind of force.'

'How wonderful to see that you need not attribute *every* heinous act on earth to me.'

'Oh, it was your doing. Just not your hands.'

She sighed, smoothing her fingertips over the pink satin lining the gap in the dressing gown at her breast. Lips half-parted. Looking for all the world like a lazy diva being pleasured by a suitor.

'Who did your dirty work for you?' I asked lightly. 'My money is on Sean Mulqueen.'

'Poor Sean – I shall miss him. He was very useful to Seixas and Luke, and you know them to be friends of mine. One is upstairs, as a matter of fact.'

'I'm not, darling. You seemed sure enough agitated when you left. I was worried over you.'

My head snapped to the side as Seixas Varker approached us. Wearing an expensive robe that didn't fit him – probably had never fit any man who'd been forced to throw it on in a heated moment – and freezing in horror at the sight of me.

Silkie Marsh forestalled any insult I might have lobbed about their sleeping together by winking at me in a roguish fashion and then smiling at Varker adoringly. But suddenly I couldn't manage to pay Madam Marsh quite so much attention. I've read her cover to cover already. She's constructed out of porcelain and rot – exterior flawless, interior remarkably uncomplicated. Money, power, and vengeance are all she knows.

Varker, though. I wondered about Seixas Varker. All his high rhetoric about *civic duty*, about saving runaways from our heartless streets. He'd been smug but earnest. As if convincing himself it were true. That half smile, his terror of physical harm, the way he carried himself as if always vaguely afraid of falling. Sins are only burdensome to people with scruples, and I suspected Varker owned an inconvenient conscience he'd long been smothering. He was so repulsed by his own mortality, so averse to risk. His diseased attempt at serving justice hung so wrongly from his shoulders that the man was grotesque at first sight. Here was a God-fearing slave catcher, I reasoned, one with an appetite for wealth and an easy means to come by it, who'd no idea where he'd wake up when the Reaper divorced him from his plump hide.

'My word, but you're an unlooked-for nightmare,' Varker gasped. His wrist was still braced with wood and pale linen. 'I suppose you're here to break other pieces of me as yet left intact?'

'Oh, Seixas,' Silkie Marsh purred. 'That isn't Mr Timothy Wilde's forte. Just look at him. You're thinking of Valentine. But he really ought to be leaving now.'

'Where are Delia and Jonas?' I questioned, approaching the slave catcher. 'The pair you kidnapped. Where are they now?'

He backed away smiling, pudgy frame all aquiver. 'Why in heaven's name should you think—'

'Answer the goddamn question.' My fist had closed over the crossed lapels of his dressing gown before I quite realized how it had arrived there. 'I want them back. They don't belong to you.'

'My goodness. Anyone would think they belonged to *you*,' I heard coolly stated from behind me.

Varker's back struck one of the Venetian mirrors an instant later. The glass shivered violently but failed to shatter. I closed my eyes, impelling rational thought by sheer force of will.

This isn't about you. None of it is about you. Calm the fuck down before you ruin it all.

When next I looked at Varker, sweat trickled down his neck like tears from a frightened kinchin. I hated him for it. Even as I was bruising his sternum, my fist lodged against his damp, doughy chest.

'I presume you took Julius Carpenter simply because he's a nuisance to you,' I said. 'Was there another reason?'

'No, no. I swear it. What other reason did I *require*?' he whined. 'That wretched boy costs me more time and trouble—'

'Then I'm going to ask you once more where Delia and Jonas are.'

'And then you're going to leave,' Silkie Marsh added, as if to a recalcitrant child. 'Do answer him, Seixas, he's growing very tedious.'

'But I don't know!' he cried. 'Do you suppose I wish to encourage you to – to abuse me in this manner? Do you think I *want* to be mauled like a savage, when I could simply tell you the whereabouts of two niggers? I *don't know*. I wish I did, so that you'd consider unhanding me.'

Around then, I let him go and he slid down to the floor. For all I knew, every word spoken to me inside that brothel had been a calculated lie. Strand after strand thrown out, every line woven into a net to drag me under. But I was either going to be the sort of copper star who crushed wrists to get what I wanted or the sort who didn't.

Anyhow, Varker was telling the truth. Or so the chalky, fear-dulled whites of his eyes told me.

Hardly closer to my goal and sick at heart over it, I headed for the front door. Steps sounded behind me. Soft, prettily measured steps. The footfalls of a dancer or a devil. When I'd crossed the threshold into the blinding midday sunshine, I turned back to Madam Marsh.

'Only tell me *why* Lucy was killed,' I said.

'Is that question a torment to you, Mr Wilde?' she asked. Her fairness of hair and of complexion were radiant in the reflected snowlight, hovering above scarlet velvet as supple as the best French wine.

'Yes,' I admitted. It was a thorn in my side, tight skinned and swollen.

'How marvelous,' she concluded, shutting the door.

Sitting on a bench in the long, narrow hallway of the Catholic Orphan Asylum that afternoon, hands resting in my lap, I allowed my mind to wander. Flat-faced saintly icons surrounded me. I wondered whether the Catholic God actually preferred His martyrs ornately adorned following their gruesome deaths. And whether the martyrs themselves might find it all rather superfluous. I'd just conjured an image of Lucy Adams in the blue garb of a Madonna, a shimmering halo illuminating the brutal purple neck bruise and the still more brutal inscription carved into her chest, when thankfully I was interrupted.

'Mr Wilde? Are you all right?'

Bird stood before me, her small square face aghast, with a set of schoolbooks tucked under her arm. She wore shallow-necked blue serge with vertical black stripes, and it made her freckles stand out against her pale skin like pink pepper on an egg.

'Don't worry a bit over it. I'm fine.'

'But can you *see*?'

'More or less. And anyhow, I won.'

'Why have you a new greatcoat?'

Explaining that my previous greatcoat had been drenched in rancid cooking oil would have been about as pleasant as telling her that my previous jacket had burned in my chief's fireplace. So I refrained. Anyway, the new garments were better than the ones I'd bought when penniless. I pulled open the greatcoat's dark green collar.

'See? I've a new jacket too. There's reward money to be had, on occasion. I'll be a rum-togged swell before you know it.'

She sat down beside me. As usual, I came blessedly uncoiled a bit in her company. And, as usual, we began by not saying anything. It suits us.

A cluster of girl kinchin passed us by, giggling and tugging one another's threadbare sleeves, chanting an ancient rhyme about counting crows. As much a spell as a number game, and one I'd always found sinister.

One for sorrow,
Two for joy,
Three for a girl,
Four for a boy.
Five for silver,
Six for gold,
Seven for a secret, never to be told.

A silly, harmless incantation, I grant, but given my all too present predicament, even the thought of *blackbirds* raised my hackles. *Blackbirder* in flash patter, though I'd never ruminated much over the word, was a cruel term for a crueler practice. And

233

an apt one. As the high, reedy voices faded, they left a bitter feeling in my pate, an ache all along the edges of my unsolved problem. Quelling a dark sigh, I directed my attention to the Bird I had actually managed to protect on occasion, the one at my elbow.

'Who came at you on the muscle?' she wanted to know at length, nudging my ankle.

'I don't think you're meant to speak flash,' I reminded her.

'I don't think I'm meant to have visitors with black eyes.'

Smiling, I replied, 'A man I had an argument with.'

She slammed her books on the bench in an exasperated huff. That was fair, I reasoned.

'Fine. He wanted to capture a black woman and sell her for a slave. And I objected.'

Leaning back against the wall, she kicked idly at the air with worn brown leather boots. 'Father Sheehy says to the nuns when he thinks we're not minding him that slavery is an abomination against the soul. That it'll cause a war. Will there be a war?' she asked softly, an unsettled line appearing between her eyes that was regrettably all too familiar to me.

I hesitated. Picturing Bird Daly in the midst of a metropolis turned battleground, Manhattan occupied by a callous army who took what they wanted when they wanted it, as had happened during the Revolution. It rattled my skull considerably. George Washington Matsell wasn't a cold-hearted Democratic bully, I realized. There were just one or two people, maybe more, whom he cared for very much. That was all.

'I hope there won't be a war, but Father Sheehy is right. Slavery has to be ended.'

'Why are there slaves in the Bible, in that case?'

'I'm no expert. But I don't think God much cares for everything that happens in that Book.'

Bird shifted to peer up into my face. 'Are you a Catholic or a Protestant? You're not Irish, so I s'pose you must be a Protestant, even if you are a dead rabbit.'

Linking my fingers, I meditated on this question. Kinchin, I have been learning, greatly tax the adult brain. At twenty-eight, I could barely keep up with Bird. By the time I was forty, I'd never savvy a word she said. And while I could certainly understand why she thought me a dangerous sort, I'd never asked myself whether I was Protestant or not. The whole query was pretty confounding.

'I'm just a copper star,' I told her. 'God and I get on fine, but we don't palaver much. We're . . . neighborly.'

'Eamann who lives over in the boys' wing says that the Negroes aren't the same as humans – that they're thicker in the head, like a monkey or a horse, and that means that they're happier as slaves.'

'Well, Eamann is repeating something told to him by a ripe idiot. Colored people are people. Would *you* be happier as a slave?'

A brief silence fell.

'Don't be warm at me,' Bird whispered thickly. 'I've never spoken with a colored person. I didn't know.'

Glancing down at her, I mentally kicked myself seven or eight times over. Bird was never fragile. But she went from working a profession I wouldn't wish on anyone to living for a month with Mrs Boehm and myself to being an orphaned asylum student – and all in a summer thunderstorm spell of time. It makes for a volatile personality. She used to fling teacups, ready bottles, anything breakable within smashing distance. Still does on occasion. On the night before she'd moved the short distance to the orphanage, she'd destroyed Mrs Boehm's sole cobalt vase whilst sobbing that we only wanted to be rid of her. And each separate time she sees me again, a little wave of glad surprise passes through her from head to toe. In short, our problems weren't about to be solved by my turning snappish enough to make her cry.

'I'm sorry, Bird. Of course you haven't. You lived in a house, and then were hidden in another one, and now you're at a Catholic school. You ought to be warm at me and not the other way around.'

I think I'd have heard her response better if her face hadn't

235

suddenly been mashed up against my vest. My arm fell around her shoulders in alarm.

'Bird?'

She remained there, half under my coat lapel – shaking, muscles knotted and face invisible – for two or three minutes. I didn't grudge it to her, but something obviously troubled the girl beyond my predictably clumsy endorsement of abolitionism. Waiting to discover what it was grew excruciating. By the time she'd settled, I'd planned out exquisite revenges on whomever was tormenting her.

'I wake up wrong,' she murmured.

'What?' I asked, certain I'd misheard her.

Her freckled face reappeared, grey eyes brimming and nose red. 'I know I live here,' she whispered, nodding tiredly at the nearly empty hallway. 'I savvy it's real when I'm awake. But in the morning, before my eyes open, I don't sometimes. In my head, I still work. For *her*. There's no Father Sheehy, or Neill, or Sophia, or my new pal, Clara. There's no Mrs Boehm. There's only the work and the madam just before I open my eyes, so I don't want to open them at all. You're gone too. You're *gone*. I think I still live where I did before, and it *hurts*.'

She was right. It hurt like the devil.

And how wonderful it would have been to tell her that one day she'd cease recalling brothel work. I'd have given a great deal to say so with any certainty. Considerably more than I'd have given for the assurance of never again screaming at the sight of my own charred bones, only to discover my body was, in fact, abed and drowning in cold sweat. But what is carved in our skin – though not always visible – can be equally as permanent for not being seen.

'I'd not wish to scrape against the likes of you,' I informed her instead, carefully schooling my voice. 'To think that you've been waking up wrong all this time and never told a soul. Anyone else would have been blubbering all over the school. Hell, *I'd* have been scared witless.'

Sniffing indulgently, she pulled away a fraction. 'You're ribbing me.'

'I'm not. Most folk are unadulterated milksops next to you.'

Bird heaved a great sigh.

'But don't do that anymore, all right? You know you don't need to lie on my account. You don't need to keep mouse either, if something eats at you. Tell me, or Mrs Boehm, or anyone else you like. Being brave and being alone aren't the same thing.'

'There's nothing I'd not do to keep from going back there,' she muttered. 'I'd die sooner.'

'That's not going to happen.'

'I'd do terrible things, Mr Wilde.'

'You'd not need to. I'd do them for you.' I gave her shoulder a squeeze. 'Listen, I've a very difficult case I'm working on. The one I just told you about. If I miss seeing you during the next week or so, that's the reason. I'm hard at the copper starring, but I'd rather be keeping you company.'

'You're still warm at me.' She frowned. 'I hate when you're warm at me.'

'I'm warm at the slack-jaw who schooled your friend Eamann to parrot trash. Never at you.'

Bird hopped off the bench. I only hoped she was minding me thoroughly. *Never at you.* A fair percentage of my small friend's life had been a wide-awake nightmare. But if I could remake her into simply a little girl with grey eyes and high cheekbones and a splash of freckles across her face and shoulders instead of a melancholy adult with the untroubled complexion of a child – I'd do it in a heartbeat, but that doesn't make me any less fond of the Bird who exists now.

She hoisted her books and tucked them back under her arm. A doubtful shadow lurked at the edges of her eyes.

'Do you really believe that, Mr Wilde?' she asked, dabbing her face with her sleeve. 'That being brave isn't the same as being alone?'

'Every word of it.'

Bird took a long moment to gaze at me. Thinking nigh-bottomless thoughts with a mind that had been wrenched wide open long before it was ready.

'And you call *me* a liar,' she concluded as she walked away.

Chapter Seventeen

A negro, who had escaped with a boat from Virginia to New York, was reclaimed; and was condemned, upon his return, to be hanged for stealing the boat. It was exactly as if a man whose horse had been stolen had gone off with the horse, and had afterwards been executed for stealing the bridle that happened to belong to the thief. He had a wife and eight or nine children in New York.

E. S. Abdy, *Journal of a Residence and Tour in the United States of North America, from April 1833 to October 1834*

I decided that speaking to as many associates of Lucy's as was possible would quickly solve my problems.

It didn't. Not quickly, that is.

Over the course of the next four days, from February 18 to 21, I avoided the Tombs. That wore me a bit rawer every hour, which was an unexpected confirmation of fondness for the horrible place. Each evening, I met with the Vigilance Committee. First at the Reverend Brown's comfortable parsonage, then at Julius's ken, and last at the fashionable apartments north of Washington Square belonging to one George Higgins, who owned an art collection that young Jean-Baptiste would have swum the Atlantic for. But no significant progress was made. Lucy and Delia's neighbors were all questioned; their friends contacted; their homes watched. None of it proved profitable. Delia and Jonas were still as vanished as possible, Lucy unavenged, and the rest of us a long and weary day older.

George Higgins, for my money, had about a week left before he came unstitched like a poorly made stocking. The tracks at the edges of his eyes had deepened, and his costly shoes went unpolished as he tramped through the mire in search of her.

'Get some sleep, George,' Julius would advise every evening.

'When this is finished,' he'd answer.

We'd all part with solemn handshakes and unspoken oaths to try again next morning. Then we'd make our dull ways homeward, avoiding the avalanches that had begun sliding off the townhouses. Already feeling about as buried as the poor devils who are dense enough to walk under the eaves of rooftops in February.

I made repeated efforts to see my brother and was told by the men at his station house that he was *out doing a spot of delicate investigating*. That I didn't know the specifics maddened me, but Val can smell danger the way wolves smell blood, and I received the odd note from him, and thus knew him to be alive if not well. The first said, in his very civil hand:

Heard about the mitten mill down Five Points way. Try vinegar poultice on the eye. Mulqueen is lucky to have died so easy.

A recipe followed. Whether or not having your head fried with cheap grease was an easy death by comparison to whatever Val had in mind didn't bear mulling over. But I did make the poultice. My swollen eye deflated to a lurid but perfectly functioning organ within half an hour. The next, two days later, read:

Getting somewhere, though this business is dim as glimsticks. Heard from Matsell – it's a close shave you aren't sacked yet, and you're to keep clear of the Tombs. Best greetings to your landlady.

The matter was, just as Val said, about as dim as a bad candle. I interviewed as many relevant individuals as I could, and a few irrelevant ones. The information collected made for the most baffling picture I'd ever tried to squeeze into a sane shape. So on the afternoon of February 22, a mere six days before I'd be forced to attend my first official Democratic Party event, I spread a sheet of butcher paper over the floor of my room, half listening as Mrs Boehm's pleasantly grainy voice crooned a Bohemian song in the kitchen below. Next to the butcher paper, I opened my notebook so I could stare simultaneously at the appropriate statements.

Then I threw myself facedown on the floor in trousers and rolled-up shirtsleeves. The boards were plenty warm on account of the evening rye loaves, my windows frosted over with floral sprays of improbable ice. A cozy setting for some serious thought.

Selecting a bit of charcoal, I started sketching. First came Meg, the cook who'd been manhandled by the likes of Varker and Coles on the day of the kidnapping, as she'd looked in the Reverend Brown's parlor with him and Julius and Higgins and me staring thirstily at her. Parched for knowledge. Her body was divided as if on a plumb line: half a hale black woman of around forty, half a curled-up root of an arm with a stiff hip and a turned-in foot. She'd a pretty face, dark as could be, with a flat nose and a too-small chin that lent every expression an elfin quality.

As I sketched Meg, I read my notes. She'd been subjected to outlandish church rumors about the murder, and so her testimony emerged as much a defense of her household as a statement of facts.

Mrs Adams hired me, some two years back. Yes, sir, Mrs Charles Adams, and don't you say otherwise. People are gossiping something terrible – that she was only his mistress, that he threw her out on the streets and she died there, that she'd taken a shine to a new man. It's not right, not a bit right. Mr Adams loved her plenty.

Mrs Adams, she was looking for colored help, but the quality cooks get snatched up plenty quick, you understand. The way she

looked at me said I seemed too good to be real from my references
and here I was a cripple! How was I to do for them? I said you give
me one day, ma'am. Just one day. I can clean faster than any pert-
headed Irish miss, and I can fricassee a rabbit good enough to shut
your eyes and then melt down your throat. Well, she smiled, and
said any help could face her down with that sort of vinegar didn't
need any 'day' to test her mettle. Worked there ever since.

Sure enough, I cooked for Mr Adams's parties. Made it all
ahead of time and he'd go on and hire the servers. Do I look like
I'm fit to serve at table?

But that can't be the way of it. It can't. When Mr Adams got
home of an evening, he never did have eyes for a thing save her.
Used to trail after her like a puppy. It made me blush to see them.

Oh, he was kind enough to Jonas. The boy was from another
marriage, though, from when Mrs Adams was young. It's hard for
a man to raise a strange chick in his nest. But he wasn't ever harsh
nor cold to the child. Just . . . distant, maybe. Distance isn't cruelty.
There's those who can tell you firsthand.

Rutherford Gates? No, I never did hear that name.

No, I tell you. Not once.

Oh, Lord have mercy.

I forced a bit of air through my teeth, shading the turned-in crook
of her withered hand.

Meg wasn't helping.

As I'd been told not to disturb Rutherford Gates, I'd lost no
time in wringing his sister like a wet mop. Miss Leticia Gates of
Twelfth Street and Third Avenue greatly resembled her brother.
Pink-cheeked and fresh, with nut-brown hair, delicate pince-nez,
and a direct manner. Beginning with her raised hand as she'd pulled
the wool of her needlepoint through the canvas, I drew Miss Gates
sitting on her settee, answering my many questions.

Yes, it's a dreadful business about Rutherford's housekeeper. Oh,
I've heard, of course I have. He can hide nothing from me. We've

adored each other since we were little, you know. And I'm the elder, so it's always my first instinct to mother him, and he seemed so very distraught the day he found out. His reaction to her death was . . . well. I don't suppose I should say any more.

I'd smiled sadly, and poured her more tea, and confessed I knew just how she felt, I'd a brother too – leaving out that he discovered an interesting German tonic called *morphium* at the age of sixteen and may possibly be a molley – and within half an hour we were fast friends. Miss Leticia Gates, spinster, was right back to the natural order: shoveling confidences in my ears as if I were a tale-burning oven.

I began sketching her face, with its even, almost handsome features, framed by sleek brown hair done in an unassuming knot at the base of her neck.

A sister can always tell, you see. Perhaps it's the same for brothers, though I do suspect a part of it may be womanly intuition. But I'm so attuned to Rutherford. When he was a boy, I'd know at once when something vexed him – I could sense it, as if his distress were a scent or a sound. He was always such a sensitive little chap and wouldn't hurt a fly, the dear thing. I recall once – but you won't wish to hear an old maiden lady's sentimental stories.

She'd been mistaken. I'd eaten a ratafia cake (reeking of almond and rosewater, no comparison to Mrs Boehm's airy delicacies), announced it perfection, and said by all means, tell me a story.

If you insist, Mr Wilde. Oh, do take another – you're a bachelor, I see, and I make them small just for the purpose of guests eating more of them. Well, we were rambling through the woods – goodness, that would have been our summer home on Long Island, of course – and we came upon a puppy that had been caught in a game snare. Half-starved, the poor creature. All white, with blue eyes and a single floppy ear marked with brown. After extricating it, my brother nursed it back to health, and he couldn't hear a word about finding it a new home without tears coming to his eyes. Our father, who was never an animal lover, insisted. And it seemed there was an end to the matter.

The night Papa meant to give it to a neighboring farmer, I woke from a dead sleep certain that something was amiss, and I raced downstairs to find the house turned upside-down, and both Rutherford and the puppy missing. Knowing all my brother's hiding places, I was soon able to find them in the eaves above the horse stalls, with a week's supply of food stolen from the pantry. Rutherford meant to wait it out, you see, the rest of the holiday. But a spider had crawled from the straw and bitten my little brother upon the hand. Can you believe it? That was why I had felt the jolt of panic, Mr Wilde. I will always believe so. His hand was already dangerously swollen, and still he hadn't wanted to seek help at the house, he loved that puppy so. I screamed for my parents, and thank God I did. Rutherford nearly died of the fever stemming from the wound.

Oh, please don't mind me, I always get a bit carried away when I tell this story. It frightened me so, the sight of his tiny hand swollen into a ghastly red paw. He was only six at the time. You're very kind. There. Now I'm quite cheerful again. Rutherford had his way after he recovered, of course. That dog was his inseparable companion until he departed for university.

So you see . . . I know Rutherford. I'd assumed . . . oh, it's so difficult. I'd imagined he had a mistress, you see. In Albany. There was something about his step, about his smile when the softer emotions were spoken of. My brother was in love, I knew it in my bones. And I confess it to you – my reasoning led me to believe that this mysterious Albany woman I'd invented was some kind of actress or musician. The wildly lovely, untamable sort who'd have made a very poor match for a politician. So I allowed him not to tell me about her, for fear of embarrassing him.

If only he'd confided in me that Lucy Wright was, in fact, his paramour. We dined together on the day he learned of her death, *you see, and I can hardly bear to think of how anguished he sounded when he spoke of it. Far more distressed than he would have been at the tragic loss of a domestic, however capable. He said nothing directly to the purpose – but Rutherford hasn't been the same since. I can't bear to think of him alone in those first hours of mourning, with no solace save his own strength of character.*

Met his housekeeper? No, never. The poor soul. Murdered . . . I can't bear to think of it. No, Rutherford visits me habitually, but not the other way round. He says he misses me and my little domestic touches – I am known for being an exceptional hostess, Mr Wilde, and I say so with neither pride nor false modesty – but now I cannot help but wonder if he meant to keep me well away from her. I'd have known, of course. If I'd seen them together. I'd have known in an instant that there was no Albany woman.

Oh, must you? Return anytime you wish, Mr Wilde, and you'll find yourself most welcome. I do pity the poor woman, you must realize – I picture her often. Blonde hair, soft blue eyes, efficient but graceful. I regret not meeting Lucy Wright, Mr Wilde. I wish Rutherford had trusted me. No matter how low her birth or her station, I would not have disappointed him.

She certainly hadn't disappointed me.

No, if what I wanted was a better picture of Rutherford Gates, I'd gotten a mural. As for Lucy's true portrait, I'd kept it to myself.

I pored over the drawing, chin in hand.

Gates, I thought, was a very good suspect from almost every angle. A suspect who lied. A suspect with *motive*.

But if I believed his sister, he'd once nearly killed himself to save a puppy.

I added a finishing flourish to her hair, scrubbing my free hand over my face before pushing myself along my deliciously warm floor to reach more blank paper.

Next I tried my luck with Timpson, the owner of the flower shop where Lucy had been all too briefly employed. Timpson resembled the world's most affable cadaver. Grey skin, grey hair, greying teeth. The only patch of Mr Timpson that wasn't grey was his nose, which drew its sunlike glory from the little flask of spirits within his pocket. He was a Manchester man, before. And anxious enough over Lucy to be happy to see me. I told him little enough of her murder, but what I did tell him shook his frail bones.

I drew Mr Timpson arranging a vase as he spoke with me, the stifling perfumed hothouse flowers just a half-rendered mass of charcoal fumes.

I cannot begin to tell you how sorry I am to be informed of this dreadful news. And in Ward Eight, no less – positively shocking. I have always been of the vocal opinion that this neighborhood, this very integrated neighborhood – ah! I see, Mr Wilde, that I do not shock you by speaking of integration. All to the good, my dear boy.

As I was saying, I have always trumpeted its safety at every polite opportunity. One does not win a battle of public opinion in a day, sir. You're a copper star, so you understand me perfectly. Copper stars are new, yes? They are mistrusted by the masses. You must earn their trust, as must proponents of general integration. When integrated neighborhoods are seen to be free of crime and vice, they will become desirable. When the copper stars are seen to protect the citizenry and serve the public, they will become heroes.

The way I read the map, Timpson's dreams coming true were about as probable as Piest donning a straw bonnet and winning the beauty contest at the county fair come summer. I liked the stooped little florist, though. I took a pull of rye beer purchased from the Germans next door before continuing to sketch his antennae-like eyebrows.

I can begin the tale only a month ago, regrettably. She came into the shop and – Lucy's full name? Why, Mrs Charles Adams, I believe, though I never met the husband. She spoke of him only occasionally, but she seemed quite taken with the lucky fellow.

Yes, I'm certain. Undoubtedly Adams was the name.

Actually, she was already known to me, as she'd purchased flowers here for her own household several times. And she was quite unforgettable, Mr Wilde. A month ago she approached my counter with a certain boldness in her eye I'd not been accustomed to seeing there, as she had always appeared a shy – not to say timorous – lady for all her great beauty. She confessed to me that her little boy spent his days away at lessons now, and that she found herself lonely, and that she knew flowers very well indeed. Had raised them, arranged them, helmed Christmas parties and marriage ceremonies. And I have been in need of assistance for quite some time – my age and rheumatism make repetitive work rather arduous, you see, and it was a great stroke of good fortune that such a capable applicant showed an interest.

She readily described her previous experience for me. I was much struck by the detail with which she described a wedding celebration she'd worked on – fresh gardenias arranged into an intricate coiffure for the bride, shocking pink azaleas framing sprays of white moss roses on the tables, magnolia centerpieces – she knew of which she spoke. I hired her on the spot.

I last saw her on St Valentine's Day. It's the busiest day of the season, of course. She stayed quite late. She oughtn't to have been there so long, but she insisted upon remaining until the crowds had thinned. There wasn't an inkling as to any trouble. Lucy was conscientious always, but I can't imagine she'd have lingered if something was truly troubling her. She appeared quite at peace.

I have been so horribly worried all this time, Mr Wilde. I made inquiries, you see, but could discover nothing. None of the other merchants in the area were personally acquainted with her. It seems she kept herself quite private. By the time I realized I didn't even know her exact address, days had passed.

Other stories? Told to me by Lucy, you mean? Gracious, I wish I could help you, but we talked only of flowers. Lucy was a wonderful woman, but a reticent one. It's of no use to a policeman, my relating that Lucy recalled running through field after field of wild orange coneflowers as a little girl and afterward felt as if she spoke their language.

She was such a lovely creature. Thank you for telling me of her fate at last, Mr Wilde. To know the truth is better, in the end, howsoever it might hurt us.

Poor old Timpson was mistaken about that, but I followed him well enough at the time.

Finally, I wriggled toward a fresh corner and started in capturing Grace of the Millington household. I'd begged a favor of Turley in the mournful afternoon half-light and gained a private conference in the wine cellar, our oil lamp tracing white semi-circles in the bottoms of hundreds of bottles, throwing Grace's features into sharp relief as she stood before me with her hands tucked neatly behind her.

Not kittled to see me. Nor any too gladdened that the subject I broached was *Why are you frightened of copper stars? Which? Who? Can you tell me the stories?*

I'd explained. I'd cajoled. I told her of Jean-Baptiste's carriage museum, and she relented a fraction. Finally, I related the death of Sean Mulqueen and she spoke her piece. Probably because being trapped in a wine cellar with a star police for longer than twenty minutes was going to wreak absolute havoc upon the remainder of her schedule.

It's not that I don't appreciate what you've done. Letting the boy go free and all, and no one the wiser. I've seen him hereabouts, though I've not hired him since. Not every man would have done the same.

It just doesn't matter, you see, Mr Wilde. It doesn't matter what you've done. It isn't enough.

That Irish copper star, and the slave catchers you spoke of. We know them. We know them plenty well by sight. We know others too, ones you've never heard tell of. We walk in pairs and those

248

that have little ones keep them inside after dark and we pray that something comes of our precautions. That numbers will shield us, that daylight is friendlier. None of that is true, the way I figure it. But we imagine it's so, and so live easier.

Supposing you stop them, Mr Wilde? I'd shake your hand, then, and praise the Lord for His mercies. But supposing they stop you? And hear tell as I've talked, whether from your lips or someone else's? What then?

Folk are disappearing. Melting away. They trickle up from the South too, new escaped slaves arrive every day – singles, pairs, whole groups sometimes. I'm happy for them. They get a second chance. I hope more fight their way through. What's more, I pray for it. But they don't matter either. Not to my life and whether or not I get to carry on living it.

When a man lays hands on you, you're gone. Just like that. Easy as blinking. The way back home is too long, Mr Wilde, and the light too dim. So I can't talk to your sort. Because you can't keep me safe. Maybe you want to, for all that you're white and I can't rightly see what difference it makes to you one way or another. But it comes down to luck, caution, and God. You aren't my kind, you never will be, and you don't understand what it means to think about it. It won't ever happen to you. And so I'll go on about my business and ask you not to be seen hereabouts anymore. For my sake.

Please try to picture what I mean. If we were stolen for ghosts when we were snatched up, sold for even a shadow of our former selves, that would be something bearable. I could be sold for a ghost. I'd live, I think, though nothing's certain. But you're less than a ghost once you've been taken. At least ghosts get to keep their own name.

Growling in frustration, I dropped the stick of charcoal.

I did my level best every morning not to picture Jonas chained to a wall, watching the unspeakable befall his aunt. As had nearly already happened. Likewise, I tried my damnedest not to imagine the pair of them tethered with leg irons to a narrow ship's berth, bereft of every human kindness for the rest of their lives on account of not being human any longer.

At night I pictured it, though. And darkness was fast falling. And my heart was thudding up against my clavicle because I'd tried the only trick I know and the only talent I have that's ever brought me a moment's respite from misery and *I still wasn't getting anywhere.*

Tap tap tap.

'Come in.'

My door swung to. Belatedly realizing I'd heard Mrs Boehm's tread on the staircase, my face snapped upward half a second later.

'Oh, sorry, I—' Leaping from my ridiculous prone position, I threw a blue waistcoat over my shoddily buttoned shirt and lit the oil lamp. Being reduced to a copper star with a mangled face is bad enough without losing all sense of dignity. 'I was working.'

Mrs Boehm edged forward, staring at the butcher paper. She wore the plain grey frock of the three I've catalogued, with the neat row of white lace at the hem and the four deep pleats at the hips. The one that makes her hair less golden, but her eyes marginally more blue. She placed her right hand on her tiny – really far too thin, but who am I to ask whether a baker is eating properly – waist and raised the back of her wrist to wipe a bead of sweat from her brow. Several translucent locks of her baby-fine hair had fallen in her face, but she avoided touching them, for her nails glowed with butter. How Mrs Boehm (who is almost precisely a year younger than I am, as I learned in November, making her twenty-seven) manages still to produce goose down from her head is a perennial puzzle. She brought with her an oddly calming aroma of cinnamon.

'I made *franzbrötchen,*' she answered in reply to the question I hadn't asked. 'With pumpkin seeds. Too much dough, and maybe you would like one?'

My landlady had reached the spread-out sheet anchored with four of my five books by this time and sunk absently to her knees, wiping her hands on her ivory half apron. I fell to watching her.

'These people, they are to do with your problem?'

I nodded, sitting Indian-style on the opposite side of the brown paper. About two feet divided us. Two feet and four carefully rendered faces, staring back at me in vivid, accusatory detail. I traced the edge of my scar and then dropped my hand. Annoyed. Instead, I picked up the charcoal again and let my fingers wander.

'You think with your hands.' The edge of her liberal crescent-moon mouth lifted, and her angular cheekbones had pinkened from the heat of the ovens. 'I think also with my hands. But with bread.'

Glancing up momentarily, I continued drawing.

'Bird, she, I believe, thinks with her eyes. When closed, when open. Always looking, always remembering, always busy. Filling her head with more thoughts.'

'There's plenty of thoughts in that pate already,' I sighed.

Adjusting her dove-colored skirts in a small fan, she leaned forward. What interest she held in my portraits I couldn't fathom before remembering Mrs Boehm loves stories. And my drawings, God help me, are nearly as florid and emotive as is Mercy's fiction.

'I worry over that kinchin,' she owned. 'But Bird, she is strong. She can handle more thoughts than many children are capable.'

'Did she tell you about waking up wrong?'

She tilted her head, a pained *yes*. Liking the interest of that angle better, I shifted my wrist accordingly.

'I told her she needn't be alone to be brave.'

Mrs Boehm's head cocked the other way. There was a tiny track of sweat making its slow descent from her neck past her collarbones and downward. Nearly as elusive and shimmering as her hair in the waning daylight. It arrested the corner of my vision for senselessly long.

'Truth, I think that. One needn't be alone to be brave.'

'She said I didn't believe so myself and then called me a liar.'

'And *are* you a liar, Mr Wilde?'

'Probably. I'm enough other undesirable things.'

I thought about the manuscript hidden in my sleeping closet under my five books. Those words I'd spent, the hours of effort, all

251

in search of what truly happened last summer. Never having intended for any living soul to read it, I must have been telling the truth therein. Mustn't I? Could I believe myself truthful when utterly alone? Copper Star 107 had written the same events in police reports, but Tim Wilde had once been told that books could be cartography. They were maps for Mercy, anyhow. Always had been. So why did I sometimes feel as if even that effort was meaningless, merely the blurred vision of a half-blind, sentimental fool?

One for sorrow, I thought, absently recalling the chiming girlish voices at Bird's school and the dark augury of seeing a single blackbird. There was a reason that number heralded pain. There's always a reason, I think, behind the doggerel kinchin chant.

'*Tch.* Easy enough to tell if you are a liar,' Mrs Boehm chided. 'You are brave already. Are you alone?'

Her eyes, when I met them, were entirely colorless as the sun angled lower. Uncanny, the pallor of them, and yet how warm they seemed, softened by a hint of blonde lashes and an indulgent expression as she finally smoothed her hair back behind her ear. Not a thing about Mrs Boehm's eyes, I realized just then, made an ounce of sense.

'Perhaps, as Bird thinks, you walk through life alone in the middle of company. Always a stranger. Only you can know for certain. I don't give *franzbrötchen* to strangers,' she added.

My hand froze.

She sounded a bit breathless, but surely I was conjuring that myself. Surely men who stride casually about as if their hearts are in their chests and not on the other side of the Atlantic Ocean miss key signals, invent others on the merest whim. Surely she meant to be kind. Mrs Boehm *is* kind, after all. She's one of the kindest women I know.

Kindness can account for literally thousands of otherwise inexplicable things, I decided.

I managed a comradely smile. 'I don't draw strangers either. Unless I'm working.'

Our attention dropped to the paper river between us. The one that now included Mrs Boehm's face, planes softened by frostlight and the unearthly sheen of the atmosphere beyond my window. With her head angled and her hair edged in silver.

Pale eyes scrutinized my person. Both from the picture and from the woman before me, kneeling unselfconsciously on my floor.

'*Are* you working?' she asked me.

Bang bang bang.

Mrs Boehm began to rise, but I caught at her bony wrist without quite knowing why. Stepping over the paper, I passed through my open door to the top of the stairs.

'Who's there?' I called out.

'Timothy, it's freezing. You want to see me – I promise.'

Taking the stairs two at a time, I unlocked the door to discover Julius Carpenter. Well wrapped, a wary look about him. My pulse quickened. Something had changed. The fact that *anything* had changed was nigh miraculous.

'Tell me you've solved it,' I requested of my old friend.

'Not today,' he owned.

'Varker and Coles have caught smallpox.'

'Damned if I wouldn't dance a jig at that prospect, but no.'

'Then tell me Delia and Jonas are alive and well, and like to remain so,' I groaned, leaning against the door in near defeat.

'I can't speak as to the future,' he answered, lips quirking. 'But regarding Delia and Jonas, why don't you ask them yourself?'

CHAPTER EIGHTEEN

I felt the stripes, the last I saw,
Red, dripping with a father's gore;
And, worst of all, their lawless law,
The insults that my mother bore!
The hounds are baying on my track,
O Christian! will you send me back?

E. Wright, Jr, 'A Fugitive Slave to the Christian'

Julius Carpenter and I traveled in a hack northward along the Bowery as the ailing afternoon gave up the ghost. A hack I'd hailed, of course, while he'd stood two feet behind. We didn't dwell on that, though. Not when we were about to see Delia Wright and Jonas Adams again. Not when *answers* hovered before us in the air, simple and alluring as hummingbirds and just as elusive to the touch.

The Bowery is a broad, careless, hedonistic street, full of mindless laughter at eight in the evening and the muffled whimpers of lost drunks at two a.m. Packed with revelers lurching helter-skelter in pursuit of unhealthy distractions. Spies and traitors seemed to glide through the slush, their glances arrowing into our hack's windows. The hotels' brass-fitted restaurants gleamed maniacally – hotels asking no questions when their patrons returned at four in the morning keeping different company to their companions of the daylight. Upper windows blazing, every guest seated at a skirted table with a mountain of faro chips. Afterward, we came to the seedier gambling halls. The dens masquerading as coffee cellars or poultry vendors by day, floors still littered with burnt grounds and soiled feathers. Places where thin men gathered, betting their families' suppers on raffle tickets and strings of numbers that would break their hearts.

I asked Julius first whether he'd yet questioned Delia. He said no, he'd not even seen her or her nephew. Then I wanted to know where they were, and he informed me that he'd need to draw the blinds when we approached, no offense meant. Gnawing at the bit, I asked how the devil he'd discovered their whereabouts. He pulled a folded note from his waistcoat.

'I never discovered them. This was delivered to me yesterday.' At my glare of angry surprise, he added, 'Stop. George doesn't know either. Bad wrench, not telling him, but I was instructed to keep my mouth shut. Delia hid them both deep underground, Timothy.'

The note, in a well-educated hand that failed to align itself with the edges of the paper and hung at an eccentric tilt, read:

Mr Carpenter,

Your company and the company of your rising star is requested, after dark as is customary. Bring no one else. We've a large ham and a small ham, and in hopes you will both be pleased by our repast. The supper is to be entirely private. While he has been vouched for through multiple sources, please take precautions ensuring the star arrives safely at our establishment.

That's neither here nor there,
The Candlestick Maker

My friend pulled the blinds down. The remaining light was dim but steady, shining from the hack's four safety lanterns through broad cracks in the shades. Julius was doing all he could not to smile at my confusion. It can't have been easy.

Then the spark hit powder.

'You said *underground*,' I realized. 'Underground Railroad. My God. Are you part of that network?'

'Please. My ken wouldn't hide a cockroach. The Vigilance Committee keeps people from being sent in the opposite direction. George, though – George is a stockholder.'

'So he said.'

'No,' Julius corrected me, 'a financial contributor to the Underground Railroad system. As is the rest of his family.'

'Why leave him out, then?'

'I don't know her mind, but it troubles me too.'

'I can't read this message. Are all communications coded?'

'The interesting ones.' Julius allowed himself a small smirk. 'Can't read it? You're better than that, Timothy.'

I hoped he was right, so I looked again.

'*Rising star* is a play on words. Star police. Me, presumably.'

He said nothing, but he seemed pleased. So I sallied forth.

'Large ham and a small ham can only be Delia and Jonas. *Precautions* . . . you already said I'm not to know where we're going precisely, though I imagine you'd be taking more care about it if we didn't know each other so well. But I don't see why this fellow dismisses everything at the closing.'

'How so?'

'He says *that's neither here nor there*.'

'But that's just where we've arrived.' Rapping at the hack's roof, Julius made to jump out as the cab rattled and slowed. 'Neither Here Nor There. Do me a favor, will you Timothy, and don't tell me about it if you know where I've taken you?'

That we were in the northern suburbs of the Chelsea neighborhood was clear, for the wind spoke more of forest elm than of animal remains, and the Hudson murmured away to my left. Anyway, I'd recognized the subtler glare of Fourteenth Street when we'd turned left off Bowery. But the dwellings, like so many upright redbrick soldiers, were unremarkable. Anonymous.

Kerosene lights flickering behind white curtains, cleanly swept wooden doorways featureless above their ash-strewn steps.

Julius approached a house with a pair of red candles in the window. He'd somewhat recovered by that time, though the shoulders that had been knotted with pain days previous were still not merely raw, but tense with worry.

The door opened to a colored servant girl in a neatly pressed uniform, carrying a third candle.

'Always best to have another lit, lest one go out,' Julius said.

She smiled, blew out the taper, and stepped aside.

We were led into a small sitting room, nicely populated with dark-leafed plants and a white cat presiding over the Indian rug before the fireplace. The chamber's sole occupant sat in a rocking chair, sewing a button onto a man's shirt. I'd have been arrested by her appearance anyhow, for she was a black woman of advanced age, with a crown of white hair piled atop her head. But I noted almost immediately that she was stone blind. I might have realized when she never glanced in our direction, only took on an air of listening. Her stitch work was conclusive, though. In the needle thrust, tapping with expert skill at the thimble she wore, never meriting the smallest glance downward.

'Is that Julius Carpenter?' Her voice was strong but rasping. A pleasantly abrasive sound like the skitter of dry leaves.

'Mrs Higgins,' Julius said warmly, bending to kiss her lined cheek.

'Higgins?' I exclaimed.

'And you must be Timothy Wilde. I can smell the metal copper star from here. It needs polishing.' She smiled in my friend's direction, revealing teeth as white as her hair. 'I fooled him, didn't I, Julius?'

'You fool everyone, Mrs Higgins. Timothy, this is George's mother, Mrs Adelphia Higgins. She's better known as the Candlestick Maker in some circles.'

I took the hand that had apparently written the note I'd just perused. Her sightlessness explained the odd orientation across the paper, her quiet force the fact I'd stupidly mistaken the writing for a man's. George Higgins was visible in the regal line of her jaw, the navy sheen of her black skin. Mrs Higgins's eyes were focused in the middle distance and slightly to my left, her hair pearlescent in the firelight. She lingered over my hand – reading me, no doubt as well as I could read a stranger with sight intact.

'I can't tell you how relieved I am that Delia Wright and Jonas Adams are safe, Mrs Higgins,' I said.

'They will need your help, I fear. They will need every ally they can muster. The danger of their position cannot be underestimated.'

Hesitating, I glanced at Julius.

'Doubtless you wonder why my son is not present.' Setting her sewing down, Mrs Higgins rose and smoothed her elegant eggplant-colored skirts. 'Delia's wish, and she will explain it to you. Mr Wilde, I needn't tell you to speak of this place to no one, I trust?'

'On my life I won't.'

'So I have been told, by multiple parties. You wouldn't credit how very difficult it is to gain the respect of Grace Stackhouse, employed by my not very distant neighbors the Millingtons, for example. But you have. Follow me, then. Please keep your conversation as low as is possible; I am entertaining more than one guest at present.'

Mrs Higgins walked with sightless ease to the mantel, passing her fingers along its marble lintel before arriving at a door in the far corner. The room beyond proved to be windowless, lit with a single kerosene lamp throwing every manner of shadow, and appeared to be a miniature museum of sorts.

The collection it housed was unlike any I'd ever seen. Every wall was lined with taper holders and pocket lamps, from the humble bull's-eye to the most delicately scrollworked silver candlesticks. I spied night lanterns with iron flaps, candles with flared shades to amplify the light, gold-plated chambersticks etched with bountiful wildlife. Simple pewter stands, elaborate sconces that appeared from their floral embellishments to have sprouted from tiny metal seeds. Every variety of illuminative device I could imagine glinted at me from the shadows, their shapes guessed at by reflective edges and half-formed curves. And nary a candle or a box of lucifers in sight.

Mrs Higgins walked to a glassed-in shelf full of miniature wall chandeliers and reached behind the display. We heard a small, well-oiled *click*. The shelf swung open. Our hostess descended a flight of steep stairs in near-total darkness. We followed more carefully, at an uncomfortable disadvantage without light.

'George's late father owned a very successful chandlery business,' Julius informed me under his breath. 'His collection is often shown as a museum. It's perfect, really. Why suspect a room serves a double purpose when it's used for public tours? There's a handrail along the wall.'

To my surprise, my knuckles struck smooth paper and not the packed earth or mortared stone of a cellar. No gusts of chill air rose to greet me, no sickening hint at the laughable state of our metropolis's sewage system. Treading in Julius's footsteps with my fingers tracing a waxed wooden handrail, I made for the glow at the bottom of the staircase.

When our feet reached level ground and a thick carpet, we turned a corner. And a sight I'll never forget if I live to be a thousand years old appeared before me.

New Yorkers almost never see escaped slaves. For plentiful reasons, most of them obvious. Refugees keep to the woods for fear every stranger they meet may be a bounty hunter with a bloodhound. And anyhow, they're ill equipped for cities. They've no chink, no proper clothing, and no notion of how to scavenge for food in a weird world of zigzagging streets and towering straight lines, a godless forest built of brick and stone. A man adept at stealing farm eggs to save his skin doesn't necessarily have the skill to raid an iron-barred grocery after hours. Cities are dangerous. Packs of roving urban dwellers inhabit them, their glances calculating and feral. So we see runaways but seldom. And most are glad of it.

This particular escaped slave, a woman of no more than twenty, inhabited a bed sheltered from the rest of the room by a Chinese screen. The room itself was low ceilinged and underground but otherwise a study in normalcy. Framed pressed flowers, braided rugs over pine floors, chintz wall hangings printed in russet and turquoise. The woman rested uneasily atop the coverlet in a nightdress and soft dressing gown, tossing her braided head to and fro on the goose-down pillow, both feet bandaged in thick cotton matting. I didn't have to ask what had happened to them. She'd fled from the South through fields and swamps and thickets and rivers in the dead of winter without any shoes. Her eyes flicked open just as I entered the room.

'Are you the doctor?' she asked me. Her voice was heavily accented, drawl so thick it spilled like molasses from her cracked, ashen lips.

'He's been and gone, dear.' Mrs Higgins peered around the screen. 'You'll keep both feet, we think. We were so glad of it. Do you remember?'

'However did she make it here?' I marveled.

The bravery of the concept – the geography, the risk – left me smaller than usual and tongue-tied with admiration. Aside from ferry travel to Brooklyn and back, and rare journeys to Harlem and Staten Island, I've never left New York in my life. It's a common local ailment. And here she'd traveled hundreds of miles. Equipped with, presumably, *nothing*.

'She'd the Railroad signals – lanterns and such, when she neared towns. Otherwise she followed the stars,' Julius answered.

'Weren't stars, most nights. I followed the moss,' she moaned.

Mrs Higgins's mouth twisted worriedly. Feeling for the bedside, she placed the back of her hand against the sick woman's brow.

'This is Sugar,' she said, voice directed at Julius and eyes trained on the wall. 'Sugar, you're very warm. Do you need me to call for the doctor again?'

When Mrs Higgins pulled back a fraction, I saw Sugar's face entire. Her eyes wandered feverishly, bandaged hands feeling all around her on the surface of the quilt. What she was searching for

I couldn't fathom, nor could I begin to calculate the size and shape of what she'd lost in order to gain her freedom – her family, friends, the space she'd slept in, the unmatchable blue of the sky outside her door.

Julius pulled at my elbow, and we entered a short hallway. Away from the gentle comforting sounds and the stifled whimpers that pierced them. I stopped my friend when he reached the next door. A question burned at the back of my throat.

'Do the kinchin ever survive the journey? I don't see how it would be possible.'

For far too long, he simply looked at me. 'In spring and summertime, yes. In the winter, with luck. But you can't very well wait for summer if you're to be sold away from your kinchin on the morrow.'

It made sense. It all made logical, heartless, insane sense.

'Think on what we can do, not what we can't,' Julius advised, entering the next room.

Delia Wright sat in a combined bedroom and sitting room, her elbow on the table before her and her eyes pinned to her nephew. Having met the pair only once, my relief at seeing them hale swelled admittedly out of all proportion. Jonas was curled in the double bed, clutching the edge of the blanket though for all appearances he slept. Delia's hair had been neatly arranged atop her head, and the forest-green day dress Varker had abused repaired meticulously. She was perfectly buttoned and hooked, brown eyes wracked and raw. I saw in her a general who has suffered unspeakable casualties planning his retreat in dress uniform. Seeing us, she rose, nodding a warning toward the kinchin. Julius embraced her, quick but fierce, and she led us through to still another room.

We found ourselves at last in a subterranean library. Well lit, replete with heavy armchairs and heavier bookshelves. Delia closed the door behind us.

'He's hardly slept,' she confessed. Her tone was clear, but so very, very low.

'We can't tell you how sorry we are, Delia,' Julius said. 'For you

261

and Jonas, for your sister.' Hesitating, he searched for words of comfort. 'She's with God now, if sooner than she should be.'

'Is she?'

A cruel shudder passed through Delia's torso, and she crossed a hand over her stomach. Going to the fire, she added a small log, though the blaze crackled brightly already. When she turned back, she'd swept the thoughts from her eyes.

'We searched everywhere for you,' Julius told her. Urgent, but not reproachful. 'Never dreamed you'd be Neither Here Nor There – how could we have guessed you were with George's *mother*? He's nigh out of his mind.'

'As have I been.'

'I've only managed to keep it from him by avoiding him. Mrs Higgins is a better liar than I am. And why should you have asked that George—'

'I'll explain it.' She seated herself in a fireside armchair. A candle burned beside her, and she moved the taper to the low table in the middle of the room. 'Mr Wilde, there is a favor I must beg of you.'

'I'm at your service.'

'As reparation?' she asked, dry as chalk. 'Or simple goodwill? I do read the newspapers, you know.'

I'd seen it coming. But knowing you're about to suffer a blow doesn't lessen the effect, I've found. On the contrary. Either Delia Wright had been present and afterward taken hostage when her sister was murdered, or she had discovered the body in Val's bed and fled with her nephew. No other explanation for their absence was sensible. Apparently, the latter had taken place. But I'd no words to explain why I'd dropped her loved one's corpse in the rank snow under a pile of piss-stained newsprint.

'I hope you can forgive me for moving her,' I said fervently. 'Though I don't expect you will. What I thought was right at the time isn't easily—'

'Please, Mr Wilde.' She adjusted her hems in aggrieved impatience, and I recalled how decisive Delia Wright was in actual life. She was riveting. 'Spare me your explanation of what it feels like to have a sibling. I recall it. Do sit down, you're both unsettling me.'

Finding no further words, I obeyed. Julius and I took the settee, and we all leaned forward an inch or two. Three conspirators, bending toward a tiny open flame.

'The man who murdered your sister will pay, Miss Wright,' I vowed. 'Only tell me how and who.'

Delia's mouth opened upon a mirthless gasp of hysteria. 'Ah, Mr Wilde.' She was still smiling. Shaking her head in a pitying way, beautiful and exhausted and clearly inches from the end of her rope. 'How I wish I *knew*.'

The silence that settled was thick with disappointment. I'm not proud of that, and Julius took a brief look at his boot toes. But we wanted vengeance by that time. For Lucy, for Delia, for the boy gripping the edge of his quilt as if it were a sword hilt.

'You needn't make useless protestations of your brother's innocence either, now you know I'm at as much of a loss as you are.' Delia's fraught smile at last faded. 'I will forever remember that Captain Wilde was kind to us, and I cannot credit that he suddenly returned to his home in a murderous rage. Not after all he had done. We could scarcely believe our good fortune that night – that the Committee, Mr Carpenter, and the star police, Mr Wilde, had taken such drastic measures to free us. And then to *house* us, no less. Well. But I shall tell you all I can, and then perhaps you'll see some light where I see none.'

It can't matter that she doesn't know the culprit, I thought above the unmanly protests over the unfairness of fate shrieking in the back of my head. *When you know what happened, you'll understand who.*

Of course you'll know the murderer's identity. You'll finally know Lucy's name.

And this is the story she told me.

Delia and Lucy had remained in Valentine's home for all of the first day and most of the second. There had been eggs for frying, salted pork, mysterious spices, and a jug of table wine they reasoned they'd pay him for after returning to their homes. The sisters talked while Jonas constructed a fleet with kindling masts and newsprint sails, only to decimate his armada in a fiery battle within the small sea of Val's hearth. When conversation wearied them, they perused the clean but otherwise neglected library (why Val owns books when he reads them but once and remembers them perfectly puzzles me extremely) and watched the passersby braving drifts in Spring Street. Then it belatedly occurred to the women that, should Meg have given the alarm, there must surely be people worried about them.

'George often misses church for business reasons, and it wouldn't have occurred to either of you to reassure our congregation if poor Meg appealed to them in hysterics, and so I suggested attending Sunday night services.' Delia took a slow breath, gazing into the fire without seeing it.

'Your sister was against the idea,' Julius surmised.

'Lucy was frightened.' Delia dashed an errant tear from her eye with an angry little swipe. 'But I will tell you something about my sister – on each occasion she was frightened around *Jonas*, she either compelled herself to stop or sent him away. She couldn't bear the thought that she would influence him in a cowardly direction. It haunted her perennially. As if she could help her instinctual reactions! On that particular evening, she couldn't work herself up to leaving through the back alley and walking to our church in West Broadway. And so she *insisted* that I take my nephew. Lest he grow to startle at shadows.'

Delia's voice remained measured during this account of her sister's unique stamp of courage. Nevertheless every word, piece by piece, built to a soaring monument. She hadn't simply loved her sister. Lucy had been Delia's heroine.

'But no one at the Abyssinian Church saw you,' Julius prompted.

'No.' She shifted her eyes in my direction. 'Someone followed us. After we had reached Spring Street.'

I moved forward again, aching for fresh material. 'Go on.'

'We ducked into an alleyway. I pulled Jonas through the back door of a chophouse and we rushed across the crowded dining area. When we reached the street again, we simply ran. I took us in circles. Perhaps twenty minutes passed, all told. By the time we arrived back at the alley behind your brother's house and raced indoors, I saw no one behind us.'

The rabbity flutter of my pulse heightened. 'Can you describe your pursuer?'

'I caught the hint of a copper star on his greatcoat shining in the lamplight. Tall as Julius, maybe. I'd the impression he had red hair.'

Sean Mulqueen, I thought. Not at all surprised.

'When we arrived back at the house, we were quite shaken. But my sister wasn't alone. There was a woman with her. She was strikingly beautiful – pale, almost angelic, with blonde hair and a sweet, assured manner.'

Apparently I started in shock, for Julius cast a questioning look at me. I'd told him all about Silkie Marsh and her blessedly rare species of malevolence, of course. Though they'd never met apart from Julius's mockery of a fugitive-slave trial, he'd a vivid recollection of the woman who'd almost stolen his life.

'She'd introduced herself as a Miss Marsh, and she was on her way out already.' Delia's expression pulled taut, her freckles standing out in stark constellations. 'I'll be very brief, for the subject . . .' Her eyes fell shut. 'Charles Adams was not who we thought he was. Perhaps you're aware already—'

'There, take a breath, now,' Julius said.

'Rutherford Gates was his name, apparently.' Standing, Delia crossed to the mantel, running palsied fingers over its framed illustrations. 'It was a lie. All of it. Lucy's marriage, her *life*. Or so we were told. Miss Marsh claimed Charles Adams was a state senator. God, to think of it, of Lucy's face . . . she was devastated. Heartbroken. I was witness at her marriage ceremony in Massachusetts. You can't imagine how happy she was. Miss Marsh left soon after warning Lucy.'

'*Warning* her?' I exclaimed.

'Lucy said she'd advised us to flee the city. We couldn't know if my sister's marriage held any claim – if she was Lucy Adams or

265

Lucy Wright. But Miss Marsh insisted in very feeling language that we run for our lives, for danger – Varker, Coles, worse perhaps, but she wouldn't say how or why she knew of it – waited to pounce on us every instant we remained in town.'

Delia peered at my lips as if expecting me to comment. She was disappointed, though. Of the many questions that swarmed in my pate, angry and stinging as individual blood flies, none would have made sense to the woman before me. *Why in holy hell would pure vice in the shape of a pretty brothel madam warn you of danger?* wasn't practical, though it was to the purpose. *What game was Silkie Marsh playing in your head?* wouldn't solve my worries either.

So I kept my mouth shut. Listening.

'We were no way prepared for flight, however,' Delia murmured. 'Lucy and Jonas's free papers were at West Broadway, and to travel without them . . . we may as well have surrendered to Varker. Lucy was in such a panic that she proposed I take Jonas at once to a safe house. Here, naturally.' She gestured, a sad and futile spasm of the wrist. 'I was to return and accompany her to West Broadway after I'd fetched my own free papers from my lodgings. We knew you'd arrive that morning, Mr Wilde, and trusted you'd do us the courtesy of escorting us there and seeing no harm would come to us for it. I won't prevaricate with you – Lucy also wished to see Charles. To see her husband, if he was such. She could not have abandoned him, on the word of a stranger, without ensuring the allegations were true.'

'Nor could you leave without her and your nephew's free papers,' Julius agreed.

'But by the time I'd arrived back at Captain Wilde's residence after leaving Jonas here . . . you saw what I saw, Mr Wilde. You must have, since my sister later ended up in an alleyway. You were due to call on us that morning, and who else had reason to move her?' Delia stroked her fingers over her throat as if over the purple stain across her sister's neck. 'I fled. We must have missed each other by minutes.'

Exhaling slowly, I stitched together facts as the fire hissed to itself and Delia paced. Bits of truths and half-truths, fragments of stories, the earnest accounts of those I trusted and those I didn't. Motives, actions, consequences. None of it could be heard above the blaring fanfare of unanswered questions. So I asked a few key ones.

'When your sister found work last month, did Gates raise objections?'

'I see your mind, but I can confirm nothing. He asked her if she thought she could handle the strain and Lucy said yes, she was certain she could. Then he ordered a brace of pheasant and two champagne bottles from the restaurant down the road to celebrate her success.' She fluttered one hand exhaustedly. 'But we also believed him to go by the name of Charles, so I suggest you ask me more useful questions, Mr Wilde. Time runs short.'

'What explanation did Silkie Marsh give for knowing you were at Val's?'

She paused midstep, raising an eyebrow. 'Is she not your brother's mistress, then? Lucy said Miss Marsh claimed—'

'Of course she did,' I muttered disgustedly.

Silkie Marsh, I thought, *is a snake charmer who had four vipers in her basket. Varker, Coles, Gates, and Mulqueen. If only I knew which of them sank his fangs into Lucy the next morning.*

I shook my head, clearing it. 'What favor did you wish to ask of me, Miss Wright?'

She sat down again and faced the pair of us. 'I want Jonas's free papers. They're in Gates's house, and I'm effectively trapped here. I want you to bring them to me. I retrieved mine on my way back to Spring Street.'

'And why didn't you ask George to accompany us?' Julius asked.

This provoked another laugh. A species I couldn't identify – shadowy and deep. 'Because I need to borrow a considerable sum of George's money,' she owned breathlessly, 'and if he were here, he'd have simply said yes. My teaching salary amounted to little more than room and board. I've nothing remotely sufficient to make a fresh start. I could drag Jonas through fields and forests, could flee like a criminal along the riverbanks, hungry and ever desperate for the next Railroad station, but—'

'But you could much more easily be caught that way,' Julius said simply. 'And so, if George was willing to pay for a private coach—'

'Then I could imagine just for an instant that we'll arrive safely.' A spasm borne of grief and regret clutched at her throat, and she shook her head. 'George Higgins doesn't want me to live out the remainder of my days in Canada. So asking him to fund the enterprise is degrading enough without forcing his answer. Standing before him, as you see me now, would force his answer. You pose the question, Julius. And thank you both for your help – I imagine you can guess what it means to me.'

I could think of nothing further to ask, and our conversation had drained the golden glints from her eyes entirely. 'We'll return with his papers,' I said, rising. 'Within a few days, if not less.'

Delia nodded and fell into the armchair. Silent. All but spent. I couldn't imagine the hell she'd passed over those few days – but it had wrenched her, tugged her lovely face into a grim drape of sackcloth and mourning weeds.

On our way out – past the feverish runaway woman now tended by a black doctor and Mrs Higgins – I inexplicably thought of magnolias. Of Lucy's hands working gardenias into hair ornaments for another wedding long ago, the one Timpson had described to me. I could see the summer sun cutting through the window where she worked, feel the caress of a clover-rich breeze sliding lazily in through the half-open door. In my mind's eye, the blooms began to wither as she touched them. Disintegrating.

'This is a nightmare,' Julius mentioned as we stepped down into icy streets once more.

'Worse,' I said. 'We're not about to wake up.'

Leaning back against the seat of the hack we found, I allowed myself a single uncharitable thought.

I just learned next to nothing, I realized.

Settling further into the dim, I took a deep breath and let it out again.

Fine, I thought. *Far be it from me to let* nothing *discourage me.*

But I couldn't for the life of me shake the feeling that something worse – more specific, perhaps – was amiss. I'd had such premonitions before, a bell in my head signaling something was *wrong*, and knew there was a mismatch somewhere. An error like a wall unevenly papered. It was in every way sensible that Delia preferred an intermediary when making a painful, humbling request. Laudable, in the circumstances. In fact, I suspected that Miss Delia Wright was more honorable than most of the people I'd ever encountered. Her high character explained everything about our fellow Committee member's exclusion.

Didn't it?

And if George Higgins seemed to me a bold man – one who was no stranger to raw force, would have fought Julius's captors with pistols at dawn, took what he wanted when he wanted it simply because he'd been told he couldn't – what of that? I liked such men, admired them.

Delia wasn't *afraid* of him. Surely.

George Higgins, I thought as the hack carried us further away from Neither Here Nor There, *bears further study.* And then fell to wondering why that should be.

CHAPTER NINETEEN

$50 REWARD. Ran away, from the subscriber, on Thursday last, a negro man named Isaac, 22 years old, about 5 feet 10 or 11 inches high, dark complexion, well made, full face, speaks quick, and very correctly for a negro. He was originally from New-York, and no doubt will attempt to pass himself as free . . . JNO. SIMPSON, MEMPHIS, Dec. 28.

Theodore Dwight Weld, *American Slavery as It Is: Testimony of a Thousand Witnesses*, 1839

I'd like to say that the scant few days prior to my entire investigation falling to splintering shards of fiery disaster around my ears were in any way pleasant. Restful. Conducive to clarity of thought.

They weren't, though. They were exhausting. And they were heralded, as so many dusty events likewise make their debut, with the reappearance of Valentine Wilde.

The Liberty's Blood – the cozily barbaric Democrats-only saloon my brother frequents, to which he summoned me two days after I'd spoken with Delia – was less quiet than it ought to have been on a Tuesday morning, February 24 to be precise. Its front bar, burnished with the oil of thousands of greasy fingers, was well populated with Val's typical crowd. Irish grateful for a watering hole where Party camaraderie rather than native scorn tints the atmosphere, dead rabbits whose notion of breakfast is a pint of ale and a knife fight, and the sycophants who envy the rabbits' style and chink but don't have the spine to muscle their way into politics. I didn't bother to search for my brother in the front room under the countless American flags hanging from the ceiling and the cobwebs dangling from the flags. Pushing past a knot of cartmen taking a pine-beer respite, I tugged at a flag hiding a doorway and entered the back area.

I squinted at the familiar specters of its furnishings. The kerosene fixtures on the walls serve the dual purposes of creating soot and shadows. They're useless otherwise. I picked my way past plush couches where rogues employ their lips for sweet nothings and far worse after clandestine Party meetings. So early, the place was deserted. Save for Valentine's mountainous silhouette, half curled on his back exactly where I expected him to be, on a divan beneath the most ridiculous taxidermied American eagle I have ever seen. Having seen many, many taxidermied eagles in my time.

I sat in the armchair adjacent to the small couch, as usual. Val had clearly not yet reached an amicable truce with daylight. Lamplight. Any light at all. Reaching, I tapped him on the forehead.

'Oh, for God's sake, *why?*' came the mumbled response.

'You summoned me. Where the devil have you been?'

He twisted from the hip and rolled into a seated position, staring balefully into the gloom. Wincing, he passed a quiet moment with the stars behind his lids. 'Albany.'

'Truly?' Of all the possible answers, there was one I hadn't expected. It was pretty tantalizing, though. 'What was in Albany?'

'Some of the purest cut opium I've ever blown, for one, courtesy of our state senate. Made it back into town yesterday evening. That's when I scratched you the note. I think. Have I got that properly?'

Sighing, I left my hat on the table and shoved my head past the flag into the front saloon, calling for a bucket or two of coffee and a plate of rashers from the dining hall next door. Realizing who I wanted them for, the fantastically scarred-up barman shouted for the errand boy. Within half an hour, Val was wiping his fingers on a napkin in our murky lair and making considerably more sense.

'All patched up, then?' he asked.

Comprehension lagged slightly. 'Oh,' I said, brushing my fingers over the back of my hand. Only a shiny red spot remained, and my eye – well, the blackened one – was en route to respectable again. I poured myself a second cup of coffee. 'I'm fine. Why did you go to Albany? That's a hard ride in such a short time.'

'Because that's where the trouble was. Is. See here, Tim.' My brother looked more drawn even than his usual. 'You're going to be a cow about this, but you need to let me run the lay alone from here. So far as investigating the *murder* is concerned.'

'No,' I replied. 'What did you discover?'

'I'm dead beat on the subject, Timothy, you—'

'Matsell hasn't even taken me off the case, and he likes it little enough.'

'He doesn't savvy what I do.'

I waited. Ominously silent and profoundly irked.

'All right, here's a sketch, supposing a sketch will make you any less oafish. Though it won't.' Val settled back against the divan, finding a cigar end in his waistcoat pocket. He didn't light it, only twirled it in a meditative fashion, like a card sharp with an ace. 'I'm known to a good many of the bushy-tailed partisans at the state capitol. From considerably far back. Ran with any number of them as a young Jack dandy, before they dealt in slogans and banners and ribbons and such. I stood for a few drinks and let my old pals buy me a few more. And rumor has it, Rutherford Gates is a silver-tongued cull on the senate floor if there ever was one. Not to mention an essential vote, numerically speaking. And up for re-election against the smuggest Whig bank baron ever to – fine,' he growled, when my looks began to reflect how grave I found these concerns. 'You don't give a rat's arse. Fine.'

'So far as it's relevant to investigating the murder, of course I do.'

'How about preventing your own, you codfish-brained infant?'

His tone was so snappish, I caught myself short.

'You pitched me exactly the same flux last summer, over the kinchin murders,' I protested, spreading my hands. 'Nothing happened.'

'And you saved the Party from a thorough lacing when you discovered a bloodthirsty Irish Catholic lunatic *wasn't* roaming the streets hacking kids apart. As I have now *reminded them. In person.*'

'But I can't—'

'Cross them, and they will hurt you before you die and piss on your grave afterward.' Val abruptly returned the cigar end he'd been studying to his pocket. 'You've already stolen from blackbirders, disrupted court proceedings, fought a slave-catching Irish copper star to the death, though that wasn't your doing exactly, and antagonized half the police force. I told the Party bosses I can manage you. Tell me I'm right.'

I shook my head in disgust. 'We found Delia and Jonas. They're hidden in an Underground Railroad station.'

To my surprise, Val clapped his hands once in apparent delight. 'Now, there's a patch of sunshine. Sing me the tune.'

There was a time when I wouldn't have breathed a word of it to my savage and Party-entrenched sibling, but I'd like to think those days are past. Anyhow, no part of my tale surprised him. Not Mulqueen's trailing Delia and Jonas, not even Silkie Marsh's mysterious warning. None of it.

That worried me in ways I can't possibly express.

'They're for Canada?'

I nodded, polishing off the coffee.

'Already struck out?'

'No. The Railroad needs to make arrangements with the conductors and the stations en route for such hot cargo. It'll be four or five days.'

'Never to return, though?'

I glared at him.

'Safer, don't you savvy? Gates, whose importance in Albany I wish to firmly stamp on your coddled little mind, was being groomed for a governor's daughter. They've been throwing him in her direction after every fete and oyster soiree.' Valentine checked his watch and shot me a meaningful look after snapping it shut again.

'That lying weasel,' I concluded with deepest conviction. 'Did he kill her, then? His *wife*? Is that why you—'

'That's yet dark to me. It's just . . . I've a feeling this is a bigger pail of rotten eggs than we thought.'

'Bigger than a corpse in your bed?' I demanded, thoroughly flummoxed. 'Bigger than Silkie Marsh's plan to ketch us?'

Val considered this briefly, then shook his head. As if he were speaking flash and I could only comprehend Chinese. It wasn't a new expression – a single contracted eyebrow, lungs braced as if stifling a martyred sigh. But an urgency I hadn't seen him wear often riveted me nevertheless.

'Listen.' My brother leaned forward, lacing his fingers. 'I gave some thought to what you said, before. About what that old scar means. *As many as I love I rebuke and chasten, be zealous therefore and repent.*'

Fighting a shiver, I managed to confine it to my lower back. 'And?'

'They're from Albany, yes? The Wrights? Well, I looked for their kin. People who could help hide them if the Party comes out firing. No one would admit to knowing them, Tim. This is bigger than I savvied. Every colored I could find by the name of Wright did their best to convince me they'd never heard of a Delia or a Lucy. Swore it up, down, and sideways and then tossed me out on my ear with vigor.'

This was admittedly disturbing. 'Someone's frightened them, obviously. All right, so the conspiracy is wider than we supposed. You think the murder is about Lucy's past and not her present?'

'No, I think you need to sit on your meddling hands and let me manage from here.' Valentine stood, setting his hat on his head. 'You'll be at the Party gala come Saturday?'

My grimace of excruciating distaste answered in the affirmative.

'Bully. We'll have you back at the Tombs in no time, with a sprucer office and the wind at your back. Watch me. You'll be a captain within a year.'

'Val, I'm not about to give this up. Swear that if you do work it out first, you'll tell me everything.'

Valentine was shrugging into his fur-collared greatcoat, tucking bits of expensively tailored fabric into the folds where he desired them. Wiping his kerchief over his still-haggard face, he frowned. 'I sent a message to the Capitol. When I get a response, I should know more. And so will you.'

'That's fair, then. I'm going to help Delia and Jonas make their escape from Manhattan. Don't tell me not to. I'm getting them away from here.'

I didn't say, *I'm going to retrieve Jonas's free papers for him.* Neither did I say, *I have every intention of breaking into the Gates residence with the help of the Committee of Vigilance, which means robbing a state senator for the Democratic Party in the company of Africans. A state senator I strongly suspect murdered his wife.*

My guess was that information would have been the sort to ruin a remarkably civil conversation. For us, anyway, it was civil. So I kept my tongue in my head. For two days, I'd been wracking my brains over it. Sleepless, anxious sweat prickling along my brow. But I'd dined the night before with Julius after engaging some friends in a spot of reconnaissance, and despite the enormous risk, he agreed with me. Housebreaking was our only tenable option.

'Of course you're helping them escape.' Val chuckled in his pained way, donning leather gloves. 'You're an abolitionist. A *quiet* one. Yes?' he asked.

'Yes.'

He swept out of the room.

I meant it too. If we didn't manage to keep mouse over cracking Rutherford Gates's ken, we were all in for trouble of the permanent variety.

* * *

275

We convened the following evening, February 25, at George Higgins's residence. Five men seated at a round table inlaid with ivory and shell and honey-colored wood, planning for battle. We were cautious, to be sure, but likewise gladly determined. At last, we were actually *doing something*. It felt like a mercy at the time.

Julius had at once informed his childhood friend that Delia was alive following our visit to Neither Here Nor There, counseling patience. He'd put off the matter of her request, however – I think due to an ardent wish that Higgins sleep through at least one night that week. And so now I watched as he repeated Delia's desire to borrow funds for the Canada journey, as I'd decided Higgins required inspection. It's not decent to study a chap over when he's just realized that he is the only person who can send the woman he loves – and for her own good health – to a faraway land. No one was looking at me when I did it. But study I did.

I saw only heartbreak of the common garden variety. George Higgins turned to stare out his parlor window – an enormous window, with a mountain of sage cushions – looking in the reflection of the pane as if he needed a moment to cobble himself back together with sticks and twine. To my left, the Reverend Brown sat with his hands folded, thinking or praying. To my right, Jakob Piest drummed his spindly fingertips against the inlaid tabletop. I needed someone I could rely upon, trusted by the Committee, with an unconventional, not to say bizarre perspective on our dilemma. That was Jakob Piest from electrified mane to mud-crusted boots.

Julius, across the table from me and seated between Higgins and Piest, gripped his friend's arm. 'Think on the fact she's alive, George. That's better than we feared at first.'

'Alive and unwilling to speak with me in person.' Higgins extricated his arm with the excuse of rubbing his hand through his beard.

'Didn't want to cause you undue pain, did she,' Julius reasoned.

'Or herself undue discomfort.'

'She'd no wish to bully you.'

'She can bully me all she likes and she knows it, it's her refusal to face that fact square on that I can't abide.'

Hear, hear, and a three cheers besides, I thought before I could help it, pulling my stub of lead from my pocket. My fingers were positively itching.

'I didn't like keeping you in the dark, George, but you see how it stood,' Julius added, frowning.

'Oh, yes. I imagine that if anyone ever openly defied an instruction from my mother, they would be struck down from on high within seconds. And the autonomy of her guests is her cardinal rule – they're guided, arrangements are made, but they're never dictated to. Delia would be treated no differently than a barefoot runaway. Whether or not I've been courting her for nearly two years.' Bitterness was audible at the back of his throat.

'Is Mrs Higgins called the Candlestick Maker because of your late father's profession?' I inquired, redirecting the conversation.

'Actually, no,' Reverend Brown answered when his congregant failed to speak. 'It's because she takes souls and conveys them to where their light need not be hid beneath the bushel of slavery. *Candlestick Maker.* I've always been fond of that title.'

A silence fell.

'Have you any paper?' I asked Higgins next from the clear blue.

The man didn't even blink. But it's extremely disconcerting to have a woman's countenance emblazoned on the backs of your eyelids, so I didn't fault him. 'Look in the desk, just there.'

Returning with a sheet, I started scribbling. 'Reverend, what did you discover while ostensibly distributing tracts door to door?'

Coughing, Reverend Brown pushed a pair of spectacles up his nose. 'I was received at five neighboring residences by means of the rear yard, and both servants and their employers proved most amiable people. Very gracious about my pamphlets, and one woman even made a donation to the Abyssinian Church after serving me tea. On the whole, they were as curious about the boarded house as was I. Many eyes are on the place. But I'd not say it's *watched.* No more than any other empty building, for fear of vagrants occupying it and inviting fire or theft. And to their knowledge, Gates has not returned a single time.'

Eighty-four West Broadway had begun to appear before me in neat charcoal lines. My activity was inviting some bemused glances, but I couldn't bring myself to give a damn. When I'm wound so tight brainwork actually *hurts*, drawing is the only way I can manage to think at all. 'Mr Piest?'

'Yes!' he exclaimed, lunging awkwardly forward and jarring the table. 'Oh, I beg your pardon.'

'Never mind.' Hiding a smile, I asked, 'How went your investigations?'

'I inspected the fortifications of Eighty-four West Broadway to the minutest degree, all the while taking obvious notes and in broad daylight. That was to a purpose, Mr Wilde – if seen, I would have been thought a copper star evaluating the security of the residence for a fee, and not a skulking villain seeking an opportunity for rude gain. Windows, doors, locks, back area, side entrances, cellar ventilation – *nothing* escaped my most intense scrutiny. Every brick and smear of mortar is indelibly marked upon my mind, and in my notebook.'

The Committee stared at him. Struck dumb. Whether with admiration or because they'd never seen a star police who resembles a talking crayfish wax poetic over housebreaking, I'm not sure.

'And?' I prompted.

'The place is impenetrable,' he announced. With passion and finality.

'I – wait a moment. What exactly—'

'The windows are barred with iron to prevent paupers from breaking and entering. Ventilation holes for the cellar are like-wise fortified with very thick boards. And were we to attempt entrance via the front or back doorways, we would require either an ax or a battering ram.' He raised a hand, as if for pardon. 'I must put the question once – is it possible to *ask* Mr Gates for permission to enter, without informing him of the whereabouts of the refugees?'

'With Lucy in the ground?' Julius shook his head. 'The risk is too high.'

George Higgins scowled in complete agreement.

'Free papers can be forged,' Reverend Brown said cheerily. Earning my eternal respect and a puff of appreciative amusement from Jakob Piest.

'Delia and Jonas are at enough risk already, whatever in hell is going on here, without bad documents hastily come by,' Julius argued.

I went back to my sketch. The others fell to murmurs, suggestions between themselves I half listened to.

If you force your way in with a cannon and a copper star, the Party will apparently kill you if Val doesn't get to you first.

If you ignore the question and go back to your life, it will haunt you until you are, in fact, dead.

If you break into the Astor House and steal Rutherford Gates's keys—

The pencil fell from my hand. I'd just reached the roofline of the brownstone, the snow-crusted edge of its tiles.

'Gates boarded his dwelling in February.' My voice sliced through the low chatter. Higher than usual, really nothing like my normal tone. 'A cold February. This has been a *very* cold February.'

'Yes?' Higgins drawled, the question somehow both mocking and hopeful.

Finding the nub of lead again, I tapped it against my rendering of the impenetrable house. 'The kidnapping was the night of the storm. When all those ships foundered. Dozens of them. It was the worst gale in years.'

'It was and then some,' Julius agreed.

'We all met at Eighty-four West Broadway before setting out for the docks, and we left in a tremendous rush. No one, in a practical sense, used the place thereafter. It was simply closed by hired men.'

'What on earth has that to do with *cold?*' Reverend Brown asked.

'He's coming to it,' Mr Piest answered, beaming.

Staring down at the sketch, I began to smile myself.

279

It was a very dangerous idea. It was the only idea, however, that I appeared to have wrestled from the ether. And considering the weather and the often slipshod behavior of workmen hired to secure a private house, it had every possibility of working.

'Is there generally space for applicants at the Colored Orphan Asylum?'

If Mr Piest was an object of wonderment before, this query sealed my status as resident curiosity.

'They take whatever orphaned and half-orphaned charges they can, but winter is difficult. Money is always a useful commodity, if time is pressing,' the reverend replied when no one else could find his tongue.

I nodded. 'Suppose I knew of someone who can get us into this place, but who would require an immediate change of address afterward for safety's sake? If I did, would one of you be willing to bribe his way into the Colored Orphan Asylum?' Angling a look at our host, I continued, 'I ask as a salaried copper star with a secondhand coat, addressing my question to a gentleman of substance. Mr Higgins.'

He thought about being amused. In fact, a quick smirk appeared on his lips before he'd managed to whisk it away again.

'Take the whole sodding pile and gladly, Mr Wilde,' he announced.

'Mr *Higgins*,' the reverend objected, mildly shocked.

Higgins shrugged and fell back to scrutinizing his house. It was well furnished, embellishments designed for comfort not snobbery. He'd shelves and shelves of books, the scope of reading material I'd used to enjoy at Mercy's residence. I'd have loathed him for those books if I were that sort of man. And I realized that – while the room's décor had once been a mark of status, maybe – he'd transformed it in his mind into a jewel box. Higgins had conjured Delia's brown eyes keeking out through the window, the crook of her arm grazing the table over buttered toast of a September's morning, on countless occasions. Now the house was merely a house, its color bleached away into faint shapes that once had been gifts for a loved one. Every vibrant thread superfluous, every delicate tassel stripped of meaning.

I'd the evening previous, in a ruminative episode typical of me for being utterly useless, forgotten the name of Mercy's first published short story – the premier installment of *Light and Shade in the Streets of New York*. It couldn't possibly matter to anyone save myself whether I knew the title, and yet *I* was the one punishing myself over it. The workings of my brain were beginning to resemble the exertions of a man at hard labor, turning a heavy wheel for the benefit of no one.

Looking at George Higgins, I watched in silent dismay as his own gristless mill began to grind.

What about you troubles the woman you love so? I wondered past a rush of fellow feeling.

But there was nothing to be done about love, anyhow, and there was a kinchin to consider. Two, if I was counting my chosen collaborator in crime. When I leaned forward in my chair and traced a small triumphant circle around the chimney, Mr Piest began to cackle wildly, giving me a slap, hard and congratulatory, on the back.

After all, I told my already-grumbling conscience, *it isn't as if you'll be teaching Jean-Baptiste how to steal.*

Chapter Twenty

It is a subject of deep regret to me that proper measures
were not taken to ascertain the cause of the death of one of
the unfortunate youths, at the time the rest were stopped.
There is no doubt upon my mind, but that he was cruelly
and barbarously murdered.

Richard Stockton regarding kidnapping victim Joe
Johnson, who was flogged to death with a cart whip,
African Observer, 1827

The following night we set out to find Jean-Baptiste Jacques
Augustin. The living black chimney sweep, not the dead
French painter. Whether our oh-so-orderly plans would be met
with abject failure in the form of a locked chimney grate, we knew
not. But my hopes were high. The last people to use the sitting
room, presumably, were those assembled on the night of the
abduction. And God knows we hadn't bothered with securing the
fireplace. That meant, supposing flue safety had occurred to neither
Gates nor his day laborers, a clever sweep could break into the
place without breaking anything whatsoever.

An elegant solution. Though a perilous one. I liked the risk to
our small friend about as much as I liked being forced to rob a
house.

'He can still say no,' I remarked to Jakob Piest and Julius Carpenter as we snaked through alleyways. Too narrow for horses, plenty wide enough for rats to scuttle across our feet.

'Of course he can,' Julius replied. He was just ahead of me, his blue winter cap bobbing along through alleys festooned in grime. 'But this is the only decent notion we've come up with.'

I skidded on a patch of snow melt that had frozen, melted, mixed with putrefying slime, and frozen again. Several times. We were in Ward Nine not far from the Millington residence, heading southeasterly away from the Fifth Avenue shrines to lucre, back toward humbler terrain. The neighborhood where Grace Stackhouse claimed Jean-Baptiste's sweepmaster held court.

Crossing Greenwich Lane, we found ourselves in the labyrinth off Factory Street, traveling under a stone archway. We picked our way through used books spilling helter-skelter from the passage. Their motionless owner thrust a box of more marketable items – corn plasters and odd buttons – in our direction. He'd no customers, nor did he seem likely to find any. Overhead the darkening skies shifted queasily.

'Do not suppose for an instant, Mr Wilde, that I like this either,' Piest remarked. 'But I do suspect that the child knows his business by now well enough to wish to be rid of it.'

I agreed. Jean-Baptiste must have been talented at scaling chimney walls to remain yet unscathed by them. But who would want such a life, given a choice? Thinking a silent plea that we'd not be the cause of his first irretrievable mishap, I skirted a horde of patchy cats yowling over a rubbish barrel. Half-starved and better than half-frozen.

'Here we are.' Julius came to a halt in the middle of the passageway.

Political posters covered the surface of what I assumed was a very drafty wooden door. Slogans of yesteryear dissolving, the words FREEDOM and CORRUPTION disintegrating alike in dangling peels of streaky paper. It's a cheap method of windproofing, but it works and costs only a few pennies' worth of horse glue. Knocking, we entered, Julius in the lead, this time, I and Piest at his heels.

'Clear off. We're closed for the night. Copper stars,' the sallow-faced mulatto sweepmaster added in disdain, noticing the pins Piest and I wore. 'Christ almighty, what this city is sinking to. I paid the tax already, last week. You'll shake not another penny out of me.'

Neither Piest nor I could claim surprise at this assumption. We did exchange a dark glance, though, and Piest's nose twitched in repugnance.

'We're looking for a sweep. It's urgent,' Julius explained.

'Caught wind of inspectors coming tomorrow, eh? Unless you've a down payment for a rushed appointment, all the lads are booked through the week's end.'

The sweepmaster sat behind a desk. *Desk* being descriptive of the function. I could equally have described it as a *pile of cast-off bricks*, with a tabletop crowning it. He took a sip from a tumbler resting next to a ceramic jug. His face was dour and jaundiced beneath the natural bronzing of his mixed blood, his hair held neatly in place with bear grease, his mouth cruelly slender, his eyes calculating. Not that he looked at us a second time. He merely scribbled away at an accounts ledger.

'We've a down payment,' Julius assured him. 'But we need a particular sweep.'

'Ah.' Setting the bedraggled quill down, he linked his hands behind his yellowed shirt collar. 'A *particular* sweep, is it now. Well, for *particular* sweeps, the rates are higher, naturally. It's Tomcat you'll want, then, yes? He'll not mind, supposing you give him extra coin as well and offer a drink or two first to take the edge off. He's like to scratch otherwise,' he concluded, winking.

The sourly curdled feeling in my stomach was wholly familiar. My work as a copper star had occasioned it time after wretched time. But always previous, I'd either arrested the bastard who'd caused it or else made off with every kid I could find trailing along behind me. *Tim's stray cats*, my brother calls them, though I believe he approves of the practice. But now . . . now we were on a mission, and I was banned from the Tombs. So I fixed my tongue between my teeth and commenced furiously scheming.

'That's not the way of it,' Julius said, a thin stripe of steel running under his tone. 'We need a boy about six years old – mute, though not deaf.'

The sweepmaster tilted his sullen face back, bewildered. 'The Cockroach? What can you possibly want with the Cockroach? Well, it's none of my business, if you fancy the little freak. He's never been asked for after hours, but we'll persuade him, won't we? Right this way.'

I watched my feet follow after my friends. Along a corridor, through a doorway, and down a flight of dank stairs, as the shadows fled from the sweepmaster and his swinging lantern. The cellar had a ceiling of about four and a half feet. Ancient roots halfheartedly scraped from the walls reached out like sinister fingers. The cave had been dug to house potatoes and cured pork in the winter months, a cold haven for summer apples and salted cheese wrapped in bright wax.

Instead, the frozen hole in the ground boasted two levels of bunks crammed up against either frigid, flaking dirt wall. And it housed tiny colored boys instead of foodstuffs. The adults crowded forward, bent at the waist and keeking as best we could through the consuming darkness. A thick stench of coal dust suffused the cavern. Not because fuel was stored there, but due to the sweeps themselves.

'Cockroach!' the sweepmaster yelled, sending a wave of disquiet through the sleeping chamber.

Several hollow, red-rimmed sets of eyes stared back at us. An older boy of perhaps eight with the characteristic forward-bending spinal deformity pushed himself up to see what the trouble was. Another, who'd been caught out of bed, shuffled back to his bunk, his knees and ankles fused permanently outward.

Then the tiny shadow of a body rolled off a lower bunk from beneath his thin cotton sheet, landing sprawled in startlement on the raw earth. Half a second later, he straightened, walking toward the conscienceless churl holding the lantern. Blinking, obviously frightened. But not very surprised.

'Cockroach, see?' The sweepmaster was pleased. 'Quick as lightning, but never makes a sound. Same color too, the inky little pest. Cockroach, these people want you.'

Jean-Baptiste's hands curved into angry talons.

'Come on, then.' The sweepmaster turned back to ascend the stairs.

'Jean-Baptiste, is it?' Julius whispered.

The lad's mouth dropped, forming a circle as the light retreated. He took two steps toward Julius, uncomprehending. Then his sleepy and inflamed eyes lit on myself and Piest, and he gasped.

'We'll explain in a moment,' I told him.

Jean-Baptiste trotted willingly enough up the stairs. Ahead of us, a *clang* from the sweepmaster's lantern hitting his tabletop sounded just before a furious flipping through of accounting ledgers. When we entered the front room, our host was running a thorny finger down the columns of a separate book, one taken from a shelf. Grunting, he wrote the words *Cockroach: Private Services.*

'That one had better be healthy enough to climb a chimney tomorrow,' he advised.

Grinding my teeth to sand began to seem imminent when Jean-Baptiste shot us a glance of alarm. Piest placed a finger aside his nose with a subtle wink, and the moment passed.

Clucking sadly, the sweepmaster took another swig of liquor. 'I mean it. Nothing to ruin the next day's wage. Trust to your own natural delicacies where he's concerned and think feelingly of my sorrows, gentlemen. I lost another to the cancer last week, and we're short till I can find another.'

The cancer, my ever-helpful brain supplied. *Chimney sweeps' cancer. Cancer of the scrotum due to sweat mingled with soot that's never washed away, beginning in an open sore and ending in death.*

Julius paid for Jean-Baptiste's time. How much, I've no idea. The chink belonged to Higgins, anyhow. Words were exchanged. Not that I listened to them. I was busy with my usual dilemma, wondering whether to clap the nameless sweepmaster in irons, evacuate his establishment and raze it, or else to attend to the actual business at hand.

Before I quite knew what had happened, we were all in the alleyway, Jean-Baptiste looking up at us with a mystified expression. Piest sank to his haunches with a hideous, overwhelmingly kind smile.

'What a scoundrel you work for. You remember me and Mr Wilde, yes?'

Jean-Baptiste nodded.

'We've a proposal, Jean-Baptiste, and we hope that you will consider the mission with due care,' my fellow copper star continued. 'We wish you to climb down one last chimney and remove some papers from a house. Papers that belong to noble parties unable to retrieve them. It would be hero's work, the essence of chivalry, and afterward you would be placed in a school and never sweep a chimney again. God and fate willing. What say you?'

He said not a word, of course. It took us ten minutes, in the mouth of that unholy crack in the sea of brick, to convince the boy that we truly meant to take him away from his sweepmaster. That we were copper stars, lawless lawbringers, and so cared not one whit about indentures or apprenticeships. That he didn't 'belong' to anyone. And that I wanted him to steal something when I'd explicitly instructed him *never again*. The challenge of speaking half English and half bizarrely comprehensible sign didn't aid matters.

My ethics didn't help either. I'd not known, not until seeing it, the sort of scars he'd earn in that dungeon. And by the time we'd near to convinced him, I felt filthy. I didn't blame Piest or Julius; they're good men, the best of men, and kinchin drift through our streets like so many bits of river trash along the shore. I'm not exceptional, on the contrary.

I've simply been river trash. And I can't abide bullying.

'Stop,' I said at last. All eyes swept to me. 'Stop all of this. Jean-Baptiste, you're leaving that bastard's employ either way. You don't have to help us. I'll find you a new ken.'

My friends shifted their feet.

'He's right.' Julius smiled. 'You're not going back.'

The boy's eyes made every effort to widen, but scratched against coal dust and blinked frantically.

'As to the quest – it's once, and once only,' Piest said. 'You make the choice. There's risk, but we'll do everything we can to protect you.'

'It's for someone the same age as you,' I said softly. 'Another boy, called Jonas. This is wretchedly unfair and I'm sorry for it. But you can rescue him. Are you willing?'

The kinchin drove the back of his wrist into his watery eyes and rubbed hard. Gave a little heave of his shoulders. Smiled faintly.

'You have to say yes or no,' I admonished.

He nodded.

'Good man,' Julius said to the boy, shaking his hand.

We fell into a line as we set off for West Broadway. A moment later, my friend Mr Piest noticed that I was in serious difficulties. He sidled over and touched my arm.

'You want to throw that soulless wretch in the Tombs on brothel-keeping charges. But you're . . . not presently capable of making an appearance at our workplace.'

Forcing the stifled air from my lungs, I nodded. Attempting to expel the mad responsibility that I personally rid New York of adults who suppose undersized kinchin bodies to be bartered and sold, small slaves of every color and description. I'd thought to exhale my self-imposed duty and focus on Jonas's free papers.

It didn't work.

'Don't worry about that pimp another instant, Mr Wilde. You need not trouble yourself.'

'Why not?'

'I'll arrest him for you at daybreak,' Mr Piest trilled, charging into the gloom. 'I'll put the scurrilous blackguard in the westernmost cell block, on the ground level where the floor never dries.'

'Lord, but you're a prize,' I exclaimed. And meant it.

If Piest wasn't a grown man – and a peacekeeper at that – I'd have sworn that he giggled.

'Come along, Mr Wilde,' he called. 'And do stop pretending as if you're still a mystery to me, following a six month association. I may not be quite so gifted at unraveling enigmas as you are, but I've considerably more practice. And you aren't so very puzzling, you know. Now, quick march! There's work to be done.'

There comes a point at which events leave your control. After the hard push on the sled over the icy crest of the hill, after the reins have broken and the horse has abandoned its wits. After your foot leaves the cliffside and your balance can't be regained and you're falling, a wide emptiness in your chest and only the rush of gravity and the salt spray on your lips where once you could still have said no.

You can't always feel that moment, though. I certainly didn't. Not on this occasion.

I stood with Jean-Baptiste in the rear yard of 84 West Broadway, which boasted several long flowerboxes wreathed in white. Our breath visible, hearts beating in a rapid duet. The moon had revealed itself, leering with crooked teeth. I wanted to drag the clouds over the distant lamp illuminating all our designs. Pulling out my watch, I was able to see the time. That was infuriating. Not the hour, the visibility. Herding the kinchin back underneath the stunted awning above the servants' entrance, I shook my head in the general direction of the sky.

I was minutes away from sealing a number of fates, as it happened. Though I was blissfully unaware of it at the time.

Jean-Baptiste arrested my sleeve and aimed an eyebrow at me.

I held up a single finger, meaning *wait*.

Tapping his palm against the wall of the building at a furious tempo, my small friend indicated his impatience.

But there were procedures in place. Signals. Schemes as intricately rigged as the sails of the great ships in our harbors. Patting the lad's shoulder, I watched as a raccoon slunk over the gate opening onto the rear alley. Paws silent, eyes yellow and dark

ringed, searching for bones. Then two sets of human feet passed by
– a pair of men, by the sound of it. For a harrowing instant I thought
that they slowed. But it was only my restless energy, for the steps
crunched away.

When they'd passed, I sank to my haunches and repeated very
low, 'You'll come straight back if the flue seems to be closed?'

Jean Baptiste nodded. He drew the long shaft of a flue in the air,
ending in a sharply angled space that I'd soon enough guessed to be
the chimney pot. When he showed me a particular angle of attack
and shook his head, followed by tracing a shallower progression
and a nod, ending with the full stop of his palm in the air, I'd an
excellent notion of the sorts of spaces he generally contorted
himself into. I knew without being told that they were dark as
death, and all too often baking from the recently doused fire in the
grate. But apart from that, chimneys are about a foot wide. When
they're not smaller. For me, the act of crawling into one would be
a personal nightmare.

'But you're usually climbing *up* them.'

He smiled, shrugged. The boy's hand made a *whooshing* gesture
of sliding down the flue and landing, with a *puff*, in the soot pile.

'There won't be a soot pile. You've not cleaned it. I'm serious
about you taking care – it's three stories down.'

Ducking, he mimed bracing his back against one surface and his
knees against the other, shuffling downward to the hearth using his
arms.

'Doesn't that hurt?'

He pulled up his sleeve. The skin at the back of his arm had been
polished with something abrasive, likely vinegar or acid scrubbed
in with bristles and vigor. His elbows were shiny, like halfshells.
Like scars.

'He did this to you?'

Jean-Baptiste spread his palms wide.

He does this to everyone.

I was half tempted to murmur *Forget the sodding chimney, someone
needs killing* when the faint sound of music reached my ears. The

tune was a spiritual, the voice rich and affecting, genteel in accent if not in execution. As a matter of fact, the singer could be nothing save half a jug deep in rum or corn whiskey.

> Oh, carry me away, carry me away, my Lord
> Carry me to the burying ground.
> The greens trees a-bowing . . . Sinner, fare you well!
> I thank the Lord I want to go,
> To leave them all behind—

'Halt, if you please, sir!' came a much shriller warble from the sidewalk before the front entrance to 84 West Broadway.

There. Our pair of watchmen had taken position before the house.

I lifted a finger toward Jean-Baptiste's nose. 'You're never going back to your sweepmaster, no matter what happens. Be *careful*.'

He nodded. Beyond, Julius Carpenter's raucous singing continued. Punctuated intermittently with Jakob Piest's voice raised in hearty lawkeeping protest.

In retrospect, I ought not to have been worrying about my small friend's climbing skills. In retrospect, I ought to have been anxious over literally everything else.

In retrospect, I am very nearly as sharp as I pretend to be.

Treading silent as I could, I whisked a crumpled sheet away from the building's rear wall and retrieved the ladder I'd deposited there the night previous. Setting it against the side of the house, I pulled a small grappling hook attached to a rope from an empty cistern, a tool I'd likewise planted. I clenched the rope, wound it a few times around my fingers, and commenced climbing. It was a tall ladder, and it creaked beneath my weight, though Jean-Baptiste would doubtless have an easier time of it.

'I tell you, I *must* see some identification,' Piest squeaked from the roadway. 'Public drunkenness is a crime, but however you crawled into the bottle, sir, I've no wish to drag you to the Tombs whilst you find your way out again.'

Ping.

I'd missed. I hazarded a glance down from the top of the ladder, saw Jean-Baptiste staring back, and tried again.

Ping.

The hook lodged in the chimney.

Thin scraps of cloud drifted above us, as if the sky were peeling, moonlight shining through the sickly grey ribbons. Testing more than half of my weight on the rope, I determined it would hold a boy who could probably count the hearty meals in his history on one hand. Then I swiftly descended, half listening to our watchdogs as Julius allowed Piest to harass him in the least apt display of efficient police work to date.

When Jean-Baptiste was three rungs up, I spoke in his ear.

'You recall what Miss Wright told me – once you get in through the parlor, go up the stairs to the left and into the master bedroom. In the back of the wardrobe is a teak box, unlocked. Bring every paper inside to me. If that chimney grows too dangerous for *any* reason, come back. Use the rope for as far as you can. Yes?'

He scurried away. Up the ladder like a fireman, up the rope like an acrobat, onto the roof's lip like a bird coming to rest. By the time he was down the chimney's mouth, taking the rope along because I'd told him to, I might have dreamt him. A sooty spirit drifting through the night like smoke from a ninepin cigar.

'It's a damned *outrage!*' Julius's voice cried. 'Since when have *star police* the right to manhandle *free citizens*? What's a cheering song on a winter's night to do with you? I've half a mind to knock you down.'

'I'll have you for violence, as well as for drunkenness.'

'I'll have your teeth in the mud!'

'Do not try me too far—'

'I'll send you flat on your face and the crowds will line up to shake my hand!'

Smiling at the exceedingly peaceful fray at the front of the house, I slung my hand over a rung of the ladder and commenced waiting.

Waiting, for a man of my temperament, is next door to unbearable.

A whistle like the distant shriek of a forgotten teakettle rang in my ears beneath the sound of my friends blithely quarreling. Meanwhile, my eyes were pinned to the chimney bricks, neck craning as I willed Jean-Baptiste out of the lightless shaft. So close. *So close.* I smelled the bright tang of success in the very air around me, felt the bittersweet ache of *finally getting something right, goddamn it* pulsing beneath my fingernails.

So close.

Minutes passed. Insults were exchanged in the icy street beyond. I waited, statuelike. As if I'd been carved centuries before and the smallest breath could shatter me.

Then Julius, after shouting a furious expletive I'd never heard emerge from his lips in my life, commenced singing again.

'Oh, carry me away, carry me away, my Lord . . .'

'Christ,' I hissed under my breath. My skin frosted over, hairs prickling in fright.

For of course that was the *other* signal. The one that I'd been keen to avoid.

'What's all this about?' called a new voice. 'By Jesus. Piest, is that you, you scoundrel?'

Beardsley, I thought, gripping the ladder rung as a jolt of recognition rattled my teeth. *And with McDivitt, no doubt.*

'Is that boy after givin' you a bit of trouble, then?' McDivitt's brogue chimed in. 'Isn't it *lucky* we came along. Ye might imagine that we'd be sore after having a *gun* waved at us, but the honor o' the copper stars demands we come to your aid.'

'I can see to this, gentlemen!' Piest crowed, his voice gone reedy and anxious. 'And I hope you understand I was acting on behalf of a friend when we quarreled at the Tombs. As were you, I gather. Professionally, we are all brothers in arms, eh?'

'Oh, so you *don't* want help from the likes of us, then?' McDivitt's voice sneered.

'Don't you like us, Mr Piest?' Beardsley added in a marrow-

293

freezing tone. 'I think he doesn't like us, McDivitt. I think this doddering old maggot doesn't like us at all.'

'That's very unkind,' McDivitt lamented. 'Strikes me right in the heart, it does. To hear such a thing.'

The inky seep of fear that gripped me commenced flowing outward through every channel it could find. Twin urges of *Don't leave your post* and *Don't allow your friends to be thrashed senseless without you* tore at me. Meanwhile, I removed the ladder from the wall and raced to cover it. It was a risk, but also a shortcut, for I couldn't possibly leave it there when we fled. A rope dangling from the side of a building that doesn't nearly reach the ground would be mistook for a snapped laundry line. But a ladder propped against a wall meant broken windows and an infestation of Irish. The alarm would have gone up at once if I'd left it.

Just as I'd hidden the blasted thing, I heard from beyond the repulsive crack of a fist hitting bone. Followed by a muffled moan that could only have emerged from Mr Piest.

I was flat against the edge of the rear wall an instant later, chest thumping as I listened to cackles from the other copper stars. I was almost ready to act as hotheaded as I generally do. But then a shout of inebriated glee went up and a pair of feet flew away down the street.

'That darkie *bastard*! After him!' McDivitt shouted.

More bootsteps rang out in pursuit. More cries echoed through the quiet. I couldn't imagine what had happened, couldn't know if Piest was badly injured or not. Quivering on the edge of taking a dive streetward for worse or for better, I stopped to look up at the roofline.

A tiny face stared down at me, mouth wide in soundless surprise.

I ran the few paces back into the rear yard. Jean-Baptiste had pulled the rope up after him and flung it over the edge of the tiles to reach the ladder, which of course was no longer there.

'Come on, I'll catch you,' I hissed, going to the wall.

The lad lost no time in grasping the cord, and it was the work of four seconds for him to slide halfway down the building. When he neared the end of the line, however, he hesitated – instincts demanding he clutch it for dear life rather than take the freefalling plunge he spent all his waking energies avoiding.

Understandable. His nightmares consisted of a sudden drop and a sharp stop. But I hadn't the time.

Jump, I mouthed up at Jean-Baptiste, pleading.

His eyes said he'd as soon throw himself headfirst down a chimney.

Leaning with my palms against the brick, I stared up in mounting dismay. The child's shirt had rucked up against the rope, and I could see where he'd belted a number of papers to his skeletal chest.

This kinchin just accomplished the impossible for you, and he's determined to live the rest of his days dangling from the side of a townhouse.

'Jean-Baptiste, *please*,' I insisted softly.

Screwing his swollen eyes shut, he let go. Abandoned himself to gravity and tumbled through the air.

What I remember about catching him wasn't how courageous he'd just been or how perfectly he landed in my arms. It was that he weighed so little, composed of spirit and ash as he was, that he might have been the charcoal drawing I'd made of him. Just an infinitesimally thin portrait of a sweep and not a boy at all.

'All right?' I asked, setting him on his feet.

He swayed for an instant, but soon recovered. Looking up dizzily, he nodded. Then he laughed.

'Then run,' I said, taking his hand and flying for the alley.

I first spied George Higgins half an hour later, mindlessly patrolling the rear yard of his own townhouse. The lights within his residence were blazing very nearly as brightly as the eyes of their owner as Jean-Baptiste and I shut the gate. Reverend Brown sat on a neat pile of firewood, gloved hands folded in his lap. And to my boundless delight, Jakob Piest rested on the steps before the back door, holding a small slab of beef to his jaw.

'Thank God,' I exhaled. 'You've no notion how close I came to joining the mitten mill. Are you all right, Mr Piest?'

Piest's mottled complexion was pale, his mouth actively bruising. 'Reveling in the triumph of high adventure and most gratified to hail the conquering heroes,' the Dutchman answered readily.

Higgins had rooted himself to the ground at the sight of us. 'You have them, then? The free papers?'

Jean-Baptiste reached into his shirt and produced a bundle of decidedly soot-smirched documents. They were among the most beautiful things I'd ever seen. They were without any question the most beautiful things George Higgins had ever seen. For an instant I almost didn't want him to touch our ill-gotten trophy, though I couldn't have begun to say why. He reached forward, almost angry in his haste, and the kinchin hastily shied away, dropping his prize. Frightened of a blow. A kick. Something worse.

When Higgins had shuffled through the stack and found the free papers, however, his face changed to something nearly approaching fondness. Or awe in the presence of a miracle. Akin to both.

'You took these?' he said to the boy.

Jean-Baptiste nodded.

'God bless you. You'll stay with me from now until we find a proper home for you.'

He was beaming so wide, the filthy kinchin staring back at him in bewilderment, that scarce anyone heard me say, 'Tell me Julius Carpenter is inside.'

The Reverend Brown coughed, clasping his hands a bit tighter. 'I regret to say no. But I must.'

The silence that spread was much colder than the air surrounding us. And the night was already deeply bitter. Jean-Baptiste looked as if he was failing to shiver only because he'd learned how not to, and Higgins wore the faintest hint of frost upon his coat collar. He passed me back the free papers for safekeeping. Possibly because I hadn't yet managed to prise my eyes off of them.

'What happened?' I questioned Mr Piest as I hid the documents inside my greatcoat. Already cursing myself and my clever, clever plans.

'We were accosted by Mr McDivitt and Mr Beardsley.' Piest shifted on his stair. 'They were . . . extremely combative. They demanded a fight. When they began one, I . . . I am not proud of this, Mr Wilde. But I was found lacking.'

'You weren't either,' I protested, seeing visions of nooses and impromptu bonfires and simple drowning with stones tied to Julius's ankles. 'What *happened?*'

'Mr Carpenter assaulted Mr McDivitt somehow. When they and Mr Beardsley all took to their heels . . . I cannot apologize enough.' Piest looked as distressed as I'd ever seen him. 'I don't know what happened. One instant, I was floored, and the next . . .'

'I'd stolen a little remembrance from that leech McDivitt,' Julius interrupted.

The gate swung closed, creaking mournfully. We all of us wheeled about to peer into the gloom. And there stood Julius Carpenter. Winded, hale, self-satisfied, with his breath puffing into clouds before his lips.

'I'm not very fast, Timothy, but I'm faster than the rest of your force,' he told me, leaning briefly on the metal of the gate as he recovered himself.

'Why did they chase you?' I exclaimed, going to him. 'It was perfect, however you distracted them. But what on earth . . .'

He reached into his coat pocket and flung something on the ground. It had many points and a dark, brassy hue, like a fallen oak leaf half-hid in the cracks of the paving stones.

It very much resembled a copper star.

'Give that back to the blackguard, if you like,' Julius said with a heartfelt smile. 'I don't mind in the slightest. I can't keep it, after all. Since we're together again at last, shall we go inside?'

CHAPTER TWENTY–ONE

When we eat rice white man no give us to drink . . . when
Sun Set white men give us little water . . . when we in
havana vessel white men give rice to all who no eat fast he
take whip you . . . a plenty of them died.

Letter written to New York abolitionist Lewis Tappan
by *Amistad* survivor Kale, 1840

As a reward for my successful plan, I was elected one of the
party to deliver Jonas's free papers the next morning and
trusted with the actual address of Neither Here Nor There.

As a punishment for his foolishness over falling brutally in love,
George Higgins elected himself to accompany me.

I met him before his mother's residence in the spun-sugar
February dawn, sunlight pale as an oyster shell and the dull little
sparrows trilling pleasantries to one another from the naked
treetops. Higgins finished a thin cigar as I alighted the hack, tossing
it in a puff of sparks on the cobblestones, clearly having just walked
from his own rooms near Washington Square. After I'd paid the
driver, I swung my eyes to Higgins and inspected him again.
Considering.

He looked about as well as most condemned men at the Tombs
do when their breakfast arrives on hanging days. Near enough to

the end to decide brave façades aren't particularly useful. 'How is Jean-Baptiste settling in?' I asked by way of greeting.

'My housekeeper and I have bathed him upward of ten times. He needs seven or eight more, but at least he's amenable. Splashes about like a fish, laughing when we try to drag him out again.'

'Well, there's a glimpse of the world as it should be.'

Higgins sighed. 'Perhaps you're right. But I can't help but think it should all have been different somehow.'

My jaw tensed, because that was just it. *Different somehow.* I agreed with Higgins. Some aspect yet eluded me, some mistaken figure was ruining the balance sheet, and the world entire was beginning to look slightly askew. Meanwhile, the poor man's beard was lengthening around its architectural edges, and there was a fragile, tender look to his active eyes. Tucking his striped silk cravat farther into his vest, he shook his head at his mother's house. 'And not just because I wish it so. I can't trace where it began to go so utterly wrong.'

With Lucy Adams's murder, I thought, surprised.

Then, *No, the initial kidnapping by Varker and Coles.* And after that, *Vicious words carved into a beautiful woman long ago.*

As Higgins glared in anguish at his family home, I realized I hadn't the faintest notion either. And that alarmed me.

Something is missing.

'We can still get them away from here.'

'And what does that make us? Sending them off into the wild because they've asked us to?' Higgins peered beneath my hat brim with fresh interest.

'I don't know, Mr Higgins. Worthy of them, maybe?'

'Hmm.' He started toward the door. 'Really, we've been through enough by now . . . call me George, nearly everyone else does. Even that Inman rascal down at the 'Change, confound him.'

My step hitched. George Higgins was as much fortress as man, composed of walls and moats , and his tone suggested I was being given a password to call down the drawbridge. 'Really?'

'Unless you want me to keep addressing you as Mr Wilde, in

which case I retract the offer.'

'No, call me whatever you like. Anyway, I'd supposed you called me *that whey-brained copper star* or something similar. Worse.'

'I did indeed.' He gave me a tight smile, removing his hat and gloves as the door swung open. 'But I've decided that *Timothy* is considerably more efficient. Don't think me too admiring of our police force, now – I'm not about to start voting Democrat anytime soon.'

In the parlor, George Higgins kissed his mother warmly on her wrinkled cheek. If he was angry at her failure to tell him Delia's whereabouts, he failed to show it. As for Mrs Higgins, she sat with a small tray before her, finishing spiced tea and a buttered biscuit, wearing a red shawl tucked neatly about her shoulders.

'Hello, Mr Wilde,' she said before I'd announced myself. 'George, dearest, you won't be tiresome? Betrayal of a confidence—'

'I'm not being tiresome, Mother.' His voice might as well have emerged from the bottom of a well. 'You did what you thought best. But I'll see Delia before she goes, if she's to be relying on me for the means to settle up north.'

'She expects you,' his mother assured us, wiping crumbs from her fingers. 'The arrangements are quite settled – Mr Wilde, if you would do us the favor of seeing that their departure goes smoothly, I'd be much obliged to you. It will be two mornings from this one. March the first.'

'I'll be here.'

'I warn you, Mother, I'll be in attendance as well, if only for my own peace of mind,' Higgins said. Though his tone indicated he'd never possess the commodity *peace of mind* again.

Reaching, she found his hand. 'I wish you'd been spared this, my boy. Much more than you know.'

Pressing her fingers, he made for the door beyond. We passed through the museum, the shrine to illumination with its countless lamps and bright hints of crystal. No one greeted us upon the narrow hidden staircase, and the sickroom that had so recently housed the escaped slave was quite empty. When we reached the inner sitting-room door, Delia's voice called us through.

She sat in the widest armchair, with Jonas's small body tucked up against her side, reading to the child. Delia had rearranged her hair, passing one strand about her head in a braid like a coronet, the effect quite queenlike. The arch to her brow wasn't superior precisely, and the slim bow of her lips was far from aloof or unfeeling. But she appeared to have molded herself into the shape she wished to be in when the blow fell. If Lot's wife had been given time to craft the exact attitude of her transformation, had she adopted an insolent spine and a sweetly curved hand when cruelly transformed into salt, she might have looked so. She might have glanced back at the only home she had known with just such an expression. I spent a meandering moment attempting to recall the name of Lot's wife before realizing she hadn't been granted one.

'Mr Wilde.' She placed the book on the table and passed a hand over Jonas's cheek. 'You remember Mr Wilde, Jonas. He's done it, I think. He's taken back what we need to get away.'

'I don't care.' Jonas's eyes looked similar to Jean-Baptiste's, so swollen were they with weeping.

'You *will* care, love.' Rising, she kissed him on the top of his head. 'Doing as I asked doubtless must have required enormous effort. I apologize, Mr Wilde. And I thank you.'

'You needn't do either.' I pulled the free papers from my coat pocket and passed them to her.

When she took them, her hand faltered. She smoothed the other across her hip, swaying a little. At last she smiled. A broken smile, as if a gemstone had cracked down the middle. It hurt to look at.

'Hello, George,' Delia whispered without meeting his eyes. 'I thought you would come yourself.'

Taking her wrist, he lightly kissed her cheek. There was such a force of affection in that minuscule gesture, it could have felled armies. I stepped toward the fireplace, wanting to notice less about my surroundings.

But I was still missing something. The hairs at the back of my neck whispered so.

'I've brought what you asked.' He produced a quantity of paper money. Rather than giving it to her, he went to the nearest table and set it down. 'There's extra here, in case of later emergency.'

Delia had begun to look faint. 'I'll pay you back when I reach Canada. I can find work teaching. I must, for us to live. I'll pay it all back.'

George Higgins huffed another stony laugh. 'This is a gift.'

'No, it must be a loan. I will make you restitution.'

'I insist.'

'I am aware of your opinion of loan defaulters and bad creditors,' Delia shot back, sounding almost angry. 'It is not a fond one.'

'Don't insult me.'

'It isn't an insult. It's my life. It's paying you what my life *costs*.'

'Don't *fight*, you make me *sick*,' Jonas shouted.

The kinchin tore out of our sight. He left behind him the feeling that an enormous clock had chimed. An immediacy entered the room when he left it, breathed down our spines with fiery gusts and stale teeth. A child's future was at stake. He was free only so long as we kept our heads.

Higgins flinched at the carpet. 'Please accept my apology. Surely you know yourself to be priceless in my estimation. Only tell me if you want anything further of me.'

Delia's lips began to quiver. The barest vibration, like the tremble of a candle flame.

'I can ask nothing more of you, George. You've been so generous already.'

Wrong answer, I thought.

He backed away, gazing at her. Placed the hand that still held his gloves on the door frame and allowed himself the slightest shake of his head, jaw clenched. The last hot meal before the executioner's arrival had clearly ended. George Higgins twisted his gloves with an expression of finality and then struck them hard against the wood.

'Godspeed to you both, in that case. Timothy, I'll see myself out.'

When he had disappeared and the echo of his feet above our heads had faded into nothing, Delia Wright sat upon the chair and covered her mouth with her hands.

'Miss Wright, I'll not trouble you much further. Though I will be present day after tomorrow, to see that you depart safely.'

I received no answer. She rocked back and forth once, pressing her fingers to her lips. Then she stopped. Dropping her hands to her lap, she forced herself to look in my direction.

'Does George Higgins frighten you?' I asked. 'Please tell me the truth.'

'He frightens my pride,' she rasped. 'I've a considerable stock of it, and he treats me as if I were a champagne flute.'

'That isn't all,' I insisted.

'No.' She bit at her nail, then pressed her hands together hard. 'But Lucy's death had nothing to do with George, if that's what you're implying. He has offended me personally, in a way I'd not wish to discuss.'

Since she appeared wholly sincere, I'd no answer for her. Instead I offered her the rest of my plunder. When she saw I held another paper, her brow furrowed – but as she took it, bemusement faded. With a single finger, she traced over the letters her sister had written.

'I never meant it for a trophy,' I said. 'Keep the marriage certificate between Lucy Wright and Charles Adams if you like. Only tell me, if there is more to discover. That's all I ask. I owed you the free papers, but . . . please, Miss Wright. If there is aught to tell me, *tell me*.'

Refolding the Massachusetts State certificate of marriage, she extended her arm, and I took the document back. It had been in the precious pile along with one or two old letters and receipts, the small stack of paper Jean-Baptiste had stolen.

I'd thought that it mattered, somehow. Counted.

'We imagined it real,' she answered. 'I don't want any part of that piece of paper. It isn't my fault Charles Adams never existed, Mr Wilde.'

And no – it wasn't. She was manifestly a good person, had worshipped a sister who was taken untimely away, and *What are you still doing here, Timothy Wilde? Demanding she wrest clues from marriage certificates?* My own failures seemed stacked about me like walls. Was I so desperate for a rope to be thrown down that I expected Delia to solve my mystery for me?

I shook her hand. And for good measure I kissed her hand. Because I liked her and I'd liked her sister, maybe more than I should have for crime victims I was aiding, if I'm honest, and then I stalked to the door.

When I'd reached it, I thought of Mercy as last I'd seen her. Before she'd left me and then swiftly learned that the deep waters of a boundless sea can seem one's friends if one is wracked enough, and suddenly I couldn't bear to leave the room. Mercy had been drained, grief-sick. Beautiful. She'd been my whole world, and she'd stood there and let me send her away, she'd thought that better, the wiser route, she'd taken my offer of help and watched me turn from her, she'd gazed at my back as I retreated and she'd *gone to London*, and in the ugliest hours of fitful nights, that makes me angry enough to want to stab something.

'Is this the only way for it to end?' I asked.

Something shifted in Delia's throat. Then she tilted her shoulders at me. The cautious, self-measuring shake back and forth to loosen the muscles before a boxer enters the ring. I ought to have recognized it.

'How dare you ask me that?' was all she said.

It should have been enough. That tone would have frozen me solid, had I not already been hot enough under the collar to barge in where I wasn't desired or – in fact – effectual.

'You can ask anything of George Higgins,' I told her, knowing myself a fool even as I said it. 'He wants you to. It's none of my business, but – Miss Wright, he doesn't want to give you money. He wants to give you *everything*.'

304

'How can I request that of him?' she cried, half-closed fist working at the base of her slender throat. 'Here he has wealth and stature. Here he has a claim. *Here*, in New York. A life of his own, a *place*. I won't ask him to abandon it.'

'You do love him,' I realized. 'How can you not understand that you're what he wants?'

She smiled at me pityingly. 'George wants a figment of his imagination – a fine lady to preside over his realm and pour tea for guests who talk of tariffs and play sophisticated card games and drink French wine.'

'He doesn't,' I protested. 'He wants you.'

'Well, then. He'll have to track me, won't he?'

By this time, her small hand had lit upon my breastbone and she was forcing me out the way I'd come. There was a hard object in it, and when I reached up, curious, she slapped it into my palm. Valentine's house key. I'd forgotten about it entirely. It seemed a relic from a past age.

'If he wants me so badly, he'll follow after like a good American hound dog,' she continued as she ushered me out. 'That's a point in favor for dogs – the sincerity. If they snap after a piece of meat, you know well enough that they mean it.'

I realized when I awoke next morning that it was the last full day that Delia and Jonas would spend in New York. That oughtn't to have felt disheartening. But seeing as I'd still not managed to inform them who murdered their kin, it did feel *wrong*.

Then I recalled that I'd a Democratic political function to attend that evening, which felt *perverse*.

Sitting up with a groan, I kicked away my quilt and set about washing and dressing and generally loathing the particular character of February 28, 1846. I continued absently hating my life throughout shaving, and dressing – in the best togs I had, which weren't good at all – and marching down the stairs to scare up bread and coffee. But when I'd reached the bakery, I replaced quiet distaste with curiosity.

Mrs Boehm sat with a steaming mug of tea before her, staring in befuddlement at a letter, my morning copy of the *Herald*, and a package wrapped in brown paper. When Mrs Boehm is befuddled, she scowls at objects as though they've insulted her mother's honor. She looks like a pale, thin, kindly woman about to slap a blackguard in the face with a leather glove. It's remarkably endearing.

'What's this?'

'Three things. For you, Mr Wilde.'

'Why are you glaring daggers at them? Are we at war with Mexico or with Britain?'

'Who can say anymore. Both, neither. I do not understand,' she explained in her always hoarse, lightly accented voice, 'how it comes to be that letters from over the ocean should arrive without any postage.'

I dove for it. Mind awhirl with calculations.

It takes more than two weeks to receive a missive from London, which meant that Mercy had fired this one off before ever seeing mine. That was . . . a thought to be filed away for later. Of tremendous importance. Meanwhile, while this one was enclosed in an envelope and addressed to me in her fantastical scrawl, my landlady was perfectly right; it hadn't any postage. That was twice, now, that correspondence from the only girl who'd ever made me want to spend the remainder of my days memorizing the whorls on the tips of her fingers had arrived by magic.

'Are we losing our minds?' I asked.

Mrs Boehm shrugged, jutting her pleasantly square chin at the letter. 'Read it. I will bring the tea now. I am thinking you will need the tea.'

That was inarguable, so I thanked her and tore the missive open. It was near as long as the first, and every bit as illegible.

Dear Timothy,

I had convinced myself that it would be better to await your response and thus know as many of your thoughts as you wish to tell me – what color they are, I suppose, whether black or red or a pale, peaceful blue. Whether you wish to describe them to me. Whether you wish me to pen notes to you at all. And I still agree with myself – waiting would be better. But I found myself dwelling over my own recently mailed correspondence, you see, because I made a point of not forcing myself to pick it over like poor needlework, and now I worry so. Over what I said, or failed to, and how receipt of my tale may have affected you. I am not so stupid – you have said it yourself, the last thing I am in the midst of a teeming jungle of faults is stupid – that I can pretend a letter from me would affect you not at all.

It is all the more maddening to fret over your possible responses because I'd used to know how you fared more or less daily, and what's more, I'd been able to predict you fairly well even when you weren't in sight. Now the thought of having very likely sent you a dim and cobwebby sketch of my little life here, and not seeing at once your brows folding in on each other, and at once distracting you, feels a bit like holding a hand to a heating kettle – bearable at first, but then. Oh, then. And all the more so because when I read my own words lately, I've not the foggiest idea who wrote them. Anyone could have written you that letter. I only hope she treated you well.

I am near certain I forgot to say thank you. Thank you. I'd not be here if it weren't for you, in so very many senses, and of course you'd no wish for me to depart at all. To say that you've been kind to me would be to put very small words to something enormous like the curve of the horizon, so I shan't. But thank you.

If I was very morbid before, do your best not to pay me any undue attention. One day I'll stop seeing mortality stamped like the mark of Cain on every passing stranger, and one day the ticking tocking ticking of my own survival will be less loud, I pray. My heartbeat is quite grotesque at the moment, but I will try to muffle it. I promise. I will write more words. Sensible ones. I will draw better maps of my mind. I will try harder. I will drown the ticking in a sea of ink, and yesterday I saved a young boy from a terrible *case of pneumonia, and what else can I expect to be given? Aside from good work and blank paper? I've reached the conclusion that the balance of my charitable deeds in New York had more to do with being absent from Papa's presence – his house, his air, his eyes, his everything – than to do with being present for the needy. But there are worse escape routes, are there not? Death ought to mean something, as lives do. Mine will. No matter how loud the ticking.*

You deserve my apology, as well. I never felt half so beautiful or mysterious in any other company by comparison to yours. But I supposed you chased the irresistible unknown – that because you had never exchanged hope for action, you therefore remained intrigued. I might have shattered it, gone in like a barbarian army and razed the temple. I never did. To be honest, I believed you'd lose regard on the instant you achieved mine, so preoccupied were you. If I'd been at all brave or selfless, I'd have smashed my statue and pedestal, crushed that Mercy to a faceless powder and replaced her with this one. Please forgive me for polishing her and setting her ever in the best light – she was an illusion, but she made my life more bearable at times, though at other times she infuriated me. And please rip her down. Supposing you haven't yet. She was terribly uncomfortable, so petrified and dry and liable to crack.

Words come hard today. Every day, now. I hope you know what I mean. I never wanted you to see the grime in the sill if you opened the window. But now I'm not myself any longer, maybe you'll come to know someone new, and like her enough to write her in London? She still resembles me, after all. If not, you've already done far more for me than you know.

If you cannot be well and be close to me at once, tell me to stop. I do remember nonsense about letters in bottles and correspondence burned unopened, and I am braver than that, though only just.

Sincerely,

Mercy Underhill

How long I stared at that letter, I've no idea. How many pulses of the extremely inconvenient organ in my chest lanced against my rib cage, I've no notion either. I think it was quite a spell. Then I read it again, and I realized something that tore a messy hole right through me.

Mercy wasn't merely despondent. For all the passion her words had always owned, the bright chaos and the rage and the teeth beneath the smile, they'd been orderly. Sensible. And they were like her children – she could quote verbatim sonnets she'd written when twelve years old. The thought of her staring at her writing without recognition was akin to God mistaking man for a serpent. Barring the possibility that she'd been merely exhausted on both occasions she'd written . . .

Mercy was unwell.

Mechanically, I reached for the tea. Tea wasn't going to help. But I felt as if a butcher were scraping the meat from my bones.

'Not good news,' Mrs Boehm said quietly.

'Not all of it,' I agreed, voice strained.

'What is inside of this package? It's from your brother.'

'I probably don't want it, then.'

'No? I like him, your brother.'

'Absolutely everyone else does. I do occasionally. Open it if you like.'

She did, with enthusiasm better befitting Christmas morning as experienced by a six-year-old than a package from my inexcusable sibling. When she'd pulled away all the string and paper, her broad brow cleared, and her face lit up in delight.

'Krásný,' she exclaimed. It was a Bohemian day and not a German one in her head, apparently.

Despite my sincerest effort not to, I leaned forward.

She touched a set of used clothing. Used, but not factory slops – the fabric and stitchwork were sumptuous. I could simply tell, from a frayed buttonhole there or a crease here, that it had been worn previous. There was a white shirt, pale and soft as goose down. A double vest of sapphire velvet. A trimly fitted set of buff trousers. A silken scarlet cravat. Finally, a frock coat of dove grey, with some of the longest and most sweepingly cut tails I have ever seen.

It was all smallish. As if cut for a lean man, and not a very tall one.

Mrs Boehm, eyes sparkling, passed me the accompanying note.

Embarrass me at a Party function, and I will alter where your nose is oriented on your face.

It was about then that my head hit the table. I shook it, rolling my ruined brow to and fro against the wood. That felt nice. Comforting.

'What are you thinking?' Mrs Boehm asked worriedly.

'I was wondering when the moment would come that my life is ruined entirely. More so than my life is already ruined, I mean.'

'And?'

'It's here,' I sighed. 'I can stop waiting. It has arrived.'

CHAPTER TWENTY-TWO

*The chastity of my daughter cannot be protected as an
American citizen, because African blood courses her veins,
consequently she has 'no rights that a white man need
respect.' She has no virtue that a white man need regard.
She has not honour that a white man need admire. No
noble qualities he need appreciate.*

William M. Mitchell, *The Under-ground Railroad,*
1860

I donned the togs, and I went to the Democratic fete.
It proved considerably more eventful than I had anticipated.

The festivities were held at Castle Garden, which is at the
southernmost tip of the island. I'm particularly fond of the shoreline
– of the Battery where you can feel the wind as if you were midriver,
and of the small pleasure grounds surrounding Castle Garden
where you can see the wide, wide bay for what it is. It used to be a
fortress, a redbrick circle of civic defense built on a manmade
island with a lengthy bridge promenade spanning the waves. I've
been there dozens of times.

That didn't spare me any shock when I arrived that evening, in
a chattering, clattering mass of other guests.

They'd carpeted the entire bridge span in scarlet. A bespectacled gent in a fur coat jostled my elbow when I froze in disbelief. Castle Garden is gaslit and every lamp was blazing, kindling smaller blazes in the countless gemstones – some diamond, some paste – arrayed in the hair of the ladies who passed me, all leaning on the arms of ponderous men with side-whiskers and gold monocles. I crossed over the water, breathing the rich brine of the bay mingled with the fresh spruce boughs adorning the lampposts. Many attendees were obviously Fifth Avenue aristocrats – landowners and trade barons and such. Others, though, were Bowery types – bruisers with greased curls escorting laughing molls in watered silk skirts, keen for liquor, dancing, and then after-hours copulation in the private rooms of the downtown coffee houses.

It didn't get any better when I went inside.

They roofed over the circular space within the fort's walls when they transformed it into a pleasure garden. But I'd never seen it so thickly slathered with gilt and bunting. Areas had been roped off for dancing, already being put to merry use. Another space boasted dozens of silver oyster platters, festooned with curling ribbons of lemon and coldly glittering ice, and a team of colored oystermen in livery were cracking shells as if their lives depended on it. Meanwhile, trays of boiled tongue in aspic and hot corn fritters swept continually past my head, as did waiters bearing enough champagne to put out last summer's fire.

I'd known, in the abstract, that the Party had money. Of course I had. I just hadn't been aware that the Party was *made of money.*

I took two champagne glasses and drained them, then took another. The waiter, bless him, didn't so much as flicker an eyelash. It greatly endeared me to the man.

The opera stage featured a cake my head wouldn't have measured up to if I'd been standing on the dais. In front of this monstrosity stood a politico of no little personal charm and a frankly alarming physical presence, with poison-green eyes and a sinister curl to his lip. Valentine was declaiming thanks, congratulations, patriotism, and continued donations to a group of smiling Party officials and their wives. He wore an azure jacket and when I peered more closely, I was given to understand that his waistcoat was populated by embroidered hummingbirds.

Clearly not the direction in which to go.

I was en route to a dimmer part of the amphitheatre, equipped with couches and coffee and cigar smoke and a piano being very aptly played, when I was recognized.

'Still with us, I see, Wilde.'

If you've never viewed an elephant outfitted for a ball, it would be difficult to grasp the effect a formal grey swallow-tailed coat has on Chief George Washington Matsell. He held a whiskey glass, swirling the liquor in the crystal tumbler. Eyeing me. I grow uncomfortable when Matsell is eyeing me. Everyone does.

'I'm sorry for all the trouble,' I offered. 'I'd apologize about my office, but that wasn't my doing.'

'No, I can't really see you inscribing your own lynching on your wall. Anyhow, you can spell *miscegenation*.'

I relaxed a fraction. 'Maybe when this has blown over . . . I could . . .'

Chief Matsell took a sip of spirits, boring termite holes in me with his eyes. 'Get back to police work at the Tombs?'

My neck commenced burning. But I nodded.

'Supposing you don't do something characteristically rash or brainless anytime soon, I don't see why not.' Matsell took on the distant expression he gets when he's weighing whether you're worth smiling at. 'Ceaselessly streaming vexations build my character. You're quite keen at that. Anyhow,' he added, gesturing lightly at first my attire and then the room at large, 'this counts. The effort to be *reasonable*.'

'It doesn't come naturally.'

'Oh, I'm well aware. The Millingtons just donated eight hundred dollars to the Party. They mentioned you by name, most appreciatively.' He slapped me on the shoulder in farewell. 'This is the system, Mr Wilde. Come to like it, or it will cease liking you.'

Biting my lip, I blinked in frustration. I'd never held any respect whatsoever for politics, but considering the Adams affair, now I was about as likely to grow fond of the Party as I was of bedbugs.

That was the moment I spied Rutherford Gates.

He stood in profile to me, twenty or so yards distant, in a herd of flounced skirts, looking dapper as usual and with his thumbs tucked into his braces. But Gates appeared . . . diminished. The eager boyishness of his gestures had faded, and a brittle layer of tension, like a glaze, covered his once-animated face. Aching to know the true reason, love thwarted or guilt discovered or any shade in between, I reached for a fresh glass just as Silkie Marsh swept up to the state senator.

Madam Marsh again wore black satin, elaborately beaded on this occasion, with a train and a low neck that showed the full swell of her porcelain skin. She wore black because she'd known no one else would, presumably, and the effect made her look a priceless piece of statuary in a yard full of bedraggled peacocks. She spent a brief time greeting Gates, her exquisite features alive with warmth, concern, and affection beneath the corona of her flaxen hair.

Then she spied me, and a guillotine blade flashed through her eyes while the smile remained fixed.

I tilted my champagne flute in her direction. A challenge, not a greeting. Her smile never faltered, but the hand resting on Gates's forearm twitched. It was pretty satisfying.

She excused herself from Gates, who still failed to notice me. Moments later, Silkie Marsh had procured a pair of fresh drinks and was sweeping in my direction, striking hazel eyes aglow.

'Mr *Wilde*. What a shock. To see you looking so well, and in honor of the Party – I can't help but think we'll be friends at last one day.'

Taking the drink, I let that monstrous notion die unheralded.

'And how goes your investigation?' she added sweetly. 'So touching, the way you've grown attached to this family. So very *personally* involved.'

That merited a sharp look. 'And aren't *you* personally involved, Madam Marsh?'

Laughter looks very fine within the complex hollows of a white throat, and thus Silkie Marsh angles her head away when she succumbs to mirth in front of a man. When she'd got her breath back, she leaned close, murmuring in my ear. 'I've been involved personally in only the most trivial fashion. But I've enjoyed myself quite disproportionately. And Rutherford Gates is a great friend of mine, so I will admit to being deeply invested in his well-being and the success of his upcoming campaign. He is a wonderful man, when you come to know him, and has done much for our fair state. I hate to see him suffer. I've been doing all that I can to keep up his spirits in the midst of this inexplicable tragedy.'

Her breath alive in my ear, I thought of her visit to Val's rooms that night. About reasons for murder and the flavor of lies. Nothing fit. *Nothing.* Aside from Delia and Jonas's departure for Canada the next morning, I'd failed in every way possible.

'So you won't tell me how you're getting on?' she cooed.

'Badly. You know as much.'

'Well, never fear, Mr Wilde.' She touched my hand, and it shot a slick eel from my neck to my toes. 'Doubtless your investigation won't last much longer.'

She was gone an instant later. Leaving me with the eerie sensation that I already knew she was right.

You're missing something enormous. Something right before your eyes.

The next twenty or so minutes passed in an unpleasant blur of glad faces, swirling coattails, raucous laughter, and impending doom. Everything was more bearable with a champagne flute at ready service, though I was careful. Delia and Jonas were to depart at dawn, and I was to be there. A protector. A public servant. What the copper stars are *supposed* to look like, to the best of my admittedly patchy ability.

Just get them away from here, and as for the rest, come what may . . .

'If I'd known you'd look quite so spruce decked in that rigging, I'd have invited you to pass out flyers.'

Valentine landed on the sofa beside me. Likewise equipped with champagne, happily afloat in his natural Democratic element. The piano player appeared to have taken a short break, but my niche was still pretty snug and situated next to a drinks table. I have my priorities, same as Val.

'I'd have invited you to sod off,' I replied. Not unkindly.

Val chuckled, eyes drifting over the room.

'Matsell hinted I'm still employed.'

'Of course you are. Steps have been taken.'

'By you, I suppose.'

Valentine adjusted his ridiculously expensive avian-themed vest with considerable self-satisfaction.

'Oh,' I said, handing him the house key that Delia had returned.

'That's a relief, I've been using my pocketknife all this while. Thank you. Everything else running on oiled tracks?'

Feeling communicative – miraculously communicative, if I am honest – I shook my head.

'I've had a pair of letters from Mercy. Under mysterious circumstances. The gist of them suggests she's not . . . faring well overseas.'

Val nodded, squinting contemplatively. 'She's a sensitive moll. But she'll muddle through – iron spine, and all that. Don't fret overmuch, not from New York. It doesn't fadge in the geographic scope, you savvy.'

This seemed sage advice. I considered it accordingly.

Then I noticed that my sibling wasn't surprised by the news that Mercy had twice written me. Which I thought odd, since the news was . . . surprising. At least it was *newsworthy*.

'Well, I'd best be off,' he sighed. 'Hands to shake all round.'

And then I put two and two together and realized that they spelled *Valentine*.

'Oh my *God*,' I cried, leaping up as he rose to depart.

Valentine quirked a brow, resting his hands on his hips. 'What?'

'You,' I hissed, pointing furiously. '*You've* been delivering Mercy's letters. I can't believe it took me this long to puzzle it through.'

'What the devil are you talking about?'

'The fact you're an infuriating bastard.'

'Don't be a nimenog, I've no notion what you're on about. She mailed them to you, didn't she?'

'They had no postage! Neither of them. The first had no *envelope*, for the love of Christ!'

Val laughed, rubbing a hand over his face. 'Really? Bollocks.'

My expression must have been daunting, for it compelled him to further speech.

'All right, all right, it was me. She wrote them herself, of course – every word. But she didn't have your new address, did she, and I've lived in Spring Street for years. She figured sending them to you via my ken a neat fix. I'd meant to put them in envelopes and address them to you, deliver them in passing. You'd never have been the wiser, I'm a dab hand at imitating penmanship. What a slubber I am, though, forgetting the postage. Damn. There was plenty of morphine involved the first time, as I recollect it, and the second—'

The world was awash in red. I would have his blood for this. I would make him *pay*.

'That's why you came to my ken on the morning of the murder,' I realized in awe. 'When you called on Mrs Boehm and I was at the Tombs. You weren't *stopping by*, you wanted to see the bloody floor show after I'd heard from her again. Watch me squirm.'

'What about *check all was well*?'

'You mean *pick about in my brains*. Did you read them?'

'Of course I read them. Are you daft? Mercy Underhill is your version of religion and here she starts up scribbling you cracked messages from abroad and expecting me to deliver the dross. I'm not any too kittled with her at the moment, come to that, I had half a mind to burn them and be done with it. But read them? Yes, Timothy. I couldn't very well predict how likely you'd be to take a nap in the East River without *reading* them.'

'Spying!' I snapped. 'Forgery!'

'Why in hell are you counting?' he wanted to know, staring at the two fingers I'd just counted off on my left hand.

'Narcotics, alcohol, bribery, violence, whoring, gambling, theft, cheating, extortion, sodomy, spying, and forgery,' I spat back. 'A nice even *dozen* now.'

'Oh.' He smiled, teeth gleaming. 'Nacky system you've got there. Add *lying*, I'd no intention of ever telling you. How else could I have kept on reading them? That'll be a baker's dozen.'

'I'm going to murder you right here, in front of the entire police department.' My fists had sunk deep in his lapels by this time, and I gave them a vicious shake.

'You are *adorable*,' he said fondly.

'Fuck you.'

'If you don't let go of me, my Tim, I'm going to put your pate in that punch bowl yonder,' he advised. 'You don't want that to happen. Neither do I, come to think of it.'

He walked away.

Describing my mental state for the next quarter hour wouldn't be to any purpose. Suffice it to say that I located a dripping champagne bottle along with my green greatcoat and decided I preferred a river view to an interior one. I found myself sitting on a bench under the stars. Watching both the intoxicated passersby and the waves all smashing mindlessly against one another in the dark. The promenade was cold, and someone had vomited in the snow a few feet from my bench. But it was better than any building my brother occupied. Guests milled about, taking the air or resting on benches gazing out at the bay.

I'd spent ten minutes planning vengeance when I spied a slim silhouette coming down the walkway. Likewise woolgathering, in a black London-cut suit with a white waistcoat and wearing a rose in the buttonhole of his open greatcoat.

'Jim?' I called.

When my brother's friend spied me, he cautiously approached. 'Why, Timothy. May I?'

Seating himself at my behest, his sharply chiseled face softened. 'What a surprise. Had I expected you, I should have sought you out. Don't think me unmannered, I beg.'

'I hadn't expected to see you here either. How did you come to be in bed with these scoundrels?'

The instant I said it, I must have winced, for Jim favored me with an indulgent smile.

'How, indeed. I work for them. I don't suppose you had reason to pay especial note to the piano, but—'

'I did.' I smiled back at him. 'It was very good. Not that I'm any judge, but . . . I liked it. Is that how Val knows you?'

He nodded shyly, pulling a thin pipe from his coat pocket.

'Gentle Jim, the Democratic Party's official pianist,' I mused.

'Only Val calls me that, actually.'

'Oh?'

I waited. He pulled at the pipe. So I leaned my elbows back against the bench and linked my fingers in an easy, attentive posture. Badly in need of a distracting influence. And frightfully curious about the one beside me.

'Well,' he said at length, 'I was playing for a group of donors at a private club – I say donors, but I mean brutes, really, Timothy, let us be sincere – and sometime around four in the morning or thereabouts they decided to stage a dogfight.'

'Ah,' I said. Being helpful.

'Within minutes they'd procured a half-starved street mutt and one of the guard dogs from the Bloomingdale Insane Asylum wing of New York Hospital. I suggested they let the stray go, or I'd fight them. I was about to have my nose broken when Valentine bet twenty dollars against the stray that he could win it in a billiards game. And there you are. He then teased me over my . . . refined sensibilities. We restored the creature its freedom to piss all over Broadway an hour later, of course.'

Morphine and hemp weed, I thought, regarding the night in question. Hemp weed makes Val magnanimous.

'Timothy?'

'Sorry. Yes, that sounds like him.'

'You weren't wondering how I came to be associated with the Party, however. You would fain know why I'm polluting New

York with my presence and not London.'

'I'd not put it like that.'

Again I waited, the cold breeze ruffling our hair. He intrigued me severely, and he was going to talk within seconds. It was like watching a tightly wound, ornately detailed clock winding up to the midnight chime.

Fifty-eight . . . fifty-nine . . .

'I don't imagine you've ever been banished.' Jim assumed a bright, optimistic look that seemed hewn out of marble. 'I shouldn't recommend banishment, Timothy, for all there's something . . . oh, I don't know. Romantic about it.'

'Romantic?' I repeated, stricken.

'Shakespearean, perhaps. Charmingly quaint.'

'It killed the equivalent of ten thousand Tybalts.'

'It did at that. There you are, then. Very old-fashioned and impracticable, to die over such nonsense.' He pushed his fingers through his dark hair. 'Val didn't tell you about this? No, silly of me, I wouldn't come up in polite conversation.'

'Don't be ridiculous. My brother's conversation is never polite.'

He laughed sharply. 'Granted.' Jim fiddled with the pipe, considering. 'My family is an influential one. Cabinet ministers and useless titleholders and the like, trailing most of the alphabet after their names.'

'What *is* your name?'

'Oh.' He looked somewhat discomfited. 'James Anthony Carlton Playfair. How d'ye do.'

I shook his hand again, amused.

'Are you capable of actually opening this?' He glanced down at the champagne bottle resting between us.

I had it uncorked within five seconds, with a sharp push and a steady wrist. That being how it's done. Taking a drink, I handed it over to my companion.

'God, thank you.' He tilted the bottle at me before taking a swig. 'Your servant. Anyhow, there was a gentlemen's club I'd used to frequent that catered to men of my . . . persuasion. Beautiful little place, all drawn curtains and tiny pink hothouse roses and finger sandwiches and the latest newspapers. They'd a piano, and I confess myself to having been rather popular among the young rakes. One young rake in particular, a bright-eyed boy with pale curls who bred hounds at his family's estate. He wasn't in London often, but on the fourth occasion he visited, we spent twelve days together, and I decided by the end that I could not exist in his absence, that I would shrivel to a rind, et cetera, and that steps would have to be taken. Then I did something quite uncharacteristically stupid, I'm afraid.'

'What was that?'

'I told him so. In a letter. What a monumental imbecile I was, you're thinking. You are thinking it is a miracle I manage to shave of a morning without slicing my head off.'

'I'm thinking you're a man who wrote a love letter,' I answered quietly.

'Apparently his valet was in the habit of reading his mail. Typical story, quite a dull one, really. The valet rudely demanded a meeting and then rudely demanded a great deal of money. I politely invited him to go to hell, not believing the coward would have the bollocks to make good his threat. Unfortunately, I was wrong. Father threw me out on my arse with a ticket for a steerage berth on a ship bound for America and three hundred pounds. When I arrived, I bought a piano so as to give private lessons. Soon after, I was hired to play at a Democratic Party meeting and that proved rather more lucrative. As for my family, I haven't spoken to any of them since, though I've been writing for two years now. I miss my mother and sister rather dreadfully,' he added in a polished-brass voice that failed to mask the bleakness beneath. 'But this is the sort of life men lead when they have once been very stupid.'

'Not deservedly.'

'I was terribly lucky, actually,' he corrected me. 'Buggery is a capital offense in London. I'd hardly have been the first molley strung up by the neck and sent to hell that much faster. Oh, I beg your pardon.'

'No, it's not you.' I shook my head, echoes of *London, London, London* pounding inside of it. 'It's just . . . the more I know of the world, the less I like it.'

'Ah.' Jim's clever blue eyes studied my features, looking for I knew not what. 'Forgive me, but which . . . element met with your disapproval? Christ, what a rotter you must think me. I've really no wish to offend you, and—'

'You haven't,' I insisted. 'I'd simply not have wished to see you hanged.'

Gentle Jim, or James Playfair as I could now name him, froze and then released a small exhalation. Thanks or relief I couldn't say, though I believe something of each was at work. It was rudely unsettling. Realization dawned that a fellow who apparently bore lifelong banishment with grace and philosophy would have been unsurprised if I'd spit in his eye. Jim gave me a well-bred nod, and I saw him as he must have looked gliding about Westminster, a Vivaldi tune pursing his lips into a breezy whistle.

'Timothy, is that why you work as a copper star? Because the world runs helter-skelter?'

'That's to do with poverty and owning a fractional face.'

'No, that's why you *became* a copper star. That isn't the same thing at all.'

The objection was mildly stated, I grant. But mildly stated by a chap who could have leapt out of an illustration advertising milled soap. It was all I could do not to take him by his perfectly hewn chin and shove my face into his and force him to comprehend me.

'For God's sake, you of all people haven't the slightest idea what looking like this feels like,' I grated out. 'Everything – work, women, all of it – has to do with my finances and my looking like a marauding barbarian.'

Jim began to chuckle heartily. I'm endeared to the man for a number of reasons. But being snickered at by a fine-featured sophisticate during a conversation about severe fire scarring is plenty mortifying.

'Do you truly suppose that scar renders you at all unpalatable?'

'I don't suppose it, I know it.'

'Oh, if you *know* it, I shan't trouble you further,' he said airily. '*Know it.* How silly of me. But I wonder why the girl exploring the grounds just now, the one with the obscenely large brown eyes, was studying you so assiduously before she departed with her chaperone? Perhaps you reminded her of her dear departed brother lost at sea or some such coincidence. No matter. Do you see that fellow in the grotesquely fashionable orange breeches? He's a molley by the name of Augustus Westerfield, runs an insurance concern. Just over there, on the bench?'

I glanced in the indicated direction to discover a pair of eyes staring directly back into mine. I blinked. And then returned my attention to James Playfair with all speed.

'Poor Auggie, such a lonesome boy. I suppose you remind him of his dear departed brother lost at sea too,' Jim sang teasingly.

'Evening, gents.'

My head shot upward in startlement.

Directly before us, wearing ordinary street togs with copper stars pinned to their jackets, false smiles pinned likewise to their faces, stood McDivitt and Beardsley. Beardsley looked pleased from his blushing baby cheeks down to his muddied boots, and McDivitt's black Irish glare blazed forth in perfect counterpoint. His copper star was new. Of course it was – Julius had stolen the other, and I'd left it in the mud where it belonged.

I slowly stood, sensing Jim rise behind me. But he wasn't involved in my troubles. And so that needed fixing.

'Jim, go back inside,' I said.

'Do you know these men?' I felt Jim shift closer. 'But of course, they're your colleagues.'

McDivitt shifted the tone of the conversation when he caught Jim by the arm and yanked him bodily forward. I didn't require Val's friend to tell me verbally he'd just discovered a knife blade was tracing his ribs. There's a pinched look of terror about the eyelids, a small gasp as the point registers.

'Let go of me *at once*. What the devil do you mean by it?'

They ignored him. I thought about apologizing but decided to spend my energies saving his hide instead. Supposing I could manage it.

'Your pal stays,' Beardsley informed me, puffy cheeks glowing. 'For now. Let's walk to shore.'

Hanging back, I nodded.

'And wouldn't that make for a fine time, you trailin' along after. You're going first, Mr Wilde,' McDivitt snapped, jutting his chin, 'and don't think I'll not loosen this fellow's kidneys from their moorings.'

As I returned to Manhattan along the ridiculous carpeting, followed by Beardsley and McDivitt and a silent James Playfair, I adopted and discarded a number of plans. But when we'd reached the darkness of the area abutting the bridge entrance, I realized I'd been played doubly for a fool. A hacksman with a chestnut mare glanced up at our footsteps. As if he'd been paid to wait.

'You saw the man. Quick march,' Beardsley ordered.

Knowing that if either myself or James were placed in that carriage, our odds of survival would drastically lower, I spun abruptly on my heels instead.

By the time I'd turned, the knife in McDivitt's calloused hand had shifted from Jim's back to his throat.

'Don't,' I protested, raising my hands. 'He doesn't mean you any harm.'

'Go along with us, and we'll readily enough agree with ye,' McDivitt growled.

'I'll go where you wish, but let him alone.'

'No!' Jim thrashed once, which only accomplished a trickle of red running from the blade down into his cravat. He stopped, wincing.

'Jim, hold perfectly still and shut your head,' I suggested with deep feeling.

'I will not stand by and *watch* while—'

The knife point deepened, widening the scarlet stream.

'Jim, *stop moving*,' I cried.

We'd run dry of options. In another moment, James Playfair would be dead, and I would have been the death of him. So I stepped up into the hack. Jim's wide blue eyes followed. Helpless to do aught save resist the invasion of metal into his flesh.

Just as the wall of the enclosed carriage cut off my view of the scene, I heard Jim bite back a cry of pain. McDivitt climbed up after me and swung the door closed. The knife blade he held was red. It had gone deeper than I ought to have allowed. Just *how red* and *how deep*, I realized, I couldn't bear to know at that moment. I only knew Jim had cried out, and that I ought to have leapt headfirst into the goddamn hackney.

When Beardsley followed his cohort into the vehicle from the opposite side and shoved a chloroform-soaked rag into my mazzard, I only managed an instant of struggle before I began the descent into blankness and black.

'Where are you taking me?' I muttered as my eyes slid shut.

'You've an appointment you've been neglecting, Mr Wilde,' Beardsley answered. 'Pity. And when we could all have been such fast friends too.'

'They'll be giving him a proper welcome anyhow, won't they?' McDivitt remarked with icy amusement. 'They always do at Tammany Hall.'

CHAPTER TWENTY-THREE

I never knew a man of color who was not an anti-Jackson
man. In fact, it was their respectability, and not their
degradation, that was the cause of their disfranchisement.

E. S. Abdy, *Journal of a Residence and Tour in the*
United States of North America, From April 1833 to
October 1834

I dreamed of a wedding at which the magnolias were all a glistening black. Black as the murder of crows at rest in the branches of the flowering tree. Lucy Adams was a bride with a long lace veil that fluttered like an ivory shroud. She smiled, awaiting a man I couldn't see. Happy. Longing. The bouquet in her hand gleamed dark as onyx, and the sable blooms writhed softly in the sunlight. They horrified me, because I knew they were wrong somehow. But I couldn't think why, only watched as they multiplied in her hands, twisting and entwining and finally engulfing her. All the while, until her face had been wreathed over with black tendrils, she smiled and smiled still more.

A brief interlude passed when I thought I was dead and being carried to my funeral on a long bier. But after that I fell, and it was colder than it had been previous. A sharp pain pierced my ribs, more than once, and I slipped back into oblivion.

I didn't wake up due to any overt curiosity as to where I was. It was bound to be someplace unhealthy. I awoke because my head had been replaced by a swollen globe with very thin skin, possibly a bulging oiled sack, and it hurt to keep the sloshing contents within my skull, and generally when my pate is giving me trouble, I press hard at the skin around my scar. Making to do so, I found that my arms weren't working as they normally did.

Peculiar.

I heard voices and detected the aroma of cigar smoke. Half of me battled to wake. The other half distinctly preferred not to be in a world where my head now resembled an overripe melon, rotten-sweet and oozing flesh from its cracks.

In the end, I didn't make the decision for myself. A man said, 'You see, sir? There. He's coming round.'

And then he gripped me by the hair and bashed my head into the back of the chair I sat in.

Air flooded my lungs in a gasp, but otherwise I can't recall how I reacted or how long it took for me to recover. The unfocused origins of returning consciousness are lost to me. All I knew just then was that my skull had exploded like a ship under cannon fire. Minutes or seconds later, I was fully awake.

I appeared to be skillfully lashed hand and foot to a chair. Raw hemp scraped over my wrists. I pulled at the bonds anyhow, everything in me shrieking to *get out*. My fingertips, I noted, were already cold. The room could equally have been the study of a rich man, the antechamber of a clubhouse, or the library of a small university – stately armchairs, portraits of men in high collars who didn't much care for my looks, leather-bound tomes. I registered decanters on side tables, papers strewn over a rolltop desk. Blinking, I counted the glow of three cigar ends filling the room with haze.

A trio of unfamiliar Tammany men sat before me. All were dressed as if they'd just been summoned from the ball at Castle Garden, in floral silks and cutaway jackets. One was tall and thin and bald, with an imperious hooked nose on which rested a pair of pince-nez. The next was fair-haired and dashing in appearance, though he seemed not much younger, and he glared balefully at his pocket watch. The third had sharp eyes framed with crow's feet, the body of an ex-pugilist, and a scar across the bridge of his nose where an antagonist had split the skin.

Pocket Watch cast a look at me and then to the side of the room. 'You can't pretend it's not very annoying. There were dignitaries present, *patrons*. Wasting half an hour after being called away because the man you delivered has been drugged unnecessarily and then bashed in the skull—'

'Begging your pardon, it wasn't unnecessary.' Beardsley stood off to my left, his hat in hand. Behind him, McDivitt looked no less cowed. 'That man there is *dangerous*.'

Scarred Nose sniffed in amusement. 'Really, gentlemen. He's the size of my accounts manager.'

'He's the reason as Sean Mulqueen rests in the ground,' McDivitt protested.

Pince-Nez keeked down his nose in my direction, openly annoyed. 'What we all mean to say is that this business has grown tiresome, and it's absurd to waste still more time nursing a man back to consciousness because the pair of you were too lazy to wrestle him into a pair of handcuffs. You're dismissed. Should we require you, we'll call you back.'

McDivitt opened his mouth to protest and Beardsley scowled. Nevertheless, the door shut with a well-oiled *snick*, and four of us remained.

They pondered me. I considered them in turn.

I was distracted, though. And not just because something sticky was trickling through my hair.

My thoughts were full of Jim and a red knife, as well as Delia and Jonas and the private carriage ride that could be . . . hours away? Seconds? Already passed? I'd have been scared witless by the odd triumvirate, I imagine, if I hadn't already been quite so hellishly angry.

'Since you've tied me to this chair, I expect we'd better get to know each other.' The plan was to go down fighting, I decided. I'd disgust myself to death otherwise. 'I'm Timothy Wilde. Copper star one-oh-seven, if it interests you.'

'We know who you are.' Pince-Nez smiled coldly, shifting in his seat.

'Fine. Who are you? And why the chair?'

'You've not exactly been acting in our best interests, have you?' Pocket Watch asked tiredly, glancing again at the time.

'Is that my job?'

'Yes,' Scarred Nose answered. He looked amused.

'I supposed you wanted me to solve crimes, which I've been doing to the best of my admittedly thin ability,' I replied with all the terseness a recovering chloroform victim can muster. 'Which bit chafed your tender parts?'

Scarred Nose started to laugh, a wheezy and rustic exhalation I found not entirely malicious.

'I like him,' said Scarred Nose.

'God, I don't,' said Pocket Watch, taking a pull from his cigar. His arrogance was diluted by a faint note of petulance.

'He's a unique specimen,' Pince-Nez said thoughtfully. 'But I suspect he might be useless to us. And you know how I feel about useless people.'

A silence fell. The calculating sort.

Scarred Nose leaned forward. 'You're a square player, my man. Yes? So answer me plain: we want you to stop harassing Senator Gates. Is that so much?'

'I'm not harassing him, I'm investigating the murder of his . . . housekeeper.'

'You robbed his home! Or you attempted to, anyway. Do we really have time to argue with this ant?' Pocket Watch asked his colleagues. 'McDivitt and Beardsley have been following you for weeks. They're very old hands at shadowing – Madam Marsh recommended them to us, and they've proven most efficient. This all needs to *stop*. It should have stopped *long ago*.'

'Answer the question, Wilde,' Pince-Nez interrupted icily. 'We want you to stop. Is that so much?'

My skin had turned entirely cold by then. So it was a difficult job answering. I recalled the two sets of footsteps in the alleyway behind Gates's ken and McDivitt and Beardsley's appearance at the front of the building minutes later.

McDivitt and Beardsley have been following you for weeks.

And where else had I gone?

'Ah, see?' Scarred Nose asked. 'He's clever. I like clever ones. Yes, Wilde, we are clearing the city of Wrights. Seixas Varker and Luke Coles are en route to the Higgins residence. We don't give a damn it's a Railroad station, but that family knows far too much about our Senator Gates. He always was the sentimental sort – to an alarming and dangerous degree, we're discovering.'

'Don't,' I gasped. 'They're . . . I'm getting them out of your way. This morning, in fact. That job is already done.'

'And what of your own precious convictions, Mr Wilde?' Pince-Nez queried pointedly. 'We know your abolitionism to be most passionate. What guarantee have we that you'll act with discretion, that you'll not expose the good Senator Gates for the romantic idiot we now suspect him to be? He is a highly important figure. An asset. You are not the former, and you may not be the latter either.'

'There are people bitter over Sean Mulqueen's death, but I'm a reasonable man,' I protested.

'Are you?' Pince-Nez mused. 'I'm just wondering. In light of your wrists, you understand.'

I failed to follow him, and I think he guessed that.

'You could certainly be a *reasonable* abolitionist and we'd have nothing further to discuss here. A measured, sedate, effective abolitionist, with a free conscience. Beholden not just to his ideals but to his employers. And here you are scraping your wrists off the instant we mention a pair of Negroes who've been causing *you* grave woes. Is that *reasonable?*'

I didn't need to see myself to feel pain, didn't need their ironic exchange of glances to know that chloroform, a likely kick or three to the ribs, and a head injury had all done their dirty work on my poker game. Which isn't generally so abysmal as the one I'd just displayed. I didn't need to feel the rope burn to understand these people already appreciated my loyalties.

I did need to solve it, though. And fast.

'I'll leave Gates alone if you leave the Wrights alone,' I attempted.

'Regrettably, this isn't a negotiation, Mr Wilde,' Pince-Nez replied.

'Why can't it be? You'll lose nothing by it.'

'Oh, we intend to lose nothing by it. Gates's position is most crucial. And a colored mistress kept as a wedded wife . . . Whether he's guilty of actually legalizing the union or not, and we still aren't certain, I shudder to think of the scandal that would rock this Party. It would be widespread, divisive, ruinous. Quite unthinkable.'

'I'll forget all about Gates, but it can't matter to you whether the Wrights live in Canada or Kentucky,' I pleaded.

'And why does it matter to *you?*' Pocket Watch sniffed.

'Loyalty is important to us, Mr Wilde,' Scarred Nose declared. 'It might even be of primary importance to us. Well, to me, anyhow.'

'It is to me too.' I forced myself still and lowered my voice. 'So is decency, though.'

'We want a personal pledge, Mr Wilde,' Pince-Nez said, drumming his fingertips against one another. 'If it involves a degree of sacrifice, well, that is precisely the means by which we will know you trustworthy. Is that so difficult to grasp?'

'No, it isn't. But it proves me untrustworthy in quite another direction.'

Pocket Watch glared with time-pregnant emphasis at Scarred Nose, who sighed. Pince-Nez pulled his eyepiece from his nose and wiped it clean with a cloth. Then he likewise angled a look at Scarred Nose, twitching one shoulder in a minute shrug.

'Oh, very well, though it is a pity.' Scarred Nose appeared disappointed in me. 'I hate killing the clever ones.'

'Sometimes killing the clever ones is very interesting indeed,' Pince-Nez observed.

'Let it be one of us, though – McDivitt and Beardsley are out for vengeance. They'll botch it, try to break every bone they can find first. It's tedious and unmanly. One of us should get rid of him the quick way.'

'I'll take care of him,' Pocket Watch said, eyes glinting. 'You'll both be wanting to see to the Castle Garden donations.'

'I can't make this right for you, nor for anyone else, if I'm dead,' I choked out.

They weren't listening.

'You don't think painful cautionary tales have meaning?' Pince-Nez wondered philosophically.

'Certainly cautionary tales have meaning. I've watched you slice all ten toes off a rabbit, send another's hand through a sausage grinder, but they both lived,' Scarred Nose argued. 'Yes, that was valuable, but the story had a narrator. This won't.'

'I'm putting the wretch in the river where he won't trouble us further,' Pocket Watch grumbled. A door opened behind me. 'We haven't the time, so nothing of the sausage grinder ilk is going to happen.'

The door closed again.

'No. It won't,' announced an unnaturally calm voice.

My eyes slammed shut.

The newcomer was a shock, to be sure. But only because I own – deep down, beneath my speech and even beneath my thoughts maybe – an optimistic soul. And had supposed the situation could not possibly deteriorate further.

I was wrong.

Valentine walked easy as you please into the room and swung a small chair toward us, resting his hat on the carpet and sitting down as if we were all in a café ordering coffees. His leaded stick he rested against his knee. When I realized that his presence meant Jim was alive and had given an account of my abduction, I did manage a single breath of relief on that score.

The rest of me, meanwhile, was about as stupid with fright as a fox in a trap. It can rip a fellow open a bit, fighting such strong dual urges to scream *Help me* and *Get out of here*.

'Captain,' Scarred Nose said. Cordial but measured. 'With respect, you weren't called for.'

Val crossed his legs, flashing the Tammany men a smile. He pulled a matchbox and half a cigar from his pocket and added his smoke to the sickening aura of dread in the room. His eyes lingered on the flame, as they always did, before he waved the lucifer out.

'I know. Figured it for an oversight, what with me such bang-up company and all. What a night, eh? I'll not flam you, I'd my doubts about the venue, but you've gone and proven me a goosecap. We're pulling in thousands down Castle Garden way.'

Pocket Watch shifted in his seat. 'Captain Wilde, we'd like you to leave now. This matter doesn't concern you.'

The flinch that crossed my brother's features when he laughed looked positively excruciating. 'My lord. I've been watering at the wrong punch bowl this evening. Your tangle-foot must have been fit to fell a bear. Are you lushy or just brainless?'

Flushing with rage, Pocket Watch began to rise. He was prevented by Scarred Nose, who caught his arm.

Pince-Nez, having finished his cigar, ground the end into a gilded tray. 'Quite right. I see no point in mincing words. Captain, the painful fact is that your brother here has been making an unbearable nuisance of himself.'

'He has a habit of doing that,' Val agreed.

'And the more painful conclusion we have reached is that safety calls for us to eliminate this . . . hazard.'

'He's been all this while disposing of hazards.' Val waved a vexed little zigzag in the air. 'I *told* you. The colored family is legging it with a will, and that innocent in my bed didn't up and walk away on her own, did she?'

No one expressed shock that Val's bed had once contained a corpse. Save for me, at him voicing the fact. That was a shock of the stomach-spearing variety.

'You told them that—'

'Tim, press your teeth together and keep them that way,' he growled. Sighing in a martyred fashion, Val resumed smiling at the

Tammany men. 'Silkie Marsh leaked it, they tell me. She thought they should be posted. I'd like to savvy how *she* knew, but that's another matter. Never fear, we're all fast enough pals for them not to panic over a stiff one in my sheets. It isn't as if I know how it got there. The point is, this tune has carried on too long, and the band ready for home. Untie my brother and we'll call it square.'

'Your family feeling is admirable,' said Pince-Nez, 'but he's intractable. We are disposing of him.'

'You aren't,' Val said quietly.

He began to twirl the walking stick. Tender half circles, turning the point on the carpet. You could barely see the motion. It's one of the subtlest deadly gestures in his repertoire. Not that I was comforted by that. If I hadn't already been bleeding, I think blood would have forced its way out, my heart was racing so.

'I think you're forgetting who you're speaking to,' Pince-Nez said, glowering down his Roman nose at us.

'Oh, no.' Val smiled. 'I think *you* forget who *you're* speaking to.'

'Of all the . . .' Pocket Watch spluttered.

'And just who do you think you are, Captain Wilde?' Scarred Nose asked. Under the anger, he sounded grudgingly impressed.

'I think I'm the boss of Ward Eight.' Valentine, I realized, never looked at Pocket Watch, but divided his attention between Pince-Nez and Scarred Nose. 'I think I'm the flashest goddamn boss of Ward Eight ever to breathe, and I think one of you is up for re-election as our alderman come spring. There are more starving Paddies than you can beat with a stick washing up every day. Thousands of them – more than any man could count. And I'm the cull who feeds them, finds them a steady graft and a ken with a roof, flashes his ivories at their snot-faced kinchin, and they *worship me*. They'd jump in the river on my say-so, and you think I'll tell them how fond of you I am if you go through with this? I have slaved for this Party every day since I was sixteen years old. Doing ace work. And for what? To have my kin stolen from a fund-raiser and trussed up like a chicken? Last week I was in Albany, and there are Democrats there who'd break a cove's skull if he so much as looked at me cutty-eyed. You do *not* want me peppery at you. Timothy Wilde is off the table. Permanently. Give me back my fucking brother before I lose my temper.'

Pocket Watch's chest heaved with fury at the end of this speech. Pince-Nez's eyes had gone glacial, half homicide and half intelligent calculation. As for Scarred Nose, he looked to be battling a smile.

'I begin to fear,' Pince-Nez said slowly, 'that you are as intractable as your sibling, Captain Wilde. Are you willing to face the consequences?'

'Get the hell out of here, Val.' God help me, it wouldn't stay in any longer.

Valentine stood, resting his stick against the chair. The cigar stump he tossed into the fireplace. Pulling out a pocketknife, he approached my chair and began sawing at ropes. The hemp was so tightly fastened that it snapped readily, audibly. The three Tammany men watched him. Pince-Nez aloof, Pocket Watch livid, and Scarred Nose allowing himself a rueful grin. Blood rushed back into my fingertips. It hurt.

But then, there wasn't much of me that wasn't hurting by that time.

'You need me,' my brother told them. 'You haven't even dreamed up all the ways you need me yet. Am I right?'

Scarred Nose tilted his head. 'I think very possibly you are.'

'Bully. We can palaver over some new ones, then. Offer me a drink, for Christ's sake, it makes for better conversation.'

Laughing openly, Scarred Nose reached for a decanter and poured a glass.

My brother hauled me up by one arm and dragged my none-too-steady carcass to the door. Throwing it wide, he said, 'Go out through the front, I've left it unlocked.'

He launched me through the opening as if firing me from a rifle. Predictably enough, I fell. Seconds later, the lock slid into place behind me.

And I was alone.

* * *

Thanks to the chloroform, the head injury, and the ebbing panic, I lay stunned for some few seconds. Unsupported, I felt faint. The hallway I'd landed in had a waxed floor, and the building's lights were out. Those were the two facts I managed to absorb as I lay there, debating whether Val's odds were better if I left as he'd instructed or if I started up flinging myself against the locked door.

My instinct was to put my shoulder to it until they let me back inside. Since that was my instinct, I reasoned, it was probably a bad idea.

You have been remarkably useless, and he's gotten you out of their sight. Do not ruin it.

You ruin so very many things.

Through my semi-conscious haze, I recalled that Neither Here Nor There was presently under siege. Shoving my hands against the floor, I pushed myself viciously upward.

As I crept along the wall, sentences drifted at random through my rearranged brains. One of them recurred, though. A sentiment I'd not examined with near thorough enough care.

Silkie Marsh leaked it . . . I'd like to savvy how she knew, but that's another matter.

So I thought about that question. Since my visit to the Greene Street brothel, I'd been aware that Madam Marsh knew where Lucy died, but so much had been at stake since, I'd failed to dwell on a frankly bizarre instance of omniscience. My assumption had been that the murderer had told her – acted at her behest and reported back. But that line of thinking had gotten me nowhere.

Was another explanation possible?

I pushed through a door, dizzy and lost, and found myself in a deserted restaurant, pale starlight edging the windows. I'd never been to Tammany Hall, but it's a popular gathering place, where concerts and lectures and Punch and Judy shows are held as well as political rallies. The ceiling loomed high above me, chandeliers hanging like nocturnal predators. Quick as I could, I picked my way past the potted ferns and the upside-down chairs.

I was midway across the room when one possible theory

explaining Silkie Marsh's strange prescience occurred to me, and I nearly set the whole place crashing down like a row of dominoes when I walked into a table.

'No,' I said out loud, gripping the edge. To steady it or myself, I couldn't guess. 'No, that isn't right.'

All the air seemed to have left the room. There were stars behind my eyes again, the chamber lurching in sickly spins and contortions like an asylum inmate caught up in an ecstatic dance.

Because I'd just recalled something else.

You're what he wants, I'd said to Delia Wright regarding George Higgins. Though I shouldn't have, for it was none of my affair.

George wants a figment of his imagination, she'd answered.

Telling me, as usual, far more than the speaker intended for me to know.

Memories flooded back to me. Of speaking with every relevant party I could muster and wrongly supposing they'd told me nothing useful. Of reasons people kill and die and which are the strongest. The simplest. Of waking up time after time from dreams of magnolias with an uneasy feeling I didn't understand. Of asking Silkie Marsh, face to face, whether Lucy's name had been Wright or Adams.

That question is impossible to answer.

Screwing my eyes shut, I pictured the seven free blacks whose lives had needled and pierced and threaded into my own – the three Committee men, Lucy and her son and her sister, and Jean-Baptiste – and with a faint surge of hysteria it occurred to me that antique omens about sighting blackbirds ought not, could not, be trusted. Particularly when we were speaking of people. Not ravens on the wing at all.

And yet, in this particular case, I could have worked it all out from a nursery rhyme. Were I a different man. A mad one.

Seven for a secret, never to be told.

'It isn't real,' I whispered. 'None of this is real. It was all a lie.'

Charging for the door, I found it unlocked as Val had said it would be. The man clearly possesses a great many keys. I plunged into the intersection of Nassau and Frankfort that faces diseased City Hall Park at an angle, touching Chatham Street. Desperate for a hack. I could tell it was nearly dawn, for a milkman with a wagon full of jugs was drawing water from a nearby Croton pump to lengthen his profits, topping off the milk and the cream. Approaching five in the morning, then.

I was only late for my appointment by half an hour.

Perhaps there was still time.

She's with God now, if sooner than she should be, Julius had told Delia.

Is she? the sister had replied in a voice like her own spectre's.

'Stupid, *stupid*,' I whispered as I ran.

Finding a hack proved simple enough, and within a quarter hour I was in Chelsea, the stars fading above me as the night began to wash away, facing the doorway of Neither Here Nor There.

It was open.

I went in, my footsteps far too loud. The silence – God, that silence. It was suffocating.

Hesitant, I stopped in the hall.

'Mrs Higgins?'

No one answered me.

'Is anyone here?'

The quiet wrapped itself around me, from head to foot like a white winding sheet, over my nose and my mouth and my ears. Freezing me in place.

I thought a cry sounded from a distance. But it was so faint the direction couldn't be determined, nor if it was simply the soft mewling of the cat. Unable to bear the stillness any longer, I raced through the parlor, through the museum and down the secret stairs into the hidden Railroad station.

As with much of the rest of this investigation, I never made a police report about what I found below.

But it was important, so very important, the story, what happened and why, more important to me than I can begin to convey, because I don't have a great many confidants to my name.

338

One of them, and one of the brightest and the bravest men with whom I've ever shared company, was born a free black in New York City and christened Julius Carpenter. He wasn't like a brother to me, because Christ knows how terribly complicated I find that particular simile, but he was something I'd needed nearly as much – he was my friend. From the day I met him, he was effortlessly kind, the sort of person who makes you less alone in the world without leveling demands or challenges, who is so at home within himself he needn't question why or whether you're fond of each other. He was once ordered to give up his name, and he refused. I'll never forget that.

Julius Carpenter died in the early morning on the first of March, 1846. He was felled with a gunshot wound to the chest, and I discovered him still warm on the floor of the subterranean sitting room.

Ten feet away lay the equally lifeless corpse of Seixas Varker, whose head had been smashed in with a nearby poker.

Long Luke Coles was slumped with gangly arms askew against the far wall, a bullet hole in his head.

Delia sat very still in the middle of the carpet, surveying her surroundings. The gun she held was a Colt revolver, and it had belonged in life to Varker. I'd once stolen it and then given it back.

'I told you I'd kill them if they touched Jonas,' she said when she looked up at me.

I slumped to my knees on the rug before her. Too horror-struck to answer, at least at first. Anyhow, speaking with her was problematic for another reason entirely.

I didn't even know her name.

CHAPTER TWENTY-FOUR

Another woman, to save her children, who would all have been doomed to slavery, if her claims to freedom had been rejected, precipitated herself from the top of a house, where she was confined, and was so dreadfully mutilated and mangled that she was suffered to escape, because she was no longer fit for sale. There was no doubt that she was a free woman; but she knew a whole family of young slaves was too valuable a property not to turn the scale against her.

E. S. Abdy, *Journal of a Residence and Tour in the United States of North America, From April 1833 to October 1834*

At first the ticking of the clock was the only sound. I listened. Just breathing, my hands on my legs as I knelt on the carpet. Seeing the gun. Seeing Julius in my periphery. Surrounded by death, though only one that I'd grieve over.

I reached for the sofa, leaning, and I pulled a cloth from its arm. Coles and Varker could be sprawled like so many slaughtered chickens, but not Julius. Carefully draping the lace over his features, I pressed his hand for a moment. It was still warm, still pliant. Just no longer *him*.

When I had to speak or go mad, I posed the question.

'Will you tell me who you are?'

All the blood had drained from Delia's warm complexion, leaving her grey. Drawing her fingers over the gun she held limply in her lap, she gave me the briefest of glances.

'Varker and Coles gave me away to the Committee just now. But however did you find out?'

'It was Mr Timpson, partly.' My tongue felt clumsy, overlarge. 'He told me about a wedding Lucy had worked on – magnolia centerpieces, gardenias in the bride's hair. It was a Southern wedding he was describing, where such things grow. He even mentioned a memory of Lucy's, running through fields of coneflowers when she was a little girl. Though he didn't know it, he was painting a picture of the South. Where?'

'North Carolina,' she whispered.

Closing my eyes, I nodded.

Silkie Marsh hadn't said it was impossible to answer whether Lucy's name was Wright or Adams because she didn't know if the marriage was legal – Lucy Wright never existed. I thought about Long Luke whining to us weeks before that the women were escaped slaves and realized that, if I'd listened to the right party, I could have known the truth all along. I'd been charging into battle with flaming sword held high, assuming all the righteous anger of the law was on my side when, in fact, I was classed with cracksmen and sneakthieves.

'We didn't realize until I was fourteen and Lucy sixteen, you know.' Her voice was as lifeless as the gun in her hand.

'Realize what?'

'That we were slaves, of course.'

I stared back at her, mute. The woman I knew as Delia Wright was fine-boned and lovely, as lovely as Lucy had been. Her pear-shaped brown eyes with the gay freckles surrounding them were clear, her hand quite steady. I thought about Bird Daly suddenly, and what she'd said to me about returning to brothel work.

341

*There's nothing I'd not do to keep from going back there . . . I'd die
sooner. I'd do terrible things, Mr Wilde.*

'Is Jonas all right?'

I went to sit before her, seeing the room as if from a great
distance. As if I were viewing a *Herald* sketch of a crime I'd never
set eyes on. As if it weren't my life at all.

'He's in an upper bedroom with Mrs Higgins. She's trying to
settle him.'

'Where's George?'

'George went for help,' she said. Then, tears spilling onto her
cheeks unheeded as she glanced at Julius, she added, 'They grew up
together. George isn't well.'

'I'll listen if it helps. If it's useful. Not otherwise.'

Delia's face twisted in surprise. Finally, she pulled her knees
into her chest, resting her chin on them.

She looked very young just then. In the way that Bird had once
looked very young and endlessly sad. Sadder than health and youth
ought to allow.

'Our father was a wealthy white doctor in a small town. The
coneflower field was part of his property. I used to run through it
too.'

I nodded. Recalling when Greenwich Village was a village and
my parents alive and how I'd run through switchgrass by the river.
Run for no reason at all.

'He hadn't many slaves,' she said, frowning, 'and we lived in the
house with the doctor and my mother. We'd lessons, though not at
the school – he hired a private tutor from Philadelphia.'

'I did wonder about your accents.'

'Did you? My father studied medicine in the North. Much of
our time was spent at our lessons, and our father appreciated that
we spoke so well. Differently from our friends among the slave
children. We'd no idea we were just like them. My mother was a
quarter African . . . the doctor called her *darling* and us his little
sweethearts. Then another doctor arrived in town. One with, as it's
said, airs and graces. He laughed at my father for living with a black

mistress, mocked him relentlessly among their colleagues and began stealing his patients, and my father decided to take a white wife instead to save his practice. He was bettering himself, I suppose.'

To say I am as ignorant of the realities of slavery as I am regarding the realities of New York City politics would be a bald lie. Mercy and her late father the Reverend Underhill had kept me well informed. They'd told me repulsive things. Things I'd wanted to pluck gently from Mercy's whimsical mind as if removing a worm from an apple. So I'd heard tales of unspeakable cruelty.

I wasn't inured to such stories, however. On the contrary.

'He also decided that he needed improved furnishings,' Delia continued. '*Doctors* ought to maintain *a certain standard*. So he sold my mother to a man traveling home to Missouri and my sister to a neighboring plantation, and I was put to work with his other house slaves. I often saw my sister, when she could manage time away. If I hadn't, I think we'd both have gone mad.'

'Lucy was also a house slave, I take it.' Regardless of her true name, she would always be *Lucy* to me. 'She arranged flowers and helped with banquets and celebrations.'

'All the vases and arrangements fell under her care eventually. She'd always been clever with flowers. She loved them.'

'If I could kill the son of a bitch who carved words into your sister, I wager I'd do it,' I swore under my breath.

Wherever Delia's mind had been, I'd jarred it badly. She started, lifting her chin from her knees.

'Whatever do you mean?'

'Those words.' *As many as I love I rebuke and chasten, be zealous therefore and repent.* 'The man who punished her by carving a Bible verse into her chest ought to be shot like a dog.'

Delia laughed suddenly. It was such an incongruous sound in that room, she might as well have fired the revolver. When she kept laughing, she tried to stop, covering her mouth with her hand. Eyes shining with fright at the unnatural peals of mirth fighting to

343

escape.

'I'm sorry,' she said a moment later. 'No man carved that message into my sister's skin. She did it on her own with a dirty piece of metal. She was so beautiful, you see.'

Delia's words came clearly. Marched straight as foot soldiers who no longer fear death as they did once. If I live to be a hundred, and God knows that isn't going to happen, I'll never erase the image of her giving me the key to a riddle I'd never had any right to try to solve.

'Everyone on that plantation wanted a piece of her, of something beautiful. Everyone wanted her, and a great many of the men in the house took what they wanted. She said that they wouldn't look her in the eye when it happened, and they wouldn't speak to her either, her masters, and so she left a message where they couldn't miss it. I think when they sold the children their violence inevitably produced, she lost her mind a little. I've two nieces and another nephew, all auctioned while she lived in that hell. I'll never see them again.'

My throat worked, but no sound emerged. Nothing visible about me changed that day. I was the same scarred copper star at the end as the beginning, for all I'd seen and heard. But almost without meaning to, I made a decision.

If a war was required to end such stories, then I wanted a war.

'Something happened to alter everything. You were sold, weren't you? And to the same plantation?' I reasoned when I could speak.

She sighed. 'My father decided a new horse and buggy were also required. Yes.'

'How soon afterward did you leave that place with Lucy and Jonas?'

'I was an unbroken nuisance, my sister unbalanced, and Jonas valuable. We were given to a broker after barely a fortnight, to be auctioned in the Capitol.'

'And how did you escape?'

'My sister saved us. She was very brave, or . . . I thought she was. She didn't know that she was, she thought herself a coward, but – I'm sorry. Wasn't she brave, though? Wasn't she?'

Delia wept into her sleeve for several moments before I reached out and touched her wrist. It was a tiny, inadequate gesture. But I feared offering more. When she looked up again, shoulders shaking, she took my hand.

'She was braver than I'll ever be,' I told her.

The rest of the tale was simple. The slave brokers entrusted with the women and child were crude, underhanded men. They were en route to a District of Columbia slave pen to auction the family and return to the plantation with the money, pocketing a percentage as a fee, when Lucy had spied Rutherford Gates riding in the same direction. Though she was near to the breaking point and chained in the back of an uncovered wagon, she had seen something in his eyes. A sympathy, perhaps. Perhaps a weakness. In any case, she had screamed to Gates that the three travelers were kidnapped free blacks from Albany and not slaves at all. She had begged him for help.

And to her shock, he had actually believed her.

'The look in his eyes,' Delia remembered. 'As if he'd been given a sacred mission. I'll never forget it. When he threatened to drag the slave agents to the nearest magistrate, they hatched a scheme. They explained – always in sideways language, dropped hints – that magistrates were very busy people. That witnesses would have to be called, that weeks would pass and everyone the worse for it, since the three of us would be forced to pay for food all the while we awaited adjudication – that's the law in the Capitol, and naturally we hadn't a cent. The brokers were right, meanwhile, and so Charles – Gates – took out his purse and paid them two hundred dollars for the three of us.'

'As a bribe,' I clarified. 'Not as payment for property.'

'Precisely.'

We fell briefly silent. There wasn't much remaining I didn't know. But that didn't mean I was overeager to reach the conclusion.

'We stayed in his house in West Broadway for three months,

living out the story we'd told him, writing letters to imaginary kin in Albany,' Delia recalled. 'Shushing Jonas whenever he spoke of the plantation. I honestly don't think he remembers it any longer. At first we were terrified and grateful in equal measure, but Gates was kind to us, and seemed . . . I still can't believe he never cared for my sister. It's monstrous. In any case, he proposed, and she liked him very much by that time. I think no less she reasoned it would be . . . sensible . . . to be married. To have her new name on another official record.'

Gates had arranged for them all to be given new free papers, doubtless through the Party, having been told that the kidnappers destroyed their Albany documents. Lucy agreed to marry him in Massachusetts, and the family had traveled across Connecticut and celebrated with a small ceremony at an abolitionist church in the rolling countryside. Upon returning to Manhattan, Delia and Lucy had joined the Abyssinian Church, where Delia taught and Jonas learned alongside other colored youth, and they had been reasonably safe. Contented, though Lucy still suffered attacks of nameless, overwhelming fear.

Then Lucy found work at Timpson's Superior Blooms, Gates departed on one of his journeys, and all fell to pieces.

'Varker and Coles were engaged to get rid of your sister,' I said to Delia. She was gripping my hand in a frenzied clench. 'One black woman and her child, residing at Eighty-four West Broadway. They mistook you for her.'

She nodded. I passed her a far better handkerchief than I'd any right to own, which I'd discovered inside the costly jacket, and she pressed it into her eyes.

The next subject was nigh impossible for me to broach. Not due to my white Northerner notions of abolitionism, and not due to my great regard for the quietly weeping woman before me. Not even due to my guilt over having witnessed a tragedy unfolding whilst unable to halt the inevitable collision – indeed, having led the wolves straight to their door. The problem was more personal.

I know what it's like to have a sibling. And sympathy was

burrowing a tunnel right through my ribs.

'Your sister sent you away with Jonas on the pretence of getting your free papers.' I stopped, eyes burning, then forced myself to go on. 'When you returned to Val's apartment alone, Lucy had left you . . . instructions, I take it?'

The shudder that passed through Delia's body could have broken her back, had she been a different sort of woman. But Delia was formidable. Deadly. And she'd done precisely what she'd had to do in order to save her nephew.

'I'm sorry,' she whispered. 'I never meant your brother any harm. Not after he was so unaccountably kind to us. Lucy's note was quite clear. I didn't understand a syllable of it, but I obeyed. I don't think I want to understand it. I only knew she had done it for us.'

She pushed her fingers into a pocket of her day dress and passed me a short letter. The writing was palsied, very difficult to read. But read it I did.

Dearest sister,

I pray that this reaches your hands. All is not yet lost. But we are set upon from every direction – last night I was told just how dire our situation has become. I am in the thick darkness now, but recall that where dark is thickest, there is our Lord best felt. When you find me, I will have gone home. Dwell on my release from the shadows that plague us, and be at peace. I love you, and I love Jonas, beyond your comprehending.

Follow my instructions to the letter, I charge by all we have endured together: it must appear that I am the victim of a violent brute. Make it look so in haste. Do this for me and for Jonas. It is your part in the bargain I have made. Set the scene as for a murder and you will both live. I know not why this must be, but trust that I believe in the messenger, and do as I tell you one last time.

Then run, my darling girl. Run and never look back.

I thought about Mercy's second letter to me. Mercy, who had

always known an unaccountably great deal about human nature.

Death ought to mean something, as lives do. Mine will.

'Lucy hanged herself while you were out, and you took her down.' I passed Delia back the note I'd refolded. 'You would need to have cut the rope, I imagine, and you used the knife I found sitting on the counter. Did you dispose of the rope later, on your way out?'

Delia nodded, looking me clear in the eye.

'Your sister told you to make it look like a violent brute had attacked her – so you removed her clothing and arranged Val's dressing gown tie to look like the murder weapon. You turned over a table and smashed a decanter and pulled down a painting, none of it very systematic. You were too grieved to do it other than quickly, then run for safety. But you trusted her. So you obeyed.'

She added a second hand to the one clasped in mine. Peering at me through long wet lashes, she shook her head in disbelief. 'Captain Wilde could have hanged as surely as she did. I want you to know it's been a terrible weight on me. I can't think who could want such a thing or why.'

I knew why. But it was a terribly long story.

Footsteps fell in the room beyond. I whisked the gun from her lap, pivoting. But the woman I'd known as Delia Wright had no real need of me. George Higgins came through the door. His eyes were a wreck, his mouth pulled downward as if recovering from a stroke. The carefully sculpted man looked quite lost. Adrift on a sunless sea.

'Help is coming,' he told Delia. 'Timothy.' He hesitated. 'God help us, I realize you're a copper star. But in light of—'

'I was never here.' Rising fully, I rested the gun on the table. 'What steps are being taken?'

'My mother has resources. Many others have died here, of various ailments. Only not . . . in this fashion. It's the river for Varker and Coles. We'll bury Julius at the Abyssinian Church with no one the wiser.'

A spasm passed over Higgins's face – violent, inexpressibly

grieved.

'Tell me,' I said.

'We'd just arrived to take them to the carriage,' he answered. 'Varker and Coles burst in on us. They were very full of themselves – swaggering, making boastful speeches. They said you were in the Party's hands, Timothy, and likely already killed. We were frightened for you – when I think of the look on Julius's face. Are you all right? There's blood at the back of your head.'

I couldn't care, not when my friend's was forming a small lake in the carpet. Not when Julius and I wouldn't be worrying over each other any longer.

'Please, go on.'

'We were ready to fight them, but no one had yet moved. Jonas was crying, and Varker lifted a hand to slap some silence into him. Julius stepped in front of the boy as a shield. Not aggressively, just – decisively. That yellow-hearted coward started like a hare and then shot him. Just shot him point blank, in the chest.'

That was as I'd imagined. But none of it was quite bearable. I was near to undone, living only in the silent spaces between heartbeats that chanted, *your doing, your doing, all yours, your—*

'Was it long?' I asked, trying to breathe slower. 'Before Julius—'

'No, not long,' Delia answered swiftly.

'It was over seconds later.' Higgins wiped a hand across his haggard brow. Sweat stood out at his temples, and I could see the blue veins in his dark skin quivering with rage. 'Varker hardly knew what he had done. He'd the gun aimed at me an instant later, and this . . . this young lady lifted the poker in my defense. Varker fell like a stone. She'd snatched up his revolver and turned it on Coles before—'

'Before you could stop me?' she demanded.

I could hear whole histories in that voice. Scores of them and from many narrators, as hoarse and as heavy a tone as chains being dragged along the ground. So too could Higgins. He studied her, curled into herself there on the floor. Her polished-oak curls, her eyes blazing through her tears. After choosing words reverently as

349

talismans, he went to the woman who'd called herself Delia and knelt before her. Her lips parted. She hadn't looked terrified when I'd walked into a bloodbath partly of her making.

She looked terrified now.

'Before I could shoot him for you,' Higgins said. 'I'd have spared you that, if I could. I've a friend upstairs called Jean-Baptiste, I've just fetched him and . . . we're leaving New York. I can't stay here any longer. This city is like an illness that seeps in through your skin. I'll see you and Jonas to Toronto, and after that, you need have nothing further to do with me. I'll find my own way. I know you supposed that I'd turn my nose up at you if I learned where you came from. I understand why you imagined so, what with all my peacocking, how dandified and pretentious you must have thought me. Bragging about my education, my work, my plans. Bragging about *money*. I'd thought to impress you, and you thought me an arrogant fool of no constancy or substance. That was my fault. You were wrong, though. Mistaken.'

'How exactly was I mistaken?' she whispered.

George Higgins smiled sadly and shook his head.

'I'd follow you to the edge of the world if you asked me,' he told her. 'I love you. I only wish I knew your name.'

The carriage that departed from the alleyway behind Neither Here Nor There that dawn contained Jean-Baptiste, who'd signed on for the adventure with enthusiasm; Lucy's son Jonas, whose name I never doubted was real, as it's impossible to teach a kinchin a new moniker instantaneously; George Higgins, after he and I had seen Julius shrouded and delivered into the shaking hands of Reverend Brown; and a woman whose name I'd no right to ask.

And so I never learned it.

I hope, though, that George Higgins learned it. Hours or weeks or minutes later. I hope that very much.

When the others were safe in the vehicle behind drawn curtains, it proved weirdly difficult to let him go. He stood there finishing a thin cigar while I stared at alley muck, both wondering what to say to each other. As if we'd snagged hooks in each other's skin and feared tugging at them. Maybe that's because I respected him and wished him well. Maybe it was because we'd just spent a quiet minute staring into the same waxen face as it grew ever colder, standing on either side of our fallen friend. And that can make you need a person. Someone who's seen a portion of your mental map – knows where the rapids and the plummeting moss-edged wells are.

I felt as if, when George Higgins departed, Julius would be dead. And I wasn't doing a man's job at facing that.

'You'll write us when you're safely to Toronto?' I asked when he threw the stub to the ground.

'Of course.' He reached for my hand, and I took it. 'I'd not even object if you wrote back. Will you?'

'If you want me to. Though I'd make a paltry substitute for hearing from Julius. He was the best of us, I suspect.'

'I suspect you're right.' Clearing his throat, he added, 'We'll just have to trust to his sound judgment that he tolerated misfits like you and me for a reason, eh?'

It grew useless to even attempt speech about then. So I swallowed, and he stepped toward the carriage.

'Goodbye, Timothy. By the way, I mean to write my housekeeper that you can have your pick of my library.'

Clearly, I'd misunderstood. Chloroform and a gash that likely resembled a traffic accident had quashed what little was left of my faculties. It only remained to check myself into an asylum and have done.

'You – but – *why?*' I stammered.

He smiled, dark eyes gentling. 'Because you were staring at my books as if you were looking at a vault full of bullion. They'll be cumbersome and difficult to ship and worth little enough. They aren't rare or even old. I'll simply buy new ones.'

'But I can't—'

'Are you going to be dense about this?' he asked pointedly.

It was, as usual, a fair question.

'No,' I said. 'Thank you. It means a great deal to me.'

When Higgins opened the carriage door, he cast another, shrewder look back in my direction. Pulling his fingertips down his clipped beard, he paused.

'I don't get the impression that you let go of things easily. Timothy, are you about to do something dangerous?'

He sounded concerned. I was more than a little touched. But the smile I attempted must have been a death's mask variety, if his sudden look of dismay was any judge.

'Goodbye, George,' I said, turning to go. 'Be well.'

After several lingering seconds, I heard the carriage pull away. I didn't look back. Looking back, as Lot's wife learned, can prove unhealthy. I know my new friend wanted to stop me. That he even considered it. But I'd put fleeing to Canada with two kinchin and the woman I love pretty high toward the top of the list myself, and he felt likewise. So he let me go.

That's how it happens that, about half an hour later – and even dressed as if I belonged there – I paid a call at the Astor House.

CHAPTER TWENTY-FIVE

If the lineal descendants of Ham are alone to be scripturally enslaved, it is certain that slavery at the south must soon become unscriptural; for thousands are ushered into the world, annually, who, like myself, owe their existence to white fathers, and those fathers most frequently their own masters.

Frederick Douglass, *Narrative of the Life of Frederick Douglass, an American Slave,* 1845

I'm usually fairly sharp at recalling trivia. When I didn't remember Rutherford Gates's room number – possibly because it seemed someone had taken a flaking rust-orange railroad spike and driven it through my neck and into my brain – I was vexed at first. Then I looked down, recalled what I was wearing, and loftily demanded his room number from the desk clerk, citing secret Party affairs.

Within five minutes, I stood outside his door.

If someone had asked me why I was determined to speak with Gates, I'd not have managed a sensible answer just then. But I'd been given a panorama, a mural of stories leading one into the other. In short, I suspect I wanted to see Rutherford Gates because of his sister, Leticia.

She had said, *It did frighten me so, the sight of his tiny hand swollen*

353

into a ghastly red paw . . . Rutherford had his way after he recovered, of course. That dog was his inseparable companion until he departed for university.

I'd a question to pose on that subject: I wanted to know the dog's whereabouts. And I meant to have the answer.

The railroad spike drove a bit farther into my head with every step I took. I tested the door. He hadn't locked it, so I stepped inside.

Astor House living quarters happen to be as splendid as we're all led to believe. My boots sank into a Turkish carpet, and the morning sunlight nosed its way into soft folds of mossy curtains. I entered a parlor – nothing like the Millingtons' showy monstrosity, but carefully decorated with patterned paper and soft blue furnishings – and discovered my quarry.

Gates sat in an armchair, smoking. The man who'd once struck me as healthy-complexioned had been coated in the fine silt of grief and fear. The silvering goatee remained waxed, the brown hair combed, the spectacles neatly placed on his nose. He didn't give a good goddamn that was the case anymore, though. If not for force of habit, I don't think he'd have donned a waistcoat and attended the Castle Garden soiree at all. He'd been out all night, for he hadn't changed clothing, and his brown eyes stared through a misty wall of regret and champagne at me.

'Mr Wilde. To what do I owe this surprise?'

'Pretend to me that it's a surprise and I'll fight you here and now in this hotel room.'

I meant it wholeheartedly, but that didn't stir Gates much. He gestured to a chair opposite. I ignored him. If I sat down, I didn't like my odds of getting up again.

'Do you want to explain to me how you *accidentally* arranged to have your wife murdered?' I asked him. 'And don't tell me the Party found out you'd married an African by chance, and this was all their doing. You knew those women to be slaves. And you told Madam Marsh as much.'

That galvanized him. Gates's head snapped toward me. If I was being careful – and I wasn't, not by that time – I'd have said he was now privy to new information.

'How on earth can you know that?'

'Because I've worked out how your wife died. You needed a safe distance from her suddenly, and you confided in Silkie Marsh. Surely you realize that terrible things started happening immediately afterward.'

If I'd slapped him in the mouth, he couldn't have looked more appalled. 'I did . . . I did relate to Silkie the sad truth of my situation. She's a dear friend. But—'

'You must have told her of your new troubles that day we found you at the Astor. Told her Lucy was murdered. What did she say to you?'

'That she was sorry for my loss, sorry that slave catchers had harassed members of my household. She tried to console me,' Gates protested. His liverish complexion was pinkening in dismay "She knew nothing of how Lucy ended up strangled.'

'It's very simple. After a failed attempt by Varker and Coles to capture Lucy, Madam Marsh simply walked into my brother's rooms and ordered your wife to kill herself so her kinfolk wouldn't be sent back to North Carolina. Marsh accomplished this in large measure by telling Lucy that you'd spilled her house slave origins.'

The letter Lucy wrote to her sister had revealed relatively little about her plight, but what I could manage to extrapolate was very telling indeed: *Do this for me and for Jonas,* she had said. *It is your part in the bargain I have made. Set the scene as for a murder and you will both live.* That meant that an agreement had been reached, a pact so deep I was only beginning to guess its dimensions. A pact orchestrated by none other than Silkie Marsh, who had paid her fateful visit the night before. And who'd realized that the fact Lucy was hidden at Val's, of all places, was an engraved invitation to foster another sort of unholy mayhem entirely. It must all have looked very neat in Madam Marsh's head: Lucy would send her family away on a pretense. Lucy would die. Delia would orchestrate the evidence. Mulqueen would arrive shortly thereafter. And then . . .

I didn't feel much up to musing over what would have happened then.

I know not why this must be, Lucy had admitted, *but trust that I believe in the messenger, and do as I tell you one last time.*

I wonder to this day precisely what Silkie Marsh said to Lucy, but the situation that must have been presented was obvious: *as a free woman married to Senator Gates, you are unspeakably dangerous. You have escaped us once already. Slavery or death: make your choice.*

Lucy had thought about running, and she had thought about going back. Running would lead to capture. Slavery likewise meant death, a piece at a time. Not the thick darkness where God lives, but the thin, silvery hell in which she could hear nothing beyond her own shrieking. Then she had considered the new option presented to her by Silkie Marsh. It was no less terrible a way out. It was simply the only unspeakable path she could tread alone. And if love for her sister was world encompassing, Lucy's love for her son was universes of stars with their satellites. She would have done anything, everything, to spare Jonas. Her death had been a gift.

'Does it surprise you that betraying your wife's origins got her killed?' I asked.

Sadly, it shocked him right through to the spine.

I've never been in a war, cannon and brimstone howling all around me. But I think Gates looked as blasted, just then. Ruin had been held at bay with battlements of uncertainty and self-delusion and dumb force of habit, and my news had stripped his remaining defenses. And when the clarity did arrive, it fragmented him. I have done very stupid things in my life, and I've also witnessed tragic ones. Never yet, though, has the former directly caused the latter.

Gates didn't happen to be so lucky.

When the few wails had ended, and the muffled sobs, I demanded information. I thought I needed more. In truth, I was a train divorced from its tracks, flying downhill in a smoldering blaze. I could still see Julius's face before me, still recalled what it felt like to *carry this man's dead wife* and bury her in newsprint. I got my wish after a little reviving brandy and some truly alarming tremors.

'Silkie was to arrange everything,' he moaned, squeezing his skull in his hands. 'I never meant for Lucy to be hurt. Dear, affectionate Lucy. I was mad to keep her in my own home, mad to marry her in the first place. Even if under a false name. But to think of her cold, in a pauper's grave . . . God help me.'

'I think you'll have a better chance with the devil,' I growled. 'Tell me. *Now*. What vile arrangement did you enter with Marsh?'

Lips quivering, he capitulated. 'I arrived home one Sunday night when Lucy had been out with her sister. Lucy threw her arms around my neck and told me that she was ready, finally, to leave the house regularly – that she couldn't conscience Jonas learning to fear the world as she did. Of course in that first instant, I was proud. Enormously so. And Timpson's isn't so very far from my residence.'

'You supported her,' I said through my teeth, recalling Delia's account. 'You asked how her nerves would fare. You ordered champagne. But afterward . . .'

'I realized how insane my situation was in truth. Lucy would be seen five days a week working at the flower shop, then returning. She'd be discovered within the fortnight – by her own circle, by men who know me, and I was terrified.'

'Really? What in holy hell *terrified* you?' Those words snapped out like the crack of a lash.

He quailed. 'Disgrace, yes, public evisceration, *yes*, but none of that was paramount – I've many political obligations. Some are to monstrous people, vultures. Mr Wilde, they are conscienceless creatures you'd not believe possible.'

'Oh, I'd believe them possible, all right.'

A quake of revulsion passed through him. 'You think me the same as the rest of the Party. Grasping, vicious.'

'No, there's a difference. You're too cowardly to do your own dirty work.'

'It was never meant to be dirty work!' he cried, tearing his spectacles off as fresh moisture rushed to his eyes. 'I met with Silkie one night, as an old confidant, one who has ever had my ear and I hers, and we shared a wine bottle and talked. I'd never before unburdened myself of my secret. It felt giddy and sickening at the same time. I once raced a trap when I was terribly drunk, as a boy. It felt like the same. Like falling, flying. All at once. If Silkie hadn't always supported me so ardently, in my life, my campaigns . . . I'd have shattered apart. And it didn't seem wrong either. Lucy had lied to me too, after all.'

'I suppose Jonas gave them away,' I ventured.

'I wish he had done.' His voice sank to a whisper. 'When we married – Lucy was hesitant over intimacy. We didn't consummate the vows for some six months, in fact. I never pressured her, never dreamed of causing her distress. But we did sleep together and when Lucy dreamed . . . she didn't dream of Albany, that much was clear.'

I have battled the urge to strike a man in the face many times. On that occasion, I'd have done it and gladly had I not been saving all my strength for another task.

'Let's have the rest of it,' I ordered.

'Silkie – she's wonderfully sympathetic. I confessed to her that I needed Lucy out of my house. I needed her to disappear. If I'd told Lucy the truth, she would have been angry, perhaps even bitter enough to expose me, God knows what she might have done out of vindictiveness or hurt. But if Silkie could find her a fresh place to start – a real housekeeping position, work as a seamstress or a florist, perhaps, away from the city – then I could even visit her there. As Charles Adams.'

My vision wasn't wide and glimmer edged at this point because I could barely stand. No. Human selfishness can be staggering. And every word, every asinine fantasy, had been God's honest truth in his head.

'I suggested to Silkie that Lucy be told they needed protection from vicious anti-amalgamationists who'd found us out. That there was no time to lose, and she and Jonas must pack their things. It was more than half true, you realize. If my voters had discovered us, they may well have torn Lucy in pieces or burned down our home. And the Party – they're capricious, hellishly vengeful, and I'd deceived them. When you told me slave catchers took Delia and Jonas, and that Lucy had been murdered, I felt as if I was dying.'

'You are one of the stupidest men of my acquaintance,' I said. 'I need you to grasp that. My friend was killed over this. Over the fact you are *witless*.'

He shook his head frantically. As if that would shake death off him the way a dog shakes off droplets of Hudson water.

'I never wanted her hurt,' he pleaded. 'I loved her. I only wanted her gone. I'm sorry.'

I just stared at him. That level of mewling naïveté could have rivaled a steaming colt's, and here it was emerging from a grown man. An educated man, who knew his Party and their capabilities. The same man, I reminded myself, who after meeting and growing infatuated with a beautiful black woman, supposed that through caution and careful manipulation of her fears he could encase her in a pretty prison cell *for the rest of their natural lives*.

He isn't too stupid to live, I decided. *He's far worse.*

Gates's imagination could grasp nothing outside of his own interests. He supposed every story ever told was about him.

'What did you pay your friend Silkie Marsh to make Lucy disappear? Oh, I beg your pardon – to see her *spirited away in safety*?'

'A hundred dollars.' A mouselike whimper escaped his throat.

'You may not have strung up that rope, but you killed her all the same,' I hissed. 'Lucy was a lit match set to a political powder keg, and the person you consulted was the Party's unofficial mascot? You paid a viper of a woman to make your wife vanish, and you are going to jail.'

'Please,' he whispered. 'I've committed no crime, save for the crime of trusting in the wrong ally. Yes, I paid Silkie, but I never told her to hurt Lucy. You can expose me, perhaps. But not arrest me.'

'I'm not arresting you for murder.'

Pulling Varker's still-loaded revolver from my pocket, I trained it on the terrified politico. My arms were clumsy, cotton-stuffed limbs, my vision dark as a button-eyed doll's. But I managed. Touching that gun was repulsive in every sense, as if I'd accidentally run my hand along Varker's living skin. But I lacked the physical strength to wrestle a man to the Tombs, and I thought I might walk him against the muzzle of a pistol.

'Wait,' he gasped. 'If you aren't arresting me for murder . . .'

'I'm arresting you for forgery, violation of corporation ordinances, and spouse abandonment. Your marriage certificate is filled out in your own hand, and I've possession of it. It's no matter to me how you come to be locked in the Tombs. The fleas are just as friendly there with falsifiers of government documents as they are with murderers. They're very democratic.'

The look he leveled at me was extraordinary. One I'd never seen the likes of, in fact. Half was more or less leprous with self-disgust, the other half flushed with gratitude.

He didn't have to make decisions anymore. Standing up, he shrugged into his greatcoat and headed for the door.

'I've one more question,' I said as we quit the hotel room, my gun trained on his kidney. 'I spoke with your sister. You once rescued a dog you were very fond of. You sheltered it in a barn loft, and a spider bit you. She said you and the dog were inseparable until you went away to school.'

'Yes? What of that?'

'What became of the dog you loved so entirely?'

I'd puzzled him. He peered back at me, eyes full of Lucy and a hundred dollars changing hands. 'I don't know. I think my parents gave it to a neighboring farm. I could never have kept him at a boarding school. Why?'

Seizing his elbow in a rough grip, I led him down the hallway to the stairs. I didn't answer him, and soon he subsided into miserable shock. I thought about what love looks like, and the fact that to Gates love resembled a leash, with the beloved object trailing alongside him in a haze of delirious joy. He felt a finer fellow with an adoring mutt at his side. He walked taller through the streets with a beautiful girl waiting in his home, cupped within his shell like a pearl. He wasn't an evil man, merely a hopelessly selfish one.

I wondered, as we journeyed to the Tombs, which sort are capable of the most damage.

George Washington Matsell, when I burst into his office half an hour later, was composing a letter. He dropped the quill when he saw me, half standing and then slowly sinking down again.

'I need your help,' I said.

Despite carrying the weight of one of our healthier frontier bison, Chief Matsell had me deposited in his own chair within seconds. I wondered why I should be in his chair and not the wooden one his guests are generally offered. And then, limbs as loose as a jellyfish's, I realized it was because the chief's chair had arms, and I was less likely to spill myself on his floor like a burst feed bag that way.

'What in Christ's name is going on, Wilde?'

I passed him the key to a Tombs cell. His eyes flew down to the metal in his fingers. Then I set the gun on his desk. I don't think he could have been any more flummoxed if I'd produced a sack of leprechaun gold.

'This was Seixas Varker's weapon. Three people are dead, including Varker and Coles. It's being taken care of, you can tell the Party. Discreetly. Bodies already disposed of. The colored family in question has left New York, and they're not returning. Supposing Tammany won't miss Varker and Coles too keenly, I've fixed it all up plumb for them.'

'Then why do you need my help, and who've you arrested?'

'Rutherford Gates.'

The troughlike furrows at either side of Matsell's nose and mouth tensed, then shook with a mix of outrage and alarm.

'I had to,' I whispered. 'He paid Silkie Marsh to eliminate his wife, and she was bullied into hanging herself. It was crueler than murder. I know someone will free Gates before a trial is even spoken of, that it isn't a crime to terrify a woman to death. If you hurry, he'll have been jailed for under ten minutes. I'll never say a word, on my honor.'

Cursing under his breath, Matsell pocketed the key in his sack coat. Instead of running for the cells, however, he went to a pitcher of water sitting beside a small bowl and came back with a wet handkerchief.

'Hold this in place,' he said, guiding it to my head. 'If today is the day you finally faint in my office, Wilde, I will assign you to patrol the Five Points for the remainder of your natural life.'

Fending off a wave of nausea, I nodded. Pressing the cool cloth into my head felt wretched and heavenly at the same time. The final sound I heard as Matsell departed was the scrape of the lock on his office door.

Rutherford Gates, it seemed, wasn't the only man newly locked in the Tombs.

In an effort to remain conscious, I thought about the lockup: it's 148 cells of about seven feet by fifteen. A male wing and a female, each featuring cast-iron water closets, ripely pickled bedding, and a strong stench of despair. When you can smell the despair beneath the reek of seeping sewage, that is. What comes up from theoretically solid ground in these parts smells as if Hades needs expanding and is annexing more territory via fissures in our prison floor. They're vile little holes.

Putting Rutherford Gates in one ranked with the most satisfying experiences of the previous month.

My vision began to swim again. The clock ticked and the sun rose and snow began to fall outside the window, the tiny gems that deal a sting like pinpricks. Soon I'd lost any delineation between the spreading clouds in my eyes and the storm in the city beyond.

It'll be no easy task, digging Julius's grave with the ground frozen, I thought. And then lost still more of my sight for an entirely different reason.

When I heard the door unlocking, well over an hour must have passed. And it wasn't Matsell who entered.

Valentine strode inside in a hurry. Whatever spirits I might have been keeping up crashed into a ravine when I saw his face. His mouth was set in a grim line, eyes darkened by resentment so profound the pouches beneath twitched in disgust. Everything about him was angry, from his ramrod spine to the bullish angle of his neck. My brother looked as if he planned to hack someone to death with a hatchet and enjoy the exercise. And when he's in that humor, he isn't shy over starting dustups that leave people with their brittle bits splintered.

I swallowed hard, pressing my sleeve to my eyes when I realized Delia had kept my handkerchief. I'm almost never afraid of him now I'm grown. But I was then.

'I'm sorry.'

Val didn't answer me. He pulled the cloth away from my head and shifted my hair with careful fingers. Parts of it stuck together in a nasty fashion, but he took considerable time about the project. Doubtless finding the spot that could deck me with a single swing.

'Matsell fetched me here,' he said. 'Gates has been released, though he looks to be contemplating a stroll in the Atlantic. This split needs needlework.'

God help me, even his voice was furious. If I was judging by appearances, he'd eject me from Matsell's office and then plunge into the hearty business of never speaking to me again. Panic sent dark tendrils streaming along my skin.

'Please,' I choked out. 'I'm sorry, so sorry, but I couldn't stop myself. Gates as good as murdered her, and Silkie Marsh made it look your doing to spite us.'

Val took the cloth to the basin and started rinsing and wringing. Refolding it, he turned back. Even his stance crackled with disdain.

'I'm not angry.'

363

'Of course you are, why wouldn't you be, you're practically gnashing your teeth you're so bloody furious! Don't look at me like that and then tell me you're not cursing the day you ever made me a copper star. Just say it, damn you, I – '

'Hush.' Pressing the cloth lightly back in place, he perched on the edge of the desk. 'For God's sake, Timothy. I'm angry. I'm not angry *at you*.'

I pressed my fingers into my eyes the way Val often did. It didn't dislodge the spear through my skull, but it went a fair way toward hiding my expression. Or such was my fervent prayer. I'm ninety percent sure it would have troubled him.

'I'm sorry anyhow.'

Val deemed silence the best response to my continued apologies.

'And that was . . .' Wiping my hand over my face, I sat up a bit. When I pictured what my brother had done at Tammany Hall, I realized I hadn't the words for it. 'Thank you. But you still look like you're going to croak someone and then cure his hide for boots.'

Val shook his head, seeming ninety years old instead of thirty-four. 'Christ, but you exhaust me. You're my kid brother. I honestly can't imagine – Tim, I met you ten minutes after you were born, making about as much sense as you do now. How do you want me to look when I find you hog-tied and bleeding?'

I shook my head with my eyes squeezed shut, saying the only relevant thing I could summon that wasn't still *I'm sorry*.

'Julius Carpenter is dead. So are Varker and Coles.'

My brother sucked a breath in and then whistled it out again. 'Anyone get out of it in one piece?'

'Lucy's family left this morning. They're as safe as circumstances allow.' Glancing up at him, I added, 'You told me at the Liberty's Blood that you'd sent a message to the Capitol. Have you gotten a reply? You asked someone you trust to question the auction pens about missing deliveries two years back, didn't you?'

Val's eyebrows tensed. 'I did, yes. Tim, those people—'

'They really were escaped slaves. Don't tell me their names,' I requested. I needed that, needed it in ways I didn't even understand. 'Just leave them be.'

Valentine shrugged. 'When no one in Albany would admit to knowing them, I started to have my doubts.'

The wind in the streets was picking up, tumbling through the road like a runaway carriage. Val shifted and clapped me on the knee.

'Come along, bright young copper star. We'll find a sawbones and patch you back together. It wasn't a straight flush, dragging Gates here, but it wasn't a pair of twos either. The Party bosses have been watching him unravel for weeks now. The chief will say that you delivered him here for safekeeping. They'll probably give you a medal.'

Before I knew quite what was happening, my arm was over his shoulder and we were halfway across the room. That was plenty mortifying. But I was clearly in no state to make my own escape, and I'm not exactly popular at the Tombs.

'What would you have done?' I asked. 'If those Tammany men hadn't listened to you.'

'I'd have worked out a different lay.'

'And if that failed?'

'I'd have thought it out again fresh. And I'm the leery sort, you know, plenty active between the ears. I'm even capable of keeping my mouth hinged and thinking at the same time, which is a trick I should teach you.'

'I know you are. You always did take more after Mum.'

I don't quite know why I said those words. I only knew it mattered to me very much that I did. My brother's step hitched, and I think he produced a perplexed little cough before we moved on.

Maybe I said it because he was all that I had, and we shared a history that couldn't be mentioned between us. Maybe I possessed a string of mad fantasies about Mercy Underhill and an equally mad anchor back to myself by the name of Valentine. He was my entire context. Maybe I was grateful and wanted him to know it in absolute terms, because I hated the fact that neither of us took our alliance for granted, neither accepted it without question, and the doubt was half my fault, and I loathe that skepticism more than I have ever hated any single thing, bar none.

It's difficult to be certain. I can't recall quite what I was thinking. But after that there were only miles of looming stone, and wind with sharp fangs, and rays of sun like tiny arrows through the endless air.

Chapter Twenty-six

Margaret was the first that met me. She did not recognize me. When I left her, she was but seven years old, a little prattling girl, playing with her toys. Now she was grown to womanhood – was married, with a bright-eyed boy standing by her side. Not forgetful of his enslaved, unfortunate grand-father, she had named the child Solomon Northup Staunton.

Solomon Northup, *Twelve Years a Slave*, 1853

Since last summer, I've a habit of waking up in my brother's bed with head injuries. It's unspeakably tiresome. On this occasion, at least I didn't also find myself permanently disfigured for the second time.

So there's a blessing, I thought, gingerly sitting up.

The painting of Thomas Jefferson had been righted and the decanter replaced. My boots and cravat and jacket were gone, but I still wore the shirt and trousers I'd been given for the Party ball. Touching the back of my head, I'd a vague recollection of someone stitching me together as if I were a rag doll. According to the clock, only a few hours had passed. I faced late Sunday afternoon, the first day of March, and I yearned to erase ninety percent of it as if it had never existed.

Something was roasting. I could smell it sending thick trickles of brown fat into the pot.

When I wandered into the kitchen, I found my brother pulling an iron cooking vessel from the fire and James Playfair sitting at the table wearing an anxious expression. More than usually pale. Around his neck he'd arranged a gleaming yellow scarf that failed to quite hide the strips of bandaging. I wondered whether he might likewise have a key to Val's rooms and then decided I didn't care. I'd never previously experienced happiness when encountering one of Val's friends. It seemed prudent to cherish the occasion.

'Oh God, sit down!' Jim leapt to his feet and shoved a chair under my legs. It was startling but well intended. 'You aren't meant to be wandering about willy-nilly like a street cat. The doctor said—'

'I feel much better,' I told him.

Val cocked a dubious eye at me and then used a fork and knife to lift the roasted lamb leg onto a carving board. It had been stuffed with rosemary sprigs and bits of amber garlic. My brother was dressed in red flannel and black trousers, so a shift at the firehouse appeared to be imminent.

'I feel wretched over—' Jim began.

'If only I could have, I'd—' I said at the same time.

We paused.

'There was nothing you could have done save for what you did. And it was damnably good of you to do it. Are you all right?' I asked.

Jim flicked his fingers as if dismissing a soured wine bottle. 'It's a scratch.'

'A *scratch*,' Val growled, apparently not having recovered his good humor. 'It isn't a scratch, you mincing little twit, it's a gash in your fucking neck, and last I saw you, you looked like you'd taken a bath in your own ruby. If I have my way about it, McDivitt and Beardsley will be kissing their careers farewell if not their bollocks, preferably both.'

'My gracious, but you're terrifying, Valentine,' Jim said pleasantly, winking at me. I couldn't help but smile back at him.

'I don't like my own meddled with, and if they touch either of you again, I'll lace them personally. I'm keen to lace them now, but the Party might manage it better.'

Jim flushed ever so slightly. 'Shall I give you my handkerchief to protect you in battle?'

My brother sniffed in sardonic amusement, covering the meat with a bowl. Entirely oblivious to the fact it had been only half a joke. I wondered whether he'd yet cottoned to the notion that molleys engaged in sincere affection in addition to widely reviled deviances. Because I was sold that they did. That seemed a long conversation, though.

'Why are you doing that?' I asked instead, nodding at the covered roast.

'Because after ten minutes, it's better that way. Matsell said to tell you he'd released one other prisoner, colored fellow by the name of Tom Griffen. According to the chief, no one has pressed any changes against the man, so he's free to go. Any story there?'

For an instant, I couldn't recall. Then I did and felt about as grateful toward the chief as is possible.

'Tom Griffen killed Sean Mulqueen,' I answered.

'Did he now? I'll have to post him a thank-you.'

Val revealed a loaf of bread and passed it to Jim, who'd already found a knife. On the instant a crust had been sliced, I appropriated it. For some reason, I was suddenly ravenous. My brother pulled a cork from a wine bottle and began setting out glasses.

'You need to spill what happened this morning,' Val announced. 'Best get it off your chest sooner, and I think I'm entitled to that story, you know.'

I did. And crossing Val seemed like bad luck just then.

So after we'd migrated to the parlor for supper, I told them. Quietly, I wove a picture of magnolias at a sun-soaked wedding. Of people who were figments of their friends' imaginations and a mother who was unspeakably brave. Between my brother smoking

369

furiously and Jim looking appalled, I was at least blessed with an audience who shared my sympathies on the subject. And the roasted lamb proved helpful, as did the first bottle of wine, and the second.

By the time we'd tidied up, the sun was setting. Jim wandered over to the window and twitched the curtain back, staring out into the gathering night. My brother reached for his jacket. Then he shot me a look I couldn't get to the bottom of.

'She'll have to be dealt with,' he said. 'One of these days.'

Ah. Silkie Marsh and her affection for heartbreaking chaos.

'I know,' I said.

'I'm for the Knickerbocker Twenty-one, then. Jim, stay for a spell if you like, but I'd be grateful if you were clear by tomorrow.' He smirked wickedly at me, donning his gloves. 'The Society of Young Irish Widows is planning a fund-raiser and means to pay us firedogs a call. I've been angling for a piece of one in particular for weeks now. Not *too* grieved, you understand. She asked to speak me privately afterward, and I don't think she means to say much. Anyhow, you're likely better off snug home and resting, eh, Jim?'

'Doubtless,' Jim said evenly, about as composed as an Astor House flower arrangement.

It didn't fool me for an instant.

'Tim, keep what little wits you have about you, yes?' my brother admonished.

And then he'd disappeared. I walked across the room to where Jim stood staring at the closed door.

'I don't know how you do it,' I noted.

Jim turned toward the window again, pulling his scarf tighter with one slim-fingered hand. Outside the evening grew steadily colder, crystallizing into frosted shadows as the living things huddled together for warmth and the unliving things grew brittle and fragile.

'It doesn't matter who Val thinks he is,' he answered. 'I know who he is to *me*. That's something. And I know who *I* am. That's

370

something too. And not a soul in the world can take either one away from me.'

I stared into the afterglow beside him, doubtful that I'd ever heard that particular sentiment laid out in quite that fashion. He said nothing, and I said still more of nothing, until the nothing had twined thickly between us.

'I feel so alone here,' I heard myself murmur at last.

'Really?' Jim answered with a small smile. 'I never do.'

'How is that possible, in a city like this?'

'Look at it,' he said, gesturing. 'This window looks down upon hundreds more panes of glass, and behind those panes live thousands upon thousands of lost souls. When I feel cast down and helpless, scores of other men do as well, and when I am bitterly angry at feeling cast down and helpless, countless other people languish in concert with me. When I'm happy, it's the same. It's a bit like . . . I used to play chamber music. It's like a vast orchestra. And so I shan't ever be alone.'

Looking out along the brick void of the street, I tried to conceptualize what he was saying. I imagined doubles of myself everywhere, matched my mood in my mind's eye with that of faceless others, and found he could only be in the right. If I felt alone, I could not possibly be alone in that feeling. Not in a metropolis as cruel as ours. Feeling the comfort he derived from city dwellers he would never meet, however . . . I wanted that brotherhood so very badly and instead grew only disgusted at the immenseness of our inability to help one another.

'I can't tell you how much I envy you,' I confessed. 'I've never felt such a thing from New York.'

'Of course you haven't.' Jim touched me on the shoulder, a brief but comforting gesture. 'You were born here.'

James Playfair and I quit my brother's house after a little brandy and soft, unhurried conversation. I was unsurprised to learn he had a key, and he was surprised to see I didn't plan on remarking over it. He went back to his new digs, I imagine.

I hailed a hack and headed straight for Greene Street and Selina Ann Marsh.

And for once in my life, it wasn't out of stupidity or impatience that I waltzed open-eyed into the lioness's lair. The way I saw the chessboard, the latest match was a draw. On the one hand, Lucy and Julius were dead and I'd mourn that fact for an indefinite period punctuated by my demise. On the other hand, Val was never directly implicated, and the beleaguered family was well on their way to Canada with a man who loved at least one of them. And so far as ruining me goes, she'd not yet quite managed it. But she'd come close.

I needed to know what was necessary to make it all stop.

I found Silkie Marsh alone in her mirrored parlor, sitting in an armchair reading a letter. She seemed profoundly distressed by its contents – gnawing at her lip, her striking hazel eyes skimming the lines while she twisted a piece of her golden hair. It was down, falling about her shoulders like light piercing through a cloud. She smiled upon seeing me. That's due to my being an enemy. If a friend had interrupted her during a private moment, she'd have scowled like the very devil.

'Mr Wilde.' Her attention flickered between me and the page before she folded the paper, resting it on her lap. She wore the crimson dressing gown, its folds spilling graphically onto the carpet. 'You aren't wanted just now.'

'What would happen if we stopped?' I asked, removing my hat and sitting on the sofa.

Passing her tongue over her lower lip, Silkie Marsh considered this query. Since it had surprised her considerably, she took her time.

'I was expecting questions, but not that one.' She pressed her nail along the letter's crease and then set it on an adjacent claw-foot table.

'I've answered most of the others on my own. You were paid a hundred dollars by Gates to get rid of his wife, for a start.'

She gazed at me, silent.

'It can't matter now whether or not you tell me the rest,' I argued.

'What do I get in return?'

'I'll leave your brothel sooner rather than later.'

She blinked at me, jaw tight with impatience, and began to glance at the letter again before fixing her attention on her embroidered slipper. 'My poor friend Rutherford was so worried. And I quite understood – the Party is cruel when they want to be, as cruel as a mob, and either one might have gone after him if he'd been found out. The situation was unacceptable. Bad for Rutherford, dangerous for his wife, potentially disastrous for Tammany. I was asked to assist, and I did.'

'But a paltry hundred wasn't enough for you,' I returned. 'If instead of relocating them, you arranged for Varker and Coles to sell the family, you'd earn a fat share of the proceeds. When that scheme fell through, you lit on a new one. I don't know how you realized Lucy and Delia were hiding at Val's, admittedly. But I do know Gates told you they were slaves.'

She sighed. 'When Seixas described the men who assaulted him, I knew of course it was you and Valentine. Sean Mulqueen searched a number of colored hotels as well as Eighty-four West Broadway for Lucy the next day, but that was a wash. When I asked him to have a look at Val's residence instead . . . well. The sisters weren't careful about windows. And Val isn't careful about beautiful women.'

Silkie Marsh was right, so I didn't bother to argue with her.

'Mulqueen was always your man, wasn't he? I thought he worked for Varker and Coles at first, but I'd lay money that you invented the whole filthy system. Mulqueen the copper star, Varker and Coles the dealers, and all you had to do was appear in court when they needed you.'

Adjusting a fold of her exquisite robe, Silkie Marsh shrugged. She seemed tired. Worn. 'I didn't like losing Sean – he was quite capable. He signaled me when the woman calling herself Lucy Adams was at last alone in the apartment as well. Delia Wright or whatever her name was led him in plenty of circles thereafter, but Sean had already done his duty.'

'Who gave Gates away to the Party?'

'I did, of course, after the sister and son disappeared. They appreciate the power of secrets, as I do. Exposure could have been devastating for multiple campaigns, the scandal would have rippled endlessly – better to be prepared for the worst. It would have been madness to leave Tammany in the dark. From the moment Rutherford told me of his endangerment, I saw an opportunity to be of use to them. I took it.'

'Along with his blood money.'

'All money is blood money, Mr Wilde,' she snapped, impatient rather than hurt.

'You told Lucy the truth that night, didn't you? That Gates was being groomed by the Party, that the job in the flower shop was too public, that she was an escaped slave who had to be eliminated from the picture. And then you were inspired to strike a deal. If she made my brother look a heartless killer, you'd leave her kin alone. You as good as held them hostage – their lives for one faked garroting.'

'She agreed soon enough,' Silkie Marsh said, picking at a thread that clung to her robe. 'It was childishly easy. It was the least messy option left to me, in fact, compelling the problem to solve herself.'

'Why in hell's name would you make it seem Val's doing?' I didn't quite mean to ask the question, but it bloomed forth of its own volition. 'You once loved my brother, and you walked into his rooms and instructed an innocent woman to frame him for murder.'

'To see what you'd do, of course.' She yawned, blocking her mouth with the back of her delicate wrist.

I'd guessed so. Imagined that Silkie Marsh had seen a marked woman in Val's home and grasped at a singular opportunity for destruction. Still, it numbed me to the bone, hearing it said so carelessly.

Smirking at my obvious dismay, she touched her fingertips to

374

her collarbone. 'You didn't disappoint, Mr Wilde. Your moving the body was *vastly* entertaining. Not as entertaining as watching you sit through Valentine's arrest would have been, but overall this has proven a thoroughly delightful experience. I've heard Seixas and Luke are missing, which is a bad sign. But they really weren't very bright. I'm terribly pleased overall.'

I clenched my fingers over my leg, mind awhirl. The question *Are you pleased with yourself?* wasn't the one I wanted answered. It was of enormous importance, though, to learn whether her loathing for me had infected her feelings for my brother. Because if affection for Val lurked somewhere in the echoing cavern of her own emptiness, then I thought it just possible to call a cease-fire until I could decide what to do with her. If I could make her see that her sick notion of sport could have ended in a noose and a trapdoor, then maybe more people wouldn't have to die because of me. I could visit Julius's grave, stare at the fresh churn of earth with the worms burrowing through it, and tell him, *I'm endlessly sorry. But I promise you that this is never going to happen again.*

'Valentine could have hanged.'

'Oh, that was hardly likely, was it?'

'Hardly *likely*?' I cried. 'God, *listen* to yourself. Half of police work is best guesses, convicting obvious suspects, and you painted him a killer without a second thought.'

She rolled her head on her neck, cupping a hand over her nape. 'If I got Val arrested for murder, I could have gotten him off again just as easily. Bribed his way out, or testified for him perhaps. He'd have been so grateful to me.'

'He could as easily have been sentenced to death.'

'If Val had been hanged for murder, I'd have mourned him. But I'd have survived it. Would *you*?'

Silkie Marsh commenced braiding her hair. She did it unhurriedly, as if bored with the conversation. It was such a simple, womanly activity, so natural the way she wove the pale strands together. The easy domesticity of her fingers in her tresses ought to have been pleasant to look at. Instead, it was horrifying.

'You are unspeakably cruel,' I said.

Her hands froze. Regarding me dispassionately, the little blue circles within her eyes alight, she smiled.

'I'm merely a businesswoman. And you are very, very bad for my business, Mr Wilde.'

I stood up to go, already knowing what bottomless loathing looked like. My ribs ached, my head yet pounded, and my scar burned eerily, an echo of past hurts. Silkie Marsh reached for her letter, and I reached for my hat, knowing that impossible choices were ahead of me and somewhat awed at the paths my mind was wandering. I'd never previously been quite so keen on the notion of cold-blooded murder.

'What are you reading?' I asked offhandedly.

'Rutherford is planning to withdraw his bid for re-election, citing nervous exhaustion. All that mayhem was for nothing after all. What can possibly have gone wrong?'

When she'd said it, she looked startled, as if the words had flown from her mouth unawares. I smiled.

'Oh, I can explain that. I threw him in a Tombs cell and it ketched him a bit. But the Party will be told it was all in their service. That will likely endear me to them, I'd wager. And I've been wondering what it would be like to go on endearing them to me. Because one way or another, whether through flood, fire, plague, or Tammany, I am going to bring you down.'

'A *Tombs* cell? You've ruined everything, you beastly little worm,' she growled, all pretence of civility gone. 'He was my only link to Albany. Rutherford was invaluable, and he'd have been re-elected come spring. Do you hear me? I could have expanded my connections, my clients, my – you *imprisoned him*?'

'You'll come to know what that feels like. One of these days.'

And that parting shot could have been the end of the interview. I'd like to say that I left Silkie Marsh with a snarl on her lip and the letter crushed in her fist. The sole owner of the last word.

I can't, though. Because one riddle remained unsolved. By the time I'd belatedly realized the fact, Madam Marsh had schooled her fury into a mocking smile, hidden the crushed letter in her skirts, and was deftly continuing the braid in her hair.

'There's one thing I don't understand,' I admitted. 'Beardsley and McDivitt were always Mulqueen's thugs – the Party claimed you recommended them personally. So you must have known where the Wrights were all this while. After I gave away their location, you could have sent Varker and Coles to recapture them at any moment. Instead, you allowed them to remain hidden until the Party gave the word. That gained you nothing save risk and a lost commission. Why?'

Silkie Marsh had finished with her plait. She dropped the braid and let it hang loose, sliding gentle fingers over it. A tiny line formed between her sculpted brows as she considered. Looking for all the world like a lost girl, wandering dappled summer forest paths in an unhurried search for the right direction. She'd assumed that expression for my sake on countless occasions. But I knew this to be true bewilderment. Flesh and bone and no trace of art. It prickled down the back of my neck as nothing else had.

'Lucy was lovely, wasn't she?' Silkie Marsh wondered softly. 'All the while I was speaking with her that night . . . I'd never met her, of course, and I couldn't believe how lovely she was. You'll never believe it of me, but I offered her what comfort I could. She was so frightened, but resolute nevertheless, and . . . I think it was that, her resolve, and naturally I pitied her having thrown her lot in with a weakling like Rutherford, but, oh, how lovely she was, and I do cherish beauty, you see. I took her hand, and when I felt it shaking, I swore to her if she did what I asked, I would help her family. When I went to the Party and told them to make use of Sean's friends, I asked them to be patient if anything should come of it. To wait for you to manage things yourself, Mr Wilde. I'd made a promise, and I thought you could devise the best end for them, you see. But Tammany can be so impatient. How did it end, after all?'

From the next room, a clock chimed, reverberating from the

many mirrors. I stood in silent wonderment with my hat in my hand and felt the warm flush of my anger creeping away like flood tides. Dazzled and not a little sick. Her words had wound around my throat somehow, soft as a cashmere glove.

'I can't possibly tell you that,' I breathed.

'Ah.' She nodded, still pensive. 'I can see why you would think so, though I do hope they escaped. You had better leave, then, hadn't you, Mr Wilde?'

Somehow, I reached the door without faltering. Somehow, I found myself on the street once more. Staring up at the sky and wondering whether the stars were reeling away from us, or I'd simply lost my earthbound bearings. My pulse throbbed in my ears, a faint reminder of the sharper pain in my head.

After all that she'd done to me, it's mad to say that a small act of mercy made me more frightened of Madam Marsh than I'd ever been before. Kindly whims thoughtlessly acted upon shouldn't turn a man's stomach over in his belly. But hers did. I'd thought I understood her, right down to the gouged-out center. I'd thought I could predict what she wanted if not how she'd act.

I'd been wrong.

I forced my feet to move. Soon, I found myself striding at top speed. And seconds later, I broke into a light run, dodging potholes and frozen banks the color of lead. Because going to Greene Street had reminded me how I'd gotten into this mess in the first place, and I needed to conduct a long-overdue conversation. One I, at last, understood well enough to form the right words.

Checking my watch and seeing that evening mass at the Catholic orphanage would end in half an hour, I hastened through the ugly winter streets in the direction of the little girl who had started it all.

The wind turned as dry as old bones after the snowfall. Standing with my hands in my pockets, I awaited Bird Daly in the open courtyard between the chapel and the dormitories. The sandlike flecks had frozen in queer drifts against the benches, glittering wickedly in the shadows of marble archways. An owl perched on one of the parapets hooted softly, a mournful and lovelorn sound. Drifts of cloud cover concealed and revealed the moon, leaving me one moment a silhouetted copper star and the next merely a deeper patch of nightfall.

Then the peace of the evening was rent by the clatter of kinchin's voices mingled with the stamping of small boots.

Bird marched in a disorderly line with her schoolmates. She'd just found a long stick, the variety begging to be a sword or a wand or a scepter, and she carried it in slack fingers. Her face was so neutral, so . . . not happy . . . *accustomed* . . . that I grew still more acutely aware of my surroundings. From the particular pulse of my headache to the specific grind of my boots against the paving stones, because this moment was important to me. Her maroon dress called back the gore of our first encounter, when she'd been covered in a boy's blood and running for her life, and she was perfect. That was what I needed to say to her. Lucy Adams had taught me a lesson, though one I'd never be able to thank her for. Bird, like Lucy, could never go back. And Bird, like Lucy, was perfect. As beautiful and heartbreaking as an unsent letter.

Everything about her.

Seeing me, she smiled. Waved to the nun and started running. And before I knew quite what I was doing, one of my knees was on the grimy stone and I'd an armful of Bird Daly. For a moment, she froze.

Then she hugged me back. Just about as hard as she could.

'I didn't tell you because I didn't know how,' I said over her shoulder. She smelled faintly of liturgical incense and of something warm and entirely her own. 'But you don't wake up *wrong*. You wake up *you*, no matter where you suppose you are. I'd erase it all if I could, but that doesn't mean I want *you* to be different. The Bird here now is the right Bird. Do you understand what I mean?'

I wanted her to know what I meant as I've wanted very few things. And every bit as much as the ones that were for me.

When I'd managed to stop strangling the poor kinchin, she pulled back a little. Eyed my scar and clearly thought about touching it. She didn't, though. She just smiled in her sober, measured fashion. Set her small hands on my shoulders and squeezed.

And then she said, 'I understand.'

There's a reason, I thought, pulling her close again, *that the number two means joy in the blackbird poem.*

There always is a reason, after all, in children's rhymes.

CHAPTER TWENTY-SEVEN

Men may write fictions portraying lowly life as it is, or as
it is not – may expatiate with owlish gravity upon the bliss
of ignorance – discourse flippantly from armchairs of the
pleasures of slave life; but let them toil with him in the
field – sleep with him in the cabin – feed with him on
husks; let them behold him scourged, hunted, trampled on,
and they will come back with another story in their mouths.

Solomon Northup, *Twelve Years a Slave*, 1853

Having slept until afternoon at Val's ken, and with thoughts swarming my head like a cloud of midges, I walked a great deal after parting from Bird. Aimless, grieving. But still here. Even in the middle of the night, the streets were alive with sinners, circling one another in a dance of nameless strangers.

When I arrived home very late, the lights in the bakery were aglow. Odd. Elizabeth Street was quiet, though the Germans next door had located an accordion and a man who knew how to use it. Shrill, happy strains of a waltz pirouetted out of their windows and leapt down the street. The first stair before my front door creaked, and I mulled over finding a few nails and fixing it on the morrow. I pulled out my key.

The door flew open.

Mrs Boehm stood before me. Eyes wild, unleashing a torrent of the most guttural and emphatic invective I've ever heard. Still more emphatic than Mrs Boehm's languages generally sound, that is. Which is saying something. When she stopped, I stared at her stupidly for several seconds.

'I don't speak Bohemian,' I said, baffled. 'Or German. Was . . . was that *both*?'

Snarling, she turned on her heel and I followed, shutting the door.

Mrs Boehm stormed into the bakery, hands perched on the hard ledges of her bony hips. She wore the third of the dresses I've catalogued, the snow-white wool with the small bands of grey lace at the low neck and the short sleeves. The one that heightens her coloring, makes her hair nearly blonde and her eyes nearly blue.

Turning, she aimed a finger at me. It was like staring down a rifle barrel.

'That you are in danger, I know,' she snapped. 'Men chasing you everywhere, men hitting you. And you go to this ball, where are dancing and drinking these men who want to break your bones, and you *disappear*. No note! No message! All night and all day, and now night again. Nothing. I am thinking to myself, *Find Mr Wilde*, and I wonder how, and then I am thinking, *Mr Wilde would know, he is police*, but you are *gone*. How can I send you to find you if you are not here?'

Sighing, she straightened her shoulders. 'I was worried,' she admitted.

I kissed her so hard she took half a step backward before I caught her around the waist, my other hand traveling from her shoulder up her neck to the shell of her ear. I'd have pulled away to make sure of my welcome, but her head tilted almost instantly, her wide lips parting even as I felt their edges lift into a familiar smile.

The fact it was already a *familiar* smile sent an aching but golden twist through my chest.

I found out a number of important facts about my landlady just then. For instance, her tongue is something of a marvel. Warm, inviting, pliant. Vaguely joyful when it brushed the roof of my mouth. Or it was that night, anyway.

So I kept kissing her. I kissed her until her thighs hit the bread table and she parted them and I lifted her onto the floury pine and stepped between her knees and broke away from her lips to find out whether the hollow of a baker's throat tastes like hot buttered bread.

It does.

'I never want to get married again,' she gasped. 'I loved Franz.'

I stopped, looking up at her with my fingers tracing her jaw.

'I'm in love with a girl called Mercy who writes me mad, beautiful letters.'

Mrs Boehm's response to this information was to push my coat off my shoulders. So the clear thing to do was to go back to kissing her.

I make a great many hotheaded decisions as a copper star. But that one, I think, was the right choice.

Elena Boehm smokes very small cigarettes. She rolls them herself, carefully tucking fragrant tobacco into tiny sheets. When she smokes them, her eyes half close on the inhale, and her lips press gently into the slender tip of the white paper. When she smokes them in bed – my bed, as I'd no wish to make any presumption of being welcome in hers – she holds her left hand above her head, between the bedposts, so as not to get ash on the sheets.

It ought to look awkward. It doesn't.

I was spending my time on the depression created at the edge of her hipbone when she lies on her back. There's a little white spot there, like a freckle reversed, and I was tracing the edge of it with my thumb. It had been so long since any female had expressed an interest in my perusing their anatomy, I was keen to take as long a spell over it as was possible. And an ardent, hasty, splendid tumble with a sweet-faced woman propped on a bread table with her knees around my waist while we both remained almost fully dressed was not going to be sufficient to the grand cause. No. I like Elena tremendously and was keen to provide her with evidence of the fact. So I now know that there is a white spot beside her left hipbone, and that brushing my fingers across the inside of her elbows provokes a breathy laugh, and that beneath the covers where all is dark, she tastes of a tea brewed from the soft white hearts of meadow grass.

'What are you thinking?' she asked. Watching me and alternately watching the smoke from her cigarette slither through the air.

'I'm thinking that the gentlemanly thing to do would be to clean your kitchen table for you.'

Elena chuckled. 'I have been with no one since Franz. I am thinking we should leave the table as it is for now, yes?'

I didn't feel like arguing over that. Outside my window, the sky was turning a melancholy shade of lavender. I wondered what the reversed freckle tasted like and saw no reason not to investigate that matter further. As any self-respecting copper star would do.

'I will tell you something,' Elena announced. 'Silly, you might think it. But your London friend's stories – I imagined myself in them. The scullery maids and shopkeepers and princes. After Audie and Franz died, I ran from my life. Hurt was always in front of me, always behind me. Running from the hurt only to meet it halfway. When I read *Light and Shade* – I wasn't anymore. You see? No past I'd buried, fading. No future, alone. Only feelings from other people borrowed. I liked that.'

She was speaking of the short tales Mercy had penned and then published anonymously in a long-running series. The ecstatic fables and homespun fairy tales populated by ordinary people doing extraordinary things. Something pricked at the back of my eyes.

'I didn't know it was her when I read them,' I confessed. 'Until the last. But I always dreamed of living in her tales. Not just feeling them through a page.'

Elena thought this over. When she thinks hard about something, her slender mouth tucks down at the edges, though it looks nothing like a frown. Her cigarette finished, she crushed it carefully against the bedpost. After realizing she'd nowhere to put it, she frowned at the stub in earnest. I plucked it from her fingers and threw it against the wall.

'You are in her stories,' she concluded, passing her fingers over the boot marks on my ribs. 'You were part of her life, so you were part of her words. What I am remembering is the apothecary from maybe two years ago? You recall it?'

I recall all of them. But I'd no notion what she was talking about.

'In that installment of *Light and Shade*, there is an apothecary who makes for people medicine. Very popular. They talk to him while he blends their tonics, measures their pills. They tell him all about their lives, then take home the powders and syrups. They feel better. A mistake one day happens, a woman gives her baby the wrong tonic and the baby dies. She blames the apothecary. Innocent he is, but the people are sad for the mother and so they believe. He is thrown in jail and a new apothecary takes his place. The people go to this new man for their drugs, but they do not feel better. They still feel ill. Bad humors. They felt better before not because of the medicine, but because the first apothecary helped them feel less alone. That was you.'

Shifting forward, I settled myself above her. Elena blinked calmly up at me. There's a little scar on my shoulder from where I caught myself on a nail in the stable as a boy, a scar I don't mind thinking of because my mother patched me up again. She pressed it experimentally with her forefinger and I liked the chalky mark still more.

'That apothecary was an old Russian man,' I pointed out.

She shrugged.

'He was you anyway,' she told me. 'You are now old Russian man, with great yellow-stained beard.'

What must have been a peculiar smile crept over my face. I didn't believe that matters were quite so simple as my landlady had made them out to be. Just because I often feel like an unwilling confessor doesn't mean that Mercy ever noticed. I spent my days collecting her smallest details, and not the other way around. Still.

If Elena was right, even partially right . . . then maybe I hadn't been such a tangential shadow after all.

'When you are looking like that, sad and smiling at once, you should be kissing me,' Elena suggested.

She's very clever, Mrs Elena Boehm. So I kissed her while the sun was rising. And for a blessedly long string of minutes, everything else went away.

Though the following day proved bright and razor sharp, what snow remained had been largely trampled by pedestrians and street pigs, and the cries of the Rockaway sand vendors had been replaced with grocers hawking sweet Carolina potatoes shipped up from the South. I haggled my way into buying a bushel of them for seventy-five cents and left the creamy yellow knobs in Mrs Boehm's larder, knowing she'd find them there. Afterward I fixed the front step, noting with absent pleasure that an emerald green crocus blade was keeking out from a crevice in the none too regular sidewalk. Then I sat at my desk and I wrote a letter. A lot of thoughts yet plagued my head, and I needed to tell Mercy Underhill about them.

The problem, as I saw it, was that I'd never been able to speak to her in plain English. Before, I'd been terrified of upsetting the delicacy of our equilibrium, and after . . . there simply wasn't time. But I was through with standing in the front row with the groundlings, the bearer of a permanent free ticket to watch myself act like a fool.

So I decided to tell her the truth.

When I was through writing, I traveled back to Castle Garden.

The shoreline was whipped by a bright March wind that late afternoon, reddening the noses of passersby and stealing hats from careless dandies. The carpeting was gone, but the decorative boughs remained. They'd been buffeted by salt air and looked about as festive as sunburned shipwreck survivors. I crossed the bridge and sat on the same bench I'd shared with Jim, staring out at the great silver monster of a river. It roiled and frothed in the wind, depths churning with secrets. I thought of the night I'd met Lucy Adams, when so many had lost their lives in the waters I find grimly beautiful. I could have sat there for hours, letting the salt blast me clean.

But I'd a letter to send. I pulled it out.

I read back over it as the pedestrians milled about me, long woolen cloaks dragging through cigar ash and spent vestas, shoes skirting the grey pools of melting snow.

Dear Mercy,

That I've been in love with you for a very long while won't surprise you much. But I've learned things since you left, new things. If words can be maps, as you said they can, then my life lately is an enormous geography, and one hard to capture in letters. I can't help but suspect you're keener at this than I am. I'll do my best.

The notion of protecting you used to occupy so much of my brain that I never realized how often you were protecting me. You may not remember, or you may have done the same for everyone, but I could scarce spend three minutes in a dark mood in your company before you'd passed your latest poem to me for frank evaluation or demanded I read with you a scene from The Tempest. I confess I can see better from a distance what your company meant to me. And I'll be grateful for the rest of my life that you were there.

And don't suppose I won't love you so long as that. Given the choice, I'd prefer to miss you permanently than to forget any piece of you. I'm going to have to learn to live without you, though. And not just for my sake.

About six months have passed with me hating every man who'd ever touched you rather than being happy you were warm. Had I been fighting for you all that while, against them and my own fears and the world altogether for your permanent affections, I could maybe be entitled to such a feeling. But I settled for being near you and hoarded so many invaluable nearnesses that I forgot you knew nothing of my collection, and so can't indulge such jealousies any longer. I built miles of ramparts in your honor, all in my head. And never showed you a one.

I could lie outright and say that, now I've a woman called Elena for a friend, you are invited to feel the same about me. You are not. I'd prefer you ravenously jealous . . . because if you can't be jealous once at least, you can never love me. Can you? You could love me on paper, perhaps. From an ocean's distance. In theory. With a quill in your hand, meditating on the breadcrumb-teakettle-washboard little details of my life in New York. None of it would be enough. I can live as a mere idea to you. But I want every minute of your every hour and if you don't want the same of me, in the flesh, then I can't need you any longer and live as I should. So I'll allow myself to think that if you never come back, I'll survive it.

Whether it's true or not.

I've nothing left to me you've ever touched save these recent letters. The rest burned seven months ago. Fragments of dramas scrawled on the backs of advertisements and Party flyers, mainly, countless notes, the stub end of a single candle after you'd wet your fingers with your tongue and put out the flame. I'm glad that's gone now. This time I'll keep only what you give me. I'll manage the rest of my life – the brown studies, the work, the weight of it – on my own.

Ask anything you like of me, as ever. I've been yours for a very long time. I'm through only with needing you in return. That would have been an extravagant repayment, I can't help but think. Having you.

Yours,

Timothy

I placed the letter in the repository I'd selected. That was that, then. I stood up and walked toward the little iron railing.

When I flung the stoppered glass bottle in the Hudson, it tumbled end over end in a magnificent arc. The sun glancing off of it, the paper within sheltered and gloriously untroubled. For a moment I thought it hung suspended, in defiance of all natural law, just as Mercy's own letters had seemed enchanted. But the world

388

reasserted itself and, making a small plume, the message plunged into the water. I lost sight of it in seconds.

Our river is nothing if not deep, and dim, and wide.

Shoving my hands in my greatcoat pockets, I turned my back on it. I struck out for New York City and the people I knew there, the ones who needed me, and the swiftly enveloping twilight that would all too soon settle like a cloak over the narrow streets.

I'd write another letter soon. It too would begin *Dear Mercy*, and doubtless I would feel every separate letter of her name as they pulsed through my fingertips. It would be similar to the first, but it would be for her. Because I know who she is to me. And I know who I am. And that's something.

But not now. Now I would find a little warmth for myself. A little comfort, and maybe even a little pool of light.

When I returned to the Tombs several days later following an all-clear note from Chief Matsell, my copper star pinned resolutely to my breast, I met with a sharp surprise when I opened the door to my cave.

My office had been repainted, for one. That was gratifying. The walls were free of vicious invective and now merely relentlessly plain. I wasn't too surprised by that, for Matsell could hardly have allowed the Tombs to remain defiled. But mysteriously, a pretty oaken desk sat in the center of the tiny room. It was utilitarian but carved with artful grooves, and behind it was a comfortable upholstered armchair.

That puzzled me.

Behind the desk stood stacks of books. Dozens of them, scores of them, piled in precarious towers against the far wall. Books of every size and description and color. A veritable mountain range of books.

That puzzled me too.

'Thank the risen Christ, there he is.'

Turning, I discovered my friend Mr Connell. His square, friendly face was active with amusement as he twisted his head behind him. 'Kildare, are ye seeing this plain? I *told* you he never knew all this was delivered, he'd ha' been prancin' with bollocks out through the halls in glee. That's a dollar you owe me.'

Shouldering through the door, Kildare sighed, then smiled at me as he passed Connell a dollar bill. 'Matsell said ye'd likely turn up this morning. We wanted to see what you thought o' the furnishings and all.'

Drawing my fingers over the polished oak and the tiny leaves carved into it, I shook my head. 'I think they're incomprehensible.'

'And what about the books, then?' Mr Connell wondered. He picked up a blue leather-bound volume, then a forest green tome with gilt lettering. '*The Plays of Christopher Marlowe*. This is naught to do wi' police work. *The Iliad*. D'ye read such things, Wilde?'

'I like to,' I said softly. There was a note pinned to the complete works of William Shakespeare, and I unfolded it. 'I like to very much.'

'But who *sent* all this?'

'I've my suspicions,' I answered. When the others crowded behind my shoulders, I spread the note out on the desk.

Dear Timothy,

We are well on our way north by stage and finding the journey much more tolerable than should be expected, thanks in no small measure to my mother's influence and planning. Having ample time for reflection, and you forming a portion of my thoughts, I had cause briefly to recall your denseness and was moved to leave this note at the Railroad station where we are presently passing the night. They have promised to mail it to my housekeeper with all speed, along with instructions for her to arrange for the items before you to be delivered to your workplace. I'd have offered you my better desk, but, having been in your office, I fear that particular item would not fit inside. And anyhow, this one will suit you better. The selection of books is haphazard, but then you are a haphazard man as well as a small one.

SEVEN FOR A SECRET

*I'll write again when we reach our destination and would be
very pleased to hear from you as well.*

Best wishes,

George Higgins

Kildare whistled. 'And who might this be?'

'A friend.' Sinking in glad disbelief, I landed in the armchair. I
gripped its arms. They were solid. Real. *Mine.* 'He's a friend.'

'Sweet Mary, but I'm in dire need o' more friends.' Connell
laughed. 'Well, there's our answer, then.'

'Ye might want to know that Beardsley and McDivitt are gone,'
Kildare added. Crossing his arms, he drew his hand over the black
stubble on his chin. 'Given their ticket o' leave and sent marchin'.
The *fuss* they made. Fit to blow the roof clean off.'

I glanced up from the note in surprise. Matsell's brief summons
back to work had made me at least reasonably confident I'd not
find myself harassed or assaulted. But as awed as I've always been
by my brother, a separate voice within me continually insists he
really *can't* be as formidable as all that.

That voice is generally mistaken.

'How are ye liking the walls?' Kildare asked with a twinkle in his
narrow blue eyes.

He didn't sound interested. He sounded proud. I gazed around
me, so muzzy with gratitude that I could barely answer him. It must
have taken several coats of paint to erase that degree of scarlet
profanity.

'You did this?'

'Oh, myself, and Connell here, and Piest. Piest was that eager,
we were sure enough afeared he'd hide us if we weren't keen. Mad
eyes the man has – we daren't have crossed him. Austin and Clare
dropped by to help, and so did Hallam, and Aldenkamp. There's
plenty more stars afterward said they would have offered a hand, to
be certain, if they'd known what we were about. Evans and King
tidied when we were through. All the while Maguire passed advice
about like a tit. But it weren't no trouble.'

'Thank you.' I folded the letter from Higgins and tucked it in my coat pocket. 'You can't possibly grasp how grateful I am.'

'We could grasp it down at the pub sometime, eh?' Connell said teasingly.

'That would be my pleasure.'

'I'm fer rounds, then, as are you if you know what's good for ye.' Connell slapped Kildare on the sleeve of his coat. 'I'm to find murderers today, certain sure. I can feel it, and all. I'm to wrestle down great ugly thugs in front o' puffy rich types who'll shower me wi' riches like Wilde here. Watch.'

'Ye'll wrestle great ugly drunks bawlin' in the streets and get showered with naught but piss for yer trouble.'

'Christ, the cheek of the bastard? I'm a hero, you brute, the pride o' Bayard Street.'

Winking at me, Connell followed Kildare out the door, merrily arguing all the while.

I sat at my desk.

It really was a very fine piece of furniture. Made from a venerable tree, I'd no doubt, and lovingly crafted. There was a gouge on one of the corners – an old one, likely from when it had been delivered to its first residence or suffered misfortune there. That gouge belonged to George. But I liked it. Spreading my hands wide, I passed them over the glossy surface in a prayerful little arc.

I was home.

Historical Afterword

When asked to supply reminiscences of the abolitionist cause for William Still's history of the Underground Railroad, New York activist Lewis Tappan provided the following account: he had been asked to warn two young brothers originally from Savannah, Georgia, that slave catchers were traveling north in pursuit of them. Tappan at once left his home in Brooklyn, posting notices in all the likeliest black churches. He was successful in finding the brothers and requested they tell him their story.

They informed Tappan that their father was a prominent doctor in Savannah, who had fathered five children by their mother, who was, in fact, his slave. After marrying a white woman, the doctor determined that all the children and their mother should be auctioned off. When the family was placed upon the block to be sold to the highest bidder, the two brothers announced to the crowd that it was a cruel act to sell the six family members and that anyone who bought them would regret it, for they had lived as free beings for so long that their new masters were certain to lose their money. All six were sold nevertheless, but the brothers proved as good as their word and escaped to New York City, where – being of extremely light complexion – they shaved their heads, bought brown wigs, and were hired as white men. Tappan's warning found them in time, and they fled before the Georgia slave agents arrived in Manhattan.

So precarious was the position of free blacks born in the North that urban people of color began to form committees of vigilance in populous areas as early as 1819. The New York Committee of Vigilance was founded in 1835 'for the purpose of adopting measures to ascertain, if possible, the extent to which the cruel practice of kidnapping men, women and children, is carried out in this city, and to aid such unfortunate persons as may be in danger of being *reduced to Slavery,*' according to their first annual report. The group consisted of Robert Brown, William Johnston, George R. Barker, J. W. Higgins, and founder David Ruggles. Ruggles made himself such a nuisance to kidnappers, slave catchers, and corrupt officials that he was subjected to multiple targeted kidnapping attempts. In one such instance, an ally informed Ruggles in 1838 that he had become so unpopular that a New York magistrate had quietly circulated an offer of fifty thousand dollars to any unscrupulous party willing to capture Ruggles and dispose of him below the Mason-Dixon Line.

Overwhelming evidence indicates that the practice of kidnapping free blacks for the purpose of selling them as alleged slaves was common, systematized, and almost entirely overlooked by courts and by law enforcement. William Parker, a resistance leader from Philadelphia, reported that this theoretical 'crime' was so very pervasive that 'we were kept in constant fear. We would hear of slaveholders or kidnappers every two or three weeks; sometimes a party of white men would break into a house and take a man away, no one knew where; again, a whole family might be taken off. There was no power to protect them, nor prevent it.' Such thieves of fellow humans thought nothing of resorting to the most barbarous measures to retain their captives. Methods employed by the infamous Cannon Gang to keep their victims in line included starvation and beating with hickory sticks and saw blades – one member, Patty Cannon, was ultimately indicted when multiple skeletons were discovered buried on her property, but she died in jail while awaiting trial.

The NYPD was founded in the year 1845, during a period of violent social upheaval and political rancor. Citizens decried the formation of a 'standing army,' and despite their lack of uniforms, the copper stars were greeted with hostility and mistrust. Due to the simultaneous occurrence of the Irish Potato Famine, the city was struggling to accommodate far more immigrants than its rustic infrastructure could support. While some tenant farmers and their families fled starvation in Ireland and continued west upon arrival in the United States, many remained in Manhattan, and it soon became clear that the Democratic Party would be courting their votes – and to that end, made efforts to assist them in finding work and housing. In the absence of a social net apart from the direst of grim public institutions, politicians wisely realized that their constituents needed help more than they needed policy rhetoric, and many destitute families were aided by the system of cronyism that later made Tammany Hall synonymous with corruption and graft.

During the period that Chief of Police George Washington Matsell headed the copper stars, the language spoken by New Yorkers was changing almost daily. Phrases culled from British thieves' cant intermingled with German, Dutch, Yiddish, and other immigrant languages to form 'flash,' a child of many mother tongues spoken primarily by the poorer classes and the more nefarious denizens of the ghettos where they were forced to live. Matsell, fascinated by social trends and a man ahead of his time, took it upon himself to record this 'language of crime' as an aid to his green star police, and as an eccentric cultural document directed at the Fifth Avenue dandies whose slumming expeditions caused slang's spread to the wealthier neighborhoods. While he approached the study of flash from the point of view of a policeman, Matsell found himself reluctantly admiring that the vernacular proved so 'appropriately expressive of particular ideas,' and fans of the English language today will find its many branches of slang no less evocative, adaptable, and organic.

ACKNOWLEDGMENTS

During the periods when I'm alone at my kitchen table, trying to siphon words from my brain onto a laptop screen with a bendy straw, it's of paramount importance to know that there are people cheering me on. My amazing husband, Gabriel, my wonderful family back West, my incredible NYC posse of artists and dreamers and benign lunatics, my worldwide Sherlockian Mafia – they all play a major role in encouraging me to sit-down-and-write-it-for-God's-sake. I couldn't accomplish my bookish endeavors without their support.

Amy Einhorn takes dodgy manuscripts and turns them into marvelous books, and it's an absolute delight to roll up my sleeves and wash my hands and dive into literary surgery with her. Thank you, Amy, not only for your skills as an editor, but for liking the crazies in my head enough to spend so much time with them. The rest of the team at Amy Einhorn Books/Putnam, including but certainly not limited to Alexis Welby, Victoria Comella, Gina Rizzo, Lydia Hirt, Kate Stark, and Elizabeth Stein, are the best allies a girl could hope for – not to mention the best company.

I'm at a loss for words as to how amazing my amazing agent, Erin Malone, happens to be – she's that amazing. Until such time as books can support animated gifs about my feelings, I'll simply say: thank you, you're amazing. One day, we will have the technology. I owe a very great deal to Tracy Fisher and Cathryn Summerhayes, who are responsible for spreading Tim Wilde about the globe. To the rest of WME, including Amy Hasselbeck among many others, thank you so much for all the many ways you help me, God knows I need it.

Many thanks to Claire Baldwin and her entire Headline battalion for being utter peaches. And thank you to all my other wonderful foreign publishers for your interest in a scrappy young American copper star.

My research for this book began, as ever, at the New York Public Library, and they have been nothing save dedicated and insightful. While I rely to a great extent on primary sources, historians always light my path for me, and in this case works by Edwin G. Burrows, Mike Wallace, Timothy Gilfoyle, Leslie M. Harris, Carol Wilson, Anne Farrow, Joel Lang, Jenifer Frank, and David Grimstead made me understand just how widespread and horrifying a practice the kidnapping of free blacks was in the antebellum North. Thank you also to Richard B. Bernstein and to my French language translator Carine Chichereau for on multiple occasions keeping egg off my face. As to the atrocities my primary sources endured, I cannot fathom how they found the courage to write them down, and I am deeply indebted to them for their biographies.

Finally, thank you to my readers. My early draft readers, my new readers, my American readers, my overseas readers, my e-readers, my shiny hardcover readers, and my used paperback readers. You're why we do this. Thanks for letting me tell you a story.